T0129255

Just One Kiss

"This unpleasant thing you must confess—is it the reason you've been hiding from me?" Nick asked.

"Yes. I've been an awful coward. I beg your pardon for refusing your calls this week. I did want to see you, but well…I was afraid of what you'd say, and I didn't know how to explain what I'd done, and I'm…ashamed of myself, Lord Dare."

She looked away from him, down at her hands, but Nick, who was truly concerned by this point, took her chin between his fingers and raised her face to his. "Don't look away from me, Hyacinth. Just tell me what's got you so worried, and we'll find a way to…"

Nick trailed off when her gaze met his, and he was horrified to find her eyes had filled with tears. "Oh, sweetheart, no." He moved closer and took her face between his hands, and all at once everything else—the strange business with the pianoforte, her mysterious disappearance this week—all of it faded into insignificance at the sight of those tears. "Don't cry, Hyacinth."

For some reason this only made her tears fall faster, until she was crying so hard she could only speak in incoherent gasps. "B-but that's just i-it, my lord. I'm n-not—"

"Hush." He caught the back of her head in a gentle grip and pressed her face to his chest, then ran his hand over her back in long, soothing strokes until at last she began to calm. "There. That's better." He tilted her face up to his again and pressed gentle kisses to her forehead, her eyelids, and the tip of her nose.

He hadn't intended to kiss her at all, and if he'd stopped there—if he'd been able to resist her trembling mouth—what happened next might not have been quite such a scandal…

Books by Anna Bradley

LADY ELEANOR'S SEVENTH SUITOR

LADY CHARLOTTE'S FIRST LOVE

TWELFTH NIGHT WITH THE EARL

MORE OR LESS A MARCHIONESS

MORE OR LESS A COUNTESS

Published by Kensington Publishing Corporation

More or Less a Countess

Anna Bradley

LYRICAL PRESS
Kensington Publishing Corp.
www.kensingtonbooks.com

LYRICAL PRESS BOOKS are published by

Kensington Publishing Corp.
119 West 40th Street
New York, NY 10018

All Kensington titles, imprints, and distributed lines are available at special quantity discounts for bulk purchases for sales promotion, premiums, fund-raising, educational, or institutional use.

Special book excerpts or customized printings can also be created to fit specific needs. For details, write or phone the office of the Kensington Sales Manager: Kensington Publishing Corp., 119 West 40th Street, New York, NY 10018. Attn. Sales Department. Phone: 1-800-221-2647.

Lyrical Press and Lyrical Press logo Reg. U.S. Pat. & TM Off.

First Electronic Edition: August 2018
eISBN-13: 978-1-5161-0533-5
eISBN-10: 1-5161-0533-8

First Print Edition: August 2018
ISBN-13: 978-1-5161-0536-6
ISBN-10: 1-5161-0536-2

Printed in the United States of America

Chapter One

London, November, 1817

Before she even crossed the threshold this evening, Violet Somerset knew there would be pain. She'd braced herself for gaping chest wounds, perhaps a severed limb or two, and a few pitiful but silent screams of agony. A graceful swoon would follow, and then the convulsive death throes of a love that had been hopeless from the start.

She hadn't expected any of it would be pleasant, but she'd hoped it would be quick.

It wasn't quick. It was death by a thousand cuts.

Dreadful way to die. Unseemly. Bloody.

Violet knew all about the blood. She'd seen a gruesome picture of death by a thousand cuts in an extraordinary book she'd found hidden in her grandmother's library. It was called *The Punishments of China*, and it was fascinating reading. A bit grisly, of course, and not at all proper for the eyes of an innocent young lady, but then nothing of any interest was. For her own part, Violet couldn't help but be intrigued by such an astonishingly creative approach to the thorny problem of crime and punishment.

Still, death by a thousand cuts wasn't at all the kind of thing one wanted to see at a dinner party.

Yet here she was, trapped between the fifth and final courses, and instead of a lovely pudding, Violet was facing a ghastly execution.

"I'd hoped for a happy marriage, of course. Doesn't every young lady? But it's so much lovelier than I ever dreamed it would be. I never imagined my husband could be my friend, but that's just what Lord Derrick is to me. My best friend."

Lady Honora looked splendid tonight, with her pink cheeks and her sweet brown eyes alight with happiness. A few weeks ago she'd become the Countess of Derrick, and if one could judge by her transcendent glow, her marriage suited her.

Violet met her dear friend's luminous smile with what was no doubt a sickly grimace. "How wonderful, Honora. I couldn't be happier for you and Lord Derrick."

Honora beamed at her and squeezed her limp fingers, but Violet could only manage a feeble twitch of her hand in return, rather like a bird with a broken wing trying to take flight.

"I don't mean to say he's just my friend, of course. He's, ah…well, he's much more than that. It's difficult to put into words, but it's rather like… like a dream has come to life before my eyes, except it's better than a dream, because it's so much more vivid and colorful than I dared imagine." The fetching pink flush on Honora's cheeks deepened. "I daresay Iris understands. Is that how you feel about Lord Huntington, Iris? As if he's a dream come to life?"

Violet's elder sister Iris, who was recently married herself, was seated across the table from Honora. "I—that is, of course Lord Huntington and I are quite…we do enjoy each other's…" Iris glanced between Honora and Violet, bit her lip, and lapsed into a pained silence.

Poor Iris. It was a trifle awkward when one's sister was in love with one's best friend's husband. Violet roused herself to fill the uncomfortable pause. "It's truly wonderful, Honora. I couldn't be happier for you, and for Iris."

I never should have come here.

"I always thought Lord Derrick handsome." Honora cast a besotted glance at her husband, who was seated at the other end of the table. "But it's only since I married him that I think him the handsomest gentleman in the world."

Violet didn't follow Honora's gaze. She didn't need to look at Lord Derrick to know he *was* the handsomest gentleman in the world, and he was no less kind than he was handsome. "He's wonderfully handsome, Honora. Truly. I couldn't be happier for you."

"It's his eyes, I think. They're such a lovely brown. Don't you think he has remarkable eyes, Violet?"

Cut.

Dear God. Compared to Honora's innocent brutality, Chinese torture felt like being nuzzled by a dozen purring kittens.

"They're wonderful, Honora, truly. I couldn't be happier about his eyes."

Iris choked on her wine, but Honora didn't seem to notice this strange reply. "Oh, I feel the same way. I adore his eyes. Well, not *just* his eyes."

Honora clapped her hand over her mouth, but not quickly enough to hide an uncharacteristically naughty giggle.

Cut.

Violet raised her wineglass, but her hand was shaking so badly she couldn't bring it to her lips. Honora had always been the most decorous of the three of them, but Lord Derrick, it seemed, had transformed their modest friend into a shameless wanton.

"He has the loveliest lips. So firm, but gentle, too."

Cut.

"He's always gentle, even when he's...agitated."

She's a monster. A murderess.

"When I say agitated, I mean when he's—"

"Honora!" Iris's knife landed on her plate with a sharp crack. "I, ah...I beg your pardon, dear, but who's that gentleman who's just come in?"

"Gentleman? What gentleman?" Honora, distracted at last, looked up as a tall gentleman in a dark blue coat and a lavishly embroidered scarlet waistcoat seated himself at the other end of the table. "Oh, that must be Lord Dare. He's a childhood friend of Lord Derrick's. He's just returned to London from a long stay on the Continent."

"Oh? How long?" Violet didn't much care how long Lord Dare had remained on the Continent, but she seized on it, desperate to turn the conversation away from Lord Derrick's firm lips.

"Two years. Lord Derrick told me Lord Dare despises England, and wouldn't be here now if he could have avoided it, but you see his black armband? His father passed away several weeks ago, so he was obliged to come home, to attend the memorial and assume the duties of the title. To hear Lord Derrick tell it, Lord Dare is quite put out by the whole business."

"Why, how rude of his father to spoil Lord Dare's prolonged Continental frolic. Pity he couldn't wait for more convenient timing to die." Such pointed sarcasm was a trifle unfair, and the words singed a bit as they rolled off Violet's tongue, but her misery had found an outlet at last, and Lord Dare never need know he was to be executed in her place.

Honora leaned forward and dropped her voice to a whisper. "From what I understand, he's had quite a frolic, indeed. The gossip has it he left a trail of broken hearts from Paris to Rome." She frowned. "It's terribly rude of him to arrive to dinner so late. For pity's sake, we're onto the dessert course already."

Violet watched as Lord Dare turned a charming smile on his dinner companions. Even from this distance she could see he was handsome, with a tall, lean frame, a sculpted jaw, and an overabundance of silky dark hair.

Too handsome.

In Violet's experience—which was, admittedly, limited to one painful season of being laced into a tight corset and forced to endure the balls at Almack's—handsome gentlemen often hid staggeringly unhandsome ideas behind their charming smiles.

No, handsome gentlemen weren't to be trusted, and especially not this one—the waistcoat alone was proof of that. Lord Dare's clothes were in the height of fashion, of excellent quality and perfectly tailored, but a gentleman only wore a scarlet waistcoat embroidered with an intricate pattern of silver vines and masses of silver roses if he wished to be noticed.

Not that he needed the waistcoat for that. One was as likely to overlook a gentleman like Lord Dare as to forget to follow one breath with another.

His movements were graceful and confident, his smile easy, and if he was a trifle unkempt, it only added to his appeal. His unruly dark hair was a bit too long, his jaw not quite cleanly shaven, and his cravat just a shade off-center, the knot careless, as if it had been tied in a hurry. Despite the extravagant waistcoat, he looked almost as if he'd just rolled out of bed, and Violet hadn't the slightest doubt he had.

Not his own bed, either.

No, one wouldn't overlook Lord Dare, especially if one happened to be a lady. Not *her*, of course, but other ladies. Less sensible ones.

Violet raised her wineglass to her lips and took a healthy swallow. "So he's a rake. How shocking."

Honora smothered a laugh. "Now, Violet. How can you say so? You haven't even been introduced to him yet."

"No, and I'd just as soon keep it that way. I don't care for rakes."

They cared for her even less. There was nothing a rake despised more than a bluestocking, or a bluestocking a rake. They were natural enemies, like a mongoose and a cobra. Rakes dealt in nonsense, after all, and bluestockings were immune to nonsense, just as a mongoose was immune to a cobra's poison.

A smile curved Violet's lips. Her knack for creating apt analogies hadn't prevented her utter failure on the marriage mart, but it never failed to amuse her.

"Well, Violet, you're right, as usual. He *is* a rake, and a dreadful one, too. It seems Lord Dare has a lovely Italian villa, and an even lovelier Italian mistress he's anxious to return to."

"I can't think how Lord Derrick should be friends with him, if he's as awful as you say," Iris said. "They can't have much in common."

"Not anymore, no, though Lord Derrick says they were inseparable as boys." Honora fiddled with her wineglass, a pensive look crossing her face. "It's rather a sad story. Lord Dare had an elder brother, you see, but he was murdered by a highwayman several years ago. Such a tragic death, and now his younger brother is obliged to take a title he never expected to have, and doesn't want."

"Oh." Violet's voice softened. "That is rather sad—" She broke off, her gaze narrowing on Lord Dare as he raised his wineglass in a flirtatious toast to his dinner companion.

Violet and Iris's youngest sister, Hyacinth.

Hyacinth had been seated in a place of honor to Lord Derrick's right. She was a favorite of his, and because of her profound shyness he always insisted on taking care of his "little friend" in this way. It was kind of him, but it sometimes meant Hyacinth was seated far away from her sisters.

Tonight, she was seated right across from the wickedly handsome Lord Dare.

He was talking rather animatedly to her, his striking face alight with interest. Hyacinth listened to him with polite attention, but Violet could see the self-conscious flush on her sister's cheeks, and every one of her protective instincts rushed to the fore. "Take the ladies out, Honora."

Honora gave her a puzzled glance. "What, now? But I haven't finished my wine."

Iris glanced down the table, nudged Honora with an elbow, and jerked her chin in Hyacinth's direction. "Now would be best, Honora."

Honora followed Iris's gaze and rose at once to her feet.

Lord Derrick leapt up to open the door for the ladies, and his expression, as he watched his wife approach...

Violet's heart lurched miserably in her chest.

She knew Lord Derrick loved Honora. He wasn't the sort of man who married a lady he didn't love. But to know a thing wasn't, alas, the same as witnessing it, and even as Violet's heart twisted with pain, she couldn't take her eyes off his face as he gazed at Honora.

His entire being was alight with joy, his brown eyes glowing with it. Honora was simply crossing the dining room, a common, everyday occurrence, and yet he watched her as if...as if his every hope and dream had come to vibrant life in front of him.

Because it had.

He didn't just love Honora; he *adored* her. One had only to look at him to see there wasn't the smallest corner of his heart that didn't echo with Honora's voice, her laughter, her smile.

It wasn't any wonder Honora inspired such profound love. She was beautiful and kind and graceful, a diamond of the first water. She was the sort of lady who could bring the most jaded gentleman to his knees.

Whereas Violet…wasn't.

She had the same dark blue eyes and fair hair that had made her sister Iris the belle of last season, but Violet's laughter didn't tinkle like silver bells. She didn't know how to toss her curls or flirt her fan. Her quadrille was a disgrace, and her musical abilities—well, even her grandmother had been brought low in defeat over Violet's tone deafness.

It wasn't as if she didn't have anything to recommend her, but the gentlemen of the ton didn't admire cleverness. They didn't fall into desperate passions over a lady who was intrigued by Chinese torture or could recite the particulars of a mongoose's immune system. No, the best such a lady could hope for was to be mocked and ridiculed.

"Violet? Are you unwell? You've gone white." Honora took her arm, her brows pinched with concern as she studied Violet's face.

To Violet's horror, tears threatened. Honora had been a true friend to her, and instead of swallowing her bitter disappointment over Lord Derrick, Violet had spent these past weeks begrudging Honora her happiness.

"I'm fine, dear. It's just a sudden headache."

Honora patted Violet's hand. "Why don't you go into the library and rest for a few moments? You can slip into the drawing room when you feel better."

"But Hyacinth—"

"She's all right. She's gone ahead into the drawing room with Iris, and Lord Huntington and Lord Derrick will join us soon."

Violet hesitated. She shouldn't abandon her younger sister, but just the thought of a few moments of solitary quiet to nurse her bruised heart made her ache with longing. "If you're certain."

"Of course I am." Honora smiled, gave her a gentle push in the direction of the library, and then turned to follow the last of the ladies into the drawing room.

Violet crept down the quiet hallway and slipped into the cool silence of the library, the faint scent of must and leather wrapping around her like an old friend. Ever since she was a child libraries had felt like home to her, and she didn't hesitate to let herself sink into the comforting embrace of this one.

She didn't bother to light a lamp, but lay down on one of the sofas in front of the fireplace. Darkness swallowed the room as the flames burned lower in the grate, until at last they disintegrated into a few glowing embers in a pile of ash.

Violet didn't mind the dark. She'd spent many evenings alone in her grandmother's library, cradling dusty books in her hands and pondering the pattern of invisible fingerprints on those old, crackling pages. And after all, it wasn't so terrible to be alone, was it? All of London might scorn the spinster bluestocking, but there was a freedom to it. Perhaps it was lonely at times, but books demanded nothing of her.

Not like people.

No, she was quite happy to be alone—

Click.

Violet tensed as the catch on the library door released, followed by a faint squeak as the door was eased open, and then closed again with a quiet thud.

Thinking Honora had come to fetch her, Violet opened her mouth to make her presence known, but before she could utter a word she was interrupted by a low, masculine growl, then a high-pitched gasp.

"Stop that, my lord! You'll tear it."

Violet heard a noise that sounded like a playful slap, and then an unmistakable feminine giggle, and she instinctively sank lower into the sofa so she wasn't visible from the door.

"No, we haven't time for the bodice, my lord. Just raise my skirts and be quick, before we're missed."

Raise my skirts? That was *not* Honora.

"Sorry, love, but I can't forego the bodice. Not when the contents of it are so magnificent. And I'm *never* quick."

The lady with the magnificent bosom let out a throaty laugh. "Yes, I remember that about you, but we haven't time for...oh. Oh, *my*."

There was a low, wicked chuckle, a faint rustle of clothing, and then what sounded like a coat hitting the floor. "Perhaps we have more time than you thought, my dear?"

Violet squeezed her eyes closed and raised her hands to her burning cheeks. Couldn't a lady enjoy a few private moments of peace without being forced to witness a disgraceful debauchery? For pity's sake, this was a *library*, not a brothel.

But surely they'd stop at a few harmless kisses? That was shameless enough—not to mention in shockingly poor taste—but even people with as little self-control as this wouldn't dare bring the, ah...business to a conclusion right in the middle of Lord and Lady Derrick's library—

"Oh, yes. Put your hand…yes, *there.* Faster…"

The lady's words were lost in a long, soft moan that made Violet's entire body burst into flames of embarrassment.

"Hold your skirts up for me, love…yes, like that. Ah, sweetheart, you're so…now let me just…"

Violet didn't get to hear what he meant to do, but whatever it was, the lady must have permitted it, because in the next moment there was a grunt, then a sharp gasp and a quiet thud, as if someone had been shoved back against the door.

And then shoved again, and again, and again in a steady, measured rhythm.

Violet pressed her lips together, then pressed a hand over her mouth to hold back…a shout of indignation, perhaps? Tears? Was she crying? It would make sense, given the circumstances, and she could feel moisture gathering in the corners of her eyes, spilling over her cheeks…

Except those weren't tears bubbling up in her chest. Those weren't sobs rising into her throat and threatening to burst through her lips.

It was laughter. Loud, indecorous, manic laughter.

Oh, dear. Perhaps she'd gone hysterical, but all that moaning and gasping, and the breathless discussion of bodices—well, it was absurd, wasn't it? And that rhythmic banging…what in the world *was* that? It sounded as if someone's head were being knocked repeatedly against the door—

The lady's. It was the lady's head. At least, that was the most likely scenario, given what Violet knew of the mechanics of the thing. Granted, she had no personal intimate experience, but there was no end to the information one could find in books.

"Oh. Oh. Oh."

Thud. Thud. Thud.

Another violent burst of laughter threatened, and Violet pressed her hand harder against her mouth and bit her lip until it split. Dear God, it would be a miracle if the poor woman escaped without a head injury. Violet could only hope the gentleman was making it worth her while.

From the way the lady was carrying on, it sounded as if he was doing something she enjoyed, but there was only one way to know for certain.

No. I can't possibly. It's a disgraceful invasion of privacy.

But then again, *they* were the ones who'd chosen to express their *affections* in Lord Derrick's library. Did they really deserve privacy, given the circumstances? And after all, she'd been here first. *They'd* interrupted *her*, and it wasn't as if she'd ever get another chance to see it.

She couldn't resist just the tiniest peek, for purely educational reasons.

Violet squirmed onto her knees, careful to keep her head low, held her breath, and peeked over the back of the sofa. She watched for a moment, squinting in the darkness, then let her breath out in a silent sigh.

Well. It wasn't *quite* what she'd expected.

In fact, if the truth were told, it didn't look nearly as interesting as it was rumored to be. But then, that was invariably the way, wasn't it? That was why Violet preferred books—they never disappointed one the way real life did.

And this was...well, a bit anticlimactic.

She'd thought the lady would be clutching at the gentleman in mindless, desperate passion, but this lady was too occupied with holding her skirts out of the way to offer much in the way of clutching. Most of the gentleman's lower body was obscured by the lady's voluminous skirts, but she had one leg hitched awkwardly over his hip, and Violet could see his pelvis moving, jerking against the lady in rhythmic thrusts. They weren't up against the door, but against one of the tall bookshelves next to it, and he was fully clothed aside from his blue coat, which lay on the floor at his feet. It was too dark to see his face, but there was just enough light coming from the crack under the door to catch the glint of silver thread on his scarlet waistcoat.

Lord Dare.

Of course. Violet didn't feel even a flicker of surprise to find he was every bit the rake Honora said he was.

"Oh, harder. Please, my lord...harder..."

Lord Dare didn't hesitate to accommodate this request, but shoved harder against her—so hard he shook the bookshelf, and a book came crashing from its place and tumbled to the floor.

Violet smothered an indignant gasp, and it took all of her restraint not to hurl a pillow at his broad back. For goodness' sake, the least they could do was mind the books.

The lady was sighing and pleading with him not to stop, and then all at once she let out a keening cry that made Lord Dare shove his hand over her mouth. Her body shuddered against his, and then a few moments after she quieted Lord Dare's hips went still, and he buried his face in the lady's breasts to smother a guttural groan.

Violet waited for something more to happen, but they only paused to catch their breath, then began to right their clothing.

She blinked. Was that it, then? The whole thing had left her curiously unmoved. It all seemed so impersonal, somehow—crass even, and it looked as absurd as it sounded, except for that one part, at the end, when Lord

Dare found his pleasure. Something about that ragged groan reverberated deep in her belly, leaving a strange aching sensation.

If any of it truly shocked her, it was the nonchalance with which Lord Dare tugged the lady's skirts back into place once they'd finished. "A delight, as always, Lady Uplands. I knew there was at least one reason to return to England."

He patted her cheek in what looked to Violet like a dismissal, but the lady—Lady Uplands, evidently—grabbed his arm. "Come to me in Harley Street later, my lord."

He gave a careless shrug. "Perhaps. Go on then, love, back to the drawing room. I'll follow in a few moments."

The door latch clicked, and Violet ducked back out of sight as Lady Uplands left the library. Once the door was closed and the room dark again, she peeked over the back of the sofa, curious to see what Lord Dare would do now.

As it happened, he didn't do much of anything at all. He made some mysterious adjustments to his falls, then retrieved his coat from the floor and put it on. He fumbled in the pocket, drew out a pocket-watch and checked the time, then closed the case with a snap and strolled over to the sideboard to help himself to a glass of Lord Derrick's whiskey. Once he was finished, he checked his watch again, pulled his coat into place with a sharp tug, and left the library.

Well. It had been a tidy night's work for Lord Dare, hadn't it?

Violet sat on the sofa for as long as she dared after he left. She had no wish to make an appearance in the drawing room *now*, but her sisters would be wondering where she was, and Hyacinth must be ready to leave.

On her way out the door, Violet stopped to pick up the book Lord Dare's enthusiastic thrusting had knocked from the shelf. He must have stepped right over it on his way, without bothering to put it back. For some reason, this bothered Violet more than anything else she'd witnessed tonight.

She turned the book in her hand. It was a collection of engraved plates bound together in a leather binding. Her lips turned down in a frown when she saw the spine was cracked, but then she noticed the hand-lettered title, and a soft laugh escaped her as she placed the book gently back on the shelf.

The Rake's Progress.

How fitting.

Chapter Two

Some chit was banging on the pianoforte, and each discordant note was crashing inside Nick's head as if she were a blacksmith and his skull her nail.

Volume was not, alas, a substitute for skill.

Nick sighed. He'd come tonight hoping for a distraction, but there was nothing here to amuse him. Not here, and not in all of London. He'd seen it all dozens of times before. He'd been away from this cursed city for two long years, and it wasn't nearly long enough.

England was as cold and wet as it had ever been, dinner parties were still deadly dull, and he would have sworn the young lady who was now displaying her dubious musical skills was the same young lady who'd performed at the last English dinner party he'd attended two years ago.

Impossible, of course, but it was remarkable how much one pale-faced English chit resembled another.

Or one English lord another, come to that.

Nick watched as Lord Derrick strolled toward him from across the room. He took the seat next to Nick on the settee and offered him a cordial smile. One thing about Derrick: he was always the consummate gentleman, no matter how awkward the circumstances.

"Welcome back to England, Balfour. Two years is a long time, but you've changed surprisingly little since the last time I saw you."

It was a simple observation, and there was no edge to Lord Derrick's voice, but Nick's jaw tensed nonetheless. The last time he'd seen Derrick he'd been so sotted he could hardly stand upright. He'd been in a filthy West End gaming hell at the time, doing his best to squander his inheritance, and Derrick had been obliged to send him sprawling with a fist to the face to drag him out.

A lot of bother for nothing, as it turned out, because his father had squandered it anyway.

That had been six months or so after Graham's death, when Nick had at last given up playing at lord of the manor and fled the West Sussex estate for London, his father's curses still ringing in his ears.

"One thing's changed," Nick bit out. "I'm not Balfour anymore, Derrick. I'm Lord Dare now."

But he shouldn't be, and Derrick couldn't help but flinch at the reminder. "Of course. I beg your pardon."

Guilt stabbed at Nick's chest, and he drew in a long breath to gather his composure. There was no sense in lashing out at Derrick. They'd been close friends at one time, and the man had been decent enough to invite him here tonight. And after all, it wasn't as if Derrick were wrong. Nick might be Lord Dare now, but he was still the same useless rogue he'd been when Graham was alive.

It was depressing, how little things changed. Two years gone, and yet here he sat in a tight cravat and an even tighter coat, a tragedy of musical incompetence ringing in his ears, and it was as if no time had passed at all.

"How does Lady Westcott get on?" Lord Derrick asked, clearly eager to change the subject. "She doesn't come out in company much anymore. I haven't see her for months. I hope she's well."

"Oh, you needn't concern yourself about Lady Westcott. She's very well, and as impatient and demanding as she's always been. She's every inch the tyrant you remember."

Not just any tyrant, either, but the tyrant who held Nick's purse strings.

His aunt was the only family he had left, and Nick adored her, but that didn't stop him from occasionally wishing he could wring her neck. She'd insisted he accept Derrick's invitation tonight, no doubt because she hoped his old friend would magically persuade him that underneath his loathing for London was a burning desire to remain here forever.

If Nick had entertained a shred of hope himself, it had vanished as soon as he'd set foot in the dining room. The moment he laid eyes on Lord Derrick, he'd been overwhelmed with the same familiar despair that had made him flee London the first time. It should have comforted him to see his childhood friend, but it didn't—it only made him feel Graham's absence more keenly.

There was no going home, it seemed. Not for him.

Not surprising, really. He should have expected as much, and so should Lady Westcott. They were both a bit too old to believe in magic.

Lord Derrick chuckled. "Ah. Her ladyship is demanding you stay in London, is she?"

"For all the good it will do her, yes." Nick had agreed to a six-week stay only, and he'd be damned if he'd stay a moment longer. "It's November, for God's sake. No one leaves Italy for England in November."

He let out a regretful sigh as he thought of Catalina, the lush, dark-haired Italian mistress he'd just installed in his seaside villa. He'd hardly had a chance to lift her skirts before he'd been obliged to return to the damp, chilly grime of London.

"Unless their father happens to pass away in November, as yours did."

This time there was a distinct note of censure in Lord Derrick's voice, but Nick dismissed it with a shrug. His father had been trying to find a way to die for nearly three years now. That he'd finally accomplished it hardly seemed an occasion for mourning.

"Death is rather a good way to escape an English winter, isn't it? Perhaps I should consider expiring of a consumption while I'm here, or a bilious cough, or some mysterious inflammation of the lungs. Whatever it is one dies of in England. Boredom, perhaps."

"Oh, I'm certain you'll find something here to amuse you, Dare. You've always been rather good at keeping yourself entertained, and London offers plenty of opportunities to indulge your vices."

London, and Lord Derrick's library, as it happened.

Ah, well. Everyone needed to excel at something, and Nick excelled at indulging himself.

He raised an eyebrow at Lady Uplands, who was seated on the other side of the drawing room, tracing a gloved finger over her swollen lips and eyeing him hungrily, much as she had the beef course at dinner.

Spectacular bosom still—not an inch of sag since he'd fondled it two years ago. But he'd explored it many times before, and a man needed variety. He couldn't tup the same lady time and time again any more than he could read a single book over and over, or eat the same meal every time he sat down at table.

Besides, the encounter with Lady Uplands had depressed his spirits. The dark library, her skirts clenched in his fists, her heaving bosom—it was all too familiar. Just like everything else this evening, it made him feel as if he'd never left England at all.

Lady Uplands caught his gaze and darted the tip of her tongue across her top lip.

Nick covered his mouth with his hand to hide a yawn.

How subtle.

She might lick her lips all she liked, and his cock might twitch as hopefully as *it* liked, but it would be best if he resisted paying her a visit in Harley Street tonight. Even if he was tempted to while away a few hours with her, a dalliance with Lady Uplands wouldn't improve his standing with his aunt. He'd already managed to drive Lady Westcott to the edge of her patience in the few short weeks since he'd returned to England, and Lady Uplands was just the kind of vice that would send his aunt hurtling over the edge.

Lady Westcott did not, alas, choose for him to spend the whole of every night engaged in debauchery, or the whole of every day asleep in his bedchamber, recovering from said debauchery. It was not, in her opinion, a proper use of the Earl of Dare's time.

The chit at the pianoforte tortured the final notes out of Moore's "The Minstrel Boy," accepted the polite applause with a curtsy, and resumed her seat on the settee.

"I thought she'd never be done," Derrick muttered. "I don't know that I can sit and listen to another bout of ceaseless pounding—"

"Miss Somerset, will you play?"

Nick followed Lady Derrick's gaze to a yellow silk settee near the back of the room, to a young lady who froze like a frightened rabbit at the request.

It was his sweet little dinner companion with the dark blue eyes, fair hair, and pretty lips. When he'd taken his seat across from her at table she'd flushed as pink as a peony, and hadn't been able to bring herself to meet his gaze.

"Ah, see how clever my wife is." There was no mistaking the way Lord Derrick lingered possessively over the words *my wife*. "We'll be fortunate indeed if Lady Derrick can persuade Miss Somerset to play. She displays her musical skills only rarely, but they're exceptional."

Nick stifled another yawn. He didn't much care whether the chit played or not. "Somerset, you said? I don't recognize the name. Who is she?" Oddly, he didn't recall Derrick introducing them at dinner.

"Hyacinth Somerset. She's one of Lady Chase's granddaughters."

Nick's gaze narrowed on Miss Somerset as she seated herself on the pianoforte bench and paused, her fingers poised above the keys. "Lady Anne Chase? I didn't realize she had granddaughters."

Lady Chase was one of a group of a dozen matrons who continued to hold considerable power over fashionable London, despite their advanced age. She was alternately feared for her irascibility and respected for her spotless character and vast fortune, but no matter what one thought of her, she was indisputably one of the grand old dames of London.

"They only came to London two years ago, to live with Lady Chase after their parents were killed in an unfortunate accident. Hyacinth Somerset is a sweet little thing, and a dear friend of Lady Derrick's. She plays beautifully, but she's rather timid, I'm afraid."

Nick stifled a snort. Timid? She looked as if she were about to fall into a terrified swoon. The delicate pink had leached from her cheeks, leaving her so pale she was gray, and her hands were trembling. For God's sake, what was wrong with the chit? Surely she'd displayed her musical skills in dozens of drawing rooms before this? Nick stifled a sigh as her fingers sank to the keys, and he braced himself for another lackluster performance.

There was a collective indrawn breath as Miss Somerset's fingers began to move delicately over the keys, and Nick went still as the first dozen notes of Haydn's final piano sonata floated through the drawing room. A hush fell as she sank into the piece, a faint smile curling her lips as the light, trilling notes tumbled over each other.

The tense muscles in Nick's neck eased, and a flush of pleasure washed over him, akin to the feeling one got when sinking into a warm bath after a day spent outdoors in the cold. He was particularly fond of Haydn, and he'd never heard this piece played so beautifully. Miss Somerset's technical skill was impressive, but she'd also captured the exuberant, whimsical quality of the music, and she took such obvious delight in playing that it was a joy to listen to her.

Joy. Now that…*that* was something new.

When she was finished she sat for a moment at the piano bench, lost in the music still, but her head jerked up at the enthusiastic applause, and her eyes widened, as if she were surprised to find a crowd of people in the room.

She rose awkwardly to her feet, and Nick half-rose himself, but before he could offer to escort her back to her place Lady Derrick hurried over, wrapped an arm around Miss Somerset's shoulders, and led her from the drawing room.

Derrick nodded at a fair-haired lady and a tall, stern gentleman who followed after them. "That's her sister, Lady Huntington, and the Marquess of Huntington with her."

"Why is Miss Somerset in London at all this time of year?" It wasn't as if it were the middle of the season, after all. "She must be off to the country soon for the holidays."

"Lady Chase has a country estate in Buckinghamshire, but she never goes. She claims it's too far. She's rather fussy, and she detests the country. She rarely leaves London, and she insists upon having her granddaughters with her at all times."

"Miss Somerset is a pretty little thing. I don't believe you introduced me to her at dinner, Derrick. Why don't you, and perhaps I'll call on her tomorrow." It was something to do, anyway, and the gesture would please his aunt. Even with her exacting standards, she couldn't find anything to fault in one of Lady Chase's granddaughters.

But Lord Derrick let out a short laugh and shook his head. "An introduction? No, indeed. Miss Somerset is a *lady*, Dare, not an opera singer or an actress, or a lusty widow looking for a protector. Introducing her to you would be like throwing a tender lamb straight into the lion's jaws."

Nick stared at his old friend, a sudden, bitter anger burning his throat. He should have known Derrick hadn't simply *forgotten* to introduce him to Miss Somerset. It had been intentional, and there could be only one reason for such a slight. Nick didn't deny he was a rogue, but for all his wicked ways, he wasn't a despoiler of virgins.

"Christ, Derrick. Do you truly believe I'd insult an innocent young lady? I may not be Graham, but I'm not an utter villain."

A dull red flush spread over Lord Derrick's face. "I beg your pardon, Dare. I didn't mean to suggest...my wife is very fond of the Somerset sisters, and Hyacinth Somerset is...unusual. I'm afraid we're all rather overprotective of her."

"Yes, well, I didn't ask you to deliver her to my bedchamber like some kind of pagan sacrifice, Derrick. It's a simple introduction, that's all. If the lady doesn't care for me, I'll leave her alone."

Of course, she *would* care for him. Ladies always did, and with little effort on his part.

As if to prove this point, Lady Uplands caught his eye from the other side of the room and began to pout and nibble at her lips. Nick let his gaze drift from her luscious mouth to her spectacular bosom, and all at once he recalled a special sensual talent of hers, one that involved her two best features:

Those pouting lips, and that generous bosom.

Perhaps he'd pay her a brief visit in Harley Street tonight, after all. His aunt didn't need to know—

"I suppose an introduction won't hurt," Lord Derrick allowed. "As I said before, she's shy, but I'll see if she'll agree to come back to the drawing room with me. If she does, you'll act the proper gentleman, Dare."

"What, you mean no leering, and no suggestive comments? No throwing her over my shoulder and—"

"Damn it, Dare."

"For God's sake, Derrick. I'm only jesting. Despite what you may think, I *do* know how to behave myself with a lady."

He simply chose not to most of the time.

Derrick gave him a narrow look, then rose reluctantly to his feet. "See that you do, then."

He left the drawing room with a resigned sigh, and Nick relaxed against the settee. When Derrick returned with Miss Somerset he'd smile charmingly, compliment her performance, and ask for permission to call on her tomorrow. She'd grant it, and he'd take care to mention the call to his aunt, to get back in her good graces.

"I wish you a pleasant evening, Lord Dare."

Nick looked up to find Lady Uplands standing next to the settee. He got to his feet and offered her a polite bow. "Are you off so soon, my lady?"

Her lips curled in an inviting smile. "Oh, I think we've wrung about as much pleasure as we can from this evening, don't you, my lord? It grows late." She waved a hand around the room. "How long do you intend to stay? Everyone else has gone."

Nick took in the empty room with a frown. Damn it, where the devil was Derrick? He wanted the introduction, and didn't like to abandon a chance to appease his aunt with so little inconvenience to himself, but he also didn't intend to wait all bloody night for the chit to work up the nerve to return to the drawing room.

"I understand you'll be in London for some time, my lord." Lady Uplands licked her generous lower lip and gazed up at him with heavy eyes. "I do hope you'll come see me during your stay. You've an open invitation to come as often as you wish."

Nick forgot all about Miss Somerset and grinned down at Lady Uplands with frank appreciation. There was a great deal to be said for a lady who knew precisely what she wanted. "I'd like nothing more than to come see you, my lady." He dropped his voice to a whisper and leaned closer to murmur directly into her ear. "*All* of you."

She let out a low, sultry laugh. "How delightful."

Nick opened his mouth to agree, but before he got the chance, Miss Somerset wandered into the drawing room, alone. Nick glanced at the door, but to his annoyance, Derrick didn't appear.

Miss Somerset arched an eyebrow when she noticed him standing with Lady Uplands, and an odd little smirk drifted over her lips, but she didn't pay them any further attention. She glanced around as if she were looking for something, then strolled across the drawing room toward the pianoforte.

"My lord?" Lady Uplands ran a finger flirtatiously down his arm. "Will you follow me in your carriage?"

"You may count upon it, my lady." But Nick had turned his attention to Miss Somerset, who'd retrieved a blue wrap that had fallen to the floor beside the pianoforte bench, and was about to walk out of the room.

Bloody hell.

His gaze shot hopefully to the drawing room door, but Derrick was still nowhere in sight. It wasn't proper for him to speak to Miss Somerset without first being introduced to her, but if he didn't take his chance now, he doubted he'd get another.

Propriety be damned. He'd never paid the least bit of attention to it before, so why should he start now? "Ah, Miss Somerset? May I have word, if you please?"

Lady Uplands and Miss Somerset both gaped at him, shocked at his lapse in manners, then Lady Uplands let out a faint hiss and turned away with a toss of her head. Miss Somerset gave her a wide berth as her ladyship flounced out of the room, then she turned her attention back to Nick.

A strange look passed over her face, as if she were trying to make up her mind whether to be horrified or amused. Her gaze swept from the top of his head to his boots, but he fancied she lingered on his waistcoat, and his...

Dear God, was she staring at his breeches?

Unfamiliar embarrassment rushed over him, heating his neck. Christ, were his falls disarranged after the skirmish with Lady Uplands? Before he could stop himself, he gave his coat a self-conscious tug to hide any irregularities. Miss Somerset made a faint noise, and his gaze jerked to her face just in time to see her expression tip from embarrassment into sly amusement.

He stared at her, dumbfounded into silence. He hadn't expected such bold assurance from a lady who'd nearly fallen into a mortified swoon after a pianoforte performance. He studied her for a moment, his gaze narrowed, but there was no mistaking the dark blue eyes and fair hair, the pretty pink lips. She was more petite than he'd thought, and there was an impish quality to her smile he hadn't expected, but then he hadn't paid much attention to her until now.

"How can I help you, my lord?"

Her gaze swept over him again, and this time she lingered on his breeches with such fixed attention that for one wild moment Nick thought she was asking if she could help him button his falls.

For God's sake, forget your falls and gather your wits.

"Forgive me, Miss Somerset." He crossed the room and sketched an elegant bow in front of her. "I realize we haven't been introduced, but I couldn't let you leave without telling you how much I enjoyed your performance this evening."

She looked appalled, and her cheeks flooded with color. "My, ah...my performance? I don't know what you...that is, I didn't see...I'm not sure what you mean, my lord."

Nick stared at her, taken aback by this odd reaction, but then Derrick had said she was timid. Perhaps she was embarrassed by compliments.

"Your pianoforte performance. The Haydn," he offered, careful to keep his voice gently modulated, lest she fly into a panic and dart from the room. "I'm fond of his piano sonatas, and you played beautifully."

"Oh." Her brows drew together in a puzzled frown, but then her face cleared. "*Oh*. Yes. The Haydn. Of course. What else could you possibly mean? I, ah—well, thank you. You're very kind, my lord."

"It gave me a great deal of pleasure to listen. I don't know that I've ever enjoyed a performance more." He curled his lips into the practiced smile that never failed to charm young ladies, and waited for her answering blush.

But Miss Somerset didn't blush. Instead she scrutinized him with an intensity that put him in mind of his aunt right before she delivered a blistering scold. "Pleasure. Yes, I daresay one doesn't always get quite so much pleasure from a dinner party as you enjoyed tonight."

It was an odd thing to say, and Nick stumbled over his reply. "Yes, well, not many young ladies play as well as you do. Might I call on you tomorrow, Miss Somerset, to inquire after your health?" He flushed at the abruptness of this request. Damn it, he was never so clumsy, particularly with ladies, but all of his smooth charm seemed to have withered in the face of Miss Somerset's forthright gaze.

She must have found his address as lacking as he found it himself, because she shook her head. "No, I think not, my lord. We haven't been introduced."

"I'm Lord Dare, and you are Miss Somerset." He bowed a second time, then held her gaze as he took her hand and brought it to his lips. "There. Now may I call on you?"

Ah, much better. That had been charming. Surely she'd capitulate now—

"No, thank you, Lord Dare." Her tone was polite but brisk, and she draped the blue wrap over her arm with a finality that indicated the discussion was over, and she was ready to leave.

Nick's mouth fell open. For such a timid little mouse, she'd dispensed with him rather neatly. But he had no intention of arguing with her. A gentleman never argued with a lady, after all. Pity, for she would have proved rather useful in his dealings with his aunt, but he'd wasted enough time on Miss Somerset.

He offered her a cool smile and a polite bow. "Very well. I wish you a pleasant evening, then."

She nodded and made her way to the door, but before she disappeared through it she paused to look back at him, and the mischievous smile he'd noticed earlier flirted at the corners of her lips. "Oh, Lord Dare? I enjoyed *your* performance this evening, as well."

"My performance?" He hadn't the faintest idea what she was talking about, but he had the distinct impression she was laughing at him.

"Oh, yes. I was greatly entertained by your...vigorous efforts."

What the devil did that mean? Nick's mouth opened, but before he could come up with a lucid reply, Miss Somerset was gone.

Chapter Three

Someone had sewn his tongue to the roof of his mouth. Nick couldn't imagine who'd do such a fiendish thing, but the villain was likely the same person who'd stuffed his head full of cotton wool.

A faint shuffling sound made him crack open one eye just wide enough to catch a movement near the bed, and a defeated groan escaped his dry, cracked lips. He'd fallen asleep in Lady Uplands's bed, hadn't he? Damn it, he was going to have a devil of a time escaping her this morning without a repeat of last night's debauchery, and the ache in his temples made further acrobatics impossible—

"Ah, very good, my lord. You're awake."

Nick cracked open his other eye to find a long, dour face peering down at him, and a quick stab of temper chased away the last hazy remnants of sleep.

Christ. He was in his own bed, thankfully, but his aunt had sent up Gibbs to chase him out of it again.

Lady Westcott had been happy enough to leave Nick to himself when he'd first returned to England, but once it became clear his dissolute behavior was habitual, she'd set Gibbs on him like a Bow Street runner after a thief.

Gibbs had been Graham's valet for the past five years, but Nick seemed to have inherited him along with the title and the country estate. Neither he nor Gibbs were particularly happy about it. Gibbs was accustomed to serving Graham, who'd been the epitome of English gentlemanliness. Nick was accustomed to being left alone to do as he bloody well wished, and he *didn't* wish Gibbs's frightening visage to be the first thing he saw every morning.

Or the second thing, come to that.

"Awake? How optimistic you are, Gibbs. I'm not certain I'm even *alive*."

"Death is, I believe, an adequate excuse for not rising before dusk, my lord. Shall I inform her ladyship you're deceased?"

Nick rolled his eyes. Gibbs specialized in sarcasm. "Certainly, if it will get you to cease plaguing me. What the devil do you think you're doing gawking at me while I'm in my bed, Gibbs? I didn't send for you."

He *never* sent for Gibbs, but the man kept appearing like an unlucky penny.

"No, my lord. Your aunt sent me to you. Her ladyship expressed some anxiety at your persistent fatigue. She's concerned you may be ill."

Nick scowled. He never rose before dusk, and he didn't intend to start today. "As you can see, there's not a damn thing wrong with me four more hours of sleep won't cure. Go and inform her ladyship I'm perfectly well, and don't come back until I send for you."

"It is her ladyship's considered opinion a healthy young gentleman does not remain abed until sunset. Do you require a doctor, my lord?"

Nick groaned. "For God's sake. *No*. No bloody doctor. What time is it?"

"Noon, my lord."

"*Noon!* Is that all? Get out, Gibbs, and don't return for at least seven more hours." Nick was willing to indulge his aunt's whims to some degree, but this was barbaric.

Gibbs didn't move. "Her ladyship has requested your presence in the drawing room in one hour, Lord Dare."

Nick snorted. "My aunt never *requests* a damn thing."

Still, there was no point in fighting it, and Nick let his head fall back against his pillow with a feeble sigh of resignation. He didn't care for his aunt's high-handedness, but it was too much effort to argue with both her and Gibbs, and he'd have no more luck refusing her now than he had when he was a boy. Either he rose from his bed at once, or this would end with a dozen leeches and a bloodletting.

He threw the blankets back with a defeated sigh. "All right then, Gibbs. Make me presentable."

Gibbs's eyebrow ticked up a fraction, but somehow the tiny movement was enough to convey a world of skepticism. "Perhaps a wash first, Lord Dare."

It took the better part of an hour and a heated argument with Gibbs over an irregularity in the knot of Nick's cravat, but at last his clothing was deemed gentlemanly enough to present himself to his aunt.

"Such a bloody fuss over a cravat." Nick's head was still pounding from the surfeit of whiskey he'd drunk the night before, and the absurd tussle with Gibbs hadn't improved his temper in the least. "Damn nonsense... refuse to wear one at all next time, and see how the old boy likes *that*."

He was still muttering curses when he entered the drawing room, but he forced his lips into a polite mask as he approached his aunt, who was seated on a settee with the silver tea service on the table in front of her, looking as serene and elegant as ever.

"Ah, Nicholas. Here you are at last."

"Good morn—that is, good afternoon, Aunt."

She graced him with a regal smile. "Tea? I'm afraid it's a bit cool now."

"My apologies. Gibbs insisted on retying my cravat until he was satisfied each fold was arranged to mathematical perfection."

"Gibbs takes great pride in his work." She swept a critical gaze over him. "You look well. Every inch a respectable earl."

"Misleading, isn't it? If proper clothing were all it took to transform me from a wastrel into a respectable earl, there might be some point in forcing Gibbs upon me. As it is, I'd just as soon dispense with him."

Lady Westcott replaced her teacup in her saucer with a quiet click. "Yes, I imagine you would, but Gibbs's presence tends to discourage too much...excess, and so one likes to keep him about, despite your objections."

Nick settled onto the settee across from her and crossed one leg over his knee. "I'm not a child, Aunt. I don't require a nanny."

"I'm afraid I don't agree, Nicholas."

Nick's eyes narrowed to slits. Her tone was carefully reasonable, but a storm had been building between them since he'd returned to England, quietly gathering strength as he'd pursued his usual pattern of unchecked debauchery, and now it was about to break over his head with a vengeance.

They regarded each other in silence for a tense moment, then Lady Westcott lifted her teacup to her lips and took a calm sip. "Perhaps you may dispense with Gibbs once you're married."

Nick managed a short laugh, but a cold sweat broke out on his neck. "That won't happen for years yet, and in the meantime I doubt Gibbs will get on well in Italy. He's too English by half, and he looks like the sort who'd wilt under the sun."

His aunt's cool gray eyes held his, and she slowly shook her head. "You're not returning to Italy, Nicholas."

Nick went still as he stared at her, but underneath his forced calm panic fluttered in his belly. "That's not your decision to make, Aunt."

"Certainly it is. Your father left you an ancient, respectable title, a dilapidated country estate, and precious little else. I hold your purse strings, and I'm afraid I can't approve another prolonged Continental sojourn, under the circumstances."

Sweat dampened Nick's cravat until it felt as if a clammy hand were gripping his throat. "And what circumstances are those?"

But he knew—of course he knew. This moment had been bearing down on him like a runaway horse for weeks now, and he was a bloody fool not to have seen it coming.

Lady Westcott raised an eyebrow, as if she were surprised she had to clarify this for him. "You're the Earl of Dare now, Nicholas, and the only surviving member of your family. As such, you'll remain in England, and do your duty to your title by marrying and producing heirs."

Nick gripped his teacup with numb, white fingers. He was aware he'd be required to marry at some point, but some point wasn't necessarily *now*, was it?

"*Duty*. Christ, what a grim word that is."

His aunt's mouth thinned. "Is that meant to be amusing, Nicholas? Because I don't find it so. The fate of the Dare Earldom lies with you, and it's time you began to behave like a proper heir."

Nick stiffened. His father used to say the same thing, except when he told Nick to behave like an earl, what he meant was Nick should behave like Graham.

Become Graham.

At first, right after Graham's death, Nick had tried—God knew he'd tried—but it hadn't taken long before it became clear to them all he'd never be the man Graham had been, and even clearer his father would never be able to forgive him for it.

In the end, it wasn't terribly painful to disappoint someone who expected no better from him, and he'd walked away from his father easily enough.

But his aunt—no, disappointing her was something else entirely.

For all her imperiousness, Nick loved his aunt with the singular fierceness of a boy who'd lost his mother at a tender age. When Nick was a child, his father had been kind enough in a careless sort of way, but the late Earl of Dare had only had enough love for one child, and he'd lavished it all on Graham, his heir.

Nick hadn't ever blamed his father. Everyone who knew Graham loved him with that same kind of intense devotion, including Nick. He'd worshipped his older brother, and Graham had always been his best friend and most loyal champion, even when Nick hadn't been worthy of either distinction.

But it had always been Nick's aunt who'd truly *seen* him. At best, his father had simply tolerated him with a kind of careless, exasperated affection, but his aunt understood him. After Graham's unexpected death, she'd been the one to suggest Nick leave England. Her insistence he journey to the Continent had likely saved his life.

He didn't want to disappoint her, ever, and yet it was inevitable, wasn't it? It was what he did, after all. She'd ask for something he was incapable of giving, and it would cause a rift between them that could never be repaired.

When the silence had stretched to the snapping point, Lady Westcott spoke. "Louisa Covington remains unmarried. She's as lovely as she ever was, and you've always been fond of her."

Nick's blood turned to ice. Surely she wasn't suggesting...

No. He must have misunderstood her. "Louisa Covington."

"She'd do honor to the title. She was born and bred to become a countess."

She had been, and not just any countess: the Countess of Dare.

"Graham's countess, Aunt. Not mine."

His aunt went on as if he hadn't spoken. "And of course the connection between the Dares and the Covingtons is—"

"I could marry Graham's former betrothed, Aunt. I could spend the rest of my days in West Sussex at the estate that should have been his, and wake every morning with his former valet looming over my bed"—Nick's voice wasn't quite steady—"and I'd still never be Graham."

Her expression didn't change, but Lady Westcott's shoulders stiffened. "I've never expected that of you, Nicholas. It's always been *you* who expected it, and it seems two years on the Continent hasn't changed that. How long do you intend to keep hiding?"

As long as it takes.

But there wasn't any point in saying it aloud. There wasn't any point in anything but negotiation now, because the problem, after all, was simple enough. He was back in England, his aunt would do everything she could to keep him here, and he'd do everything he could to escape.

He regarded her in silence for a moment, then threw out his opening gambit. "Come now, my lady. Let's get down to it, shall we? First of all, I will not marry Louisa Covington."

He had no wish to marry at all, but he was the earl now, and he was well aware legitimate heirs were not negotiable. He'd have to marry sooner or later, so it may as well be now, while he was already in England. "I'll choose the lady."

"I don't know what possible objection you can have against Louisa. She's lovely, and such a kind, agreeable young lady."

"Oh, you want to know my objection? Very well. It's a small thing, really. I object to her on the grounds that she's still in love with my dead brother."

"Even more reason for her to marry. Graham is gone, and Lady Covington is anxious for Louisa to move on. She needs a husband, and you can't spend the rest of your life running wild on the Continent. You need a stabilizing influence, and Louisa can provide that."

"Stabilizing influence? Good Lord. That sounds like a grim prospect for poor Louisa. Why not just hire the nanny, and be done with it?"

"Once again, Nicholas, I am *not* amused."

Nick sighed. No matter what Lady Westcott said, he had no intention of remaining in England, wife or no wife. He'd return to Italy at the first possible opportunity, and once he was there he'd lose himself in his mistress's arms until all the years he'd spent in this cursed place became nothing more than a distant, hazy memory.

But he couldn't wed Louisa. She'd been a dear childhood friend, and she'd suffered enough when Graham died. He could never marry her and then abandon her to a lonely fate once he'd put a child in her belly. She deserved far better than that.

No, what he needed was a businesslike arrangement with a lady who'd happily tolerate his absence in exchange for the chance to become a countess. A lady he could tolerate for a few months and just as easily forget when he left her behind.

After he got an heir on her, of course.

"I will not marry Louisa Covington, Aunt. Now that we've settled that, shall we move on?"

Lady Westcott wasn't one to waste her time with fruitless negotiation. She intended for Nick to marry, they both knew it, and now it was just a matter of settling the terms. "But you will marry, and soon."

"Yes, but I'll choose my own bride. This is not a point that's open for discussion, my lady." He didn't intend to be choosy, either. He'd take the scullery maid if it got him out of London sooner.

But his aunt must have read his mind, because she instantly crushed that plan. "Very well, but she must be a lady of impeccable birth and graceful manners. No actresses, none of your former mistresses, and no serving girls, if you please, Nicholas. The lady is to become the Countess of Dare, after all."

Nick gave a reluctant nod. "I'll find a lady you can tolerate, and I'll remain in England long enough to see to the question of an heir, but after that matter is settled, I intend to return to the Continent at once."

Lady Westcott's eyes narrowed. "The Sussex estate is in shambles. You'll see it set to rights for the sake of your tenants, and you'll arrange for a reliable steward to keep it that way. And you'll return to England for one month out of every year."

A month every year? Bloody hell.

"For pity's sake, Nicholas," his aunt snapped when she saw his expression. "Is it too much to ask I be allowed to see my nephew for a single month out of every year? I flatter myself you'll wish to see me before I die, and that's to say nothing of your children, who at the very least are owed a glimpse of their father now and again."

In fact it was very little to ask, and shame crept over Nick, as familiar as it was unwelcome. "Once a year, for one month, and of course you'll come see me in Italy as often as you like."

"Nonsense. I'm much too old to go traipsing around the Continent."

Nick raised his eyebrow at the idea she was too old to do anything at all, but she paid him no mind. Now the negotiations were over, she rose to her feet and smoothed her skirts with businesslike efficiency.

"Dinner is at seven. Do be prompt this time, won't you? You'll give poor Gibbs an apoplexy otherwise." She moved to sweep by him, but at the last moment she hesitated, and laid a hand on his shoulder. "I'm pleased you're here, Nicholas, even if it is only for a short time."

Nick nodded, and after a moment her hand slid away, and she left him alone in the drawing room with bitterness welling in his throat. He wished he could say he was pleased to be here, but as much as he loved his aunt, he couldn't offer even that small, comforting lie—not when every one of his instincts screamed at him to leave England and never look back.

But first, a wife. It should be simple enough to find a willing female. He was an earl now, after all, and heir to Lady Westcott's fortune, which was massive, but there was nothing simple about finding a bride who'd satisfy his aunt's strict requirements.

Even under the best of circumstances it could take months to find a lady she'd deem worthy of the Dare title, and these were not the best of circumstances. He likely wouldn't be able to find a bride before next season, and that was months away.

How convenient for his aunt that his father should have died in the winter instead of early spring. If he didn't know it to be impossible, he'd suspect Lady Westcott of arranging it herself, to keep him in England on a quest for a countess for as long as possible.

Nick cringed at the thought of remaining in London so long, but there was little he could do about it, unless he happened to stumble across an accomplished, well-bred young lady in London in mid-November—

He went still, his thoughts grinding to a complete halt as the strains of Haydn's final piano sonata drifted through his head.

An accomplished, well-bred young lady...

Good Lord, a stroke of luck at last.

As it happened, fate had thrown just such a lady into his path.

Hyacinth Somerset.

If he could have conjured an ideal potential bride with a wave of his hand, Miss Somerset was just the kind of lady he'd produce. She had impeccable bloodlines—even his haughty, demanding aunt couldn't find fault with Lady Chase's granddaughter—and she played the pianoforte like an angel. Her musical ability would be such a comfort to his aunt during the long, lonely English winters at his country seat in West Sussex.

A whirlwind courtship, a quick betrothal, and a quiet wedding. With any luck he'd have a boy in his new bride's belly by Christmas and be back in Italy in Catalina's bed before the spring thaw.

Memories of the Tyrrhenian Sea flashed in his mind's eye—the water sparkling in the warm Italian sun, and Catalina, her skirts hiked to her knees, her generous breasts spilling from her bodice as she crawled toward him across the bed—and they made up his mind.

He needed a proper English wife, and the sooner he secured one, the sooner he could leave London behind him for good.

Nick leapt to his feet with renewed energy, grabbed his hat, and ordered the carriage brought around. In less than half an hour he'd secured Lady Chase's address from Fulton, Lord Derrick's butler, and was thumping on her ladyship's door, one foot tapping impatiently as he waited for someone to come open it.

Now that he'd chosen the lady, he'd just as soon get on with it.

After what seemed an eternity, Nick heard the sound of slow, measured footsteps, and in the next moment the door creaked open to reveal a dusty old relic of at least a thousand years of age, with a face that made Gibbs look cheerful.

The old man shuffled backwards and pulled the door open wider. "Good afternoon, sir."

Nick stepped into the entryway. "Good afternoon. Lord Dare, calling on Lady Chase."

"Lady Chase is not at home this afternoon." The butler retrieved a silver tray from the hall table and waved it under Nick's chin. "Will you leave your card, my lord?"

Not at home? Devil take it. "Miss Somerset, then." Nick couldn't abide even a day's delay, and it wasn't as if the old man knew he and Miss Somerset hadn't been properly introduced.

The butler swept a critical gaze over Nick and his thin lips twitched with disapproval, but he must have drawn the line at refusing to admit the Earl of Dare, because he took Nick's hat and walking stick and ushered him into the drawing room. "If you'll wait here, my lord, I'll fetch Miss Somerset."

The butler shuffled across the room at a glacial pace. When he gained the door at last, Nick threw himself into a chair with an impatient sigh.

Christ, courtship was tedious.

He could only hope Miss Somerset would be reasonable about it. He'd seen very little of her last night, but she hadn't struck him as the type of lady who'd drag out a courtship by feigning maidenly confusion at every turn. He had a vague impression of fair hair, rather remarkable dark blue eyes, and modest, elegant manners—

"What in the world are *you* doing here?"

Nick shot to his feet, turned to face his future betrothed, and stumbled back a step, his mouth falling open in shock.

Miss Somerset stood halfway between him and the drawing room door, her hands on her hips, glaring at him. She was dressed in a faded blue gown, and her hair was bundled into an untidy knot at the back of her neck. She was covered from head to toe with dust, her fingers were smeared with black ink, there was a smudge of dirt on her nose, and...

Was that a cobweb in her hair?

Nick stared at her, aghast.

This was Miss Somerset? Dear God, how much wine had he had to drink last night? She looked like a maidservant who'd spent all afternoon cleaning the chimneys.

"Lord Dare? I beg your pardon, but I can't account for your presence here today. Have you forgotten we were never introduced at Lord Derrick's dinner party last night?"

Nick was striving mightily to collect his wits—or at the very least to close his mouth—but for God's sake, even his stalwart aunt would fall into a swoon if he presented a lady covered in cobwebs as the future Countess of Dare.

But it couldn't be denied Miss Somerset had a significant advantage over any other potential wives:

She was *here*, and ripe for the plucking.

Nick straightened his spine and pasted his most charming smile on his lips. "No, I didn't forget, Miss Somerset, but I was so charmed by your company last night nothing would do but for me to call on you today. I beg your pardon for doing so without a formal introduction. Can you ever forgive me?"

She would, of course. Ladies tended to be quite forgiving of even his most serious transgressions.

Miss Somerset assessed him for a moment, her brows drawn together, but then a tiny grin lifted one corner of her mouth.

Ah, there it was. Where the ladies were concerned, a grin was inevitably followed by a simper, and then unconditional forgiveness. Now, if he could just find a way to rid her of the cobwebs before she met his aunt, all might still be well—

"Tell me, Lord Dare. Does that usually work?"

Nick blinked. "Does what work?"

She waved a hand at him, from the top of his head to his perfectly shined boots. "Oh, you know, the exquisitely tailored clothing, the flattering speech, the charming smile, and so forth."

She wasn't mocking him, or asking sarcastically. She seemed genuinely curious, as if she really wished to know, and much to his dismay, her forthright manner startled the truth into leaping from Nick's lips. "Generally speaking, yes."

"Oh. How interesting." She regarded him for a long moment, her head cocked as if she were attempting to measure the impact of his charm, then she shrugged. "It doesn't with me."

Again, there was nothing ugly in her tone—no rancor or disgust—she was simply making an observation. Nick's lips twitched, and for the first time since she'd entered the drawing room, he forgot about the cobwebs. "No? Well, perhaps you'll change your mind by the time I've taken my leave."

She considered this, then offered him a polite smile. "No, I don't think so. You may as well take your leave now. Good afternoon, Lord Dare."

And then with a sweep of blue skirts she was gone, leaving a cobweb floating on the air and Nick, open-mouthed, behind her.

Chapter Four

Several days later

"Violet! For goodness' sake, child. Must you push your food about the plate in that disgusting manner? William, clear Miss Violet's place."

Lady Chase nodded at the footman, who stepped forward and whisked Violet's plate away while her fork was still hovering over her eggs. Violet blinked, then tossed her napkin onto the table with a sigh. "My breakfast seems to have vanished. I do hope my tea will linger long enough for me to taste it."

She'd been living in her grandmother's Bedford Square townhouse for two years now, and should have long since learned to hold her tongue in the face of the old lady's quirks, but she'd never been as good at it as her sisters were, perhaps because she was far too much like Lady Chase for either of their comfort.

But she had too much to do today to waste time fussing over vanishing eggs, so she gave her grandmother a bland smile and shoved her chair back from the table, ready to flee to the old schoolroom and work on her book, as she did every day.

Before she could escape, however, Lady Chase's gnarled claw clamped down on her wrist. "Just where do you suppose you're going, miss?"

"I thought I'd, ah...go to my bedchamber to work on my embroidery."

Violet had told this lie so often the prickle of guilt she used to feel whenever it left her lips had become nothing more than the merest twinge of conscience, mild and easily dismissed. She did wonder, though, why Lady Chase never became suspicious when she failed to produce any embroidery.

"Never mind that today. I've arranged for us to visit my modiste this morning."

Most young ladies would be delighted to spend the morning choosing silks, satins, and lace to be made up into dozens of beautiful gowns, but not Violet. As soon as she heard the word "modiste," her mouth went dry and her stomach threatened to disgorge the few bites of egg she'd managed to eat. "Why should you need me to go?"

"To begin fittings for your next season, of course. We must secure Madame Bell before the usual parade of mindless chits descend on her after the holidays. I think pink and yellow for your gowns this year, Violet, with perhaps a pale blue one here and there for—"

"No." Violet recoiled from her grandmother's words just as she would from a fist aimed at her face. "No."

"What, no blue? But it's so flattering with your eyes—"

"No season." Despite the deep breath she'd drawn, there was a tremor in Violet's voice. "We agreed I would be required to endure one season only."

"Yes, well, I only agreed to that ridiculous condition because I expected a young lady with your pretty face and substantial fortune would secure an earl in your first season, or at the very least a viscount. But here we are, Violet, so unless you've got a husband tucked away in the attics, I suggest you reconcile yourself to a morning at Madame Bell's."

"No. I don't want a viscount, or an earl, or even a duke, and a second season isn't going to change that. I don't intend to ever repeat that dreadful experience."

"You *will* repeat it until you're married, and no arguments, miss."

Violet's temper was rising in tandem with her panic, and both were threatening to burst into a flood of ugly, hurtful words. She gritted her teeth to hold them in. "No. I've made up my mind never to marry, Grandmother."

"Nonsense, you silly girl. Of course you'll marry."

"No, I won't. I don't like to disappoint you, but there can be no reason for me to suffer through a second season."

Violet wasn't a meek or fearful creature, but nothing of her life in Surrey could have prepared her for the malice and derision she'd faced during her one London season. It had been an utter disaster from start to finish, and so hurtful that even the idea of a second one made her shudder with dread. The only thing that had made it bearable was Iris's and Honora's staunch loyalty and support, but they were both married now. If Violet let her grandmother talk her into another season she'd have to endure it alone, with no Iris to soothe her feelings when the other young ladies treated her with mocking disdain, and no Honora to squeeze her hand when the gentlemen snickered at her graceless dancing.

No Lord Derrick, with his encouraging smile and kind brown eyes.

They'd been less than a week into last season when it became clear Violet was destined to become a pitiful wallflower. If it hadn't been *quite* as awful as she'd dreaded, she had Lord Derrick to thank for it. He'd invited her to dance at every ball, and he'd listened with polite attention when she told him of her studies. He'd been her friend when all the other fashionable gentlemen had treated her as if she were invisible. He'd never mocked her—instead, he'd done all he could to befriend her.

The only thing he hadn't done—couldn't do—was fall in love with her.

"Very well, Violet. If you insist on becoming a lonely spinster, I suppose there's not a thing I can do about it." Lady Chase gave a careless shrug, but there was a calculating gleam in her eyes. "But I want to have a few gowns made up for the spring for myself. You'll come with me to the modiste's, won't you, dear? Just to help me choose my silks for the season, of course."

Violet was far too wily not to recognize sneakiness in another, and she shook her head. "I wish I could help you, my lady, but as you know, I'm hopeless with silks and lace. Why, I can't tell Belgian from Brussels, or jonquil from primrose. Indeed, my temples are throbbing even now, just thinking about it. You're much better off taking Hyacinth."

Lady Chase's face darkened to an ominous shade of red. "Shame on you, Violet! I vow you're the most stubborn, willful, and headstrong chit—"

Violet didn't stay to hear the rest, but turned on her heel, escaped into the hallway, and hurried up the stairs until her grandmother's scolds faded to silence behind her.

She had, after all, heard it all before.

* * * *

Four hours later, Violet tossed aside the paper in her hand with a sigh. She'd been staring at her list for the better part of the afternoon, and she'd yet to come up with a plan to get the sketches she needed to complete her book.

As with everything else, it was a question of access. Through a combination of stealth and wiliness she'd managed to get a sketch of the gallows at Tyburn, and one of Newgate Prison. She'd coaxed Iris's coachman into lingering on St. James's Street in front of the bow window at White's for long enough to get a rough drawing of it, but there were a half dozen locations still on her list, each more unlikely than the last. A respectable young lady didn't just happen to stumble upon Cockpit Steps after dark, or suddenly find herself standing at Execution Dock with her sketchbook in hand. She didn't dig about in the dirt at Bunhill Fields Burial Ground on a hunt for the stray bones of plague victims, either.

Violet shuffled some papers about on the long table she'd dragged into the middle of the old schoolroom, and laid out a blank page at the end of the chapter she'd entitled, "The Black Death: London Overrun with Corpses."

She stood back, her arms crossed, and surveyed the array of papers.

No, it wouldn't do. She must have the burial grounds.

She ran a critical eye over her finished sketches, and a colored drawing she'd begun the day after Lord Derrick's dinner party caught her eye. She'd finished it last night, and now she plucked it from the pile, a quiet laugh escaping her as she studied it.

Oh, she'd done him justice, hadn't she? She'd spent hours on the rakish tilt of his head, the bored, sulky twist of his full lips, the heaviness of his eyelids over his sleepy gray eyes, as if they were weighed down by that thick, dark fringe of eyelashes.

The Selfish Rake.

Violet ran a finger over the title she'd scrawled across the top of the sketch, her grin widening. There was no denying Lord Dare was exquisitely handsome. Rakes and scoundrels generally were, but he was a shining example of the type, and she'd gotten a good, long look at him while he'd had Lady Uplands pinned against Lord Derrick's bookshelf. Her view had been limited mostly to his back, of course, but one would never know it to look at the sketch.

It was flawless.

How lovely of Lord Dare to appear in London just in time to serve as the model for her "Gentlemen, Rakes, and Rakes who Pose as Gentlemen" chapter. It was rather thin on content—so thin she'd been on the verge of scrapping it altogether—but she'd done a truly lovely drawing of Lord Derrick entitled "The Ideal Gentleman," and now that she had Lord Dare as her rake, she'd decided the two drawings taken together more than made up for any other shortcomings.

Still, as spectacular as the sketch of Lord Dare was, a dozen drawings of selfish rakes wouldn't make up for the lack of ghosts and burial grounds.

Violet set the drawing of Lord Dare aside and tapped her quill against her chin, considering. She didn't like it, but perhaps she could manage without the sketch of Cockpit Steps. But she couldn't part with the burial grounds—not on any account. If she didn't get that sketch, she'd have to scrap the pages she'd so painstakingly written on the plague epidemic, and it was one of her best. No self-respecting scholar would include a chapter on a deadly London epidemic and then leave out a drawing of a purported gravesite, but when she'd ventured to suggest to her grandmother she'd like to take some sketches of the burial grounds, Lady Chase had refused her permission, because "corpses weren't ladylike."

It was utter nonsense, of course—it wasn't as if dozens of old corpses were piled on top of each other in plain sight—but she was afraid if she insisted, her grandmother might ask questions Violet would rather not answer.

No, she'd simply have to get the sketches she needed without her grandmother's knowledge. She could try and wheedle Iris into taking her, but her sister had developed a troubling habit of confiding everything to her husband, and—

Violet froze at the quiet tread of footsteps on the stairs leading up to the schoolroom, then scrambled to her feet and dove for the table. Her grandmother rarely ventured to the third floor, but there was no telling what the old lady might take it into her head to do if she was still in a temper over the modiste.

Violet's fingers scrabbled frantically over the wood as she shoved her papers into an untidy pile and stuffed them under the cushion of an old chair she'd placed beside the table for just this purpose. Once the papers were secure, she threw herself on top of the cushion, reached under the chair to snatch a piece of embroidery with a dusty, faded image of a vase of roses stretched over the hoop, and pasted what she hoped was an innocent look on her face.

"It's only me."

Hyacinth's face appeared at the top of the stairs, and Violet sagged against the cushion with a sigh of relief. "Oh, thank goodness. I thought for certain it was Grandmother. She's been threatening to come up here and find out what 'foolish nonsense' has me so occupied."

"She nearly did come this time, but I reminded her how difficult the stairs were with her cane and offered to come myself." Hyacinth leaned against the edge of the table. "How does the book come on?"

Violet tossed aside her embroidery, leapt up from the chair, and dragged the loose sheaf of papers out from under the cushion.

She ran a careful hand over the title page to smooth it.

A Treatise on London for Bluestockings and Adventuresses.

Her beloved book. She'd written every word herself. It was, from beginning to end, her own creation. She'd even drawn the frontispiece—a lady seated in front of a fire with an open book in her hands and a serious, learned expression on her face.

She'd never shown the book to anyone. Iris and Hyacinth knew of its existence, and they'd both seen a page here or there, but only Violet knew every page by heart.

"The book comes on, but I must have the sketches, Hyacinth. It simply won't do to leave them out. One can't have a chapter entitled "Haunted London: Ghosts and Specters Run Amok in the Capital" without even one sketch of a haunted alleyway, or a chapter on the plague without a drawing of the pit at Bunhill Fields Burial Ground."

Hyacinth made a sympathetic sound in her throat, but she shook her head. "Well, you won't get it today. We're off to Iris's for tea this afternoon, remember? Grandmother sent me up to fetch you."

Oh, no. How could she have forgotten about the tea?

Violet hugged her book to her chest to try and calm the sudden, painful kick of her heart. Honora and Lord Derrick would be there. They were leaving London in another few weeks to meet Lord Derrick's family for the Christmas holidays at his country estate in Wiltshire, and they intended to stay throughout the winter.

If she didn't see them today, it might be months before she saw them again.

Months.

God help her, but the thought brought nothing but relief. That is, relief and a sharp sting of guilt. Lord Derrick had always been kind to her, and Honora was her dear friend. They both deserved much more generous treatment, but at the moment Violet could hardly bring herself to look at Honora, and she certainly couldn't look at Lord Derrick without a shameful press of tears behind her eyes.

She didn't blame either of them for her heartbreak. How could she? It wasn't Honora's fault Lord Derrick had fallen madly in love with her instead of with Violet. She didn't want to feel this way—to be selfish and hateful and begrudge her friends their happiness—and yet somehow the logic of the thing faded to insignificance in comparison to the pain of a broken heart.

"I can't go to tea at Iris's this afternoon, Hyacinth. I've, ah—I've got the headache."

Hyacinth knew very well it wasn't Violet's head that ached, but bless her, she didn't say a word. "You'll have to come down and tell Grandmother, then. She'll insist on seeing you herself."

Violet sighed. "Yes, all right." She smoothed her papers into perfect order and slid them carefully under the cushion, then followed Hyacinth down the stairs.

Lady Chase was waiting for them in the entryway, her cane clutched between her gloved hands. Violet blinked at her grandmother's hat—a monstrous black and red creation adorned with an enormous ostrich feather. It was seated squarely on top of her head, and lent a sinister quality to the peevish expression on her face.

"Well, Violet. Here you are at last, but my goodness, what are you wearing? You look as if you dragged that dress out of the dust bin, and your fingers are black with ink!"

Violet looked down at her gown. Oh, dear. She was covered with streaks of dust. She tried to brush it off, but only succeeded in smearing the ink across a fold of the faded blue skirt.

"What's to be done with you, Violet?" Lady Chase demanded in fretful tones. "You look like a scullery maid. Quickly, go up and change at once. We'll be late again, but it can't be helped, and—no, Hyacinth, dear. Don't try and brush the dust off your sister. You'll only end up covered in ink."

"It's all right, Hyacinth." Violet caught her sister's hand and gave it a reassuring squeeze before bravely facing her grandmother. "Do go on without me, Grandmother. I don't wish to make you late on my account, and I've a dreadful headache, in any case. I should rest this afternoon."

"You've a headache because you spend all your time in that dreary schoolroom, you silly child." Lady Chase's gaze narrowed on her, assessing her from head to toe, but to Violet's surprise her grandmother's expression softened, and the scold Violet expected never came. "Well, go on to your bedchamber for a rest, then. Hyacinth and I will make your excuses to Iris. Come along, Hyacinth."

Violet quivered with impatience as her grandmother and sister sailed forth, but at last they were comfortably settled in the carriage, and it was rolling down the drive.

She peeked out the window until she was certain it had disappeared, then she turned and darted back up the stairs to fetch her sketchbook and cloak. It was time to get on with the business at hand—becoming London's most notorious spinster bluestocking. She had sketches to do, and they wouldn't get done by languishing in her bedchamber.

She crept back down to the entryway and threw a nervous glance over her shoulder before easing the door open. Eddesley, the butler, had been steadfast in his disapproval of her since she'd first set foot in her grandmother's Bedford Square townhouse. Violet wasn't certain what she'd done to offend him, but she was anxious to escape his disapproving eye.

For once, fate was on her side. No one was about. The entryway was still and silent.

That was one problem solved, but she had another. Lady Chase and Hyacinth had taken the carriage. Her grandmother had a barouche as well, but Violet couldn't ask for it without alerting Eddesley, who'd gleefully report the request to her grandmother at the first opportunity.

No, she couldn't risk it. She'd have to take a hack, but that presented its own set of problems, the main one being she'd have to secure it herself, and ride all the way to Islington unaccompanied.

Well, it couldn't be helped, and fortune was said to favor the bold, wasn't it?

Freedom was in short supply in Lady Chase's household, but here was an entire afternoon of it dropped right into her lap, and Violet didn't intend to squander it. A little cry of glee bubbled up in her throat as she darted through the door, cleared the top step with one exuberant leap, and…

Slammed right into a solid, masculine chest.

"Miss Somerset!" Strong arms closed instinctively around her to keep her from toppling down the remaining stairs.

Violet's first panicked thought was that it was Eddesley, but she discarded it at once. If she'd careened into Eddesley with such force he would have collapsed into a heap like a stack of wooden blocks, and whoever'd caught her had a chest like a stone wall.

"My God, are you all right?"

A large hand settled on the back of her neck, and for a single, delirious moment Violet let her eyes close and her head rest against the hard, warm chest under her cheek. Goodness, whoever he was, he smelled divine.

A low rumble vibrated under her cheek. "Well, I'm pleased to see you as well. I confess I didn't expect quite so warm a welcome, given you practically tossed me out of your drawing room when I called yesterday."

Violet's eyes flew open.

Oh, no. Not him. Not again.

But of course it *was* him. Who else but Lord Dare could contrive to smell as if he'd just emerged from a bath warmed by a smoky fire, then walked through a forest of pine and cedar trees? For pity's sake, no *other* gentleman smelled like amber and freshly cut wood. Why should *he* be permitted to run about London, smelling so intoxicating?

She jerked free of his arms and looked up to meet his amused gaze. Lord Dare seemed always to be amused over one thing or another. Violet resented being the source of his unending glee, but she couldn't deny the glimmer of humor did wonderful things for his eyes.

They were gray, but not a common, dull sort of gray. No, of course not, because nothing so ordinary would do for a paragon of masculine beauty like Lord Dare. His eyes were a distinctive silvery-gray, with a black ring around the irises, and he had the longest black lashes she'd ever seen.

"How extraordinary," she murmured, forgetting herself as she stared up at him. Perhaps she'd have to make the tiniest adjustment to her drawing to make his eyelashes longer and thicker.

A slight smile tugged at his lips. "I beg your pardon?"

Her face heated with mortification. "I—nothing. That is, what are you doing here *again*, Lord Dare?"

She *had* tossed him out of her drawing room yesterday. She'd tossed him out the day before, as well, and the day before that, and yet here he was again, like a weed that kept reappearing after one was sure they'd yanked it out by the root.

"I came to call on you, and it seems I've arrived just in time to save you from falling down the stairs."

His warm palm was still wrapped around her neck. Violet twisted free of his touch and stepped backward, stumbling a little on the stair behind her. Yes, that was better. She had some chance of gathering her wits now that he was no longer touching her.

"Nonsense. I don't need saving."

Why did he persist in appearing on her doorstep? It was most troublesome, not only because he kept turning up when she'd forbidden it, but also because she'd been dealing him a rather dirty trick since the night of Lord Derrick's dinner party.

He'd mistaken her for Hyacinth that night, and she'd never corrected him. She didn't intend to, either, but if he kept calling at Bedford Square it was only a matter of time before he discovered the truth, and he'd made it clear he *would* keep calling, no matter what she did to try and dissuade him. Indeed, much to Violet's horror, he was behaving very much like a man embarking on a courtship.

It was bad enough a rogue like Lord Dare was pursuing her shy, vulnerable sister, but to make matters worse, he hadn't the least idea *who* he was courting. Violet had assumed he'd discover sooner or later that she wasn't Hyacinth, and would abandon his pursuit after being so ungentlemanly as to mistake one sister for the other.

It was what a decent gentleman would do.

Not that she couldn't understand how he'd confused the two of them. She and her sisters all had fair hair and blue eyes, and one of them was often mistaken for another, especially Violet and Hyacinth, who were only a year apart in age and shared their mother's delicate features. Violet was more petite than Hyacinth, but otherwise it was difficult to tell them apart, and they had been wearing a similar shade of blue on the evening of Lord Derrick's dinner party.

If he'd been anyone else, Violet might have been inclined to excuse his mistake, but she had no patience for fashionable rakes like Lord Dare, and in any case, surely a lady had a right to demand her suitor be able to distinguish her from another lady in a similar gown.

It was all nonsense, of course. Whatever reason Lord Dare had for marrying, they had nothing to do with the lady, and Violet didn't intend to let him anywhere near Hyacinth.

She eyed him now, her arms crossed over her chest. "I specifically asked you not to call on me again, my lord."

He shrugged, then gave her a crooked and utterly charming grin. "I felt certain once you had a chance to think about it, you'd change your mind."

Violet glared at him. Dear God, he was arrogant. It amazed her any lady could tolerate him, even with those lovely gray eyes and absurdly long eyelashes. "I suppose you think that smile assures you a welcome wherever you go."

His grin widened. "It always has before."

"Not this time. I already told you I'm immune to your charms, Lord Dare. Why not go bother some other lady, instead of wasting your time on me?"

"No, I'd much rather bother you. I came to invite you to accompany me on a drive this afternoon, but it seems I've caught you on your way out."

"You have, and even if you hadn't, I wouldn't..." Violet trailed off into silence as she looked over his shoulder and caught sight of a neat phaeton standing in the drive.

She bit her lip. No, it was out of the question.

Wasn't it?

Yes, yes—of course it was. He was awful, and didn't deserve her consideration, but then she would be just as awful as he was if she took advantage of his error.

Wouldn't she?

Then again, a man who couldn't even bother to correctly identify the lady he'd invited for a drive didn't truly merit her concern, did he?

Perhaps not, but careless behavior on his part didn't excuse reprehensible behavior on hers, and if she did go for a drive with him, it would only encourage him to call on Hyacinth again, and Violet didn't want the scoundrel who'd, ah...*entertained* Lady Uplands in Lord Derrick's library prowling after her precious little sister.

"Come, Miss Somerset. A drive around the park won't do you any harm."

But if she did go with him, mightn't it have just the opposite effect? It wasn't as if gentlemen enjoyed her company, or ever fell in love with her, and a gentleman such as this—a rake, with such a winning smile and such lovely gray eyes—was even less likely than most to find her at all desirable. Why, one day with her, and he'd likely never call on Hyacinth again. Really, she'd be doing it for Hyacinth's own good, and—

"I advise you to stop gnawing on your lip like that, Miss Somerset. You'll make it bleed. Now, will you come for a drive, or not?"

She gazed longingly at the phaeton, her fingers digging into the smooth leather of her sketchbook.

Fortune favors the bold...

"Well, Miss Somerset? There are only so many hours of daylight left."

That made up Violet's mind. "Very well, my lord. I'll come for a drive with you."

His eyes lit up with ill-concealed triumph. "Wonderful. Do you prefer Hyde Park, or Richmond?"

She stepped around him and made her way down the stairs. "Neither," she tossed over her shoulder as she climbed into his phaeton. "I want to go to Islington."

Chapter Five

Unusual. That's what Lord Derrick had said about Hyacinth Somerset—that she was *unusual*. He hadn't said a word about her being the most irritating young lady in London.

"Did you know, my lord, this burial ground is rumored to have been a plague pit? Bunhill Fields has quite a history. During the thirteenth century they brought cartloads of bones from the charnel houses at St. Paul's Cathedral and dumped them here."

Here. Nick blinked again, but no matter how many times he did, he was greeted by the same sight each time he opened his eyes. Weathered gray headstones, half of them tipped crazily on their sides in the mud, gnarled tree branches on bare trees, and, in the midst of this desolate landscape, Miss Somerset, a sketchbook tucked under her arm and a glowing smile on her face.

She'd taken him to a burial ground.

When she'd asked him to take her to Islington she hadn't said a word about burial grounds, but here they were at Bunhill Fields, and there she was, her hat straggling down her back and her hair falling from its pins, looking as pleased as if she were parading down Rotten Row with a crowd of besotted suitors on her heels.

"No, I didn't know that. How..."

Morbid? Distressing? Chilling? If he could judge by the fascinated expression on her face, Miss Somerset didn't seem to find it anything of the sort, and Nick was determined to treat everything she said as the most extraordinarily precious pearls ever to drop from a pair of feminine lips. In other words, this wasn't the moment to refuse to share her interest in the, ah...cartloads of corpses.

He forced a pleasant smile to his lips as he floundered for the right word. "Interesting?"

She turned and beamed at him, heedless of the rain soaking her cloak. "Isn't it? Only they didn't bury them properly, you see."

"No?" As far as Nick knew there was only one way to bury a corpse, but he did his best to sound enthralled.

"No. They just tossed them on the ground and covered them with a thin layer of soil."

Good Lord, was he trampling upon some poor devil's skeleton? Nick's gaze shot to his feet and he instinctively jumped back, half-afraid he'd find a skull crushed under his heel, but all he saw was a ruined pair of Hoby boots.

His Hoby boots.

But as bedraggled as he looked, Miss Somerset wasn't precisely the picture of ladylike modesty he recalled from Lord Derrick's dinner party. She was wandering among the crooked stones, dragging her hand over their damp, mossy surfaces as if she didn't notice that her slippers were splattered with mud and her hems a sopping mess.

Every now and then she paused to prod at the mud with her toe, as if she hoped to turn up a bone or two. "Why, I imagine they were tripping over piles of bones for ages afterwards. Oh, I wish I could have experienced it, don't you?"

Oh, yes. Of course he did. Didn't every Englishman long to have been alive to experience the joys of the great plague? "Do I wish I could have seen cartloads of bones, or shallow graves? No, Miss Somerset. I can't say I do."

Nick winced at the irritation in his voice. He'd called on her every day for nearly a week only to have her toss him out on his ear each time. Now he'd at last persuaded her to an outing and secured an opportunity to gain her affections, and his legendary charm seemed to have dissolved in the downpour.

But damn it, how was a gentleman meant to embark on a courtship when the object of his pursuit was half-drowned in mud and so preoccupied with the skeletal remains of plague victims she hadn't even noticed how utterly delightful he was?

He wasn't accustomed to being overlooked by ladies, but Nick was getting the distinct impression he might be here or not, and it wouldn't make the slightest bit of difference to Miss Somerset. If a discontented spirit happened to rise from the ground and snatch him away to the underworld, he doubted she'd even notice.

"Do you ever wonder, Lord Dare, if you can determine something about the grave's occupant by simply touching their headstone? It's a fancy of mine, that one can sense echoes of the dead."

Nick pressed his lips together to smother a derisive snort. Next she'd be trying to persuade him to believe in ghosts. "No, but I confess I don't spend much time in burial grounds."

By choice.

"Oh, well. I find them quite fascinating. The history, you know. From what I've read, the plague pit rumors are unsubstantiated. No one knows what happened to all the bones from St. Paul's, either." She shook her head with a regretful sigh.

For God's sake, he'd never met a lady more preoccupied with bones. "Perhaps we should dig about in the dirt, and see if we can find some."

Despite his vow to be pleasant and charming, Nick's voice was heavy with sarcasm.

But Miss Somerset didn't seem to notice, and she seized on the idea at once. "Can you imagine if we actually found some old bones? How fascinating that would be! But we can't do it today—we didn't bring anything to dig with."

"Yes, because of course that's the only reason we wouldn't muck about in the dirt for skeletons—because we neglected to bring a shovel," Nick muttered.

"I beg your pardon, my lord. Did you say you have a shovel?"

Did he even *own* a shovel? "No, I'm afraid not, Miss Somerset. My apologies."

"Oh." She looked crestfallen for a moment, but then she brightened. "But perhaps you have something else we could use? Not a shovel, but something else that might serve? A walking stick, perhaps?"

Nick leveled her with a hard stare. Did she truly think he'd allow her to scratch about in the dirt with his silver-handled ebony walking stick? "No, nothing. Had I known I'd be visiting a burial ground when I called on you, I might have brought something, but as it is, I've left all my grave digging tools at home."

"Oh, well. That's all right. Perhaps next time."

Next time? He gave her an incredulous look. This was his first and last visit to Bunhill Fields Burial Grounds. "I don't anticipate a second visit, Miss Somerset, and I think we'd better go back now. Your gown and hat, your hair…" He waved a hand toward her. "You're already soaked, and you look a—"

Fright. Nick managed to snap his mouth closed before the word could escape, but it was a near thing. Damn it, this wasn't going at all well. There wasn't a lady in existence who'd encourage a suitor who called her a fright.

She raised an eyebrow at him. "Yes? What were you going to say, Lord Dare?"

"You, ah, you look cold, Miss Somerset. I'd never forgive myself if you should take a chill because of my neglect." *There.* At last, an appropriately gallant speech.

Miss Somerset didn't look the least impressed with his chivalry, however. She shrugged, then turned away from him to wander down a row of headstones, pausing every now and then to peer curiously at the inscriptions. "Yes, all right. As soon as I've got my sketch. It won't take a moment, once I find the right vantage point."

"Sketch? What sketch?" Good Lord, did she intend to keep him out here all day? Nick shivered as a trickle of cold water dripped from his hat brim down his neck.

"Oh, didn't I mention that? I wanted to come today so I could take a sketch of the part of the grounds rumored to have been a plague pit, and—oh look, Lord Dare! It's Susanna Wesley."

Nick stared at her. "Susanna Wesley? You mean the Mother of Methodism? Susanna Wesley is dead, Miss Somerset. Nearly seventy-three years now, I believe."

She turned to look at him, her expression something between exasperation and pity. "Yes, I'm aware she's dead, my lord, and thank goodness for it. Otherwise it would have been a grievous mistake to bury her, wouldn't it? I meant her gravesite, of course. Her son, Charles Wesley, wrote her epitaph. Did you know? No? Oh, well. I won't be a moment."

She sank to her knees in front of a weathered headstone, heedless of the fact her skirt would be ruined with mud, but then she shook her head and rose to her feet again. "No, that won't do. It's too low. Perhaps I'll sit on Mrs. Wesley's headstone. I'm sure she wouldn't mind, particularly since my purpose is a scholarly one."

She gathered her soaked skirts around her and, as daintily as if the headstone were a throne, lowered herself until she was perched on the edge. She settled her sketchbook over one arm and moved her pencil over the paper in quick, confident strokes, her back curled over the page to protect it from the rain.

Nick crossed his arms over his chest and watched her, his gaze moving over her slender shoulders, and then lower, over the long locks of her hair lying in heavy tangles down her back. She had fair coloring, but the rain had darkened her hair to a warm chestnut color.

A dark gray cloud had moved directly overhead, and as he'd predicted the rain began to fall in earnest, but she was utterly absorbed in her drawing and paid it no mind. There was something arresting about her small, serious figure half-hidden among the tall headstones, and a strange daze descended on him as he watched her, lost in his thoughts as he listened to the heavy drops of rain fall onto the rough, cold surface of the headstones around him.

Christ, what a dismal place. So gray and cold, just like every other place in London. Everywhere he looked there was nothing but barren trees and knee-deep mounds of mud where there should be acres of soft green grass. How could anyone live in such a place? How could they bear it—

"There. That's good enough. I can finish it later from memory. I beg your pardon for keeping you standing in the rain, Lord Dare. I'm ready to leave now."

Nick's gaze snapped to Miss Somerset, and he was relieved to see she'd closed her sketchbook at last. He shook off the sudden melancholy that had descended on him and produced his usual charming smile. "No need to apologize, Miss Somerset. I'm pleased to be of service."

He gestured her toward his phaeton, and she tucked her sketchbook under her arm and got to her feet. As she made her way toward the carriage, Nick saw she'd unbuttoned her cloak when she sat down, and he couldn't help but notice her gown was clinging to her legs, revealing the distracting outline of softly curved thighs through the damp muslin.

Miss Somerset was an odd young lady, to be sure, but even covered in mud with rain dripping down her cheeks, she was rather fetching.

She didn't wait for him to assist her into the carriage, but scrambled into her seat before he had a chance to offer his hand. He swung himself up beside her, took up the ribbons, and in the next moment they were dashing through the London streets at a brisk pace.

"I'm afraid you're certain to take a chill," Nick said, after they'd gone for some minutes without speaking.

"Not at all, my lord. I'm quite accustomed to the rain and wet, and I never get ill. I beg you won't concern yourself."

She grasped a fistful of her damp, clinging skirts and tugged. Nick winced at the rude sucking sound they made as they came unstuck from her legs, but he couldn't help glancing over at her to see if he might catch another glimpse of the delicious curve of her thighs. Before he could have another peek, however, his gaze was caught by a tiny smirk on her lips.

He frowned. "For a lady who's soaked to the skin and covered with mud, you look pleased with yourself, Miss Somerset."

She cast him a startled look from the corner of her eye. "Satisfied? No, indeed, Lord Dare. I, ah…well, I'm afraid you're right, and I am a bit chilled, after all."

Nick's eyes narrowed on her flushed cheeks and those pretty lips still glowing a healthy pink when they should long since have turned blue with cold.

She didn't *look* chilled.

"Then I must insist on calling upon you tomorrow, to inquire after your health."

"What? You can't mean you still want to call, after—" She caught herself and cleared her throat. "That is, what I mean to say is, that won't be necessary, Lord Dare."

Nick turned to stare at her, incredulous.

Devil take her, she intended to refuse his next call!

Why, the devious little chit. She never had any intention of encouraging his suit. On the contrary, she'd only allowed him to take her out today because she wanted to get to Islington to get her sketch, and if she could frighten him off with all her talk of bones and disease, so much the better. She'd *used* him, and now that he'd served his purpose, she thought she could discard him without a second thought.

But Nick hadn't spent an entire afternoon standing about in ruined boots with icy water running in rivulets down his back—and discussing corpses, no less—just to be peremptorily dismissed by a crafty minx like Miss Somerset. "Oh, but I'm afraid I must insist on calling. I won't be able to rest easy until I reassure myself regarding your health."

Her health be damned. Nick didn't care if she ended up with a raw throat and a red nose. It was time to bypass her altogether, and secure an introduction to her grandmother. Once Lady Chase knew the Earl of Dare wished to court her granddaughter, Miss Somerset would have a devil of a time escaping him.

No matter how clever she was.

Whatever satisfaction Miss Somerset had taken in the success of her burial grounds mission was now dissolving into uneasiness. "I'm afraid I must discourage you from calling again, my lord. I'm not interested in…"

She felt abruptly silent as he made the turn into Bedford Square and brought his phaeton to a halt in front of the door. A low, distressed sound escaped her throat at the sight of the black crested carriage waiting in the drive.

"Ah, but here's some luck, Miss Somerset." He tossed aside the reins and turned an angelic smile on her. "I believe your grandmother is home. I've heard a great deal about her, and I'm anxious to have the honor of an introduction."

But Miss Somerset didn't appear as enthusiastic as he was, and the phaeton had hardly rolled to a halt before she was scrambling to open the door. "Oh, ah…I'm afraid that won't be possible, my lord. My grandmother never accepts calls this late in the day. Thank you for the drive, and for your diverting company. Good afternoon."

"Pity, but no matter. I'll simply keep calling until she receives me."

There was no mistaking the look of panic that flashed across Miss Somerset's face at this thinly veiled threat. "She won't receive you, Lord Dare. She, ah…she doesn't receive any gentlemen without a formal introduction."

Nick raised a skeptical eyebrow at this. He knew a blatant lie when he heard one. "How fortunate we have you to introduce us, then."

"Oh, I…well, we'll see. I can't make any promises, I'm afraid."

She tried to leap from the carriage, but he laid a hand on her arm to stop her. Damn her, she wasn't going to brush him off as if he were a bit of dried mud clinging to her skirts. If she wouldn't invite him inside, he'd keep her sitting out here on the drive until someone inside the house noticed his phaeton and came out to investigate.

"Wait, Miss Somerset. Tell me more about the plague, won't you? I'm certain I could learn a great deal from you."

"The plague? You wish to discuss the plague *now?*"

"Well, I confess I've never been much interested in the plague, but after the engaging information you shared today regarding the mountains of bones, I could hardly fail to be intrigued. Now, tell me all about it, won't you?"

She tugged at her arm to free herself from his grip. "Perhaps another time, my lord."

"Very well, but you never showed me your sketch. May I see it?"

She darted a nervous glance out the carriage window, but no one appeared, and after a moment she turned back to him and practically tossed her sketchbook into his lap. "It's nothing so extraordinary, I assure you."

"Oh, I'm sure you're being far too modest, Miss Somerset." He flipped open the book to the first page. "Now, this sketch here, for example. I could tell at once it's a headstone. You've perfectly captured the, ah…rectangular shape of it. What else have you drawn?"

He turned the pages as slowly as possible, pausing with each new sketch. He exclaimed over every straight line and every creative bit of shading until Miss Somerset looked as if she were about to tackle him to the floor of the carriage, wrench the book from his hands, and beat him over the head with it.

"Very nice, indeed," he announced as he handed the sketchbook back to her at last. "You're kind to indulge my curiosity."

She'd been keeping one eye on him and the other on the front of the house, and now she turned and snatched the book out of his hands. "Of course, my lord. I wish you a good afternoon."

She threw open the carriage door and scrambled from her seat, but before she could dash up the drive and vanish through the front door, he leapt down to follow her. "Wait. I'll escort you to your door."

"*No!* That is, no thank you, Lord Dare. Goodbye!" She tossed an anxious look over her shoulder as she darted toward the stairs, then disappeared into the house, closing the door behind her with a decisive thud.

Nick chuckled as he watched her go, then climbed back into his phaeton, took up the ribbons, and rolled down the drive with a grin still on his lips. He might not have succeeded in his quest to meet her grandmother, but he'd managed to jerk Miss Somerset from her complacency, and she was rather amusing when she was in a panic.

The day hadn't been an utter loss, after all.

Chapter Six

"Oh, just go, why don't you? Go on!"

Violet peered through a crack in the door, her heart thumping with panic when Lord Dare's carriage continued to linger in the drive. Contrary man! He knew very well she wished to get rid of him, and he'd chosen to make it as difficult as possible.

Tell him all about the plague, indeed.

But then he did seem the sort of man who'd do whatever he could to cause trouble, just on principle alone, and he was far more persistent than any dissolute rake had a right to be. He should have grown bored with his chase days ago, when she hadn't fallen into a passion and lifted her skirts for him as Lady Uplands had done.

What was the matter with the man? She couldn't account for his behavior in the least. The visit to the burial grounds alone should have been more than enough to frighten Lord Dare away, but he hadn't even raised an eyebrow when she'd suggested they dig up the skeletons! And now here he was, demanding he be permitted to call on her again tomorrow.

It wasn't fair. She'd reconciled herself to never having a gentleman fall in love with her, but she'd thought she could at least rely on her ability to repel them at will.

"Violet?" Hyacinth was hurrying down the stairs. "There you are. I was just searching for you in the attics. Have you been outside? Whose carriage is that going down the drive?"

Violet slammed the door closed and threw herself against it. "I—what carriage? I didn't see a carriage. You're imagining things, Hyacinth."

It wasn't a convincing denial, especially when Violet's voice rose to a squeak at the end, but it was the best she could do under the circumstances.

"Am I, indeed?" Hyacinth folded her arms over her chest. "I have a far more vivid imagination than I realized."

Violet's brain scrambled for something to say, some plausible excuse, but after the panic with Lord Dare her wits had deserted her. She let her head fall back against the door in defeat.

Why in the world were her grandmother and Hyacinth back so soon? It was hardly past tea time. Violet thought she'd have hours yet before they'd arrive home, but here they were, and now she was going to get caught having been out alone with a notorious rogue after claiming she had the headache.

After a long moment of silence, Hyacinth sighed. "I'm aware you're up to something, Violet, but I haven't time to wheedle it from you now. Grandmother wishes to see you at once."

Oh, dear God. If she couldn't fool Hyacinth, she didn't have the smallest hope of fooling her grandmother. "Me? Why should she wish to see me?"

Hyacinth paused on the last step and gave Violet a narrow look. "Whatever is the matter with you? You look quite wild."

"I—nothing at all. I just…why are you back from Iris's so soon? And what does Grandmother want?"

Hyacinth stared at her for another moment, a frown creasing her brow. "Eddesley sent a message to Grosvenor Square, asking us to come home at once, so here we are. You'd better go up this minute, Violet. Grandmother is upset, and—"

Dread pooled in Violet's stomach. "Upset? But it was just a carriage ride, Hyacinth! Why, I hardly said two words to him the entire afternoon. There's nothing at all to be upset about—"

"Who? What carriage ride?" Hyacinth looked puzzled. "Do you mean the carriage ride from London to Bath? She doesn't fancy it, no, but it can't be helped. Grandmother is insisting they leave this afternoon rather than tomorrow morning. I gather Lady Atherton's attack is quite a severe one, and Grandmother doesn't like to wait."

Violet gave her sister a blank look. "Lady Atherton?"

"Yes. She's had another bilious attack, this one worse than the last. Grandmother is accompanying her to Bath to take the waters. I thought Eddesley told you."

"No. I haven't seen him." He hadn't been stationed in his usual spot at the doors, despite it being calling hours, and now that Violet's alarm had begun to subside, she began to notice other irregularities.

Maidservants were dashing up the stairs, and two footmen were on their way down, dragging a huge trunk between them. Eddesley, who was as stoic as a statue until his routine was disturbed, was running to and fro from the second floor landing to the entryway, his brow damp with sweat, chasing servants, shouting orders, and adding to the general mayhem.

Relief flooded through Violet, making her knees weak. No one had even noticed Lord Dare. The house was in too much of an uproar. "How awful." Not for her, of course, but certainly for poor Lady Atherton. "I'll go to Grandmother at once."

Violet bounded up the stairs with the energy of a criminal who'd slipped the noose, her heart still pounding at her near miss.

"Oh, Violet, there you are," Lady Chase said once she'd answered Violet's knock. "Well, well, it's dreadful, isn't it? Poor, dear Lady Atherton. I'm afraid her own family is little comfort to her, so it's left to her friends, but then I'm not the sort to let a friend suffer, no matter how much her illness might be an inconvenience to *me*."

"No, of course not, Grandmother." Violet made a few soothing noises, though privately she wondered whether this new attack of Lady Atherton's was more theatrical than medical. The lady did have a tendency to imagine even the mildest stomach pain was the first sign of cholera, so this wasn't the only time Lady Chase had been obliged to make a sudden trip to Bath.

"How long do you suppose you'll be gone?" The last time the two old ladies had rushed off to Bath they'd been back within five days when it turned out Lady Atherton wasn't expiring from consumption after all, but only had a mild cough.

"At least two weeks, I imagine—likely more. It depends entirely on how quickly poor, dear Lady Atherton recovers from her attack. *If* she recovers," Lady Chase added darkly.

Violet thought the length of their stay depended far more on whether they found the company in Bath diverting than it did on Lady Atherton's health, but if her grandmother really should be gone for two weeks...

Well, she was a dreadful, wicked, and ungrateful young lady, because she couldn't quite prevent a surge of delight at the thought of all that freedom.

Two weeks! Why, she could finish all her sketches in that time. At last, after nearly two years of work, fate was smiling on her literary endeavors! It was nothing less than a triumph for bluestockings and adventuresses!

"Now, Violet, I don't like to think of you and Hyacinth rambling about alone in the house while I'm away, so you'll spend the time with Iris and Lord Huntington in Grosvenor Square, but I expect you to keep watch over Hyacinth even so. You must keep her amused so she doesn't succumb to low spirits, but don't exhaust her, either."

"Yes, I promise I will, Grandmother."

Lady Chase patted her cheek. "Well, Violet, you're a good girl, for all your foolish notions, and a most devoted sister. I know you'll keep your promise and take good care of her. Now, do go away, won't you? You're distracting me."

Violet pressed a kiss to Lady Chase's cheek. "Yes, Grandmother."

She made her way downstairs, where she found Hyacinth alone in the parlor. "Two weeks, she says." Violet threw herself into the chair next to her sister's, nodding when Hyacinth offered to pour her some tea. "Do you think she'll really be gone so long this time?"

"It's difficult to say. I suppose it depends on how bad Lady Atherton is." Hyacinth frowned as she passed Violet a cup. "Poor lady. How awful it must be to be ill as often as she is."

Violet raised an eyebrow at this. "Or to fancy herself ill as often as she does. Lady Atherton is the healthiest invalid in Bath."

"You'll feel awful for saying such a thing should she prove to be truly ill this time," Hyacinth scolded, even as a reluctant smile curved her lips.

Violet snorted. "It hasn't happened yet."

They sat for another half hour, sipping their tea in companionable silence, until Lady Chase at last made her way down the stairs. They crowded into the entryway to bid her goodbye.

"Well, girls. I'll miss you, but it can't be helped," Lady Chase fretted as she folded first Violet and then Hyacinth into her arms. "I've never been one to shirk the duties of friendship, as you know. See you behave yourselves. I daresay you can't get into much trouble in London in November, what with everyone out of town, but nevertheless, Iris and Lord Huntington are expecting you. And mind what I told you, Violet."

Then with a sweep of her heavy brown traveling cloak, she was gone.

Violet and Hyacinth stood for a moment in the sudden silence, then Hyacinth braced a hand on the newel post with a sigh. "Do you mind if we wait until tomorrow to go to Iris's, Violet? I don't like to go out in this dreadful weather, and all the fuss this afternoon has made me weary."

Violet studied her sister's pale face and forced a smile. "I don't see what harm it will do if we wait. Go rest, dear. I'll have a tray sent up in a few hours."

"Yes, all right."

Violet watched as Hyacinth made her way up the stairs, but as soon as her sister was out of sight she opened the front door and darted outside.

No, it wasn't quite dark yet. It couldn't be later than five o'clock, and the heavy rain that had been threatening all afternoon was still only a half-hearted drizzle. Violet bit her lip as she tried to decide what to do.

Hyacinth would worry if she woke and found Violet gone, but surely it wouldn't take more than an hour. She'd be back before Violet noticed she'd left, and really, there was nothing so dangerous in it. She'd take her lady's maid, Bridget, with her, and there was the carriage, still standing in the drive, beckoning her, and Eddesley was nowhere to be seen…

Violet dashed back inside, exhilaration dancing along her nerve endings. Fortune truly *did* favor the bold.

* * * *

Alas, fortune was far less kind to the faint of heart.

"I don't think this is a good idea, miss."

Violet rolled her eyes with irritation. "That's the fourth time you've said that, Bridget. For goodness' sake, it's just a little rain."

Bridget had been sitting with her nose pressed against the carriage window, but now she turned to Violet with a dark look. "It's not the rain what's troubling me, miss. It's the ghosts."

"Nonsense. There's only one ghost. Stop exaggerating."

"One ghost what's lost 'er head, and her red striped dress all covered with blood and gore!"

"I know. It'll make the most ghastly sketch." Violet rubbed her hands together with relish. "I do hope she makes an appearance. I can draw her from imagination, but the sketch will be so much more authentic if we actually get to see her."

Violet didn't truly believe in ghosts, of course, but she did like the idea of headless specters haunting the alleyways of London, seeking revenge for the crimes committed against them. And anyway, she couldn't resist teasing Bridget a bit.

"I don't want to see her, the poor, headless thing! The dead should be left to rest."

Violet was gathering up her drawing pencils and shoving them into the pockets of her cloak, but now she looked up to frown at Bridget. "Come now. Think how dull London would be if the dead didn't make an appearance now and again. We need a ghost or two, Bridget, to keep things lively."

Bridget drew in a shocked breath. "Oh, miss. Yer an odd one, but I never knew you to be a sinner before."

"Sinner? How am I a sinner? I didn't chop her head off, did I? Her husband did, and then he tried to hide her body in the lake. He's the sinner, not me. Now, stop your fussing and take these extra pencils. Unless you're so frightened you'd rather wait in the carriage?"

Bridget snatched the pencils and threw open the carriage door. "And let ye go out there alone? No. I know my duty, for all Lady Chase never said a word about chasing ghosts when she hired me. Don't suppose yer coming with us, are ye, Harry?" she called to the coachman, shaking her head when he visibly blanched. "No, I dinna suppose so, ye coward. Well, come on then, miss."

"You're a loyal old thing, Bridget." Violet hopped down from the carriage and led the way across the street toward Cockpit Steps, a dark, narrow passageway that connected Old Queen Street with Birdcage Walk. "Oh, this is so exciting! Our headless lady hasn't made an appearance in quite some time, so perhaps she will tonight. It must be lonely, after all, being a headless ghost. No one to talk to, I daresay."

Bridget snorted. "How much talking do ye suppose she can do without a head?"

"Yes, you're quite right, Bridget. Being headless *would* make it more difficult."

Violet didn't expect to see any ghosts, headless or otherwise, but she couldn't prevent her heart from sinking a little when all she found in the haunted passageway was an ordinary-looking curved staircase. "She's not here."

Bridget tiptoed up behind Violet, peeked around her, and, not seeing a headless ghost, let out a long sigh of relief. "Well, thank goodness fer that."

"Certainly, if you're satisfied with a dull sketch of a set of stairs." Violet pulled her sketchbook from under her arm and flipped through it until she found a blank page. "Oh, well. I suppose it can't be helped. I'll just have to add her in myself, and I *have* been told I draw rather nice rectangles."

What had Lord Dare said? *I could tell at once it's a headstone.*

Despite herself, Violet's lips curved into a rueful grin. She couldn't deny Lord Dare was entertaining, though she wasn't sure he meant to be. Oh, he was arrogant, too, intolerably so—only a gentleman very sure of his own charm persisted in calling on a lady who'd forbidden it—and yet one couldn't accuse him of being dull. That shameless trick he'd pulled with Lady Uplands in Lord Derrick's library had, after all, furnished Violet with enough material for a new chapter in her book, not to mention a truly exceptional drawing.

Her grin widened as she recalled what she'd overheard that evening. She was wicked to laugh, but every time she thought of the rhythmic thumping of Lady Uplands's head against the bookshelf, she couldn't stifle a giggle. Come to think on it, she hadn't seen Lady Uplands since. It would be too bad if her ladyship had suffered a head injury—

"Did ye hear that, miss?" Bridget descended a few stairs and peeked around the corner. "I thought I 'eard a noise, like a gentleman shouting."

"Oh, I'm certain there's more than one drunken blackguard hovering about. We're right near St. James's Park, and of course we're standing on the stairs that used to lead down to the Royal Cockpit, though that's been gone for a year now, and good riddance to it, I say. I despise blood sports."

Bridget hurried back up the stairs and tugged on Violet's arm. "I tell ye, I hear footsteps, miss, and they're getting louder! Hurry and finish, before a villain sets upon us."

"You'd be happy enough to see the ghost *now*, wouldn't you, Bridget? She'd frighten any villains away quickly enough. But do stop tugging on my arm, will you? You'll make me ruin my sketch, and I'll have to start again—"

Violet fell silent at the thud of uneven footsteps echoing on the stone stairs, and she and Bridget both froze at the sound.

"Dinna tell me ye didn't hear *that*, miss," Bridget hissed in her ear.

"No, I heard it. But where's it coming from? Behind us, or in front of us?" In the dark, each footstep seemed to bounce against the stone in endless reverberations, and it was impossible to tell from which direction they originated.

"In front, I think. No, behind us, miss!"

"Hurry, Bridget. Up the stairs."

Bridget crowded into her from behind and tried to push her up the stairs onto Old Queen Street where their carriage was waiting, but they hadn't gotten more than two steps before an enormous shadow fell over the stairs, and a pair of broad shoulders blocked the light.

They'd gone the wrong way.

"Well, what have we 'ere, then? A couple of doxies, out for a stroll?" A hulking man in a black cloak with his hat pulled low over his face lumbered down the stairs and threw his considerable bulk in front of Violet, blocking her way.

Violet's heart began to thunder in her chest, but she jerked her chin in the air and gave the villain her haughtiest glare. "Doxies? How dare you, sir? I'm a lady, and I insist you let me and my maid pass at once."

"Not many ladies about out 'ere, 'specially ladies alone at night, nor whores neither, now that the cockfights 'ave moved on." The man ran a filthy coat sleeve across his mouth as he leered at Violet. "But if ye came out 'ere to see a cock, I got's one ter show ye right enough, luv."

He reached out to grab Violet's arm, but she dodged his grasp and whirled around. "Down the stairs!" she hissed to Bridget, who didn't have to be told twice, but spun around and ran straight down the stairs and through the passageway that let out onto Birdcage Walk.

Violet was right behind her, but the man, who smelled to Violet like he'd drank the better part of a bottle of gin, tore after her, managed to snatch a fold of her cloak in his grubby fist, and yanked her back against his chest. "Yer a right pretty little bit, luv, but I'm jus' after yer coin, so hand over that purse, an' I'll be on my way, aw right?"

Purse? What purse? She wasn't carrying a reticule...

Oh, no. Violet's blood froze as she realized he could only mean her sketchbook. It didn't look in the least like a purse, and it had little value to anyone but her, but there was no explaining this to her attacker, who'd grabbed it and was doing his best to wrench it out of her hands.

"Unhand me at once, you villain!" Violet twisted and struggled to free herself from his grip, and Bridget, who was now shrieking at the top of her lungs, attacked the man from behind and managed to land a blow to his shin.

"Damn ye, ye little bitch." He wrapped one meaty arm around Violet's waist and sent Bridget reeling with a mighty swipe of the other.

Violet gasped as she heard the sickening thud of her maid's body crashing onto the cobblestones. "Bridget!"

She clawed at the man's arm, her fingernails ripping into his flesh, but his hands seemed to be everywhere at once, and he was too strong for her. He pinned her wrists under his other arm and held her down as easily as if she were a kitten. "Right now, 'and it over—an' I'll have that cloak yer wearing, an' yer fancy gloves, too."

But Violet didn't hand over a thing. She continued to struggle and scratch and bite until he lost patience, dragged her over to the darkest part of the walkway, and slammed her back up against a wall. "Don't know why yer taking on so, luv. I'm a' have 'em all either way, even if I gots to hurt ye to get 'em, so ye may as well stop yer fussing and 'and 'em over."

He chuckled, and Violet realized with a flash of horror that he was actually enjoying himself. Her stomach heaved both at the thought and the smell of his fetid breath gusting into her face. In one part of her brain she realized Bridget had scrambled to her feet and was tearing across the passage toward the Royal Aviary, and in another she was groping for a memory—something she'd read in a book about the proper way to clench one's fist to deliver a punch—but her mind went blank when an inhuman screech tore through the air. It sounded like...

Birds?

Violet shook her head to clear the daze, but she didn't have time to work out the birds because the despicable villain who had her in his grasp wrapped his huge paw around her neck. Panic made her freeze, but before the blackguard could squeeze the breath out of her, a low, enraged voice hissed a string of curses, and in the next moment there was a pained groan, and the hands clutching at her went limp.

The smothering weight that held her pinned to the wall was shoved aside, and Violet's knees began to buckle beneath her, but before she slid to a heap onto the cobblestones another pair of hands closed around her waist. She instinctively struggled against them, fearing the villain had returned, but these hands were gentle despite their strength, and someone was murmuring soothingly to her, telling her she was all right now, and he didn't smell like sour gin at all, but like...goodness, he smelled divine, like amber and freshly cut wood—

No. It was impossible he should be here now...

But she knew it was him, even before she opened her eyes and found that silvery gaze swimming in and out of focus above her. "Like mercury," she muttered in a daze, "or the sheen on a bird's feather."

"Miss Somerset." He was breathless, his eyes wide with alarm. "Are you all right? You're not making any sense."

"...don't approve of blood sports, Lord Dare, especially cockfighting." It seemed important, somehow, that he know this, and now that she'd told him, Violet let her head fall against his chest with a little sigh.

"I—what?" His grip grew more urgent, his arms closing around her as she sagged against him. "Are you injured? She's going to swoon," he warned, speaking to someone beside him.

Swoon? What nonsense. She never swooned. Swooning was for delicate ladies in tight-laced corsets, or dainty, graceful belles, not bluestockings.

It was the last thought she had before darkness overcame her.

Chapter Seven

She was much lighter than he imagined she'd be.

Nick stared down into Miss Somerset's face, at the long, dark lashes curled against her cheeks, the vulnerable curve of her lower lip, and only one thought penetrated the shocked fog in his brain: He thought she'd be heavier.

Somehow, between her ink-stained fingers, the cobwebs in her hair, and her sharp tongue, he'd begun to see her as solid, massive even, just from the force of her personality alone.

But he might have been holding a child in his arms—she was a feather, a cloud, an armful of mist. Christ, she was so small, so delicate and fragile, like bone china, or porcelain…

Nick choked back the fear rippling through him as he realized how breakable she was, how tender the skin of her neck. That scoundrel who'd attacked her…by the time Nick came upon them the man's fingers had been gripping her throat. Another moment and the villain would have broken her, snapped her to pieces in his brutal grip.

A strange feeling came over him as he studied the graceful lines of her face, as if he were suspended between fury and fascination. Damn it, what was she doing out here in the dark with only her maid to protect her? How could she risk her safety in such a foolish way? And why had he never noticed how pale and fine her skin was, how sweet the curve of her lips?

He curled her tighter against his chest as these confusing thoughts bounced from one side of his skull to the other, refusing to settle into anything coherent.

"…never swooned in my life."

Miss Somerset's eyes fluttered open and Nick tensed, bracing himself for tears, wailing, and hysterics. Long moments passed as she blinked up at him with wide eyes, until at last her gaze cleared and recognition flickered across her features.

She drew in a deep breath, opened her mouth, and…

Here it comes.

Said the last thing in the world Nick expected her to say.

"You're a large man, aren't you, Lord Dare?"

Nick's mouth fell open. "*What?*"

"Tall, I mean, and muscular." She reached up and ran an experimental hand over his shoulder, testing the solidity of the muscle there as if she were assessing a horse. "Yes. Quite large, and strong as well. I doubt you have much trouble with footpads and thieves on the London streets, do you?"

Nick stared at her. Not five minutes ago she'd been trapped against a brick wall with a criminal's hand squeezing her neck. Where was the confusion, the weeping, the apologetic babbling? For God's sake, she hadn't even breathed a word of thanks that he'd left her attacker bleeding on the cobblestones at the bottom of Cockpit Steps.

At that moment Nick tipped over the edge of fascination, and tumbled headlong into fury.

His arms tightened around her until she gave a little squeak of protest. "Lord Dare, you're holding me rather tightly—"

"Not another word." They'd reached his carriage, and he gave Miss Somerset's maid a curt nod. "Get in."

The servant wasn't nearly as calm as her mistress, and she dove into the safety of the carriage as if the hounds of hell were yelping for her blood.

Nick deposited Miss Somerset carefully on the edge of the opposite seat. She slid over to make room for him and he leapt in, slamming the carriage door behind him.

"Lord Dare—"

"*No,* Miss Somerset," Nick snapped through clenched teeth. "*I'm* going to speak now, and you're going to be silent and listen."

Her eyes widened at his tone, but she seemed to understand it wasn't the time to trifle with him, because she subsided at once. "Yes, of course."

"What the *devil,*" Nick began, ignoring the maid's gasp of dismay at his curse, "are the two of you doing wandering around Birdcage Walk alone, in the middle of the night?"

"Now, my lord, it's hardly the middle of the night. It can't be more than—oh!" Miss Somerset suddenly broke off and raised her hand to her mouth. "My sketchbook, Bridget! I dropped it when we ran down the steps to escape that blackguard!"

Nick pinched the bridge of his nose between two fingers. The sketchbook. Of course. He should have known the bloody sketchbook was somehow connected to this madness. "What could you possibly have to sketch that couldn't wait until daylight?"

Miss Somerset wasn't listening to him. "Everything is in that book! All my work...oh, I must go back for it at once!"

She tugged at the door, but Nick grabbed her elbow before she could leap out onto the street. "Don't even think of leaving this carriage, Miss Somerset."

For God's sake, she hadn't batted an eye over that ruffian who'd nearly choked the life out of her, but now that her precious sketchbook was at risk her face was bleached of color, and her lower lip was trembling. "Please, Lord Dare. I must have it back."

Damn it. Nick wasn't the heroic sort—gallantry was tedious, and far more trouble than it was worth—but any intention he might have had to leave the sketchbook behind fled as soon as he saw that trembling pink lip. "I'll get it. Stay here, and for God's sake, don't stir from the carriage."

Nick made his way back toward Birdcage Walk. The villain he'd felled had disappeared, but Nick found a few loose pages scattered about near the Royal Aviary. He caught them up one by one and followed their trail until he found the sketchbook at the bottom of Cockpit Steps. He scooped it up, grumbling when a few more pages slipped out and scattered across the cobblestones.

He flipped the sketchbook open, lay it flat on his palm, and started to shove the untidy pile of papers inside, but the vibrant blue colors of the drawing on the top caught his eye, and he paused.

When Almack's Fails to Entertain.

The title was written across the top of the sketch in an elegant, flowing hand, and below that was a drawing of a fair-haired young lady in a blue gown hovering on the sidelines of a ballroom, her expression forlorn as she watched a dozen or so elegant couples twirl about on the dance floor. The sketch was amusing in a way, but there was something melancholy about it, too, perhaps because the forlorn lady looked quite a bit like Miss Somerset.

He turned a few more of the sketches over, reading their titles and chuckling at some of the more creative ones.

Drunken Rogues and Other Miscreants.
Ladies Who Despise Embroidery.

How to Escape the Torments of the Modiste.

This one showed the same fair-haired lady as in the Almack's sketch. Her brow was creased with terror, and she was eyeing an evil-looking seamstress who held a tape measure in one hand and an enormous pin in the other.

Nick laughed aloud when he came to a rough sketch of a tortured-looking maiden in a prim gown slumped over a pianoforte. The title read, *Useless Pursuits: Practicing the Pianoforte.*

Odd, that a lady so accomplished on the pianoforte should despise practicing so much, but Nick didn't have time to ponder every sketch. He was about to shove the pages back inside the book when the sketch she'd done of the burial grounds that afternoon caught his eye, and he paused to study it in the dim light.

It was bleak and austere, particularly the branches of the trees she'd drawn in the foreground. She'd shaded them heavily with her pencil, and they looked bare and stark against the gray sky above. It was a lonely scene, and her sketch reflected that, but there was also a certain raw magnificence he hadn't noticed when he'd been there. It almost made him want to return to the burial grounds, to see if he'd perceive the same desolate beauty she had.

He turned over a few more of the loose pages, curious to see what else she'd done, but the rest of the pages were blank.

Or so he thought at first.

Just as he was about to close the book and hurry back to his carriage, he stumbled across an entire series of sketches tucked into the back of the book, almost as if she'd hidden them there.

And no wonder.

There wasn't a single still life of flowers or fruit, no landscapes, and no portraits. There were no drawings of kittens, dogs, or horses, or anything else one might expect to find in a young lady's sketchbook.

Nick's eyes widened as he turned the pages over one by one. There was a sketch of Newgate Prison, and a rather sinister depiction of the bow window at White's—one she must have risked her reputation to get, since it could only have been drawn from that angle if she'd been on St. James's Street, right in front of it, and...good God, was that a sketch of the execution site at Tower Hill?

Unusual. A grim laugh rose in Nick's throat.

Bunhill Fields Burial Ground was one thing. Headstones and graves, stray bones and charnel houses—they were odd subjects for a young lady's pencil, certainly, but for every belle in London there were a dozen or more aspiring artists, and there was no telling what oddity might interest a lady with an inquisitive turn of mind. He'd half-convinced himself Miss Somerset had only taken him to the burial grounds because she'd thought an afternoon spent among long-dead plague victims was an efficient way to discourage him from calling again.

But this? This went well beyond *unusual*.

Tearing about London to take sketches of gibbets and execution sites? Risking her safety in such a reckless manner? That wasn't harmless curiosity.

Nick stared down at the sketches in his hands, and a chill rushed over him as a new and unwelcome thought seized his mind.

Miss Somerset might be as mad as a bloody bedlamite.

Madness. *Christ.*

He'd overlook a few irregularities to secure a bride as quickly as possible, but the Countess of Dare, a madwoman? As badly as he wanted to leave England, he couldn't do that to his aunt, and that was to say nothing of his future children. Madness tended to run in the blood, and even he wasn't selfish enough to doom his heirs to the curse of insanity.

He peered down at the sketch of Tower Hill clenched between his fingers. She was skilled with her pencil—there was no denying that. There were dozens of sketches, most of them rough, but a few had been meticulously executed, and one or two were colored drawings of such high quality they could have been taken for the work of a professional artist.

He'd heard those who suffered from madness sometimes displayed a certain genius—a facility with numbers, perhaps, or a talent for writing or art.

Miss Somerset must be one of those.

He neatened the loose sheaf of papers and inserted them carefully into the sketchbook, then hurried back to the carriage, his chest tight as he thought of his easy, uncomplicated life in Italy. It grew more and more distant in his memory with every day he remained in this cold, dreary city, and now here was another delay.

But it couldn't be helped. He couldn't marry a madwoman.

He'd have to wait until the season to secure a bride. He'd see Miss Somerset safely home tonight, and wouldn't call on her again.

He was still a half-block away from his carriage when he heard raised feminine voices. Miss Somerset and her maid were in the midst of an argument.

Curious, he paused before opening the door.

"Even if you managed to open the aviary cages, why did you suppose the birds would swarm my attacker? Surely birds can't distinguish good from evil. Why, they might have attacked you or Lord Dare! I don't suppose you'd like to be attacked by a falcon, would you, Bridget? Though I suppose it's more likely they would have simply flown away, and left us all to our fates."

"I told ye, miss, I wasna thinking! I thought if I let the birds free they'd screech and flap about, and it would scare 'im away. What would ye have had me do, I ask? I'd already kicked 'im once, and got a clout in the shoulder for me pains."

There was a brief silence, then a soft sigh. "I know. You poor thing. Forgive me, Bridget. I never should have insisted you come with me—"

"You never should have come out at all." Nick opened the carriage door with a jerk, took the seat across from Miss Somerset, and held out the sketchbook to her with a frown. "It was a remarkably foolish thing to do. I thought you were cleverer than that, Miss Somerset."

"Oh, thank you, my lord!" She ignored the scold, seized the book and hugged it to her chest, beaming at him. "You have no idea how grateful I am."

Nick settled back against the squabs and stared at her for a moment, his arms crossed over his chest. She didn't *look* mad. Was there a chance he'd been too hasty in his determination, and she was as sane as anyone else in London?

There was only one way to find out.

"I find it…curious, Miss Somerset," Nick began cautiously, "that you would place more value on your sketchbook than you do on your person. You do recall, do you not, that you were attacked tonight?"

Her smile faded. "Yes, my lord. I haven't forgotten."

"I'm going to need you to promise you'll never do anything so foolish again." If she truly *was* mad she was unlikely to abide by any promise she made him, but he felt obligated to make the effort, just the same.

"Well, I—" She broke off abruptly, and turned to address her maid. "It grows late, Bridget. Hya—that is, my sister will be awake by now, and worried over us. Perhaps you'd better take Grandmother's carriage back to Bedford Square. I'll follow with Lord Dare. If my sister asks, tell her—"

"Tell 'er what, miss? That ye insisted on going to Cockpit Steps so ye could take a sketch of a headless ghost?"

"Bridget! Hush, will you?"

Miss Somerset cast a nervous glance at Nick, who found himself once again open-mouthed and speechless. Ghosts? Good Lord. The poor creature *was* mad—mad enough to believe she'd find a ghost hovering about Cockpit Steps!

Perhaps he should skip Bedford Square entirely, and deposit her at the door of Bedlam.

Bridget didn't say a word to Nick when he escorted her to Lady Chase's carriage—she was too busy muttering to herself about "red striped gowns spattered with blood and ghosts what have lost their heads" to pay any attention to him, and he was relieved when he'd seen her into the carriage and safely on her way.

"You don't wager on cockfights, do you, Lord Dare?" Miss Somerset asked when he returned to the carriage. "I hate to think you'd encourage such a vicious sport."

Nick blinked. What the devil did cockfighting have to do with this? Was her mind wandering? Perhaps her addled brain had confused the footpad's attack with a cockfight. Was that why she'd been arguing with her maid about birds?

"The Royal Cockpit," she explained, noticing his confusion. "They tore it down last year, but you couldn't have known that, having been on the Continent these past two years. You didn't come out tonight to see a cockfight, did you?"

Nick's brows lowered in confusion. She didn't *sound* addled. "No. I don't care for blood sports."

He'd ventured out to pay Lady Uplands a visit, but before he'd gained her doorstep he'd been overcome with weariness at the thought of another romp with her, and he'd left without knocking. Unwilling to go home and face the suffocating gloom of his aunt's house, he'd found himself wandering around St. James's Park. He'd been near Anne's Gate when he heard Bridget's screams and came running.

But he hadn't the slightest intention of explaining any of this to Miss Somerset, who, mad or not, was skilled at turning the conversation away from herself.

"Ghosts?" He raised an eyebrow at her.

She looked down at the sketchbook in her hands, avoiding his eyes. "Bridget has a vivid imagination."

"And this vivid imagination of hers led her to believe you were on a search for ghosts, without any encouragement on your part? How singular."

"Oh, for pity's sake. Very well, my lord, if you insist on having the whole of it. There are rumors the Cockpit Steps are haunted by the ghost of a lady whose husband beheaded her. Of course I never expected to see her ghost. I only came to get a sketch of the steps, though I won't deny I rather hoped I *would* see a ghost. No." She held up a hand when he tried to interrupt. "I don't believe in ghosts, my lord. I only mean to say that sometimes imagination is a great deal more amusing than reality."

It was a logical enough explanation, and she appeared perfectly lucid as she delivered it, but those afflicted with madness often had periods of clarity. "Why venture out at night if you only wanted to sketch the Cockpit Steps? Surely it would have been easy enough—not to mention a great deal safer—for you to wait until tomorrow."

Her mouth took on a stubborn cast. "I wanted to get the shadows on the steps, and truly, there was plenty of light when we set out. It's only the rain that makes it so dark."

"But why, Miss Somerset, is it so important you get the sketch at all? Why not sketch some flowers, or some kittens in a basket, and be done with it?"

"Do you find kittens in a basket stimulating, my lord?"

"No, not especially."

"Then why should you suppose I would?"

Despite his misgivings, Nick's lips curved in a reluctant grin. Miss Somerset might be mad, but she was damned amusing. He couldn't recall ever being so entertained by a woman before—that is, not a woman who was still clothed.

"Ah. So you're a true artist, then? Well, that explains why you've got a sketch of Tower Hill in your sketchbook. I can't fault your artistic skills, certainly. Pity you didn't include a head rolling about on the grass. Or wasn't there a beheading that day?"

Her lips thinned. "Did you peek into my sketchbook, Lord Dare? I'd begun to think of you as a gentleman after your gallant assistance this evening, but a gentleman doesn't rifle through a lady's personal belongings without her permission."

Nick ignored this. "Beheadings, Newgate Prison, burial grounds, and headless ghosts—not quite kittens in a basket, is it?" He leaned toward her. "They're rather...*unusual* subjects for a young lady's artistic endeavors. Tell me, Miss Somerset. What do you hope to gain from your pursuits?"

Persuade me you're not mad.

Perhaps her oddities could be explained as the antics of an overzealous artist or a determined bluestocking. After all, a gentleman could marry a bluestocking without any concern for the sanity of his future children.

He held his breath as she parted her lips to speak, but then she shook her head and snapped her mouth closed again without saying a word.

Even pressed into a thin, disapproving line, her mouth was lovely. Pink, and then she had such fair skin her lips looked like berries in a dish of smooth, sweet cream. Such delicate coloring for such a vibrant lady, but then her eyes gave her away. Determination burned in those dark blue depths.

But then maybe it wasn't determination at all. Couldn't it just as easily be the fevered mania of the mentally afflicted?

Damn it, was the chit insane, or not? Not many bedlamites had her quickness, but that sketch of Tower Hill, well…even without the head rolling about on the grass, a preoccupation with execution sites was a trifle worrying in a prospective bride. "Are you engaged in some sort of study, Miss Somerset? Are you searching London's dark streets for Drunken Rogues and other Miscreants?"

She recognized the phrase at once, and her brows lowered. "Perhaps I *am* engaged in a study, but one needn't roam the streets of London to find rogues, Lord Dare. One stumbles across them in the least likely places, don't they? Dinner parties, *libraries…*"

Nick had been distracted by the way the pink color flooded back into her lips once she'd opened them, but at this he jerked his gaze back to her eyes. "I beg your pardon?"

She waved off his question. "Perhaps it would be best if you took me back to Bedford Square now, my lord. I'm certain my sister must be worried about me."

"Yes," he murmured. "Perhaps that would be best."

He rapped on the roof of the carriage, but they'd hardly moved an inch when she surprised him by taking his hand.

"Lord Dare, I—thank you for your assistance this evening, truly. I shudder to think what might have happened if you hadn't come along. I'm very grateful to you."

"It's fortunate I happened to be near. I'm pleased I could assist you, Miss Somerset."

He forced a smile, patted her hand, then started to draw away, but she held fast to him, pressing his hand between her own. "Will you call on me tomorrow, my lord?" It was a bold request, and her face colored a little. "I, ah…you've been so kind, and I think I'd feel better about my ordeal tonight if I could reassure you of my full recovery tomorrow."

It was the most encouragement Nick had ever gotten from her. He studied her face for some sign she'd softened toward him, and he did see a tiny shift in her expression, something so strange and fleeting he could almost believe he'd imagined it, but it wasn't softness. It wasn't yearning, or maidenly bashfulness, or stark desire—it wasn't any of the things he was accustomed to seeing on a lady's face when he singled her out for his attention.

It looked like…determination.

Or madness.

Before Nick could decide which, she disguised the strange expression with a smile, and he shrugged off his curiosity. Perhaps his chivalry this evening had been enough to crack her icy resistance, but it was too late. He hadn't gained any clarity regarding her sanity, and that left him only one choice.

This courtship had hardly even begun, but it was already finished.

He thought about the forlorn look on the wallflower's face in the Almack's sketch, the bleak beauty in her sketch of the burial grounds, and, to his surprise, his heart felt curiously heavy.

But no matter how diverting she was, or how much he wished to leave England behind, he couldn't marry a lady whose sanity he questioned.

Hyacinth Somerset was not, despite his best hopes, the answer to his prayers.

Yet he could hardly refuse a brief call to inquire after her health, particularly under the circumstances. "Yes, of course."

She released his hand with a nod. "Thank you, my lord. I look forward to your call tomorrow."

Chapter Eight

If Violet imagined she could creep into her grandmother's house for a second time that day without being detected, she was sadly mistaken.

"Violet! Oh, my goodness, wh-wh-where..."

Violet's heart dropped as Hyacinth struggled to gasp out her words. Her sister hardly ever stuttered anymore, but when she did, it was always because she was dreadfully upset. She rushed forward and took Hyacinth gently by the shoulders. "It's all right, Hyacinth. I'm here now. Take a deep breath. Yes, that's it. Another one."

A humiliated flush rose in Hyacinth's cheeks as she struggled to speak. "It was dark when I woke, and I couldn't f-f-find you, and I got w-w-worried, and then Br-Br-Bridget came back, babbling something about g-ghosts..."

"I'm so sorry, dear. I never meant to worry you. I thought I'd be back long before you woke, but as you can see, no harm's come to me, and you know how Bridget exaggerates. There, another breath. That's better."

But it wasn't better, because no sooner had Hyacinth gotten a breath than she began to pant again. "I saw you, Violet." She pointed a wobbly finger at the door. "I heard a carriage, so I watched out the window, and it's the same c-c-carriage I saw this afternoon, and then when it turned down the drive I saw the crest. You were out with Lord Dare, alone, at night, in his carriage, and he's a dr-dr-dr-dreadful rake, and now I'm certain you must be r-r-ruined!"

Violet's eyes slid closed in despair. She'd made a mistake, venturing out after dark. She'd gotten her sketch, yes, but if Lord Dare hadn't happened along when he did she might very well have paid for it with her neck, and as it was she'd sent her sister into a nervous attack with her reckless behavior.

Violet patted and soothed and murmured until Hyacinth's breathing calmed. "I'm not ruined, Hyacinth. I swear to you. Lord Dare isn't a…oh, very well, he *is* a dreadful rake, yes, but he didn't do anything untoward tonight. In fact, he did me a good turn."

He *had* clasped her in his arms and carried her to his carriage, but he hadn't had much choice under the circumstances, and anyway, she hadn't been coherent enough to enjoy it, and she refused to count anything she hadn't enjoyed as an impropriety. Pity she'd been unconscious for most of it—she would have liked more time to assess how it felt to be carried in Lord Dare's arms. Or any gentleman's arms, come to that. Well, any gentleman with a chest as solid as Lord Dare's, and she'd prefer one who smelled as nice as he did.

"Wh-what kind of good turn?" Hyacinth had caught her breath, and now she was looking at Violet with dark suspicion. "What happened?"

"Well, I took Bridget out to Cockpit Steps, and while we were there, there was a bit of an upset with a…well, with a footpad, but it's nothing to fret over," Violet added hastily when Hyacinth's face paled. "Lord Dare happened to come along at just the right moment, and he was kind enough to escort me safely home."

He *had* been kind. Arrogant and overbearing, too, of course, but kind, and a good deal more solicitous of her safety than Violet would have expected him to be. Guilty pleasure swelled in her chest when she recalled the concern in his eyes when she'd roused from her faint and found him staring down at her. Of course, he'd be anxious for any lady who'd been attacked—his concern hadn't anything to do with *her* at all—but even so, it had been his silvery-gray gaze she'd held onto in those first few blurry moments she'd struggled to swim back to consciousness.

And then he'd gone back for her sketchbook, too, without knowing whether or not the footpad he'd felled had regained consciousness. The truth was, aside from pawing through her private drawings, Lord Dare had been quite gallant this evening. She wouldn't have expected it of him—not after what she'd witnessed in Lord Derrick's library—but it seemed Lord Dare had more to offer a lady than thrusting hips and head injuries.

"What were you and Bridget doing out alone at Cockpit Steps? I could hardly get a word of sense out of Bridget—she kept raving about blood-stained gowns, and some poor lady who'd lost her head."

Violet rolled her eyes. For pity's sake, Bridget was hopeless at holding her tongue. "Oh, *that*. I was taking a sketch. You've heard the rumor about the soldier in the Horse Guards who murdered his wife, haven't you? The story goes that he beheaded her, and was caught out with her body before he could rid himself of it. Now his poor dead wife drifts about, hovering between the Cockpit Steps and St. James's Park—searching for her head, in my opinion."

"What a ghastly story. No, I hadn't heard it, and I'd just as soon not have heard it tonight, because it's vile." Hyacinth paused, her gaze narrowing on Violet. "But I should have guessed this business was somehow related to your book."

Violet was a little offended to hear the word "vile" used in such close association to her precious book, and she was tempted to deny tonight's adventure had anything to do with it, but it was no use trying to lie about it. Hyacinth was shockingly perceptive, especially when it came to her sisters.

"Oh, very well—yes, it's for the book, the chapter about haunted London. I've made such good progress, Hyacinth, and now with Grandmother away in Bath—"

"She may be away, Violet, but Iris and Finn are here, and they expect us to arrive at their house tomorrow morning, so don't imagine you'll be permitted to run about London at all hours."

Violet didn't answer. In theory Hyacinth was right, but Iris was a great deal easier to persuade than their grandmother, and ever since that heartbreaking business with Lord Derrick, Iris had been particularly supportive of Violet's book.

Lord Derrick.

Violet's brows rose in surprise. How odd. Between the visit to the burial grounds and the headless ghost and being swept into Lord Dare's arms, she hadn't thought about Lord Derrick at all today.

"How did Lord Dare happen to become involved in this?" Hyacinth, who could be as persistent as any of the Somerset sisters when her temper was roused, refused to allow Violet to stray from the point. "I can't think of any reason short of ruination why you'd come home in his carriage, Violet."

Violet hesitated. Dear God, what a tangle. Still, she'd made up her mind on the carriage ride home to tell Hyacinth the whole of it, after she'd sworn her to secrecy, of course. It wouldn't do for Iris's husband Finn to discover what she was about. He was the protective sort, and likely to overreact about a tiny, inconsequential thing like a clandestine courtship. In truth, Violet didn't even want Hyacinth to know about it, but she had to tell her, because she needed her sister's cooperation for her scheme to work.

"There's no ruination. He's…well, he's courting me, except he thinks—"

"Courting you? But how can he be courting you? You've never even been introduced to him!"

Violet opened her mouth to object, but then it occurred to her Hyacinth was right—she *hadn't* ever been formally introduced to Lord Dare. It was a rather sudden courtship, and a decidedly odd one, now she thought of it. Lord Dare couldn't have any honorable reason for such a determined pursuit of a lady he hardly knew, but Violet didn't much care what his reasons were. She wasn't going to marry him. A lady didn't marry a gentleman who mistook her for her sister, and she certainly didn't marry one who'd make such shameless use of a private library at a perfectly respectable dinner party.

No matter how entertaining it had been.

But she might encourage his courtship for reasons of her own—reasons that hadn't a thing to do with marriage—particularly if he was a large, strong, and imposing man who'd make an ideal escort for a lady who might occasionally find a need to venture into the less, ah...ladylike parts of London.

Of course, any lady who would consider doing such an underhanded thing must be very, very wicked, and Violet didn't like to think of herself as a villainess. An adventuress, yes, but lying, sneaking about and betraying her family's trust, toying with a gentleman's affections...

Except there *were* no affections in this case. It wasn't as if Lord Dare were in love with her, or even with Hyacinth, for that matter. No gentleman who was truly in love mistook his beloved for her sister, no matter how alike they were. No, he had his own reasons for insisting on this courtship, just as she did, and if she chose to make the most of her opportunities, well, she was no worse than he was, was she?

And it wasn't as if she hadn't tried to dissuade him. She *had*—she'd even dragged him to a burial ground and made him stand about in the rain while she dug about in a plague pit for bones, for goodness' sake! Why, she'd done everything she could think of to get rid of him.

Well, not *quite* everything...

She hadn't told him she wasn't Hyacinth.

But if he knew the truth he might take it into his head to turn his attentions to her sister, and Violet couldn't risk that happening. Lord Dare might be a rake, but he was also an earl, and one never knew what Lady Chase might do if an earl should decide to court Hyacinth. There was a chance their grandmother might approve of Lord Dare as a suitor, and Hyacinth could end up countess to a wicked debaucher who'd nearly concussed Lady Uplands.

No, it wouldn't do. Violet was much better equipped to handle an arrogant earl like Lord Dare than her younger sister was.

"I insist upon knowing what you're up to, Violet. Tell me this instant, or I'm going to tell Iris Lord Dare brought you home in his carriage tonight, and then she'll write to Grandmother, and Iris will tell Finn, too, and then Finn will challenge Lord Dare to a duel and shoot him between the eyes, and—"

"Hush, will you?" Violet put her hand to her forehead and tried to think.

"I'm going to tell you. I'm just trying to find the best way to put it." Hyacinth's face fell. "Oh, no. If you have to think so carefully about it, it means you're about to do something you know very well you shouldn't."

"No, but I grant you it's a bit complicated." Perhaps the best thing to do was to just say it and get it over with. Violet sucked in a deep breath, threw her shoulders back, and met her sister's gaze.

"Very well. If you must know, it's just this: Lord Dare intended to court *you*, only he mistook me for you at Lord and Lady Derrick's supper party, and he hasn't yet figured out his error, so even though he thinks he's courting you, he's really been courting me instead, by mistake. So you see, it's nothing so shocking, when you think about it. Just a little misunderstanding, and we do look quite a lot alike, after all."

But Hyacinth appeared to find it shocking, indeed, because her face paled and her mouth fell open. "B-but this doesn't make any sense. Why should he want to court *me*? I don't even know him! I'm not sure I'd even r-recognize him again if I saw him, and how do you know he's mistaken the two of us?"

Violet sighed. Hyacinth wasn't taking this at all well. "Because the night of the dinner party he accosted me in Lord Derrick's drawing room to compliment me on my pianoforte performance. Have you ever heard *anyone* compliment me on my playing, Hyacinth?"

"Well, no, but—"

"He said something about the Haydn. Did you play Haydn that night?"

"Yes, but—"

"He heard you play, admired you, and waited for you in the drawing room afterwards to compliment you, but you'd left with Iris and Finn by then. Honora told me you'd forgotten your wrap, so I went back into the drawing room to fetch it after you left, and Lord Dare was still there. He thought I was you, paid his compliments, and what do you think? He called the very next day. As luck would have it, you were out with Grandmother at the time. He doesn't know you have an unmarried elder sister, so he asked for Miss Somerset, not Miss Hyacinth, and naturally Eddesley brought me to him."

Hyacinth looked dazed. "Goodness, that's an odd series of mishaps, isn't it? But why didn't you simply explain to him he'd mistaken one sister for the other when he called? It was very wrong of you not to do so at once, Violet."

Violet shrugged. "I didn't see the point. I made it clear to him I didn't choose to accept his calls. Naturally I thought he'd abide by my wishes and that would be the end of it, but I tell you, Hyacinth, the man refuses to be discouraged. He's like an insect that persists in buzzing about no matter how many times you swat at it."

"Hmm. It sounds to me as if he's enamored of you. Why else would he be so persistent?"

"Enamored?" Violet snorted. "Hardly. I'd sooner call it intolerable arrogance, but then he's terribly handsome, and charming, too, and no doubt he believes he can change your—that is, *my* mind. Whatever his reasons—and I doubt they're honorable ones—he's determined to have you as his bride."

Hyacinth reached behind her with a shaking hand, grasped the newel post, and lowered herself to the bottom stair. "B-bu-but I don't want to marry Lord Dare!"

Violet squeezed onto the stair beside Hyacinth and took her hand. "Of course you don't, dear. No lady wants to marry a man like that. He's an utter rogue. But you won't have to, don't you see? After a few weeks of courting me he'll lose interest, give up the chase, and move on to some other lady."

It all made perfect sense to Violet, but Hyacinth was shaking her head. "That's nonsense, Violet. Why, he's just as likely to fall in love with you as he is to give up the courtship. You're lovely, and so clever and funny and brave. Even a rogue like Lord Dare can't fail to recognize that."

Clever, funny, and brave—oh, my, yes. Those were *just* the qualities every gentleman wanted in a wife, especially the handsome, fashionable, titled ones. "Gentlemen don't fall in love with me, Hyacinth. You know that."

Hyacinth didn't often get into a temper, but now her brows lowered into a dangerous scowl. "I don't know any such thing! Just because Lord Derrick fell in love with Honora doesn't mean *no* gentleman will ever—"

Violet let out a quiet sigh. She didn't wish to have this argument again, so she squeezed Hyacinth's hand to hush her. "Perhaps some gentleman will, someday, but it won't be Lord Dare. He's…well, he's not the sort of man who will ever admire a lady like me."

Hyacinth's lips turned down in a frown. "I don't see why not."

Violet didn't answer, because her sister didn't want to hear that a man like Lord Dare—a man with such remarkable gray eyes and such a perfect, playful smile—would never look twice at a bluestocking like her. He was the sort of man who belonged with the belle of her season, not an odd young lady with ink stains on her hands who preferred dusty libraries to elegant dance floors, and whose playing sounded like an elephant stomping over the pianoforte keys.

Violet had accepted herself for who she was long ago. She'd never wished to be anyone else, but she also tried not to indulge in fairy tales of true love. She'd only ever done so once, and it had led to a broken heart. She didn't intend to make that mistake again.

Love might make fools of everyone else, but it wouldn't make a fool of Violet.

Still, fate had offered her other gifts to compensate for the lack of romance, and if she was a bit selfish in pursuing her love of learning, well… she wasn't any more selfish than any other young lady in love, was she?

"Lord Dare intends to call on me tomorrow, to inquire after my health." Violet turned pleading eyes on her sister. "You'll have to be gone by then, so he doesn't see you, and you'll need to make my excuses to Iris, as well."

"You expect me to hide from Lord Dare so you can continue to lie to him?"

Violet bit her lip. It sounded rather bad when Hyacinth put it that way, but it wasn't, really. She didn't intend to hurt anyone, after all. Lord Dare would doubtless be irritated to find she'd tricked him, but it wasn't as if she'd break his heart. The very idea was ludicrous.

"I wouldn't put it like that, exactly. There's no need to make it sound so underhanded."

"But it *is* underhanded, Violet! How would you put it?"

"I, ah—I simply need you to keep out of sight so he doesn't discover there are two of us."

Hyacinth's lips pinched together. "That's what I said. You expect me to hide from Lord Dare so you can continue to lie to him. Why can't you just confess the truth, beg his pardon, and send him on his way? He won't want either of us once he discovers you've deceived him."

Violet shot her sister a guilty look. "I can't. I need him."

Hyacinth groaned, and let her head fall into her hands. "I don't suppose I have to ask for what. It's the book, of course. He'll think he's courting you, when really you're just keeping him about to scare off the footpads."

"Something like that," Violet admitted, an uncomfortable pang of guilt piercing her chest. Lord Dare really had done her a good turn tonight.

She'd been terrified when she felt that blackguard's hand close around her throat. There was no telling what might have happened if Lord Dare hadn't defended her, and then he'd been so chivalrous about fetching her sketchbook...

Rake or not, didn't he deserve better than to be lied to?

Hyacinth seemed to think so, because she was gaping at Violet with a horrified expression. "I'm shocked at you, Violet! My goodness, the lying is bad enough, but to use a gentleman in such a way? It's not like you to be so devious."

Heat rose in Violet's cheeks, but at the same time a rebellious spark flickered to life in her chest. "I don't see how my behavior is any more devious than that of the young ladies who crowd Almack's in search of a wealthy aristocrat."

Ladies all over England married gentlemen for their titles and fortunes—didn't that also amount to using them? Why should she be held to a higher standard than other young ladies were, simply because her goals were different? And anyway, in a just society she wouldn't need Lord Dare at all. It wasn't her fault ladies weren't permitted to go about the city as they pleased.

"I don't care about other young ladies, Violet. I only care about you, and this preoccupation you have with your book is...well, as lovely as your book is, I'm afraid you're hiding behind it."

Violet tensed. Hyacinth had never said such a thing to her before. "How am I hiding?"

"After what happened last season, and then Lord Derrick..." Hyacinth sighed. "You're afraid of getting hurt again, but don't you see? A book is paper and ink only—it can never take the place of real life, Violet. You'll only hurt yourself if you try and make it do so, and you'll hurt those who care about you, as well."

A bitter laugh rose in Violet's throat. Perhaps Hyacinth was right—perhaps she was hiding behind her book, but it seemed she was destined to be hurt no matter what she did, and she'd rather bleed from her own hand than someone else's, and Hyacinth should know better than to think Violet would ever hurt her family.

"No one will get hurt, Hyacinth. I promise you."

"You can't make that promise, Violet. Even if Lord Dare doesn't come to care for you, what of our grandmother? She'll be terribly upset if she finds out you've been sneaking around behind her back, and what am I meant to say to Iris when you don't come with me tomorrow? Do you expect me to lie to our sister, too?"

"Grandmother won't find out. Please, Hyacinth. I only need a week or two to get the sketches for the rest of the book. I'll be done before she ever returns to London. As for Iris, just tell her I stayed behind to work on the book, and that I'll be along later in the afternoon. It's not a lie, after all."

Unless one counted lies of omission, and as of this moment, Violet didn't.

"But what about Lord Dare? What will you tell him? You'll have encouraged his courtship for weeks by then. Do you expect him to just vanish once you're finished with him? You'll have to tell him something."

"No, I won't. I won't need to tell him a thing. He'll be gone before it can become a formal courtship." Violet would be shocked if he even lasted the entire two weeks.

"What if he doesn't give up? What if he comes to care for you? He could have his feelings hurt, or worse, his heart broken."

The idea *she* could break Lord Dare's heart was so absurd, Violet laughed. "He won't fall in love with me in two weeks, Hyacinth!" He wouldn't fall in love with her at all. If there was one thing Violet could be sure of, it was that.

"I don't know. I don't like this, Violet."

"*Please*, Hyacinth. I'll do everything I can to make sure no one gets hurt."

Hyacinth was quiet for a long time, but at last she let out a resigned sigh. "Two weeks only, and then everything goes back to the way it was. Do you promise?"

Violet laced their fingers together. "I do. I promise."

Chapter Nine

"I see we still don't understand each other, Gibbs." Nick glared at his valet through a narrow slit in his eyelid. "Let's try this again, shall we? You don't disturb me until I've rung for you. Now, did I ring for you, Gibbs?"

"No, my lord."

"Then what the devil are you doing in my bedchamber? For God's sake, it's not terribly difficult. You come when my bell rings, and not one bloody second sooner. Get out, and don't come back until—no! Damn it, Gibbs, who told you to open those drapes?" Nick dove back under the coverlet before the light pouring through the window could blind him.

"My apologies, my lord, but Lady Westcott sent me to fetch you for tea."

"That's the least sincere apology I've ever heard, Gibbs. You sound positively gleeful, in your own morose, cheerless way, of course."

"Yes, my lord. I beg your pardon, my lord, but her ladyship insisted you come down at once."

Nick threw the coverlet off with a deep sigh. If the truth were told, he was rather relieved to be awake. He'd had the oddest dream. Like most dreams it was fuzzy at the edges, but he had a vague impression of gibbets and headless ghosts, and a fair-haired lady lying in his arms, her long lashes curled against her cheeks.

"Do you know any madmen, Gibbs? Or madwomen?"

Gibbs didn't pause in his task of pouring hot water into the basin, but a barely discernible hitch in his eyebrow said more eloquently than words he wasn't entirely convinced of Nick's sanity. "No, my lord."

"What, not one? Christ, Gibbs, with all the madness in London, one would think you'd be able to come up with a single example."

"Yes, my lord. I beg your pardon for avoiding those who suffer from insanity, my lord."

"Stop 'my lording' me, Gibbs. It makes my head ache."

"Yes, my lord. If I might inquire as to the reason for your lordship's sudden curiosity regarding madmen, my lord?"

Nick wandered over to the basin to wash. "Nothing, I just…I wondered what they acted like."

"I would imagine they act mad, my lord."

"Yes, thank you for that extremely perceptive observation, Gibbs. But what does someone who's mad act like? What do they do? That is, how do you know if a person is mad or not?"

"Drunkenness, my lord? Indulging in debauchery, or other immoderate behaviors? An excessive amount of time spent in bed, my lord?"

Nick scowled. "I congratulate you on your subtlety once again, Gibbs, but according to that criteria, every aristocratic gentleman in London is mad."

Gibbs let out a tiny, dignified snort, as if that had been precisely his point. "Yes, my lord. Will the green coat do for today, my lord?"

Nick waved a weary hand in the air. "Green, blue—I don't give a damn, Gibbs."

"Very good, Lord Dare." Gibbs disappeared into the clothes press and came back out a moment later with the green coat cradled lovingly in his hands. "Perhaps lack of attention to dress could be considered a certain kind of madness, my lord?"

"Or excessive attention to it," Nick shot back. "I'd be delighted to argue the point with you, Gibbs, but Lady Westcott awaits, and we both know patience isn't one of her virtues."

"Yes, my lord."

After the usual tussle with Gibbs over his cravat, Nick at last made it downstairs. He paused outside the drawing room, surprised to hear the low murmur of feminine voices, but he twisted his mouth into a charming smile and pushed open the door. "Good afternoon, Aunt. I didn't realize we had company—"

As soon as he saw who awaited him he froze to a halt, and the words died on his lips.

"Ah, here's Lord Dare at last."

His aunt smiled and held out her hand to him, but Nick hardly heard her. His gaze was fixed on a pale, dark-haired young lady who was seated to his aunt's right. "Louisa."

He knew at once he'd said the wrong thing, because Louisa's cheeks reddened with embarrassment. "Good afternoon, Lord Dare."

Lord Dare. Yes, of course. It wasn't proper for him to address her by her Christian name anymore. They were no longer children, and he hadn't laid eyes on Louisa Covington for more than two years.

Not since Graham's funeral.

"I beg your pardon. Good afternoon, Miss Covington." He managed a stiff bow. "Lady Covington," he added, with a second bow for Louisa's mother, who was watching him with a pinched expression on her thin face.

"Sit, my dear boy, and I'll pour you some tea." His aunt nodded toward one of the settees.

A sense of unreality swept over Nick as he lurched toward the settee and collapsed onto it just before his knees gave out. Louisa, Lady Covington, and his aunt, all taking tea together—it was so familiar, as if he'd somehow stumbled into the past when he opened the door of the drawing room.

But it wasn't quite the same, and it never would be, because even as the four of them sat politely sipping their tea, they were each painfully aware something was missing, no matter how hard they all tried to pretend it wasn't.

Someone.

Graham.

Graham was dead, and where he should have been there was only Nick, a pale imitation of his brother, the man who should have been Lord Dare.

"Lady Covington happens to be in town for the next few weeks." His aunt passed him a cup of tea. "Rather unexpectedly, but of course she and Louisa insisted upon calling on you as soon as they arrived."

"How kind," Nick murmured, but the muscles in his neck corded with tension. The lie fell with smooth precision from his aunt's lips, but he knew damn well there was nothing unexpected about Lady Covington's sudden appearance in London. His aunt must have written to her as soon as he arrived, and now here she was, dragging Louisa along with her like a child tangled in her leading strings.

A heavy silence fell. Nick glanced at Louisa, and his heart heaved in protest at the look of despair on her face. She was no better at hiding her emotions than she'd been when they were eight years old, and it was painful to witness her humiliation at being offered up to Nick as if she were a sweet on a silver tray.

Lady Covington was assessing Nick with pale, icy blue eyes. After a long moment, she cleared her throat with a delicate little cough. "You've had quite a long sojourn on the Continent, Lord Dare. It's lovely to have you back in England. Do you intend to stay for long?"

"No. Only long enough to tend to some business with the estate, and see that my aunt is comfortably settled—"

"Of course he'll stay." His aunt reached over to pat his hand. "He's Lord Dare now, and the Dare Earldom is too extensive to be managed from a distance. The West Sussex estate was sadly neglected during his poor father's illness, I'm afraid. It needs to be seen to, and of course there are the other, ah…obligations incumbent upon the heir of such substantial properties."

Obligations. Nick's throat went dry as the full weight of his aunt's words slammed into him. The Dare Earldom, the country estate in West Sussex, Louisa Covington…the next forty years of his life unfurled with sickening clarity before his eyes.

Except it wasn't his life at all. It was Graham's.

Nick darted another quick glance at Louisa, whose face had flushed a dull red with quiet misery. She'd been one of his dearest friends growing up—he and Graham and Louisa had been inseparable as children. He'd taught Louisa how to ride astride, and how to climb trees and catch a fish with only a stick and a bit of string.

But it had been different for Louisa and Graham. They'd been madly in love from the moment they first laid eyes on each other, and one had only to look at Louisa now to see Graham's ghost lived in every lonely corner of her heart still.

So this was to be his fate. He was meant to manage Graham's earldom, and live on Graham's estate with Graham's former betrothed as his wife. To live Graham's life, without a prayer of ever being able to do justice to it.

"Obligations, yes." Lady Covington slid at glance at Louisa, but a frown creased her brow when she noticed her daughter's expression. "I'm certain the present Lord Dare is more than adequate to the challenge. Don't you agree, Louisa?"

Louisa was well aware only one answer was acceptable, and she gave it. "Yes, of course."

Nick managed to paste a stiff smile onto his lips while Lady Covington and his aunt struggled through another half hour of stilted conversation, but both he and Louisa maintained a deafening silence. Louisa looked as if she didn't dare breathe a word for fear of bursting into tears, and Nick was struggling to hold his hurt and anger in check until the inevitable confrontation with his aunt.

By the time Louisa and Lady Covington took their leave, his smile had cracked and fallen in splinters from his lips.

He didn't mince words. "I believe I made my sentiments regarding Louisa Covington perfectly clear, Aunt. If you're trying to tempt me into a hasty marriage, you've made a rather bad start."

His aunt faced him, her back straight and her hands folded neatly in her lap. "And yet it's a start just the same, Nicholas, and far more of one than you've made on your own, I'm afraid. Unless you consider lying about in your bedchamber all day and trifling with Lady Uplands every night a start."

Ah. His aunt had found out about Lady Uplands. Well, that explained Louisa's sudden appearance here today. Either he found a wife sooner rather than later, or his aunt would find one for him, and she'd made it clear who she'd choose.

Panic gripped him in a tight fist—so tight his mouth popped open, and words began to spill from it. "On the contrary, Aunt. I've made far more progress than you give me credit for. Despite the lack of available young ladies in London, I've managed to unearth a likely countess, and I've already begun courting her."

His aunt's eyes went wide, then narrowed with suspicion. "So soon? An actress, or one of your former mistresses, I assume. I warn you, Nicholas—"

"Not to worry, Aunt. Even *you* couldn't find anything to disapprove of in this young lady."

Aside from the madness, that is.

"Indeed? Who is she?"

"Hyacinth Somerset. She's one of Lady Chase's granddaughters, and I assure you, you won't find a lovelier young lady in London."

It was true enough. Hyacinth Somerset *was* lovely, and if Nick could overlook a touch of insanity, then surely his aunt could, as well.

"Hyacinth Somerset." Lady Westcott cocked her head to the side, considering. "I don't know the young lady, but if she's one of Lady Chase's granddaughters—"

"She is, indeed. Impeccable bloodlines, intelligent, with ah...lively manners, and she's a perfect English rose, as well." Nick rose to his feet. "I'm on my way to call on her even now."

Lady Westcott gave him a cautious smile. "Well, if she's everything you say she is—"

"Oh, she is." And more, too. Much more, but after that painful half hour with the Covingtons, Nick found he wasn't much concerned with Miss Somerset's sanity anymore.

It was, after all, nothing in comparison to his own.

* * * *

The cobwebs were gone.

This was, oddly, Nick's first thought when Miss Somerset swept into the drawing room to receive him. Her fair hair was brushed smoothly back from her forehead and gathered into a simple knot at the back of her neck, and if an errant cobweb still lurked among those gleaming locks, Nick couldn't see it.

"Good afternoon, Lord Dare." A sweet smile lit her face, and she dipped into a polite curtsy before him. "It's kind of you to call on me today."

Nick had risen to his feet when she entered, but now he stood awkwardly in the middle of the drawing room, staring at her and worrying the brim of his top hat between his fingers. She'd exchanged the dingy pinafore and faded gown for a fresh bright blue one that brought out the color of her eyes.

For one baffling moment, disappointment stabbed at his chest. She looked very much as she had the first night he'd seen her, when he'd watched her play the pianoforte, and there was no denying she was lovely, but without realizing he'd done so, he'd grown rather fond of her rough edges.

For God's sake, he must have lost his mind, because he actually missed the cobwebs.

"Lord Dare?" She gave him an uncertain look when he still didn't respond, then held out her hand to him. "Are you quite well?"

Nick reached to take her hand, and a smile rose to his lips. There, on her index finger, was a faded smear of black ink.

"Ah. For a moment I feared some other young lady had come in your place, but I see you're here after all, Miss Somerset, hidden under all the elegant trappings." He took her hand and held it up, tracing his thumb from the base of her finger to the tip. "Ink," he added, at her startled look. "I see you've tried to scrub it away, but I confess I'm glad you didn't succeed, or I might not have recognized you."

"Oh." She seemed not to know what else to say, and fell silent. Color rose into her cheeks when he didn't release her hand, and she watched, mesmerized, as he caressed her fingers with slow, gentle strokes. "I, ah..." She jerked her gaze from their joined hands to his face, and whatever she saw there made her blush harder. "The ink never seems to come off entirely."

By the time she drew her hand away, Nick had gone breathless, but he cleared his throat and attempted a normal tone of voice. "I won't ask if you've recovered from your ordeal last night, because I can see you have." His gaze swept over her, and he didn't bother to hide his appreciation. He preferred her when she was a trifle disheveled, but she looked as lovely as a spring day, and a man couldn't help but be refreshed looking at her, given the gray, dreary sky still holding London captive.

She gestured him toward a settee and took the one opposite him. "I have indeed recovered, so much so I feel quite restless. Shall we take another drive today, my lord? I'd prefer it to a dull afternoon in the drawing room, wouldn't you?"

He saw at once she had a destination in mind, and he was half afraid to find out where it was. "A drive? Yes, I could be persuaded into a drive. But where shall we go, Miss Somerset? Hyde Park, perhaps?"

"No, no. Not Hyde Park."

"No? Duck Island, then, at St. James's Park? We can go and see the pelicans."

She frowned. "I'd rather not. Pelicans are such unpleasant birds."

"I thought they were meant to be quite gregarious, but we won't go if you don't like it. We could stroll along the Serpentine, if you prefer, or drive in Richmond Park, or—"

"I want to go to Wapping Old Stairs."

After the cemetery and the headless ghost on Cockpit Steps, Nick was amazed he could be surprised by anything Miss Somerset said, but he nearly fell off Lady Chase's settee. "You, ah…you want me to take you to Execution Dock?"

She nodded, her face eager. "Yes, where the convicted pirates are hung. Captain Kidd was executed there. Did you know? They had to hang him twice, because the rope broke the first time. I want to take a sketch of the gibbet."

And just like that, the madness reared its ugly head.

Nick let out a hollow laugh. "Of course you do. It makes perfect sense. Why limit yourself to Tower Hill when there are so many other charming execution sites in London?"

"Why, indeed? You understand perfectly, my lord." She beamed at him. "One can hardly stroll through London without stumbling over one gibbet or another, but you see how perfect Wapping Old Stairs is to follow the bit about Cockpit Steps. They're both stairways, and they're both haunted, so in terms of the progression of the book, it's—"

She was animated, her words tumbling over each other and her eyes bright with excitement, but now she slapped a hand over her mouth, and her eyes widened with horror.

Nick went still as her words sank in, then relief rushed over him, so profound every one of his taut muscles went instantly loose, as if he'd downed a bottle of whiskey in one long swallow. He sagged back against the settee, a foolish smile curling his lips.

A book. Of course.

He was amazed he hadn't thought of it at once. His chest swelled with hope as all of Miss Somerset's oddly shaped pieces fell into place.

She wasn't mad at all. No, she suffered from an entirely different malady. Acute intelligence.

Nick didn't admire bluestockings, but compared to madness, a powerful intellect was a minor affliction. "I must be dim indeed not to have deduced you're writing a book after rifling through your sketchbook. Tell me about it, won't you?"

She shook her head, her eyes still wide blue pools above her hand.

"In terms of the progression of the book, it's what? Please do go on, Miss Somerset." If he was truly going to court her, he may as well have the whole of it. There should be no secrets between them.

That is, no secrets but *his*.

Her eyebrows pinched together as she struggled to keep her secret for a moment longer, but then she gave it up as lost and lowered her hand from her mouth. "Very well. I *am* writing a book." Her tone was defiant, as if she expected him to either scold her or laugh at her. "Go ahead, my lord, and say whatever you wish to say about it, so we can have it over with."

"Very well, then. I think the bit about Execution Dock should precede Cockpit Steps, not follow it."

Whatever Miss Somerset had expected him to say, it wasn't *that*. Her mouth fell open in shock, and when she did manage to speak, her voice was faint. "Why should it precede it?"

"Why do you need the sketch of Execution Dock? Is it for a particular chapter? One about hanged pirates, perhaps?"

"Not just pirates, but criminals in general. It's for a chapter entitled 'The Grim Faces of Justice.'"

"I see. But Cockpit Steps must be for another chapter, since the steps are more noteworthy for the ghost than for the crime committed there. Is it for a chapter about hauntings, or some such thing?"

Miss Somerset was staring at him as if she'd never seen him before. "Haunted London, yes."

"Ah. And which chapter comes first?"

"Justice comes first, and then the ghosts. It makes more sense that way, you see, since for the most part one doesn't have the ghosts until after the executions."

Nick choked back a laugh. "Yes, I see your point. Well, then, I think you want Execution Dock first, since it's got both the element of justice and Captain Kidd's ghost. It's the perfect bridge between those two chapters, and of course as you said they're both stairways, which adds an extra touch of poetry to the thing."

She didn't say a word, but sat staring at him. When he remained silent, she raised an eyebrow. "Well? Is that it? Don't you have anything else to say?"

"No. What do you expect me to say?"

"Oh, some kind of warning about how I read too much, or about how no good can come of ladies who fill their heads with too much knowledge, or perhaps something about ghosts and burial grounds and executions not being ladylike. At the very least I expected some sort of sarcastic remark about bluestockings."

"Well, that would hardly be fair. I don't know any bluestockings, aside from you."

In truth, aside from the sort of vague distaste required of any fashionable gentleman, Nick hadn't ever given much thought to bluestockings. That is, until he'd met Miss Somerset, and discovered a knowledgeable lady was far more fascinating than he'd ever imagined.

"I don't like to generalize about any lady, Miss Somerset," he went on when she remained silent. "Just as I'm sure you'd never dream of making an unfair assumption about any gentleman, even when the gossips insist he's a heartless rake."

A guilty flush rose in her cheeks, and Nick felt a grin curve his lips.

"Yes, well, as to that…"

She bit at her bottom lip, but it was no use. The reluctant smile she was trying to suppress was determined to have its way with her mouth. Nick gazed at her lips, his breath catching when at last it burst forth.

"It wasn't the gossip, Lord Dare. It was the scarlet waistcoat."

Nick hadn't the vaguest idea what she meant, but for some reason his grin widened. "What scarlet waistcoat?"

"The one you wore to Lord and Lady Derrick's dinner party." Her eyes were twinkling with mischief.

"What's wrong with my scarlet waistcoat?" The damn thing was more Gibbs's than it was his, just like most of his elegant clothing, but if Miss Somerset liked it, perhaps he'd wear it at their wedding.

"Oh, nothing at all. It's a handsome waistcoat, and I daresay it flatters your, ah…your…"

She trailed off, looking very much as if she wished she hadn't mentioned the waistcoat at all, which only made Nick more determined to hear what she'd been about to say. "My what?"

She waved a hand at him. "Your, ah... your person."

"I see. So I'm a rake because I wore a flattering scarlet waistcoat?"

"Yes," she said, as if it were perfectly obvious. "Only a rake would wear a waistcoat so clearly intended to gain the ladies' attention."

Nick stared at her in shock for a moment, then he threw back his head and laughed until his stomach ached. "Do you know what I think, Miss Somerset? I think my scarlet waistcoat caught *your* attention, and you bear it a grudge for that reason."

"That's utter nonsense, Lord Dare." She sniffed with disdain, but a smile lurked at the corners of her lips. "But never mind the waistcoat. Hadn't we better be on our way to Wapping?"

Nick didn't stir from his place on the settee. "No. Not yet."

"Would you like some tea first? I beg your pardon, my lord." She rose and crossed the room to ring the bell. "I should have offered earlier—"

"No, no tea, thank you. What I want, Miss Somerset, is to see your book."

She froze halfway across the room. "No."

Nick raised an eyebrow at her icy tone. "Why not?"

"Because I don't want to show it to you! I can't think why you'd want to see it anyway. You'll find it dreadfully dull, I'm sure."

Nick ran a hand over his jaw, studying her. "I don't agree, Miss Somerset. I find everything about you very interesting, indeed."

He blinked, surprised to hear the low rasp of his voice. He *was* interested in her as a means to an end, but the way he'd said it, in that husky, suggestive tone, it had sounded as if he was flirting with her—

Wait. He *was* flirting with her, wasn't he? Flirting and teasing and charming her into accepting his calls so he could get on with this bloody courtship and marriage and return to Italy and Catalina's waiting arms.

Nick frowned. Christ, it was odd, but for the first time since he'd set foot on English soil he'd forgotten the only thing he wished for was to be gone again. "In any case, it's for me to decide whether or not I find it interesting. Come now, Miss Somerset. Go and fetch it, and let me have a look."

She crossed her arms over her chest. "No."

"Pity." Nick balanced one ankle on the other knee and threw his arm over the back of the settee. "Because I'm not leaving until you do, so you'll need to decide how badly you want that sketch of Execution Dock. Take all the time you need."

For several long minutes, her muttering and the soft shuffle of her slippers as she paced back and forth across the carpet was the only sound in the room, but at last she turned and faced him. "It's not...I don't let anyone...because it's private. It's just for me, Lord Dare."

Something in her voice made Nick's flesh prickle with warning. She sounded almost...no, ashamed wasn't the right word, but it was something akin to that, as if she'd done something she knew she shouldn't have, and had to keep it hidden at all costs.

"I've already seen a great many of the sketches, Miss Somerset." He made an effort to keep his voice gentle. "Would it really be so terrible for me to see the rest?"

"Yes! It's...the sketches aren't as...every lady sketches, my lord."

The warning prickle creeping over his neck blossomed into anger at this, but he wasn't angry *at* her.

He was angry *for* her.

"So the sketches are forgivable for a lady, but the writing isn't? Is that what you mean to say? It almost sounds as if you're ashamed of it."

Her face paled, and for a moment Nick was certain he'd gone too far, but then she let out a long, deep sigh. "I'm not ashamed of it, Lord Dare. Just the opposite. I'm extraordinarily proud of it, and yet at the same time I recognize it's also...people won't understand it. Only my sisters have seen it, and then only bits and pieces of it, and even they think it's...well, let's just say people would think it's odd, and leave it at that, shall we?"

"You mean they'd think *you're* odd."

It was the truth, but as soon as the words left Nick's lips, he regretted saying them. He didn't have any wish to hurt her feelings.

But she only shrugged, then gave him a small, resigned smile. "I *am* odd. As a child I always preferred the schoolroom and library to every other room in the house. Even when I lived in Surrey I was considered odd, and you may believe me when I tell you, my lord, Surrey is rife with odd characters of every sort. But here in London, well...if you judge by the ton's standards, I'm a great deal worse than *odd*."

Nick's throat closed. "How much worse?"

Her shoulder hitched in a casual shrug, but her face was tight. "Laughable. Mad, even."

Nick flinched away from her words, but he couldn't fail to hear the defeat in her voice, and he rose to his feet and crossed the room to her. She wouldn't look at him, so he tipped her face up to his with gentle fingers under her chin. "I don't think you're mad, Miss Somerset, and I won't laugh at you."

She gazed up at him with dark blue eyes and searched his face for... what? Mockery? Sincerity? He wasn't sure which, but some of the tension eased from her shoulders, and Nick was quick to press his advantage. It had become imperative, somehow, that he see this book, if only to prove to her she hadn't any reason to hide it from him.

"If you don't want to show me the whole thing, then how about just the two chapters we talked about? Justice, and haunted London? Before you refuse, remember I *did* save your sketchbook from a footpad last night."

It was a shameless manipulation, of course, but for reasons Nick didn't quite understand, it was exactly the right thing to say at that moment, because it made her smile. "I suppose it won't hurt to show you just those two chapters. I'll go fetch them, but you must promise to take me to Wapping directly afterwards, Lord Dare, with no more teasing for another favor."

Nick's lips twitched. "To Wapping, and straight to Execution Dock, with no more teasing. I promise."

Once she left the room, Nick returned to the settee to wait. He was rather surprised at his persistence, and even more surprised at the fervency with which he wanted to see her book. He was never fervent or persistent about a damn thing these days—unless it was finding a way to get out of England as quickly as possible—but somehow Miss Somerset and her ghosts and gibbets had managed to catch his attention where everything else had failed.

No one was more surprised about it than he was, but against all odds, he *liked* her.

He shifted uneasily against the settee as that sank in. It would be much easier for all concerned if he *didn't* like her, or rather, if they each liked the other well enough to marry, but not so well they chose to spend any time together after they were wed.

It was an easy enough thing to accomplish with a typical English belle interested only in his wealth and title, but nothing about Miss Somerset was typical. She was, in truth, not at all the kind of lady he'd intended to court. It might be better, after all, if he waited to find a bride at the start of the season, despite the delay—

"Here they are, Lord Dare."

Miss Somerset was standing before him with a large leather portfolio tucked under her arm, gnawing at her lower lip. She was attempting to disguise her dread under a façade of careless unconcern, but she wasn't adept at hiding her feelings. They seemed to be so close to the surface a word or a touch could call them forth.

When she handed over the portfolio, her hand was shaking.

All at once Nick realized she was taking a tremendous chance, showing her work to him. For her, it was like revealing something deep inside her, a piece of herself she'd never shared with anyone other than her sisters, and even then, not to this degree. Until he saw her face, her shaking hands, he hadn't realized the bravery it took for her to trust him with this part of herself.

"Thank you for showing this to me." He took the portfolio from her, but he hesitated before opening it, the weight of the moment lying heavy upon him. If he should do something wrong, or say the wrong thing...

She'd either slap him hard enough to make his ears ring, or she'd burst into a flood of tears. One of those reactions would be far more painful than the other, but as he grasped her cold hand in his and pulled her gently down onto the settee next to him...

It occurred to Nick he wasn't sure which one.

Chapter Ten

It was his gray eyes. She'd looked into them one too many times, or for too long, and they'd bewitched her. They had to have, because there was no other explanation for why she'd just entrusted two full chapters of her beloved book—chapters she hadn't even allowed her sisters to see—to a rogue like Lord Dare.

Handsome, fashionable gentlemen like Lord Dare had laughed at her before. They'd smirked during her torturous pianoforte performances, cringed over her quadrille—a few had even openly mocked her awkward efforts at flirtatious conversation. Her feelings had been hurt more times than she cared to count, but as painful as it had been to be laughed at, the sting had faded, because in the end Violet didn't care about flirting, or her quadrille, or the pianoforte.

But this…this was different. This was her precious book, and she cared very much about it, indeed. So much, in fact, she was willing to endure Lord Dare's derision to get the sketch she wanted. At any other time she might have appreciated the irony of the thing, but at the moment she was too busy bracing herself for his reaction.

She perched on the edge of the settee next to him, her spine rigid, and waited with a confusing combination of defiance and dread for him to open the portfolio and get on with the inevitable burst of hilarity so they could be on their way.

He took his time, but when at last he untied the thin leather string and drew out the thick sheaf of papers, it took everything Violet had not to snatch the beloved pages away before he could see them. But she clenched her hands together in her lap and forced herself to keep still as he stacked the pages neatly on the table in front of the settee and began to turn them over one by one.

He didn't laugh, and he didn't say a word.

Violet dragged a breath into airless lungs as she watched him handle each sketch—a good many of which she'd risked her reputation to get—and she tried to see them as he might see them. Some of the drawings were colored and some were simple black and white, in the manner of woodcuts. Most of them were rough still, but she'd copied a few of them over and over again from hasty sketches and mounted them on fine, heavy paper, almost like a real book.

Her sketches were quite good. Drawing was the one ladylike skill she'd managed to master, but it was the writing she enjoyed the most, and there were pages and pages of it in her neat copperplate script, each labored over with painstaking care so there were no blots or smudges of ink. No imperfections.

And still, Lord Dare said nothing.

He was going to laugh at her. Or worse, he was going to turn over the last page, then turn to her with a patronizing smile and tell her it was a sweet little book, but nothing a proper lady should be interested in. Quite a waste of her time, really—surely there was something more useful she could be doing? And now that he thought of it, did her grandmother know what she was about, or—

"Humph."

Humph? What did that mean? Violet hadn't the faintest idea, but at Lord Dare's soft grunt her anxious gaze darted from his hands to his face. He'd taken up a page to get a closer look at it. It was one of her better sketches, of a night watchman in a heavy dark blue cloak, his iron bell attached to his belt and a dog on his heels. The lit lantern in his fist created a pool of light amidst the pressing shadows of a dark London street.

"How did you get this sketch?"

Violet bit her lip. As it happened, she'd had to sneak from her bedchamber at night to get that sketch. Even now she could perfectly recall the fear and excitement in her throat as she'd crept out the door and made her way to Bayley Street. But it was a smaller side street, and there hadn't been a night watchman there, so she'd been obliged to go as far as Tottenham Court Road to get the sketch.

It wasn't the sort of adventure she wished to confess to, particularly not to Lord Dare, who'd no doubt be scandalized.

He turned to her with a raised eyebrow when she didn't answer right away. "Miss Somerset? The sketch?"

"I, ah…well, it was a trifle more challenging than some of the others," Violet hedged, determined to give him as little information as possible. "But I think it's quite a good one."

"Yes, very good. Accurate, that is. Almost as if you were standing right next to the watchman when you took it." He studied the sketch again, his sharp gray eyes moving over every detail. "On what looks to be the corner of Bedford Street and Tottenham Court Road. *At night*. But that can't be the case, because a sensible young lady like yourself would never risk her safety in such a foolish way, would she, Miss Somerset?"

Violet blinked, confused once again. For a careless, reckless debaucher, Lord Dare had a surprisingly chivalrous turn. "It's not a risk, my lord, when the young lady in question knows perfectly well how to take care of herself."

The eyebrow raised another notch. "Humph."

He set the sketch aside and picked up the first page of an essay she'd written entitled "Thief-Takers," which was a lively but comprehensive history of crime, justice, and punishment in London, complete with a detailed account of several of London's more famous Bow Street runners.

Lord Dare went quiet again, and Violet, whose nerves were stretched to the last degree by such resounding silence, darted another glance at his face to find him studying the page with fixed attention.

He read the entire essay, then gathered all the pages together, slid them carefully back into the portfolio, tied the string, and handed it back to Violet, his expression unreadable. "The Thames Police Office is in Wapping," he offered, after Violet had squirmed through another endless silence.

"Is it?" Her voice emerged in a high squeak.

"It is. You'll want to get a sketch of it while we're there, I imagine."

"Yes." She waited, but he didn't offer anything more. "Ah, is that all?"

He studied the flush on her cheeks, and a small smile teased at the corner of his mouth. "You look surprised, Miss Somerset. Did you expect something more?"

Scorn. Ridicule. Mockery. In the worst case, blatant contempt. In short, she'd expected much more, all of it unpleasant, but none of those things seemed to be forthcoming.

To her surprise, Violet found herself overwhelmed with an unfamiliar shyness, and she couldn't quite meet his eyes. It was silly of her, of course. Was she going to fall into a girlish swoon just because he hadn't laughed at her, or teased her? Had her expectations of aristocratic gentlemen truly sunk so low, or was it just her opinion of Lord Dare?

Guilt threatened, but Violet pushed it aside. If she *had* underestimated him, it was his own fault. For pity's sake, she'd witnessed him debauching Lady Uplands with her own eyes! He was a terrible rake, and that hadn't changed simply because he hadn't openly mocked her. No, it was best for all concerned if she regarded Lord Dare as a useful tool and nothing more. He appeared to be willing to take her to Wapping still, and that was all that mattered.

"Shall we go, then?" She rose from the settee and began to move toward the drawing room door. "It's early still, and it looks as though the weather might hold, so—"

"Miss Somerset." He grabbed her hand and drew her to a halt before she could take another step, and a tiny shiver tickled up her spine when his warm palm pressed against hers.

"Yes?" She turned to him, and found those strange, silvery-gray eyes fixed on her with such intensity she looked away again at once, her heart pounding.

"Your book, it's…fascinating."

Violet went still, stunned at his praise, and then her eyes drifted closed. *Fascinating.*

That word, the quiet admiration in his voice as he said it, his utter sincerity—Violet's heart soared until it felt as if it would fly from her chest. Of all the things he could have said or done, nothing in the world could have pleased her more than that one word.

She didn't trust herself to speak, but she squeezed his hand before she let it go and led him from the drawing room.

* * * *

"Oh, dear. It's high tide. I hadn't thought of that." Violet stood at the top of Wapping Old Stairs and frowned down at the water washing over the lower half of the staircase. "Well, I'm afraid the sketch won't look like much—just a half-flooded stairway, really."

Lord Dare peered over her shoulder. "Better a half-flooded stairway than a half-dead body still twitching on the noose. Or worse, a bloated corpse. They don't cut them down until three high tides have passed. I'll wager you didn't think of that, either."

No, she hadn't, and Violet shuddered at the thought now. She'd worked hard to make her book as accurate and realistic as possible, but she drew the line at bloated corpses. "Well, it can't be helped, I suppose. I'll have to do without Execution Dock, and the lower half of the staircase."

She started to make her way down the stairs, but a large hand clamped down on her shoulder. "Where do you think you're going?"

Violet turned to Lord Dare in surprise. "Why, down the stairs, of course. It will be a much better sketch if I stand closer to the bottom. The perspective is better looking up, and that way I can include part of the inn—"

"No."

"No?" Violet gaped at him. "Why not?"

He pointed down the staircase in front of them. "Because the stairs are wet, Miss Somerset, and likely slippery. You'll lose your footing and tumble head over heels, and the next thing I know you'll be underwater, and then I'll have to come in after you."

"Oh, nonsense. I won't fall, and even if I did, you won't have to save me. I know how to swim."

Violet tried to make her way down the stairs a second time, but Lord Dare wrapped a hand around her elbow and stopped her. "That water is cold, and there's no way you could manage that tide in heavy, sodden skirts. No, I'm afraid it's out of the question. You'll have to get your sketch from here."

Violet planted her hands on her hips. "Are you worried for me, or for yourself?"

His lips curled in an unrepentant grin. "Myself, of course. I don't care for a frolic in the Thames, or a soggy drive back to Bedford Square."

"Then stay where you are." Violet pulled her arm from his grasp and began to pick her way down the stairs. "If I fall in, I'll find my way back out without your assistance."

He grasped her arm again. "I know you think me a rogue, Miss Somerset, but I'm also a gentleman. I won't allow a lady to sink to the bottom of the Thames before my very eyes without lifting a finger to help."

"Don't think of me as a lady, Lord Dare. Think of me as a bluestocking. That should help to dampen your heroic instincts."

"Why can't you be both at once?" He cocked his head to the side, considering her. "After all, if a rogue can be a gentleman, then a bluestocking can be a lady."

Violet didn't recall ever having agreed a rogue *could* be a gentleman, but Lord Dare looked as if he'd relish a debate on the subject, and she wasn't going to let him distract her. "Well, I'm more the first than the second, so you haven't a thing to worry about, my lord."

Violet tugged free of him for the third time, the matter settled as far as she was concerned, but Lord Dare didn't agree, because he caught her arm again. "I don't see why that should make any difference. Why shouldn't I wish to prevent a bluestocking from drowning?"

She tugged at her arm, then glared at him when he refused to release her. "A bluestocking wouldn't drown! Any self-respecting lady of knowledge has all she requires to save herself, Lord Dare."

"Does she, indeed? Well, forgive me, Miss Somerset, but you didn't look as if you were on the verge of saving yourself when I found you at the mercy of that footpad last night."

"Do you see any footpads about, my lord?"

"No. I see one small woman about four steps away from tumbling into the Thames River, and if it came down to a contest between you, I'd wager on the Thames."

Violet blew out an irritated breath. Goodness, he was stubborn—perhaps even more stubborn than she was, a state of affairs that would have shocked her grandmother. "Very well, my lord. What would you have me do, then?"

"Take your sketch from the top of the staircase looking down, of course. Didn't I already say so?"

Violet glanced down the staircase again to get a sense of what the sketch might look like taken from that angle, and shook her head. "No. That won't do. You'll have to come up with something else."

"Oh, I already have. In another twenty seconds I'm going to throw you over my shoulder, toss you into my carriage, and drive you back to Bedford Square without any sketch at all."

Violet's mouth fell open. "I—you wouldn't dare!"

He grinned at her outraged expression. "Oh, I assure you, I would. I may strive to be a gentleman, but in your case, Miss Somerset, I find the rogue is far more useful."

He said this with the most intriguingly boyish smile, but despite his playful grin, Violet knew without a doubt he wouldn't hesitate to throw her over his shoulder and march her back to his carriage, and he'd do it without a word of argument or apology.

"Five steps only, Lord Dare. I won't be anywhere near the water that way, and it should bring me low enough to get the perspective I need."

He glanced behind her at the frothing water below, and shook his head. "Two steps."

It took all of Violet's restraint not to roll her eyes. Confound the man! Whoever would have thought a careless rogue like Lord Dare could be so infuriatingly protective? "Three. Come now, my lord. You must be able to see I can't make do with fewer than three."

He hesitated, then at last let out a beleaguered sigh. "Three steps, then." He released her arm and pushed past her, down the stairs.

Violet watched him, puzzled. "Where are you going?"

"Down to the fourth step, of course."

For all his talk of slipperiness, Violet couldn't help but notice his progress down the stairs was graceful and confident. "But why?"

Another heavy sigh. "Why do you think? To block you from falling into the water if you slip. Here." He held out his hand. "Give me your sketchbook before you come down, then take my hand."

Violet didn't hand him her book, but clutched it to her chest in an instinctive movement, her breath hitching in a strange, suspended moment of exhilaration and panic. She stared down at him, at the sun catching in his hair, and for the first time she noticed the subtle auburn highlights in the dark waves.

Thickly lashed gray eyes, silky dark hair, a hard chest, and a lean, taut body wrapped in a lovely scarlet waistcoat—it was more than enough to render any lady breathless. But Violet wasn't any lady. Oh, she'd noticed how attractive he was, of course. She wasn't blind, after all. And then he smelled so wonderful, and everyone knew scent was a vital component of personal attraction—one need look no further than Monsieur Floris's perfumery in St. James's Square for proof of *that*—but even all his attractions taken together weren't enough to make Violet's heart quicken with awareness.

But this…this was kindness, a sincere concern for the safety of someone he believed needed his protection. Whether she did or not didn't matter one whit. It was, at its very heart, true gentlemanliness—the sort every aristocrat pretended to, and so few of them possessed.

She'd fallen in love with Lord Derrick because he was a true gentleman.

But Lord Dare…

She never would have dreamed he could pose a threat to her heart.

"Aren't you coming, Miss Somerset? Don't tell me after all that fuss and bother you've changed your mind?"

He was gazing up at her, his hand still extended to help her down, and Violet's heart began to crash against her ribs as the tingle of exhilaration was swallowed by alarm. Oh, *why* did he have to be the only rogue in London who was a gentleman? She didn't *want* him to be kind and sincere—not when he had such lovely gray eyes and such a sly, playful smile. Dear God, was it too much to ask he be nothing more than a dreadful rake, and stoop-shouldered and squinty-eyed into the bargain—

"The tide is still rising, Miss Somerset. In another few minutes I'll be up to my ankles in the filthy water of the Thames, so if it's not too much trouble, would you mind—"

"You don't need to stand below me, my lord. I told you I won't slip."

"If you won't slip then I have nothing to fear, and in that case, there's no reason why I shouldn't stand here, is there?"

"But if I should slip—that is, I won't, of course—but if I should, then I'll likely knock you in, and we'll both get wet. What's the sense in that?" Violet heard the thread of panic in her voice, and her cheeks heated with embarrassment.

He gave her a curious look. "Knock me in? Unless you intend to take a run at me, I think it's far more likely I'd catch you. In case it's escaped your notice, Miss Somerset, I'm quite a bit larger and heavier than you are."

It *hadn't* escaped her notice. Indeed, she became increasingly aware of his impressive musculature with every second she spent in his presence.

"Well?" He waved his hand impatiently. "Are you coming, or not?"

Violet handed him her sketchbook, but she didn't take his hand. "I don't need your help to get down." It seemed imperative, somehow, that she not touch him.

He simply raised an eyebrow at that, but the gesture said more clearly than words that she could take his hand and allow him to assist her, or return to the carriage at once.

Violet took his hand.

His warm fingers closed around hers, his fingertips grazing her palm. When Violet reached the step above his she steadied her stance, reached into her pocket for her pencil, and held out her hand for her sketchbook.

He handed it to her, but he didn't release her other hand.

"You'll have to let go of my hand, my lord, unless you imagine I can hold my sketchbook and draw with only one hand." Violet, who'd begun to feel quite desperate as soon as his fingers wrapped around hers, gave an insistent little tug.

Lord Dare glanced at the water behind him, which was close enough to splash his boots, then turned back to her with a wry smile. He released her hand, but before she could take a relieved breath, his hands slid around her waist.

Violet froze, her breath catching in her throat as his warm fingers curled around her. "What...what are you doing, Lord Dare?"

He slid his hands down until they rested on her hips, then he eased her back against him until her back was pressed against the hard, solid wall of his chest. "Keeping hold of you, in case you slip. Go on, then. You can take your sketch now."

Sketch? What sketch?

Violet tried to gather her wits, but he was so close his lips were nearly touching her ear, and his voice...the low, husky rasp of it was...oh, dear God, had he just settled her hips more firmly against his?

Violet fought not to let herself melt into a quivering mass of willing flesh at his feet. "You, ah...you don't need to hold onto me, you know. I've got excellent balance."

He chuckled, and Violet shivered with pleasure as his warm breath stirred the loose strands of hair at her temple.

"Of course you do. Indeed, Miss Somerset, at this point, what could possibly go wrong?"

* * * *

Quite a lot did go wrong, in fact, but it had nothing to do with the Thames and everything to do with the Marchioness of Huntington.

It would have been awful enough if Iris had witnessed Lord Dare's carriage exiting the drive, and it would have been worse still if she'd come upon Violet while she was bidding his lordship adieu. But either of those scenarios would have been preferable to what actually happened.

Iris caught Violet *before* she'd bid adieu to Lord Dare.

"Well, *Hyacinth*, here you are at last."

Violet came to such a sudden halt in the drawing room doorway that Lord Dare slammed right into the back of her. "I beg your pardon, Miss—"

"I've expected you in Grosvenor Square all afternoon." Iris rose from the settee she'd been sitting on and dusted the crumbs from her hands. There was a tea tray on the table in front of her, and if one could judge from the number of empty plates, she'd been waiting for quite some time, and nibbling all the while.

Iris had developed a fierce sweet tooth now that she was carrying a child, but unfortunately, the sweets didn't have a sweetening effect on her temperament. She seemed to become crosser with every passing day, and now she sent Violet a dark look that was ominous, indeed.

"Ah, yes, well, I—Lord Dare, may I present my elder sister, Lady Huntington."

Lord Dare bowed politely over Iris's hand. "A pleasure, my lady."

Iris eyed him with ill-concealed suspicion. "Well, Lord Dare. How do you do? It's very kind of you to escort my dear sister to...to...where have you and Lord Dare spent your afternoon, *Hyacinth?*"

Violet glanced nervously at Lord Dare to see if he'd noticed the emphasis Iris had placed on that name, and found his brows drawn into a confused frown.

He'd noticed.

Oh, no. There was no telling what Iris would do when she was on a tear, and once she found out they'd been to—

"We went on a drive to Wapping, Lady Huntington, so Miss Somerset could take a sketch of Execution Dock for her book." Lord Dare chuckled. "It was nearly underwater by the time we arrived, however, and I'm afraid her slippers and my boots got rather wet."

"How unfortunate, but I'm certain *Hyacinth* will agree with me, my lord, when I say I can imagine many things far worse than a pair of wet slippers."

Lord Dare gave Iris an uncertain look. "Ah, yes, well, I suppose we could have tumbled headlong into the Thames."

"*Hyacinth* might yet find herself at the bottom of the Thames," Iris snapped, ignoring Lord Dare's frown and narrowing her gaze on Violet.

"I've kept you far too long today, Lord Dare." Violet turned to him with a stiff smile. "And I'm certain you wish to change your boots. I'll just call Eddesley to show you out, shall I?"

Lord Dare's frown deepened as he looked from Violet to Iris. "No need, Miss Somerset. I'll see myself out." He bowed to each of them, and in the next moment he was gone, and likely relieved to be so.

"Lying, sneaking about, and toying with a gentleman's affections?" Iris demanded as soon as the drawing room door closed behind Lord Dare.

Violet kicked off her damp slippers and threw herself into a chair. "Hyacinth is perfectly dreadful at keeping secrets. I should have known she'd tell you."

"Don't blame Hyacinth for your behavior, Violet," Iris scolded. "She didn't want to tell me. I teased it out of her when you didn't appear in Grosvenor Street."

"I don't see why you should have felt the need to rush over here." Violet's tone was resentful, but she didn't meet her sister's eyes.

"I *told* you why. Lying, sneaking about, and toying with a gentleman's affections!"

"What, do you suppose Lord Dare is madly in love with me? I couldn't toy with his affections even if I wished to." His affections, or any other part of him. "It was a drive to Wapping, Iris—that's all. Perfectly harmless."

"I see. So you *aren't* pretending to be Hyacinth and encouraging Lord Dare in a false courtship for the sake of your book?"

Violet opened her mouth to object, realized she had no defense, and then snapped it closed again. Dash it all, why must Hyacinth insist on such unrelenting honesty at all times? It was quite tedious of her.

Iris sighed. "I don't know what's come over you, Violet. It's not like you to be so careless with another's feelings. This preoccupation with your book has brought out the worst in you."

"But it's only for a week or two, Iris, until Grandmother returns from Bath, and it's not as if Lord Dare truly cares for either me or Hyacinth. He can't even tell us apart!"

"Yes, and it's dreadful of him, but does that mean you have to do something dreadful in return? His poor behavior doesn't excuse your lying, Violet, and you know it very well."

Violet tucked her feet underneath her and rested her cheek on her raised knees. Iris was right. She *did* know it, and after today, she knew something else, as well.

Lord Dare deserved far better treatment from her.

He *had* nearly concussed Lady Uplands in Lord Derrick's library, of course, and there was no question he was a rogue. That night at dinner Honora had whispered that Lord Dare had left a trail of broken hearts from Paris to Rome, and Violet could believe it of him. He was far too handsome and charming for his own good.

Or for hers.

But there was an innate kindness to him—a gentlemanliness, and a rare gallantry Violet would never have expected in a man like him. Today, when she'd shown him her book, he hadn't laughed at her or mocked her, and the way he'd insisted on standing between her and the Thames while she took her sketch...

Well. Lord Dare was much more than a debauched rogue with a careless disregard for the sanctity of a private library, and really, what had he done to justify her shabby treatment of him? He'd simply mistaken her for her sister. It was hardly a dastardly crime, and it wasn't as if he was the first to confuse them.

Iris must have seen the flush of guilt on her face, because she knelt down in front of Violet's chair and took her hand. "I know how important your book is to you, Violet, but this isn't the way to go about it, and you know you can always bring Hyacinth or me along if you need a companion."

Take Hyacinth to Execution Dock? No, indeed, and it wouldn't do to take Iris to such places, either. Finn wouldn't appreciate his wife and unborn child wandering about a place like Cockpit Steps, or Tyburn Tree, and Violet would never ask Iris to lie to him.

No, once she sent Lord Dare away she'd give up the chance to get the sketches she needed. A dry ache pressed behind her eyes at the thought, but she didn't know whether the unshed tears were for those lost moments of freedom, or for the loss of Lord Dare.

But it didn't matter, because either way, she had only one choice.

She pressed Iris's hand. "When Lord Dare calls tomorrow, I'll confess I've deceived him, and beg his pardon."

"Good." Iris squeezed her hand in return.

Violet drew in a breath. It was the right thing to do—the only thing—and once she did it, surely she'd feel relieved. But right now...

An image of his playful silver-gray eyes framed by those long, dark lashes flashed in her mind, and all she felt was emptiness.

Chapter Eleven

The next morning, Nick awoke to find Gibbs standing over his bed, peering down into his face like some sort of demented gargoyle.

"Good *morning*, Lord Dare."

Nick snorted at the emphasis Gibbs placed on the word *morning*. "Your impertinence knows no bounds, Gibbs."

But Nick's voice lacked heat. He couldn't blame Gibbs for expecting to find him asleep. It wasn't even noon yet, but after Nick left Miss Somerset at Bedford Square yesterday evening he hadn't been in the mood for any of his usual debaucheries. Even a foray into Lady Uplands's spectacular bosom held no appeal, and he'd ended up retiring far earlier than any self-respecting rogue should.

Still, his slumber had proved far more satisfying than a wearisome romp with Lady Uplands, because he'd had another dream, and this one was most pleasant, indeed. He could only recall snatches of it now, but there'd been a pair of wide blue eyes, and delicate white fingers wrapped around a drawing pencil, and plump pink lips curving into a smile so open and sweet it still made his chest ache hours after he'd woken.

In his dream they'd been arguing, but it wasn't the irritating sort of arguing that put a man into a temper. No, this was a different kind of arguing altogether—the kind that felt more like teasing, or flirting. The kind that made a man's heart beat faster, his breath come shorter, and his mind wander to all manner of illicit things, like brushing his thumb over the lower curve of that lip, to see if it was as soft as it looked, and then tasting it…

He'd lain awake with his eyes tightly closed for hours after he woke, trying to hold onto that dream, but eventually it faded away as all dreams did, and once it had Nick's thoughts drifted to that strange encounter with Lady Huntington last night.

A cold feeling settled in his gut.

Something wasn't right, but damned if he knew what it was.

Hyacinth Somerset wasn't mad, but something was afoot. Lady Huntington had stopped short of accusing her sister of any wrongdoing last night, but she'd been angry, and Miss Somerset had been in such a hurry to get rid of him she'd nearly shoved him out the door.

"Have you ever courted a lady, Gibbs?" Nick dragged himself upright against the pillows and accepted the cup of chocolate Gibbs handed him.

Gibbs's long face creased with distaste. "No, my lord."

"Well, why not? Haven't you ever been in love?" Nick didn't expect to gain much insight into courtship from Gibbs. His valet wasn't the kind of man who'd succumb to a heated passion—at least, not a passion for a woman. There was no telling how heated Gibbs might become over a flawlessly tailored Weston coat.

Gibbs looked horrified at the very idea. "No, my lord. I beg your pardon for my ignorance, my lord, but I don't care for messy entanglements of that sort."

"Not for love, then, but for fortune? Or companionship? Comfort in your old age?" Well, it was a bit too late for that last one now, and in any case he doubted Gibbs found comfort in anything other than a perfectly pressed cravat.

Gibbs draped Nick's coat over his arm, then stooped to pick up his waistcoat from the floor. "No, my lord."

"Well, you're no bloody help, are you?"

"*No*, my lord." Gibbs looked vastly relieved that Nick had finally caught on. "Will you have breakfast in bed, my lord?"

"Yes, all right. In an hour." Nick waved him off. "Until then, some privacy, if you would."

"Yes, my lord."

Once Gibbs was gone, Nick set aside his cup then flopped onto his back in his bed with a sigh. This business with Miss Somerset had to come to an end.

Today.

The thought left a hollow knot of emptiness in Nick's chest. Not only because he'd have to wait until the start of the London season to find another prospective bride, but also because, well—Miss Somerset was diverting, and it wasn't just the gibbets and ghosts that made her so.

She was different, and when Nick was with her, he felt different, too. After two years of running from himself, feeling different was like filling his lungs with fresh air after he'd long since reconciled himself to a slow suffocation.

He'd grown so weary of London, so tired of the dirt and grime and disease, so tired of the haunting memories, but when he viewed the city through her eyes, the shadows didn't leap out at him from behind every corner. He'd never once visited Wapping Old Stairs in the entire time he'd lived in England, yet yesterday he'd been one stiff wind away from tumbling into the Thames, just so she could get her sketch.

Tumbling into the Thames, and happy enough to do so, too.

Against all odds, and against all expectations, he was taken with her. But his fascination with her didn't change the fact that she was hiding something from him.

Lying to him.

He wasn't sure why, or what about, but it hardly mattered, and it didn't help that he was also lying to her about his own reasons for marrying.

But even putting his secrets aside, something was off about Miss Somerset.

To begin with, she had an astonishing amount of freedom for one of Lady Chase's granddaughters. Why was she always alone at the Bedford Square house? Lady Chase was notorious for her tyranny, and yet no one ever seemed to be paying the least bit of attention to what Miss Somerset was doing, or to question her whereabouts.

That alone should have raised his suspicions at once, but it was the odd encounter with Lady Huntington last night that had nudged Nick's vague uneasiness into grave doubt.

As it was, he'd simply called on Miss Somerset a few times, and taken her for a drive or two. He hadn't declared any intentions, and he hadn't been introduced to her grandmother. It wasn't yet an official courtship, and, given his reservations, the wisest course of action was to drop his pursuit now, before he could no longer do so honorably.

He'd have to stop seeing Miss Somerset at once.

Heaviness settled in Nick's chest, but his mind was made up. He rang the bell for Gibbs, dressed, and went downstairs in search of his aunt.

He found her in the breakfast room.

"Good morning, Nicholas. You're up much earlier than your habit." She offered him her usual serene smile and motioned the footman for coffee while he filled his plate at the sideboard. "You were out all day yesterday. Perhaps you've something in mind to occupy you today, as well?"

"No, nothing." He didn't have a damned thing to do now that he wasn't going to call on Miss Somerset, and a quick glance at the window revealed a dreary, wet November day.

It stretched out before him, long, endless, and empty.

"You could call on Louisa and Lady Covington."

"Lady Covington and Louisa? What, are they still in town? I expected they'd go back to the country once you made it clear to them Louisa and I will never make a match. You *did* make it clear to them, didn't you, my lady?"

"They decided to stay a while longer. You needn't look at me like that, Nicholas. I had nothing to do with it, and they don't stay for you, in any case. Lady Covington expressed a desire to do some shopping, that's all."

"If they don't stay for me, then they won't be expecting me to call." His aunt must think him dull-witted indeed if she thought he'd believe her totally innocent in this.

"It's common politeness for you to call, Nicholas. It doesn't have to mean a thing."

Nick let out a humorless laugh. "Louisa is my dead brother's former betrothed, my lady, so it damn well does mean something. How could it not?"

Her lips thinned at the curse, but instead of scolding him she hesitated, then covered his hand with her own. "I don't wish to upset you. If you don't care to call on Louisa, then don't do so. I just…I don't like to see you lonely."

The tightness in Nick's jaw eased. His aunt might not be above manipulation to achieve her ends, but she'd only ever wanted to protect him, even if it meant protecting him from himself. "I know, Aunt. I beg your pardon."

They drifted into silence then, Nick's heart kicking listlessly in his chest as he watched the rain hit the breakfast-room window in slanted sheets. What a dismal day. Whatever Miss Somerset had planned would likely have had to be postponed anyway, even if he had called on her. No doubt she was tucked into some cozy corner of her house, pawing through the pages of her book, with cobwebs in her hair and ink-stained fingers.

He didn't realize he was smiling until he heard his aunt's surprised laugh. "You look pleased, Nicholas. I must say it's lovely to see you smile. Why don't you plan something pleasant for the day, despite the foul weather? A visit to the British Museum, perhaps?"

Nick took another glance out the window. The sky was a dark, heavy gray, and it didn't look as if the rain were about to stop anytime soon. "It *is* an ideal day to visit a museum, I suppose."

Perhaps he *would* go to the British Museum for the day, or to the Royal Academy. The idea didn't hold much appeal, but he didn't have any more intriguing options. It was a pity he'd already made up his mind not to call on Miss Somerset, because she was the type of lady who'd appreciate a visit to a museum, though perhaps something less conventional than either of those places, someplace like—

Nick went still, his fork frozen partway to his mouth.

Someplace like the Hunterian Museum, in Lincoln's Inn Fields. Skulls and skeletons. Amputated limbs. Surgical instruments. Dissected animal carcasses. Jars upon jars of bizarre anatomical curiosities.

Miss Somerset would be enthralled. She'd fall into raptures, into paroxysms of intellectual bliss, and *he'd* be the one who'd get to see her face light up with joy. *He'd* be the one who had the honor of giving her that gift.

It was unlikely she'd ever seen the collection. It could only be viewed by invitation, and even if she'd been offered a ticket, her grandmother would never have permitted her to go. It struck Nick as enormously unfair she shouldn't have the chance to view it, given he couldn't think of a single person in London who'd be more delighted by it than she would.

"Nicholas? Why aren't you eating?"

Nick gave his aunt a vague nod, shoved the fork in his mouth, and swallowed his eggs without tasting them.

He'd vowed not to call on Miss Somerset again. For God's sake, he'd made the decision less than an hour ago, and already here he was, tempted to call on Miss Somerset.

But then he'd made that decision before it occurred to him how much she'd enjoy the Hunterian Museum. Everything had changed since then, and in any case, surely one more day wouldn't make any difference? It was a *single* day. What could be the harm in delaying for a *single* day? He could stop calling on her tomorrow just as easily, couldn't he?

Nick tossed his napkin aside and shoved his chair back from the table.

His aunt looked up in surprise. "Are you off, then? You haven't finished your breakfast."

"Yes, I beg your pardon, my lady. I'm not hungry, and I find myself anxious to get to…the museum."

Quite anxious, indeed.

* * * *

"The Hunterian Museum?"

Miss Somerset had looked grim enough when she entered the drawing room to receive his call. He didn't see any cobwebs today, and she was dressed in a flattering soft pink day gown, but she was pale, and she had dark shadows under her eyes, as if she hadn't slept.

But the moment he mentioned the Hunterian Museum, her entire face had lit up, and she'd clapped her hands together with unrestrained delight.

"Truly, Lord Dare? Oh, I've always wanted to go, but I never imagined I'd get the chance. Oh, how wonderful!"

"Yes, well, it's raining, so I thought..." Nick trailed off as his stomach leapt in response to the sparkle of anticipation in her dark blue eyes. It wasn't her pleasure that made him feel as if the sun had just emerged from behind a cloud, though. Of course it wasn't.

He cleared his throat. "That is, I thought perhaps you hadn't ever been, and would find it amusing."

She was gazing at him as if she'd never seen anything quite so wonderful as he. "How kind you are, my lord!"

Nick gazed back at her for a moment, then had to clear his throat again. "Well, as to that, I'm, ah...would you like to fetch your sketchbook before we go?"

"Oh! Oh, yes. I won't be a moment."

She ran from the room, then returned a few minutes later in a dark blue cloak, her sketchbook tucked under her arm.

He led her to his carriage and handed her in. She bounced on the edge of her seat with suppressed excitement during the entire ride to Lincoln's Inn Fields. "I've heard they have the Irish Giant's skeleton at the Hunterian."

Nick's lips twitched at her boundless excitement. "Charles Byrne, you mean? Yes. He was nearly eight feet tall."

"Oh, I know, I've read all about him. He was only twenty-two when he died, and he wanted to be buried at sea in a lead coffin, you know. By all accounts he was a dear man, and I feel rather sorry for him, having his bones on display for all the world to gawk at, but I don't deny I very much want to see him. Eight feet tall. Can you imagine the stress all that weight must have had on his skeleton, Lord Dare?"

Nick grinned. He hadn't even thought of that, but he liked it very much that *she* had. Damn, how is it he'd never before realized how engaging bluestockings were?

But perhaps it wasn't all bluestockings.

Perhaps it was just *her*.

Either way, it was damned difficult to regret today's outing, despite his decision to end this friendship between them, especially when she was smiling at him with those lovely pink lips. He'd dreamed about her lips, but even in his dreams he couldn't conjure such a sweet smile.

"I hadn't considered the stress on his skeleton, Miss Somerset, but I'm glad you mentioned it, because now perhaps we'll notice something when we view it. Some buckling about the knees would be my guess. Cracks around the knee bone, perhaps. What do you think?"

Nick waited with far more impatience than he'd ever imagined he could possibly feel to hear a bluestocking's opinion about an eight-foot giant's stress-related knee injuries.

She tapped her lip as she considered it. "Yes, I would think the knees would take the brunt of it." Without warning, she hopped across the carriage, plopped down next to him—*right* next to him, so his thigh was touching hers—and flipped through the pages of her sketchbook until she reached a blank page. "Like this, perhaps?"

She moved the sketchbook between them, drew out one of the drawing pencils she seemed to always have tucked into a pocket, and began to sketch a series of long lines on the page. "It wouldn't fall on his hips, I don't think, because—well, simple gravity, you know, but there's better weight distribution in the pelvic region than the knee area."

She continued to draw, and Nick continued to stare stupidly at the page, but he'd lost track of what she was saying the moment she sat down beside him. She was pressed against him, so close, the smooth top of her head level with his shoulder. If he leaned down just a bit, he could rest his cheek against her hair. He could bury his face in those heavy curls, and press his lips to the soft skin of her temples.

No cobwebs today. Her hair was in the same simple knot it had been in yesterday, but today he was close enough to notice the smooth, pale skin of her neck, and once he did, he couldn't tear his gaze away from it. She smelled crisp and clean, as if she used a soap with a mild vanilla fragrance. In a daze he leaned over her, his lips parting, his head lowering toward hers—

"What do you think, Lord Dare?"

I think you smell delicious.

"Lord Dare?" She turned to look up at him.

Nick jerked his head back. "Ah, what do I think about what?"

She tapped the pencil against the paper. "His knees." She'd drawn a rough sketch of a skeleton with a very long torso and legs, and now she cocked her head to the side, studying it. "I haven't got the proportions right, but even so, it's plain to see all the weight would have fallen in his knees and ankles. We'll have to have a look at his ankle bones, as well."

Nick, who was too distracted by the weight in his breeches to string a coherent sentence together, could only stare dumbly at her.

He'd almost kissed her neck.

If she hadn't turned at that moment, his lips would even now be brushing against that soft, vanilla-scented skin. He'd taste that delectable pulse hidden under her ear, feel it quicken against his tongue. He'd trail his parted lips across her cheek until he reached that tempting pink mouth, then he'd catch her lower lip gently between his teeth.

What would she do if he kissed her? Would she tremble and sigh in his arms, open her lips under his, or—

No. It was far more likely she'd hit him over the head with her sketchbook, then demand he take her home at once. Nick often enjoyed the attentions of a certain kind of lady, but proper young ladies like Miss Somerset tended to give him a wide berth, and for good reason.

Not that Miss Somerset had given him a wide berth—no, after her initial hesitation she seemed more than happy to receive his calls, but even so, she hadn't ever shown the slightest hint she thought of him in a romantic way. Her gaze didn't linger on his. She never flirted with him, and she didn't go out of her way to touch him.

Which was just as well, of course. She wasn't the sort of lady he fell into fits of passion over, and he didn't wish to lead her on. She might smell lovely, and have the smoothest, finest skin he'd ever seen, but she was a bluestocking, for God's sake. Rakes didn't desire bluestockings, any more than bluestockings desired rakes.

In that sense, at least, they were perfectly matched. After all, more than one happy marriage had been built on a solid foundation of mutual indifference.

"Well, we'll just have to see when we get there, I suppose." She closed her sketchbook with a sigh, but she continued to sit contentedly next to him rather than moving back to her seat, as if she wasn't even aware how close he was, and didn't notice the length of his thigh pressed against hers.

Which was, again, just as well, because it wasn't as if it mattered one way or another to him. A rake who regularly enjoyed ladies' bare thighs wrapped around his hips wasn't likely to fall into a panting froth of lust over the touch of a single curved thigh buried under five layers of thick wool.

The very thought was absurd.

And yet Nick edged toward the window, away from the disturbing limb that had shattered his peace, and leaned back against the squabs, strangely exhausted for some reason.

He'd just begun to relax again when he felt a small hand slip into his. He looked over at Miss Somerset, startled, and found her gaze on him.

"Thank you for taking me with you today." She squeezed the tips of his fingers tightly enough he could feel the warmth of her hand through her glove.

Without thinking, and without any hesitation, Nick squeezed back. "It's my pleasure, Miss Somerset."

A far greater pleasure than he'd ever dreamed it could be.

Chapter Twelve

It never occurred to Violet to scream, not even when she paused to peer into a tall, cylindrical jar and discovered it contained preserved monkey heads.

"How curious. They look rather peaceful, don't they?"

Lord Dare tapped his finger against a jar containing a monkey's skeleton. "That one doesn't, and I can't say I blame him."

He'd stayed close beside her as they made their way through the cavernous main hall, as if he expected her to swoon at any moment and was determined to catch her when it happened. Under normal circumstances it might have annoyed Violet—she was *not* the type of lady who made a habit of swooning—but, well…she *had* swooned after the footpad attacked her, and Lord Dare *had* been obliged to carry her to his carriage, so she could hardly complain.

To be fair, most proper ladies *would* swoon at the sight of a monkey's head floating in some clear liquid of undetermined origin. But even if that hadn't been the case, Violet still wouldn't have complained. In truth, she was having a difficult time keeping herself from throwing her arms around his neck and rising onto her tiptoes to kiss him on the cheek, right here next to the floating monkey heads.

Her burst of affection had nothing to do with how handsome he was, of course, or the fact that his dark blue coat turned his eyes an even more remarkable shade of silvery-gray. Violet had seen many handsome men before, after all, and she'd never wanted to kiss any of *them*, not even Lord Derrick.

Not even Lord Derrick?

She came to a halt next to a row of glass tubes displaying anatomical sections of human ears, a surprised frown forming on her lips. How odd she should be so madly in love with Lord Derrick, but never imagine what it might be like to kiss him.

But then Lord Derrick had never taken her to the Hunterian Museum.

Whereas Lord Dare, well…after only a week of knowing her, he'd somehow understood nothing could give her more pleasure than this visit today. A tiny shiver of awareness slid down Violet's spine as she watched him lean over a wooden case to study a collection of human finger bones.

She'd meant to keep her promise to Iris and refuse any future calls from him, but every one of her good intentions fled the moment she'd entered the drawing room and found him waiting for her there, his lovely gray eyes alight, tempting her with tickets to the Hunterian.

But she could just as easily refuse his call tomorrow, couldn't she? It was only a *single* day, after all. What possible difference could a *single* day make?

He stopped beside her as she paused next to another glass jar, this one holding a dissected frog. "Good Lord, he looks like he's grinning at us." A large flap of skin had been cut from the frog's stomach and pinned neatly back for display purposes. He leaned closer to study the creature's circulatory and reproductive systems. "Though I can't think what he has to grin about, considering his present circumstances."

Violet peered at the frog, her brow furrowed. "I think this one's a female frog."

Lord Dare abandoned his study and turned to her with a raised eyebrow. "How in the world would you know that?"

"Oh, um…" Violet bit her lip. It didn't seem quite the thing to discuss frog ovaries with his lordship. Perhaps she shouldn't have said anything at all, but he was waiting for a response, his gray eyes alert with interest, and she didn't like to withhold knowledge from an inquisitive mind. "Well, you see, this one has…she's…ah, the reproductive organs…"

"Never mind, Miss Somerset." Lord Dare grinned at her flushed cheeks, then took her arm and guided her past the frogs to the next display. "I can see by your blush there's no delicate way to explain it."

"Yes, well…I've never seen so many skeletons in one place in my life!" she blurted out to hide her confusion. They approached a case with three skulls displayed side by side on a set of wooden platforms. "Or skulls. Dr. Hunter seems to have been rather enamored of skulls."

"Especially those ravaged by disease." Lord Dare leaned over the display to get a closer look at the skulls and shuddered. "See those cavities where the bone has been eaten away? To be fair to Dr. Hunter, though, he wasn't simply interested in grisly curiosities. The collection taken together shows his fascination was with anatomy, surgery, and medicine."

"Yes, of course you're right." Violet was rather impressed with this observation, and relieved to be back on familiar footing. She turned away from her study of the case to smile at him. "A great deal is made of Charles Byrne's skeleton, and while it's undeniably fascinating, the rest of the collection has greater medical significance. It's not as fantastical, though, and Londoners do like their curiosities, I suppose."

"Did you take a sketch of Charles Byrne's skeleton?" Lord Dare held out his hand for her sketchbook. "May I see it?"

"It's nothing so impressive, I assure you—just a rough sketch. Once we arrived I became distracted with the other displays, but I did take a close look at his joints, and I fancy I do see some deterioration at the knees and ankles."

He took the sketchbook and turned the pages until he found the sketch. "Yes, I see just what you mean." He tapped a finger on the page. "You've put in the tiny fissures here, just at the knee bone. It's very good."

Lord Dare paused to study her drawing, while Violet walked on further, her footsteps echoing across the wooden floor. A flat case containing a small, rectangular box was beside the display of the syphilitic skulls, and Violet stopped to peer inside.

The small box contained what looked to be several long, translucent pouches. A few had been removed from the box and laid out lengthwise beside it, and she could see each little pouch had a red ribbon fixed to one end.

She'd seen something like these pouches before, in a rather vulgar black and white drawing she'd come across in one of her readings. It was a caricature of the infamous rake Casanova, and it depicted him blowing into an object of a similar shape to these pouches—the caption had referred to them as English riding coats—apparently to test its efficacy.[2]

Violet had gathered from the drawing the pouch didn't function properly if there was a hole in it, but she hadn't been able to make much more sense of it than that, so she leaned over the case to read the brief description on the card at the corner of the display, hoping it would offer more details.

Barrier device, of the dried gut of the sheep, worn by men in the act of coition, to prevent venereal infection, d. 1776.

Well, that didn't properly explain the thing, did it? The caricature of Casanova hadn't made much sense to her at the time, and a closer view of the pouches did nothing to dispel the mystery. She knew what coition was, of course, and she had some vague ideas regarding a gentleman's anatomy, but how did the pouches come into the business? How was a gentleman meant to wear them, and how, precisely, could they prevent disease? She'd like to know the answer—it seemed rather an important detail, medically speaking—but there was only one person she could ask, and he...

"What have you got there, Miss Somerset?"

He was striding toward her now, an engaging smile on his face. "You look a bit pale. I almost shudder to ask, but what is it this time?"

Oh, dear. Whatever the mystery regarding the pouches, Violet was sure she wasn't meant to discuss it with Lord Dare. She may not be a conventional sort of lady, but she'd have to be dim indeed to question a gentleman on anything related to the act of coition.

"It's not the canine tooth embedded in the cockerel's skull, is it? I read about that. Dr. Hunter maintained that the tooth grew its own blood supply once it was implanted, and...oh." Lord Dare came to an abrupt halt when he saw what she was looking at. "*Oh.*"

They stood shoulder to shoulder and peered down into the case, neither of them saying a word, until at last Lord Dare cleared his throat. "That's not...those aren't canine teeth."

"No. They're..." Violet glanced back down at the card. "They're barrier devices." She hesitated, then, "I've also heard them referred to as English riding coats."

Lord Dare didn't reply, but he made a strangled noise, and Violet wondered if perhaps she should have kept that last part to herself.

Then again, she'd come this far. "Have you ever heard of them before?"

He darted a sidelong glance at her, then looked quickly away. "Yes, I've heard of them."

My goodness, was he blushing? "Have you, ah...have you ever seen one?"

He made another choked sound, either a strangled laugh or a grunt of distress. Violet wasn't sure which.

"Yes, I've seen them."

Well, how fascinating. Lord Dare had heard of the pouches—that is, the barrier devices—and he'd seen them before, too. It stood to reason, then, that he...

Violet's teeth sank into her bottom lip, but no amount of biting was going to keep the next question from escaping her mouth. "Have you ever used—?"

"For God's sake, Miss Somerset!" This time there was no mistaking the dull red color flooding his cheeks. "I refuse to answer that."

That was as good as a yes, because if he *hadn't* ever used them he would have just said so. But he didn't seem keen to discuss it, so it would be best if she let the matter drop.

"I only ask, my lord, because, well…the thing is, I don't quite understand how it works."

Oh, dear. That wasn't letting the matter drop, was it?

He gave her an incredulous look. "Well, I certainly hope you don't think *I'm* going to explain it to you. Ask your sister, if you must know the details."

"My sister? But that doesn't make any sense. How should she know how they work? The card says 'worn by *men* in the act of coition,' my lord." She tapped a finger against the glass. "My sister is a woman. It stands to reason I'd ask a gentleman, doesn't it?"

Lord Dare ran his hands down his face. "Well, ask your brother-in-law, then."

Finn? Good Lord, she couldn't think of anything worse than quizzing Finn about such a thing. "You want me to ask the *Marquess of Huntington* about English riding coats?"

Lord Dare pinched the bridge of his nose between his fingers. "Bloody hell."

Another lady might have been shocked at the curse, but Violet found herself stifling a laugh. It was rather amusing, seeing Lord Dare put to the blush and at a loss for words. "It's not as if you need to explain it in great detail, you know. Just give me a vague idea of it, without going into anything inappropriate."

He threw his hands up in the air. "It's all inappropriate!"

"Is it, indeed?" That was even more reason to solve the puzzle, then. Inappropriate things were always much more interesting than appropriate ones, and they tended to be the kinds of things kept secret from proper young ladies.

This was just the sort of information she wanted for her book. She needed more of the sort of content that would be edifying for young ladies who would otherwise be left dangerously ignorant.

She had that chapter on rakes and debauchers, but that sketch she'd done of Lord Dare as The Selfish Rake was meant to be the centerpiece of it, and she would never use it now she realized how horribly unfair it was to him.

But if she could persuade him to tell her a bit more about the mysterious pouches, perhaps she could include a chapter on those instead, and if there was a medical component to the business, so much the better.

"*How* inappropriate?" Violet couldn't quite hide her eagerness.

"You needn't sound so thrilled about it."

He scowled at her, but Violet could sense him weakening, and she was quick to press her advantage. "I'm thrilled about any opportunity to gain knowledge. Come now, my lord. My interest is purely scientific."

Mostly scientific, anyway.

He ran a hand over the back of his neck. "It's...it goes over the gentleman's...appendage. You, ah...you understand what I mean by 'appendage,' don't you?"

"I have some idea, yes." She'd never seen this fabled appendage, that is, not the human version of it, but she'd been raised in Surrey, and there were a great many animals about.

Of course, animals didn't wear the pouches, hence the gap in her knowledge.

He blew out a relieved breath. "Then you should be able to deduce how it works. The gentleman, he...well, he slides it over his...appendage, before he engages in coitus."

Violet looked down at the pouches again, trying to envision how that might work. "But how does it stay on?"

Lord Dare muttered something under his breath about *bloody bluestockings*. "See the red ribbons on the end of it? He ties them."

"To what? I don't see how—"

She didn't get any further, because Lord Dare grabbed her arm, and without another word he hurried her away from the case, past the collection of preserved animal parts floating in their glass jars, past the skeletons in the long main hallway, and out the front door of the museum.

"Lord Dare! Wait—"

"Quiet, Miss Somerset."

He bundled her into the carriage and hardly gave her a chance to sit down before he slammed his fist on the ceiling to signal the driver to go. Violet clutched her sketchbook on her knees and stared across the carriage at Lord Dare, who'd thrown himself into his seat and was now gazing at her, his arms crossed over his chest and a pained expression on his face.

An awkward silence fell between them. Violet's gaze dropped to her lap as regret washed over her. She wasn't ashamed of her curiosity, but they'd been having such a nice time, and he'd been so kind to bring her, and then she'd gone and spoiled everything.

"I beg your pardon, Lord Dare," she said at last. "I shouldn't have teased you about it. I just...well, I'm curious, and I don't have anyone to ask about such things, and I thought perhaps you..."

Violet trailed off when he didn't reply, and she returned her gaze to her lap, quite miserable. Oh, why could she never hold her tongue?

He let out a long, low sigh. "Come here, Miss Somerset."

Violet raised her eyes to his. He patted the seat, and she didn't hesitate, but slid into the space beside him.

He held out his hand. "Give me your sketchbook and a pencil."

Violet did as he asked. He flipped through the book until he came to a blank page, and then he began to sketch. "I'm not the accomplished artist you are, but I'll do my best. This is a gentleman's torso, and the tops of his legs." He nudged the book toward her so she could see it, and drew a few more rough lines on the page. "Do you see?"

Violet herself would have made an interesting exhibit for the Hunterian's collection at that moment, because her eyes nearly fell out of her skull. Was he...goodness, was Lord Dare actually going to explain the pouches to her? It seemed incredible, but he continued with his sketch as she stared at the page, dumbfounded.

"This is his, uh...appendage, and the rest of his anatomy." He drew a few more lines until he'd drawn a shape that resembled the pouches in the case[3], then sketched in two circular shapes at the base of it. "The condom—that's the proper name for it, and I beg you *never* to use the term 'English riding coat' again—goes over him like this, then ties under here, like this. Do you understand?"

Violet cocked her head to the side to study the sketch, then nodded. "I—yes, I see how it would work, but it looks as if...couldn't it slip off the end, even with the tie?"

"It can happen, yes, but it's unlikely if it's tied properly, especially when the gentleman's appendage is, ah...well, like this."

He moved to a blank space on the page and drew two more appendages, one of them limp and dangling down between the torso's legs, and the other...

Violet caught her breath. The other was standing upright, and all at once it became clear to her just how everything worked. Not just the condom, but all the gentlemanly...apparatus.

"When a gentleman is aroused, that is, when he's ready to have coitus, his appendage is like this." He tapped the pencil next to the second sketch. "So you see, when he's, ah...well, when he's firm, the condom is far less likely to slip off, because it can be tied more securely."

Without realizing she was doing it, Violet reached out and traced her fingers over the second sketch, and when she did, Lord Dare let out a faint moan.

"How does it—the condom, I mean—how does it prevent disease?"

He didn't speak at once, but she was pressed close enough against him she could feel it when he took a long, deep breath. "When a gentleman, ah...when he's at the height of his pleasure..." He looked down at her, his gray eyes dark. "Do you know what that means?"

Oh, she knew. She'd never witnessed such a thing herself, but she'd *heard* a man reach the heights of pleasure, and not just any man, but *this* one, that evening in Lord Derrick's library. "I, ah...I have a vague idea, yes."

"When he's at the height of his pleasure, he, um...he releases an effluvium, and the lady...well, there are various, ah...fluids that occur during coitus that can spread disease. The condom prevents that, and it also prevents conception."

He fell silent, and after a moment he closed the sketchbook and handed it back to her. It occurred to Violet she should move away from him and go back to her seat on the other side of the carriage, but she didn't. "I, ah... no one's ever explained this to me before."

Certainly not her grandmother, and even her married sisters, who surely must understand the mechanics of the thing, had only offered vague information when pressed. Iris had been willing to go into more explicit detail until she'd discovered Violet intended to use the information in her book, then she'd clapped her mouth closed tighter than a whalebone corset.

He let out a short laugh. "I can't say I'm surprised at that."

"Why did *you* explain it?"

The conversation had embarrassed Lord Dare—there was no question about that. She'd felt him stiffen beside her when she asked about the condom slipping off, and she'd heard his hesitation, the strain in his voice as he'd explained the part about the fluids. She'd noticed the subtle shake of his hand when he'd drawn the appendages.

He hadn't wanted to tell her any of it.

"I told you because you asked, Miss Somerset. I didn't think it proper to discuss it in the middle of the museum with all the dissected frogs listening on, however."

Violet fell back against the seat, astounded at this response. He'd told her because she'd *asked* him to? She sat speechless, trying to recall if anyone had ever before offered her knowledge for no other reason than she'd *asked*.

Years of questions—decades of them. Hundreds, perhaps thousands of questions, and she could only remember a handful of instances when she hadn't had to argue and plead and fight to get the answers.

And now *he*—Lord Dare, of all people—had simply *given* her knowledge, offered it up to her as if she had every right to it. Not just any knowledge, either, but the kind of knowledge deemed inappropriate for delicate, feminine ears.

She stared at him, her heart in her throat. Was it possible she'd misunderstood him? "But...that's it? You told me because I asked? For no other reason?"

He looked surprised. "Well, you're a scholar, aren't you? You have an educational interest in the subject, not a prurient one. If you'd asked for any other reason perhaps I wouldn't have been so forthcoming, but under the circumstances, I thought you deserved to know."

Violet went still as his explanation sank in.

It wasn't proper, and it wasn't gentlemanly—it wasn't anything Violet could ever imagine any other gentleman ever doing for her, but Lord Dare had answered her questions because he'd decided, against every expectation she could ever have had of him, that she'd been *entitled* to the knowledge she asked for.

It stunned her. *He* stunned her.

"Lord Dare?" She touched his arm.

He looked down at her with a faint smile. "More questions, Miss Somerset? I do hope you're not going to ask me to describe the various fluids to you."

"No, I just..."

She didn't give herself a chance to think about it or change her mind. She simply turned to him, clambered onto her knees on the seat bench, and did what she'd wanted to do all day. She leaned toward him, pressed her palms against his face, and kissed him on the cheek. "Thank you."

He stiffened, but then he let out a ragged sigh, and his warm breath drifted over her lips. Violet slid her hands away from his face and drew away. Two bright spots of color stained the crests of his cheekbones, and he was watching her with dark, sleepy eyes.

For a moment she thought he'd reach for her, but he didn't. He simply nodded, once, but his gray eyes were so warm, so intense, it was almost as if he'd stroked his fingertips over her heated skin.

Violet licked suddenly dry lips. That drawing he'd done, of the upright appendage...what, precisely, did it take to make it stand upright like that? He'd explained that it happened when a gentleman became aroused, but how did one arouse him to a degree that his appendage would rise in such a demanding manner? What did it take to make him reach the height of his pleasure, and once he did, well...what was it like?

Lord Dare cleared his throat. "You're looking at me as if I were a preserved monkey's head, Miss Somerset, and you're about to take me from my jar and do an experiment on me."

"No, I—no, of course not, my lord." Except an experiment *was* the best way to gain knowledge, and he'd shown himself willing enough so far, and if she *could* get a bit more information, perhaps she could write that chapter, after all. "I only wondered..."

He raised an eyebrow at her. "Yes?"

"What does it take to make the, ah, the gentleman's appendage so... eager? I mean, what can a lady do to him, to help him reach the height of his pleasure?"

Lord Dare's lips parted. "She kisses and touches him, among other things, but it isn't a good idea—"

Violet slid her fingers up his arms and rested her hands against his jaw. It was shadowed with the faintest hint of a beard, and the tiny bristles tickled her palms. "Like this?" She leaned forward, and pressed her mouth to his.

He went still as her lips moved over his, but then he let out a low groan, closed his hands around her waist, and pushed her gently away. "This isn't like Execution Dock, or Cockpit Steps, Miss Somerset. I'm a man of flesh and blood, not one of your ghosts. It isn't wise for a young lady to tempt a man in such a way."

Tempt him? A forlorn little laugh escaped Violet's lips.

Oh, she was likely safe enough. It wasn't as if she'd ever inspired mindless passion in a gentleman before, and it was especially unlikely to happen with a gentleman like Lord Dare, who was accustomed to beautiful, tempting ladies like Lady Uplands. "All right, but first tell me, did it work? That is, are you aroused?"

He seemed to be having trouble catching his breath, and his fingers tightened on her waist. "This isn't a game, Miss Somerset. A gentleman's arousal isn't something to play with. Go back to your seat at once."

But Violet didn't go back to her seat. She didn't move. She couldn't tell if he was becoming aroused, but warmth had pooled in her lower belly as soon as her mouth touched his, and her limbs felt pleasantly languid.

So she ignored his warning and kissed him again. His lips were much softer than she'd expected a gentleman's lips to be, but they were firm, too, and so warm and lovely. She let her mouth linger on his this time, but just as she'd grown bold enough to start exploring the shape of his lips, he did the strangest thing.

He opened his mouth.

And that was when everything changed.

Chapter Thirteen

"In case it's not yet apparent to you, Miss Somerset," he whispered against her lips. "The answer is yes. I *am* aroused, and becoming more so every moment."

Violet let out a startled squeak when his tongue darted out and brushed against the seam of her lips. It caught her by surprise, and her first thought was to draw away from him, but his hand moved to her neck, and he sank his long fingers into her hair and held her still for his mouth. His grip was careful, but even as he held her gently his mouth was relentless, his tongue seeking entry with an insistence that left Violet dizzy and breathless.

"Open your mouth for me, sweetheart."

His tongue swept over the seam of her lips again, and this time she opened for him—responding instinctively to his demand without a thought of denying him.

He drew back just a fraction—far enough so his lips were no longer touching hers, but so close she could feel the warmth of them still, a mere breath away.

"Do you feel that?" His voice rasped across her nerve endings like a cat's tongue over sensitive skin, and a strangled laugh left his throat as she tried to catch his lips with hers again.

"That ache inside you, that makes you want my lips on yours? You feel it everywhere, don't you, and it makes you wild. That's arousal, desire, and when it's like this, it sweeps everything before it. It's not something an innocent young lady like you should trifle with, especially not with a man like me."

His hands closed over her shoulders to ease her away from him, but Violet curled her fingers into his coat and held on with white knuckles, her mouth seeking his, until he gave up and let his hands slide to the arch of her back, pressing her tight against him with a helpless groan.

He took her lips harder then, his hands restless in her hair, tugging her closer as he opened his mouth over hers and surged inside. And oh, the taste of him, the sensation of his hot tongue wrapping around hers, invading every corner of her mouth. The lazy, languid feeling weighing down her limbs exploded into frantic heat, and the next thing Violet knew her own tongue had darted out to lick his bottom lip.

The moment he felt the tentative slide of her tongue, his entire body went rigid against hers. His chest vibrated with another groan, and his big hands wrapped around her waist again, tugging her closer. Violet was still on her knees on the carriage seat, and she lost her balance and fell against him, her boneless body sprawled on top of his, her breasts tight against his chest and her knees between his thighs.

He let out a quiet laugh, and Violet felt the reverberation of it low in her belly. "Well, that wasn't quite what I intended, but now that you're here..." He slid his palms from her waist up her back, his movements slow and deliberate. He paused to stroke her vertebrae, shaping the delicate grooves with sensitive fingertips, each caress more maddening than the last, until he reached the back of her head and tangled his hands in her hair. He was gentle, but he held her firmly, keeping her still as his desperate mouth took hers again and again.

Violet whimpered, her body driving her on, urging her to squirm closer to him so she could feel the hard expanse of his chest against the enflamed tips of her breasts. She slid her arms around his neck and pressed tighter against him, hardly knowing what she did as she was tugged into a relentless current of desire. There was no defense against it, no way to fight it—there was only him and his mouth against her neck, her throat, his panting breath as he nipped at her ear, then licked his tongue over the abraded skin.

Some ancient instinct in the dimmest, most primal part of Violet's brain whispered a warning: this was something far more powerful than she'd ever imagined, and much too far out of her experience and control, but she could only let it sweep over her, toss her about until she either came out of it, limp and shaking, or drowned in it.

She didn't even want to fight it. She only wanted *him*.

His mouth and hands seemed to be everywhere at once, stroking, teasing, and caressing, and his hard body was shaking against hers. "I want you, so damn much." He gripped her hips in his hands and shifted her on his lap so her legs were on either side of his splayed thighs. "Do you know what that means? Can you feel me?" He held her hard against him and made a subtle movement with his hips.

It was a restrained thrust only, but it was enough.

Violet's breath caught in her throat as he moved against her, and she felt the hard length of him between her thighs, even through the heavy layers of her cloak and gown.

"Does that satisfy your curiosity about arousal, sweet? Or should I lower my falls so you can take a sketch for your book?" He sounded half angry, but even as he reproached her he moved his voracious mouth over her, licking and sucking at her neck.

"Or if that's not good enough, I can keep thrusting against you until I reach the height of my pleasure, and you can take a sketch of *that*, so all the bluestockings in London will know what it looks like when a man becomes so lost to desire he forgets his honor, and shamelessly lets an innocent ride him until he comes."

Violet bit back a plea, because *yes*, God help her, she wanted that, to feel him become frantic, to watch his face contort with pleasure.

She dropped her hands to his chest and leaned over him, fusing her lips to his as she twisted and writhed over his lap, gliding against him until he seemed to lose all control, one ragged breath after another catching in his throat as he whispered to her in broken words, begging her for…what?

For everything, and all of it at once. "Give me your mouth, sweet…*yes*, now touch me…" A harsh moan fell from his lips when her hands slid into his hair. "We can't…we can't…tell me to stop, sweetheart. Push me away…"

But Violet couldn't push him away. She could only hold onto him, the one solid thing in a world that had suddenly gone dangerously atilt. She dug her fingers into the hard, tense muscles of his shoulders and back, and nipped hard at his bottom lip.

He groaned, but in the next moment he tore his mouth from hers with a gasp, and his head fell back against the carriage seat. "This isn't…we have to stop." But even as he said the words, his hands tightened on her hips to keep her on his lap, as if he couldn't quite bear to release her yet. "I was trying to warn you not to tempt a man…but I didn't know I'd…I had no idea I'd want you so much." His eyes softened as he gazed at her. "I never should have touched you."

Violet touched a finger to his lips. "You didn't. I touched you."

He gazed at her for a moment, with eyes such a dark gray now they were nearly black.

Violet continued to trace his lips, and something tugged hard at her chest as she watched her fingers stroking him. It felt like…

Tenderness.

An experiment, a chapter in her book—how foolish it seemed now, how absurd, to imagine arousal was something clinical she could test, something she could manipulate on a whim.

And Lord Dare...

Did she truly believe she could control a man like him? The moment her lips touched his she was lost to him, drowning in desire, and it wasn't just because he was handsome, or because he knew how to touch a woman in a way that made her forget everything but his mouth, his hands, the desperate rasp of his breath in her ears.

No, it was so much more than that. Honora had called him a rake, a debaucher, and after what she'd witnessed in the library between him and Lady Uplands, Violet had thought so too, but since then...

He was so much more than he appeared to be, and why should that be so surprising? A handsome face, a scarlet waistcoat...such things were no more the whole of him than her sketchbook and pencils were the whole of her.

She should have known—should have seen it at once yesterday when he'd stood between her and the Thames River, waiting patiently while she finished her sketch.

His boots had gotten soaked.

A soft laugh escaped Violet as she thought of the consternation on his face when he'd realized they were very likely ruined.

Lord Dare opened his eyes. They stared at each other, neither of them saying a word, but something changed between them as his gray eyes caught and held her blue ones. The mood shifted, grew heavier, weighted down with something Violet couldn't define. An emotion between them they hadn't given voice to before now, some sense of expectation.

Unanswered questions.

Lies.

She had to tell him the truth, but once she did he'd never wish to see her again, and before that happened, she had to show him how much it meant to her to know there was a gentleman who understood exactly who she was, and desired her in spite of it.

Or maybe, just maybe...because of it.

Violet reached for him and trailed her fingertips over his cheekbones. She watched his eyes as she gently traced his eyebrows, his lips, and his jaw, and her breath caught at the flicker of heat in his gaze as she dragged her fingertips down his neck.

He let out a low moan, and his throat moved in a convulsive swallow. "It feels so good when you touch me, sweet."

Violet didn't answer, but she held his gaze as she settled her hands on his wide shoulders and began to arch against his lap, the movement of her hips slow and sinuous.

"No. Don't."

He gripped her hips to still her, but Violet grasped his wrists and dragged his hands away. "Shhhh. I want to. Not as an experiment, or for a sketch, or for the bluestockings." A faint smile drifted over her lips. "For you. Just you."

His thighs had gone tense underneath her, but now he looked into her eyes, and whatever he saw there made his hands go limp around her waist. He watched her as if mesmerized, his breath quickening and deepening to harsh gasps as her hips continued their insistent rhythm.

His mouth opened, and low, broken pleas fell from his lips. "Don't stop...faster, sweetheart...yes, now take me harder...*yes*...you're going to make me come..."

Violet wanted to shout in triumph when she saw he'd come too far in his passion to stop, and he gave in to her completely. A desperate moan tore from his chest as he steadied her against him, his hips taking up her rhythm until he was thrusting helplessly against her.

"Oh, God, I'm going to...you're making me—"

His words trailed off into a long groan as he jerked hard against her once, then again, and then his entire body went rigid, and he pulled her to him to bury his face between her neck and shoulder.

As he panted against her, Violet slid her fingers into his hair and played with the dark strands until he slowly regained his breath, his arms wrapped tightly around her.

When he'd calmed at last, he turned his head on her shoulder, pressed his mouth to her ear and began to speak, to tell her how much he wanted her, how she'd given him so much pleasure, and his voice, dear God, his voice, so sweet, a bit breathless still and murmuring to her, coaxing her now, a whisper in her ear, a low rasp Violet knew she'd hear in her dreams.

"I want to touch you now, and give you pleasure." He slid a hand under her skirts and wrapped his warm fingers around her thigh. "Will you let me do that for you? Will you let me touch you, Hyacinth?"

Violet froze in shock, her hands stilling in his hair, and the cocoon of warmth that had wrapped itself around her vanished with that one word, like mists giving way to a sudden rain.

Hyacinth.

A reminder, and one she badly needed, but no less painful for it.

"No, I—no, my lord." She forced herself to remove her hands from his hair, reached down and gently pushed his hand away from her thigh, then slid off his lap and crammed herself into the corner of the carriage, as far away from him as she could get.

Silence fell, and it grew heavier as the moments ticked by. She avoided his gaze, instead taking great care to tidy her skirts. When the tension between them became so thick it threatened to suck all the air from the carriage, Lord Dare cleared his throat.

"Have I done something wrong?" His voice was subdued, but it seemed loud in the quiet carriage.

No. I have.

Violet made herself meet his eyes, and her heart kicked in protest as the confusion on his face began to give way to regret. She forced her lips into a stiff smile. "Not at all, my lord. It's just…we're nearly to Bedford Square."

She waved a hand toward the window, but he didn't follow the gesture. He was staring at her, his mouth tight. "Shall I call on you tomorrow, then?"

Violet hid her hands in her skirts so he couldn't see the way they shook. "I don't think we should—"

She broke off as her gaze caught on something outside the window. Lord Dare's coachman had made the turn that led to her grandmother's door, and there, sitting at the top of the drive, with luggage strewn across the stairs and footmen swarming about, was Lady Atherton's carriage.

Violet's body went cold with dread.

Lord Dare followed her gaze. "Is that your grandmother? I wondered why I never found her at home. It looks as if she's been away."

"Bath." Violet's voice was faint. "I didn't expect her back so soon."

He'd been looking out the window, but now he turned to face her, and he must have seen something in her expression he didn't like, because his face hardened. "Well, what luck she should have arrived now, just as I've brought you home. I can meet her at last."

"I don't think now is the best time—"

"Given my current disheveled state, I'd normally agree with you." He waved a hand to indicate his breeches, and Violet's face flooded with embarrassed heat. "But introductions to your family have been rather difficult to come by, Miss Somerset, so I'd just as soon seize the chance while I have it. Fortunately for both of us, my cloak will hide any irregularities."

Violet was ready to scream, or swoon, or leap from the moving carriage— anything to keep Lord Dare from meeting her grandmother, but his lips had thinned with determination, and before she could think of a way to dissuade him, Lady Chase herself appeared in the doorway to issue orders to the footmen, and spotted the coach coming up the drive.

Oh, no. Violet shrank back against the carriage seat. She was well and truly caught this time. There was no escaping the introductions now that her grandmother had seen them, and it was inevitable Lady Chase would call her by name. All it needed now was for Hyacinth herself to appear, so Lord Dare could see for himself the depth of her deception.

The carriage came to a stop on the drive. Lord Dare leapt down at once to open the door and hand Violet out. She tried to make herself slide across the seat, alight, and come face to face with her sins, but as was likely the case with every criminal, her limbs locked in place, refusing to approach the gibbet.

"Miss Somerset?" Lord Dare stuck his head back inside the carriage and beckoned to her with one crooked finger. "Are you coming out?"

She didn't have much choice, did she? It wasn't as if she could keep hiding the truth from Lord Dare forever. He may as well find out now, and if a lie was going to be revealed, it may as well be done spectacularly.

"Yes." She accepted his hand and let him pull her from the carriage.

As soon as she alighted on the drive, her grandmother, who'd been staring curiously at Lord Dare, let out a little cry of welcome. "Well, child, here you are, and just as I've arrived. Well, come here and let me see you, and you must bring your companion, as well."

Lord Dare politely offered his arm, but he frowned down at her when he realized he wasn't escorting her across the drive so much as dragging her.

"Welcome home, Grandmother." Violet pressed a dutiful kiss to her grandmother's thin, powdery cheek. "How does Lady Atherton do?"

"Fit as I've ever seen her, dear. Astonishing, really, she should feel herself so very well after such a short stay in Bath, but then she did drink a great quantity of the waters while we were there, so I daresay that accounts for her quick recovery."

"I'm pleased to hear it, ma'am."

Lady Chase, who'd turned to Lord Dare with a great deal of interest, waved this off. "Yes, yes, I'm sure you are, but my goodness, have you forgotten your manners entirely? Who is this gentleman?"

Panic pressed down on Violet's chest. She struggled to take a breath, but her voice sounded thin as she made the introductions. "Lord Dare, may I present my grandmother, Lady Chase? Grandmother, this is Lord Dare. He's recently returned to London from the Continent."

Lord Dare offered Lady Chase a polite bow and a charming smile. "It's a pleasure, Lady Chase."

"Well, Lord Dare. How do you do? I believe I know your aunt—Lady Westcott, isn't it? I haven't seen her for quite some time. She doesn't go out in society anymore, does she?"

"No, not much, my lady."

"No, I thought not. And your father has recently passed away, I think? Sad business. I do beg you will accept my condolences, and pass them on to your aunt."

"Thank you, Lady Chase. I will, indeed."

Lord Dare and Lady Chase seemed to run out of conversation then, and Violet was too busy praying for the ground to open up and swallow her to have anything to offer, so a short, awkward silence fell.

Lady Chase, who could never tolerate silence for long, spoke up at last. "How are you acquainted with my granddaughter, my lord?"

"I had the pleasure of meeting Miss Somerset at Lord and Lady Derrick's dinner party a week ago, and she's been kind enough to receive my calls since then, my lady."

Lady Chase's eyes went wide at this. "Indeed? Well, my dear, you didn't say a word about accepting calls from Lord Dare."

"I, ah—well, you were off to Bath so quickly, Grandmother, I didn't have a chance—"

"No matter, no matter, child." Lady Chase assessed her with a shrewd eye, then turned to sweep a considering gaze over Lord Dare. "How wonderful the two of you should have happened to meet."

Violet barely managed to stifle a groan. She saw at once what her grandmother was thinking, as clearly as if she could read Lady Chase's mind. Here was a charming suitor for her most troublesome granddaughter, an earl, no less, and he'd been dropped right into their laps out of nowhere, like a tall, handsomely wrapped gift from heaven itself. The only thing that could please Lady Chase more was to return from Bath to find Violet already betrothed.

Or better yet, married.

Never mind that her precious granddaughter had been out with a gentleman Lady Chase hadn't met, without a chaperone, or that she'd been accepting his calls during her grandmother's absence, and without her permission. If Violet could only bring him up to scratch, all would be forgiven.

"I'll take my leave, as I'm sure you must be fatigued from your trip, my lady. It was a pleasure to meet you." Lord Dare bowed to Lady Chase, then turned to Violet and bowed politely over her hand, as well. "Thank you for your charming company today, Miss Somerset. I enjoyed our outing even more than I anticipated." He had his back to Lady Chase, and a wicked smile only Violet could see crossed his lips, leaving her in no doubt as to what he meant by *that*. "Until tomorrow, then."

It wasn't until Lord Dare was in his carriage and rolling down the drive and Lady Chase was fretting and fussing over her baggage that Violet realized her grandmother hadn't once referred to her by her given name.

He still didn't know she wasn't Hyacinth.

As far as Lord Dare knew, Violet Somerset didn't exist.

Chapter Fourteen

"Reducing your gown to a heap of shreds won't help a bit, Violet." Hyacinth reached over and tugged at Violet's hand, but Violet clenched at the crumpled folds of blue silk in her fist until the delicate fabric, weary of her torment, ripped at the seams.

"For pity's sake," Hyacinth hissed under her breath. "Gather your wits, will you? Grandmother will be out any minute, and you can't let her see you in such a state."

They'd been about to depart for Lady Westcott's rout when Lady Chase, fearful she'd take a chill, sent them to the carriage while she waited in the entryway for her lady's maid to fetch her a warmer wrap.

It was a brief reprieve only—just long enough for Violet to give way to the panic clawing at her with its cold, skeletal fingers. Unless she could fall into a convincing swoon and escape this nightmare, she was about to come face to face with Lord Dare.

He'd called every single afternoon since that breathtaking, disastrous incident in his carriage, while Violet, who'd never in her life avoided confrontation, and who prided herself on her bravery...

She'd cowered in her bedchamber like a shivering rodent hiding from a merciless cat.

Five days of feigning illness. Five days confined to her bedchamber, and all for naught, because here she was, a carriage ride away from facing her doom.

Her grandmother's patience with her fictional illness had run out the moment the invitation to Lady Westcott's rout arrived. Lady Chase had called in a doctor who, predictably, had pronounced Violet miraculously cured. She'd been summarily rousted from her bed, hurried into the blue silk gown, and bundled into the carriage without further ado.

"Oh, Hyacinth! What am I going to do?" She'd half-deceived herself into believing her cowardliness was its own punishment, and since her misery intensified each time she refused another of Lord Dare's calls, it seemed a sound enough theory.

It wasn't.

Even the simple rules of cause and effect had deserted her. Logic had abandoned her to fate, and fate...well, fate was unpredictable, wasn't she? Vindictive, even. Once fate took the reins, there was only one possible outcome.

Utter mayhem.

But fate was determined to bring Violet to justice, and now things had come to a head, indeed. Lord Dare would see her with Hyacinth, and thus the fact of Violet's existence would be dramatically revealed. He'd fall into a fury, order her from his sight, and once her grandmother recovered from her apoplexy she'd banish Violet to her bedchamber for the remainder of her days.

Unless...

Violet grabbed Hyacinth by the shoulders, her grip frantic. "Tell Grandmother you're ill, and can't attend Lady Westcott's rout tonight."

"What? No! I won't lie to our grandmother."

"You've already lied to her! You told her I had a dreadful cold, remember?"

Hyacinth tried to shake her off. "No, *you* told her that. I just didn't contradict you."

"It's a lie, just the same, so one more little one can't make any difference. Please, Hyacinth. Lord Dare can't see both of us tonight, or he'll know I've deceived him."

"Dear God, Violet, you're coming unhinged." Hyacinth stared at her, her own eyes widening as Violet's fingers dug into her shoulders. "Stop that! Even if I agreed to remain at home, it only postpones the inevitable. You can't keep on like this, Violet. You have to tell Lord Dare the truth."

"I know. I will, I—no, don't look at me like that, Hyacinth. I swear it this time. I will, but not tonight, at a rout with Grandmother and Lady Westcott and every gossip in London in attendance. Oh, please, Hyacinth. If you'll only help me tonight, I promise I'll confess the whole of it to him tomorrow when he calls."

"But I've been perfectly healthy all week. Grandmother won't believe I'm ill *now*."

"She will! Of course she will. She always believes *you*. Just say you've caught my cold, and have a sudden headache, and feel faint." She gave her sister a hopeful look. "If you could manage a swoon, that would be—"

"I am *not* going to feign a swoon, Violet!"

"But you will feign an illness, won't you?" Violet clasped her hands under her chin, her eyes pleading. "Please? I vow to you if you just help me this one last time, I'll set everything to rights tomorrow."

"But what will you say to Lord Dare tonight? You've spent all week refusing his calls. He's sure to demand an explanation, and then you'll have to lie to him again."

"I won't have to say a word to him. I intend to stay far away from Lord Dare."

Violet sounded more confident than she felt, but it wasn't a lie, precisely. She did *intend* to stay far away from Lord Dare. Whether he managed to find her out despite her best efforts was another matter.

So far, he'd been remarkably persistent.

"What, you think you can avoid him all night? He's going to be looking for you. Why, I daresay he's arranged this entire evening in hopes of seeing you. Indeed, he acts like a man whose heart has been affected."

Not his heart, but a different organ altogether.

"It hasn't. He hasn't…we haven't…" Heat climbed up Violet's neck. "No part of him has been affected, I assure you."

Aside from one, and a rather sensitive part, too, but Hyacinth didn't need to know *that*.

"No, Violet. I should have refused to participate in such a deceptive scheme from the start. I've made a mistake, encouraging you in this, and it ends this minute. I won't lie to our grandmother."

Violet recognized the mutinous expression on Hyacinth's face, and her heart rushed into her throat. She gulped in several deep breaths to calm her racing pulse and tried to gather her thoughts. There had to be another way out of this scrape. She just had to think…

"Wait!" She seized Hyacinth's arm again. "I've got another idea."

But Hyacinth was already shaking her head. "I told you, Violet. I won't lie to our grandmother."

"You won't have to—not to Grandmother, or anyone else. You won't have to do much at all, aside from…well, it's a small thing, really—"

"Oh, just say it, won't you?"

"Once we arrive, you'll have to hide." Oh, dear. It sounded much worse when she said it aloud, but perhaps Hyacinth wouldn't mind—

"*Hide?*"

Hyacinth's mouth fell open, and Violet winced.

She *did* mind.

"For pity's sake, Violet, where do you expect me to hide, in the kitchens? You've lost your wits!"

"Not hide!" Violet clarified hastily. "That is, I didn't mean hide, precisely. Just, ah…try and stay out of sight."

"That's the same thing! What if Lord Dare happens to be in the entryway, greeting his guests? What do you suggest I do then, Violet? Throw my cloak over my head so he can't see my face?"

"We won't go through the front door. We'll find another way into the house."

"Indeed? How do you intend to explain to our grandmother why we're creeping about Lady Westcott's house in the dark instead of attending her to the front door?"

Violet's mind was racing. "We'll tell her I'm dizzy, and wish to remain in the carriage for a moment for a few breaths of fresh air."

"I told you, Violet, I won't lie—"

"It's not a lie. I *am* dizzy."

Dizzy, nauseous, and as close to a hysterical fit as she'd ever been.

Before Hyacinth could answer, the front door of the house opened, and Lady Chase emerged and hobbled toward the carriage. Violet gave Hyacinth's arm a desperate squeeze. "Oh, *please*, Hyacinth."

Hyacinth grumbled and frowned and muttered fretfully under her breath, but at last she let out a defeated sigh. "Very well. I'll help you, but this is the last time, Violet, and I think it's very likely you'll be caught out no matter what I do."

Violet released the breath she'd been holding and gulped air into her burning lungs. "Oh, thank you."

The door to the carriage opened. The footman handed in Lady Chase, who settled her considerable bulk onto the seat facing her two granddaughters. "There now, girls. Are we ready to go?"

Violet slipped her hand into Hyacinth's and held on for dear life. She wasn't ready, and she never would be, but she nodded and offered her grandmother a sickly smile. "Yes, Grandmother. We're ready."

As ready as any criminal about to swing from a rope.

* * * *

"You look like a hungry cat crouched next to a mouse hole, Dare."

Nick hadn't taken his eyes off the front door since the first guest arrived nearly an hour ago, but now he glanced up to find Lord Derrick approaching with two glasses of punch in his hands. He offered one to Nick, who took it with a nod of thanks, then turned his attention back to the door.

Miss Somerset might be clever, and in the last five days she'd proved to be the slipperiest, wiliest lady he'd ever come across, but unless she'd found a way to render herself invisible, there wasn't a chance she'd get by him tonight.

Lord Derrick looked at the door, then back at Nick, and a frown creased his forehead. "Who are you waiting for?"

Nick took a sip of his punch, grimaced, and then drained the rest of it in one swallow. Awful stuff. "A lady."

Lord Derrick chuckled. "Yes, I suspected that much, Dare, but why do you look as though you're prepared to pounce on her?"

Nick's fingers tightened around his glass as frustration pounded through him once again. "Because she's been avoiding me, and I've had enough of it."

He'd had enough of it five days ago, when she'd refused to receive his call the day after those stolen moments in his carriage on their way back from the Hunterian Museum. When she'd refused again the following day he'd been concerned, then irritated, until at last the simmering anger he'd felt on day four had boiled over into fury by day five.

That was when he'd taken matters into his own hands, and now here he was, hovering by his aunt's door like a damned fool, ready to snatch Miss Somerset into his arms and run off with her the moment she set a toe across the threshold.

That is, if she even came at all. Lady Chase had accepted his aunt's invitation, but it would be just like Miss Somerset to find a way to elude him again, after he'd gone to the trouble of wheedling his aunt into hosting this bloody rout. He still wasn't sure why Lady Westcott had agreed, given she didn't go out in society anymore, but he was too distracted by his scheme to corner Miss Somerset to give it much thought.

"Is it Louisa Covington you're so impatient to see?"

A chill rushed over Nick at mention of Louisa, and he turned on Lord Derrick with narrowed eyes. "Why should you imagine it's Louisa, Derrick? Unless you think, as Lady Westcott does, that I should marry my dead brother's betrothed in his place, so we can all pretend he's still alive."

Derrick's face paled, and a chasm opened in Nick's chest. Damn it, why had he said that?

"No, that's not what I think." Despite Nick's ugly words, Lord Derrick's voice was calm. "I mentioned Louisa only because you and she are old friends, and I supposed you might wish to see her for that reason. Nothing more."

Derrick's quiet patience made it difficult for Nick to meet his old friend's eyes, but when he did, he saw only concern there. "Then I, ah...I beg your pardon."

Lord Derrick blew out a breath. "We both miss him. But you and I were friends at one time, too, and I'd like to be so again. Graham is gone, but *we're* still here, Dare."

Nick nodded, but he didn't trust himself to speak.

When they'd lost Graham, Nick had felt like he'd lost a part of himself, as if a limb had been torn from his body. The limb might be gone, but the phantom pain persisted. Nick had learned to live with the dull ache these past few years, but if it wasn't any longer the kind of pain that doubled him over and left him gasping, it was still always there, and it flared occasionally, usually without warning, and often just when he thought he'd made his peace with it.

Like right now.

Derrick sighed. "We're not all like your father, Nick. None of your friends expect you to take Graham's place, and you know damn well if Graham were alive he'd be the first to tell you to stop grieving and live your life."

Nick stilled as he absorbed the undeniable truth of these words. It was strange, but in the two endless years since his brother's death, he'd never once considered the situation as Graham would have done. He'd been so determined to run from his memories, he hardly let himself think of Graham at all anymore.

Derrick cleared his throat, breaking the heavy silence between them. "If you're not waiting for Louisa, then who are you waiting for?"

Nick hesitated, but it wasn't a secret. He and Miss Somerset would be betrothed soon enough. "Hyacinth Somerset."

Lord Derrick's eyebrows shot up. "Hyacinth Somerset! You're jesting."

"No. Why should I be? What's your objection to Hyacinth Somerset?" Lord Derrick was too much of a gentleman to ever disparage a lady, but Nick found his hands curling into fists as he waited for Derrick's reply.

"Not a blessed thing, Dare. She's as sweet and lovely a lady as I've ever known."

Sweet? It wasn't quite the word Nick would use to describe her. Infuriating, yes. Tempting, certainly. Intriguing, surprising, irritating, and fascinating—yes, any of those words would do, but *sweet?*

But then she did taste sweet. So sweet...

"She's simply not the sort of lady I would have imagined would suit you, Dare."

Nick couldn't argue with that, and yet he felt his lips curving into an unwilling smile as he thought of her sharp tongue. "I'll grant you she's unusual. I've never known a lady with a greater breadth of accumulated knowledge. She knows a little something about every topic imaginable— just enough to get herself into difficulties, in some cases."

Lord Derrick was looking at him blankly. "Accumulated knowledge?"

"Yes. Did you know she's read Pierce Egan's *Boxiana*? Not quite what you'd expect from a proper English lady, but I've no doubt she did read it, because she gave me a lesson on the merits of bare-knuckles over weighted gloves."

That memorable conversation had occurred the day he'd escorted her to Execution Dock. He'd teased her mercilessly by arguing with her on every point from striking with the heel of the hand to crushed wrist bones—not because he gave a damn about weighted gloves, but because he admired the way her blue eyes sparkled when he challenged her. He enjoyed sparring with her. He enjoyed everything he did with her.

"Hyacinth Somerset gave you a lesson on bare-knuckle boxing?" Lord Derrick laughed. "I think you're confused, Dare. That sounds far more like something Vi—"

"Ah, there you are, my lord!" Lady Derrick hurried into the entryway just then, a smile blossoming on her lips when she saw her husband. "Lady Avondale is asking for you. Will you come?"

"Of course, my dear." Derrick took his wife's arm, then shot one more amused glance at Nick. "I'm afraid I haven't seen Hyacinth at all this evening, Dare, but it sounds to me as if you want her sister. I haven't seen her either, but I did see Lady Chase in the drawing room just now. Perhaps she knows where her granddaughter is."

Lord Derrick wandered off with his wife, leaving Nick staring after them. Damn it, how the devil had Miss Somerset managed to slip past him? He hadn't stirred a step away from the door for the past hour. And what would he want with her sister? He hardly knew the Marchioness of Huntington.

Nick's jaw hardened, and his hands fisted with determination. He'd had enough of Hyacinth Somerset's games. Something strange was going on, and he intended to put an end to it tonight.

He abandoned his post and made his way toward the drawing room. Did she truly think he'd give up if she avoided him? He'd kissed and touched her, held her in his arms and caught her breathless moans on his lips. For God's sake, she'd *ridden* him to release in his bloody *carriage*, and made him spill in his breeches like some green lad on his first visit to a whorehouse.

Nick had been with far more women than any decent man ever should have, but he'd never in his life experienced anything as erotic as those moments in his carriage with her. Every time he thought of it his cock rose like a soldier at attention, and he thought of it dozens of times a day.

No, more than that. Hundreds. He'd had so many erections in the past five days he was afraid his breeches would require alterations.

She was *his* now, and she wouldn't escape him again—

"Oh, won't you play another song, Miss Somerset? *Please?*"

"Yes, do, Miss Somerset. A Christmas song, because it's nearly Christmas, you know! Sing the one about the sheep."

Nick was hurrying through the saloon toward the drawing room, but he paused when he heard her name, and a moment later he caught the familiar sound of her sweet laugh. It drifted through the door of a tiny, neglected music room tucked at the far end of the hallway, hidden behind the library. It was so far out of the way of the public rooms Nick hadn't even recalled it was there, but when he peered through the crack in the door there was Miss Somerset, sitting in front of the pianoforte, her cheeks flushed with laughter.

Nick's chest went tight at the sight of her. Not just because she was beautiful—though she seemed to grow more beautiful each time he saw her—but because for him, she was the beating heart at the center of every room she was in.

Her back was to him, and he didn't approach her, but remained quiet, leaning a hip against the doorframe, watching as she teased and laughed with the two children who shared the pianoforte bench with her.

"What, you mean "Shepherds Watched Their Flocks at Night?" Is that the song you want, Charles?" She reached out to tousle the sandy hair of the boy beside her.

The child shook his head. "I'm not sure. Is that the one about the angels all around, and glory shining, and the child in the manger, and all that?"

"Yes, that sounds right." Miss Somerset struck a few notes on the pianoforte. "Is this the tune?"

Nick straightened from his slouch against the doorframe as she flexed her fingers over the keys. He hadn't heard her play since Lord and Lady Derrick's dinner party, when she'd performed the Haydn so masterfully. Pleasure washed over him at the thought of hearing her again.

"Yes!" The boy gave a vigorous nod. "You're capital at the pianoforte, Miss Somerset, isn't she, Eliza?"

A small girl with light brown curls was gazing up at Miss Somerset with a worshipful expression. "Yes, and 'specially when she sings about the sheep and the angels, and that lot."

Miss Somerset tweaked one of Eliza's curls, then said with a laugh, "Oh, I'm dreadful, and all of London knows it, but you're a most loyal audience, and the only one I play for willingly. Shall we, then?"

Nick's brows drew together with confusion. Dreadful? She played like an angel, so why—

The first note rang out, and Nick's eardrums screamed in startled protest. She'd slammed down on the keys as if she were trying to flatten a poisonous spider under her fists, and the note was harsh, discordant. But then anyone could miss the first note, couldn't they? Perhaps she just needed to warm up—

Crash! Nick flinched as her fingers came down again with a vengeance, and all the melodic notes he'd anticipated with such relish fled for their very lives. The long, pale fingers that had played the Haydn so delightfully pounded onto the keys, striking one sour note after another in such a deafening cacophony it took every bit of Nick's self-control not to cover his ears.

And then, dear God, she began to sing.

"While shepherds watched their flocks by night, all seated on the ground, the angel of the Lord came down…"

An angel? Dear God, no angel had ever made such a sound. That was the devil himself, and it sounded as if he were trapped inside the pianoforte.

The children joined in happily, and the two childish voices helped to disguise Miss Somerset's tone-deaf warbling, but nothing could drown it out entirely, as she sang just as she did everything else, that is, with great enthusiasm.

Loudly.

Nick reached blindly for the back of the chair next to him. He lowered himself into it, pressed his fingertips to his temples, and waited for it to be over, but the final shrill note was still reverberating inside his skull when the children began clamoring for the song "where heaven and nature sing."

Nick, who'd heard enough by now to know heaven had abandoned them entirely, shot to his feet. "No!"

All three heads swung around to face him, the delight on the children's faces fading at once to shock, and—in the case of the little girl, fear—but neither of them looked as appalled as Miss Somerset.

Nick winced as they all continued to stare at him in stunned silence, but it was too late to repair the damage now, so he strode into the room, took Miss Somerset's arm and drew her to her feet. "That is, Miss Somerset looks fatigued, and she must need refreshment after singing so…lustily."

"I'm perfectly well, my lord, and not at all thirsty."

She stared up at him, her face pale. She made a frantic attempt to tug her arm from his grasp, but now that Nick had her, he had no intention of allowing her to slip away from him again. "Oh, but I insist, Miss Somerset."

This moment of reckoning between them was as inevitable as the sunrise, and despite her reluctance, she must have known it would come, one way or another. Either that, or she could see from his expression he'd catch her in his arms and carry her from the room if he had to.

Her shoulders sagged as the fight drained out of her. "Go on without me for now, children. I'll be back after I have a short rest."

"You shouldn't make promises you can't keep, Miss Somerset," Nick murmured against her ear as he led her through the connecting door and into the adjoining library. "I expect you'll be engaged with me for quite some time."

But once he'd closed the door behind them and turned to face her, Nick didn't know where to begin, and her agonized expression made him hesitate. Her eyes were wide and wary, and her lips were trembling, as if she were trying to hold back tears.

This, because of a few sour notes on the pianoforte? Well, more than a few, but still, it seemed unlikely.

"Did you only ever learn to play the Haydn piano sonatas?"

He meant it as a joke, to try and diffuse the strange tension between them, but if anything the dark shadows in her eyes grew even darker, and she began to wring her hands. "No, I—no. I admire Haydn too much to even attempt the sonatas."

He couldn't have said why, but the back of his neck began to prickle with dread. "I don't understand. I heard you play it at Lord Derrick's dinner party not two weeks ago."

Nick was still angry with her for avoiding him these past five days, but as her face drew tight with misery, alarm squeezed his chest, and his wrath gave way to concern. He went to her and gathered her hands in his. "What is it? You look unhappy, and…unlike yourself."

She let out a faint laugh, but it was more desperate than amused. "Unlike myself. Oh, Lord Dare, you haven't the faintest idea how right you are."

He half-expected her to pull away from him then, but her fingers clung to his as if she was afraid he was going to push her away. "I have something to tell you, my lord—something unpleasant I should have confessed to you days ago."

Nick looked down into dark blue eyes still shadowed with regret. Whatever it was she'd done, he'd just as soon have it out now, so they could move past it and begin to plan their nuptials. "This unpleasant thing you must confess—is it the reason you've been hiding from me?"

"Yes. I've been an awful coward. I beg your pardon for refusing your calls this week. I did want to see you, but well…I was afraid of what you'd say, and I didn't know how to explain what I'd done, and I'm…ashamed of myself, Lord Dare."

Afraid? The lady who'd risked a dunking in the Thames and braved the Cockpit Steps in the dark to hunt for a headless ghost was afraid of *him?*

She looked away from him, down at her hands, but Nick, who was truly concerned by this point, took her chin between his fingers and raised her face to his. "Don't look away from me, Hyacinth. Just tell me what's got you so worried, and we'll find a way to…"

Nick trailed off when her gaze met his, and he was horrified to find her eyes had filled with tears. "Oh, sweetheart, *no.*" He moved closer and took her face between his hands, and all at once everything else—the strange business with the pianoforte, her mysterious disappearance this week—all of it faded into insignificance at the sight of those tears. Nick had never been one to be moved by a weeping lady, but seeing those fat drops spill over her wet lashes and roll down her cheeks felt like taking a knife to the heart. "Don't *cry*, Hyacinth."

For some reason this only made her tears fall faster, until she was crying so hard she could only speak in incoherent gasps. "B-but that's just i-it, my lord. I'm n-not—"

"Hush." He caught the back of her head in a gentle grip and pressed her face to his chest, then ran his hand over her back in long, soothing strokes until at last she began to calm. "There. That's better." He tilted her face up to his again and pressed gentle kisses to her forehead, her eyelids, and the tip of her nose.

He hadn't intended to kiss her at all, and if he'd stopped there—if he'd been able to resist her trembling mouth—what happened next might not have been quite such a scandal, but as it was, in the next breath his mouth found hers, and then he was nudging her lips open with his, his tongue tasting the salt of her tears as her arms stole around his neck—

Neither of them heard the library door open, but they couldn't fail to hear the outraged shout that followed.

"Damnation!"

The voice was loud, masculine, and furious. "What the bloody hell do you think you're doing, Dare? Take your hands off her at once!"

Nick's head jerked up. He and Miss Somerset sprang apart, and Nick stepped away from her, his palms held out in surrender.

Standing in the doorway to the library, his entire body rigid with fury, stood Miss Somerset's brother-in-law, the Marquess of Huntington, and if his expression was anything to go by he was the protective sort, because he looked as if he were about to tear Nick's limbs from his body, one by one.

As painfully as possible.

"Lord Dare wasn't...we weren't...oh, for goodness' sake, Finn! It's not what it seems."

Lord Huntington didn't look at all convinced, which wasn't surprising, since it was, in fact, precisely what it seemed. "Are you in the habit of debauching innocents, Dare? I'd heard as much, and it seems for once the gossips didn't exaggerate."

Nick understood his lordship's rage, and he wasn't proud of his actions, but he'd be damned if he'd let any man question his honor, or, more importantly, Miss Somerset's virtue. He advanced on Lord Huntington, his hands clenched into fists. "You insult the lady, Huntington. You go too far."

"It's you who's gone too far, Dare, and you can be damn sure I'll see to it you make it right."

Neither Nick nor Lord Huntington backed down an inch. They stood toe to toe, staring at each other, and it might have become ugly indeed if Lady Huntington hadn't appeared at the library door just at that moment. She took in the scene in one quick glance, paled, and lifted a shaking hand to her throat. "Oh, no. Oh, *Violet!* What have you done now?"

Nick went still, his body going numb as one of Lady Huntington's words echoed over and over again in his head. When he turned to face Miss Somerset at last, his voice had gone dangerously quiet.

"Who the *devil* is Violet?"

Chapter Fifteen

The muted thud of Finn's boots on the thick carpet sounded like a death knell.

He was pacing from one end of Lady Westcott's private sitting room to the other while Violet, Iris, Hyacinth, and Lady Chase followed him with their eyes, their gazes flitting back and forth as if they were watching a game of shuttlecock.

None of them said a word.

Violet was under no illusions it would remain quiet. They were mere seconds away from a deafening outburst that would leave all their ears ringing for months to come. They waited only for Lord Dare and Lady Westcott, who'd adjourned to Lord Dare's study for a private discussion before they joined the rest of the party in the sitting room.

The moment of reckoning had arrived.

Violet had known from the start of this mad scheme the truth would catch up to her at last, but she'd been foolish enough to believe when it did, the only witnesses would be herself and Lord Dare.

But *this*…

Her heart crowded into her throat. In her worst nightmares she'd never imagined it would happen in Lady Westcott's sitting room, with both his family and hers there to witness her shame.

Lady Chase hadn't uttered a single word since she'd collapsed onto one of the yellow silk settees, but she was never able to hold her tongue for long, particularly when one of her granddaughters was due for a scolding.

Duping an earl into a false courtship certainly qualified as such an occasion.

"Well, Violet, I do hope you're pleased with yourself. Just look at poor Lord Huntington! Why, anyone can see he's on the verge of an apoplexy. If he expires in his sleep tonight and leaves your sister a widow, we'll have you to thank for it."

Violet wanted nothing more than for the floor to open beneath her and swallow her whole, but she forced herself to face her grandmother with dry eyes, a straight back, and hands folded neatly in her lap. "I'm sorry, Grandmother."

And she was—sorrier than she'd ever been in her life—but her misery had more to do with the astonishment on Lord Dare's face when he discovered her deception than it did with Finn's imminent demise.

But a simple apology, no matter how heartfelt, wasn't going to appease her grandmother, who dismissed it with an outraged sniff. "Well, don't tell *me*, child. You may offer your apologies to Iris after Lord Huntington drops dead."

Hyacinth, who after a prolonged search had been discovered hiding in the butler's pantry, made a faint noise of protest. "As Lord Huntington is still among the living, perhaps we can put aside the matter of his death for a moment. Surely Violet's first apology should be to Lord Dare?"

An apology, a dozen apologies—it wouldn't make any difference. As soon as Violet saw his face, she'd known he'd never forgive her.

"Lord Dare and Lady Westcott, yes, though I don't see why either of them should forgive you, Violet," Lady Chase snapped. "If Lord Dare had treated you thus, you can be sure I'd demand far more than an apology, but I suppose you've gotten your way, haven't you, miss? He won't have you now, and neither will any other honorable gentleman once this scandal gets out. You'll end a spinster, just as you wished."

Hyacinth slid her fingers into Violet's hand and squeezed. "It wasn't just Violet, Grandmother. I deceived them, too—"

"Oh, hush, Hyacinth. What nonsense. You never would have dreamed up such a dreadful scheme yourself. No, I know very well who's responsible." Lady Chase pinned Violet with a look that made Violet shrink back against the settee. "I don't pretend to know why you did it, but whatever your reason, Violet, I hope it was worth it."

She'd been so sure it would be, but it wasn't. It wasn't worth it now, and though Violet hadn't known it at the time, it hadn't been worth it at Cockpit Steps, or Execution Dock, or even at the Hunterian Museum. Her beloved book, her sketches—she wouldn't have believed it was possible anything could matter more to her than that, but she'd been wrong. Her sisters had tried to warn her, but she hadn't listened to them, and now her heart was heavy with bitter regret.

The shock in Lord Dare's gray eyes, the way they'd darkened with hurt... Nothing was worth that.

Never was that truth more painfully evident than five minutes later, when Lord Dare and Lady Westcott entered the sitting room. Violet managed to keep her chin up as she watched their grim procession, but she faltered once they were all seated and every head in the room turned in her direction. Hyacinth must have felt her begin to tremble, because she wrapped her fingers more tightly around Violet's.

For what seemed a lifetime to Violet, no one moved. No one spoke, and the silence grew colder and heavier with each passing moment, until at last Lord Dare rose to his feet and approached the settee where Violet and Hyacinth were seated.

"Miss Hyacinth." He bowed over Hyacinth's hand, and then he turned to Violet and held out his hand to her, his jaw hard and his lips pressed into a severe line.

Dear God, she could hardly bear to look at him, but he stood there in front of her, silently, his hand held out, waiting for her—they were all waiting for her—and she had no choice but to offer the tips of her gloved fingers.

"And Miss Somerset." He grasped her hand in his and bowed over it politely, his demeanor proper, his address correct.

Correct, and cold. So cold.

Violet allowed herself one quick look into his eyes, then wished at once she hadn't. There was nothing but ice in that gray gaze, and an answering shiver darted down her back. She tried to withdraw her hand, but he refused to release her. Instead he urged her to her feet and led her across the room.

"May I present my aunt, Lady Westcott? Aunt, this is Miss Violet Somerset."

Lady Westcott had a headful of thick silver hair, and between that, the severe elegance of her dress, and her regal mien, she was an intimidating figure. It took every ounce of Violet's composure, but she made herself meet Lady Westcott's gaze as she sank into a shaky curtsy.

"My lady. It's a pleasure to..."

The words died in her throat as she realized the absurdity of them. It wasn't a pleasure. Not for her, and not for Lady Westcott. Not for any of them.

Lady Westcott studied her for longer than was polite, her gray gaze cool, but just when Violet was ready to sink to her knees in the middle of the sitting room, Lady Westcott reached out and took her hand, her grip strong enough to be remarkable in a lady of her advanced years. "Miss Somerset. You have your grandmother's blue eyes."

"Yes, my lady, and your nephew has your gray ones."

A brief silence followed this statement, and Violet's cheeks heated. It wasn't what she'd meant to say at all, and she couldn't have explained why she said it, except Lord Dare's unusual silver-gray eyes were the first of his features she'd admired, and it was comforting, somehow, to know at least this one truth about him.

He'd inherited his aunt's extraordinary gray eyes.

Lady Westcott blinked in surprise, but she didn't look displeased, and after a moment she inclined her head. "Yes, he does, and so did my brother, his father. Gray eyes are a Dare family trait." She lowered her voice so only Lord Dare and Violet could hear her. "But perhaps one day soon you'll find that out for yourself, Miss Somerset."

Violet's mouth fell open. No, surely her ladyship didn't mean—

"I'm waiting for you to explain yourself, Dare." Finn had been standing beside the fireplace, watching the proceedings with narrowed eyes, but now he strode across the room to face off with Lord Dare, his arms folded over his massive chest.

Lord Dare eyed his accuser without flinching. "Oh, I think Miss Somerset—that is, *Violet* Somerset—can explain it more clearly than I can, Huntington."

Finn's scowl deepened. "You expect an innocent young lady to explain why I found the two of you alone in a dark library with your arms wrapped around each other?"

"Violet!" Lady Chase let out a despairing moan. "How could you?"

"It's plain enough what happened, Lady Chase." Finn hadn't taken his hard gaze off Lord Dare. "Dare here is a rake. He lured a naive young lady into an indiscretion, and now he's going to see it set to rights."

Lady Westcott drew herself up. "If my nephew has done something he ought not to have done, Lord Huntington, you will not need to threaten him to make it right. He's an honorable gentleman."

"Forgive me, Lady Westcott, but if he was an honorable gentleman, he never would have lured Miss Somerset into the library at all."

Lord Dare, who'd remained silent during this exchange, his gaze fixed on Violet, now took a threatening step toward Finn. "What you witnessed in the library was a single, isolated moment, and hardly the whole story of my friendship with Miss Somerset. Before you fling any more accusations about, Huntington, perhaps you'd care to hear the rest of it."

"I know enough—"

"No you don't, Finn," Violet whispered. "Lord Dare did nothing wrong. This is my fault, not his."

A shocked silence fell, but then Finn, Lady Westcott, and Lady Chase all began to shout at once.

"*Your* fault? You're an innocent, Violet. You couldn't have known what a debaucher like Dare was about—"

"How *dare* you? My nephew is not a debaucher—"

"I can well believe you're at fault, Violet! You've always been a headstrong, foolish chit—"

Only Hyacinth and Iris, who knew the whole truth, remained silent. Hyacinth buried her face in her hands, but Iris, who must have recognized the enraged look on her husband's face, leapt to her feet and hurried across the room to him. "Calm down, my lord, and let Violet speak. Indeed, she's…well, she never meant any harm, but she's not *quite* as innocent in this as you imagine."

"Just how would you know that, Lady Huntington?" Finn stared at Iris for a moment, but when she only bit her lip in answer, he threw his hands into the air. "Don't tell me Violet had your approval for whatever she did."

"Not my approval, exactly." Iris flushed guiltily. "But I, ah—well, I did know about it."

Finn pinched the bridge of his nose between his fingers. "For God's sake, Iris."

"Well, what did you expect me to do? She's my sister, and she's been in terribly low spirits ever since that business with Lord Derrick. I only thought to cheer her—"

"*What* business with Lord Derrick?"

Hyacinth was weeping, Lady Chase was scolding, Iris and Finn were arguing, and Lady Westcott was proclaiming her nephew's innocence to all who would listen, but all of them fell silent as Lord Dare's furious shout rose above the commotion.

He turned on Violet and closed his hands around her upper arms. "What business with Lord Derrick, Miss Somerset?"

Violet stared up into his face, horrified and riveted by him at once. His eyes had gone a strangely mesmerizing silvery-black, and they burned in his pale face. She'd never seen him so angry, not even when he'd struck down the footpad who'd attacked her and pummeled him into a blubbering heap on the cobblestones.

All this fuss over Lord Derrick, who'd hardly crossed Violet's mind once in at least a fortnight, and who hadn't a blessed thing to do with any of it. She tried to squirm out of Lord Dare's grasp, suddenly sick to death of this entire mess, and ready to have it over with.

"Never mind Lord Derrick. He hasn't a thing to do with this." Violet sucked in a quick breath, gathered her wits, and turned to Finn. "Lord Dare has been courting me for the past few weeks—utterly respectably, I might add. Perhaps a kiss in a dim library isn't quite as unobjectionable as *you* might like, Finn, but it's hardly a scandal, and anyway, I know you did worse when you were courting Iris."

"Violet!" Iris shot a nervous look at Lady Chase, and her face went bright red. "Hush, will you?"

"Iris!" Lady Chase made a helpless gesture with her hands, then sagged against the settee. "Hyacinth, fetch my smelling salts at once. Oh, what have I done to deserve such a wayward pack of chits for granddaughters?"

Iris hurried to their grandmother's side to soothe her while Hyacinth dug in Lady Chase's reticule for her smelling salts, but Finn remained where he was, his puzzled gaze fixed on Violet. "Courting you? No, Violet, there must be more to it than that."

Violet darted a glance at Lord Dare, but his frozen expression offered no encouragement. "There is more. Lord Dare was introduced to Hyacinth at Lord and Lady Derrick's dinner party several weeks ago. He and I weren't introduced, but we nevertheless had a brief conversation at the end of that evening, after Hyacinth left. He met us each separately, you see, and he confused one of us for the other, as so often happens with fashionable gentlemen."

She was unable to resist this last little dig, which really was unforgiveable of her since this entire disaster of a courtship was all her fault, but the petty part of her whispered none of this would have happened if Lord Dare had been paying the least bit of attention.

"For pity's sake, Nicholas," Lady Westcott said in exasperation. "You couldn't tell one young lady from the other? I was under the impression I'd raised a gentleman."

"Well, look at the two of them, would you?" Lord Dare waved a hand from Hyacinth to Violet. "If it weren't for their eyes, they'd be indistinguishable from each other."

Lady Chase had fallen into a determined half-swoon against the settee, but she raised her head at this and fixed Lord Dare with a sharp look. "What do you mean, Lord Dare? They both have their mother's identical dark blue eyes."

"No, they don't. That is, they've both got dark blue eyes, but *that* Miss Somerset,"—he pointed at Hyacinth, who froze when every eye turned toward her.—"Her eyes are soft and gentle, whereas *this* Miss Somerset's eyes are..." He still had Violet by the shoulders, and he looked down into her eyes. "Well, one only has to look into her eyes to see she'll cause no end of trouble."

A curious look drifted over Lady Chase's face as she considered this. "How remarkable," she murmured, her shrewd gaze fixed on Violet and Lord Dare. "I believe you're right, my lord."

"Let me see if I understand you." Finn, who was still dissatisfied with this explanation, gave Violet his sternest, most Marquess-like look. "Lord Dare has been courting you for two weeks, thinking you were Hyacinth?"

"Yes. I—it was wrong of me, I know. I never intended to let it get so far, but I...well, I beg your pardon, Lord Dare, though I know an apology isn't enough to excuse me."

"No, it is *not* enough, miss." Hyacinth was fanning Lady Chase, but the old woman slapped her hand away and struggled upright against the settee. "What reason could you have to trick Lord Dare with such an egregious falsehood?"

Violet, Iris, and Hyacinth glanced guiltily at each other, but it was Lord Dare who answered. "Her book, my lady. She wanted to take some sketches, but several of them took her to parts of London that are unacceptable for proper young ladies." He shot Violet an accusing look. "I happened along just at the right time to serve as an escort."

As soon as Lord Dare uttered the word "book," Lady Chase's face began to redden with anger, and by the time he'd finished, her better judgment had fallen victim to her temper. "*That book* again! I don't even know why I bothered to ask, since *that book* is invariably the reason behind all of Violet's most reprehensible behavior."

"What book?" Lady Westcott glanced from one Somerset sister to the next. "What's it about?"

"Oh, it's terribly clever, Lady Westcott. It's called *A Treatise on London for Bluestockings.* Or is it 'for Adventuresses' now, Violet?" Iris shot Violet a questioning look. "She keeps adding chapters to it, you see, and so the title keeps changing."

Lord Dare let out a grim laugh. "You're quite right, Lady Huntington. In fact, I suspect she added another chapter just recently, all about how to arouse a gentleman into attempting a seduction. Miss Somerset is quite protective of her book—she doesn't like anyone to read it—but I'll have to insist on reading that chapter. She can hardly refuse, since she wouldn't have been able to write it at all if she hadn't had my help."

An appalled silence followed this statement, then a small, choked sound escaped Violet's lips, but her whimper was drowned out by Lady Chase's piercing shriek. "A gentleman's arousal! Oh, dear God, Violet. You're ruined!"

"No, I'm not! Of course I'm not!" Violet's frantic gaze swept the room to find every mouth dropped open in horror, and she stumbled into a breathless explanation before panic rendered her incoherent. "At one point I considered adding a chapter about resisting a rake's seduction, but I didn't—"

"But you didn't resist, did you, Miss Somerset?"

Violet gaped at Lord Dare, but he only stared back at her, his face wiped of all expression. "I—I'm not...we didn't..."

She groped for the back of a settee with a trembling hand as the room tilted crazily.

Dear God, she was going to swoon. *Again.*

Lord Dare leapt toward her as she began to sway, but before he could touch her Lady Westcott grasped her hand and tugged Violet down beside her onto the settee. She didn't spare Violet a glance, however. Her gaze was fixed on Lord Huntington, her face white.

"Have you compromised my sister-in-law, Dare?" Finn's voice was low and calm, but it swelled with such stark menace a shudder ran down Violet's spine.

But Lord Dare never flinched. He met Finn's gaze head on. "Yes."

Finn didn't move, but every inch of his body went rigid, and the air around him snapped and hummed with suppressed fury. "Then I'll see you tomorrow morning at dawn."

Violet's heart dropped to her stomach with a sudden, sickening lurch. "No!"

Iris and Lady Westcott both rose to their feet with cries of dismay, but Lord Dare raised a hand for quiet, and silence fell over the room.

"There's no need for that, Huntington. I've compromised her, and I intend to marry her."

Finn stared at Lord Dare for a long moment, taking his measure, then he blew out a breath, and nodded once. "At once, by special license, so we can have the business finished well before the ton comes back to town and gets wind of it."

Violet sat motionless on the settee, mute with shock, and listened in horror as the two men casually arranged the rest of her life as if they were tossing dice about on a hazard table.

She struggled to open her mouth, to speak, to argue with them, to say something—anything—but all that emerged was a faint whisper. "No." No one paid her any attention.

"We'll have it at Lady Chase's house in Bedford Square," Finn said. "Before the end of the week, if possible."

Lord Dare nodded. "I'll get the special license tomorrow. Once we're wed I wish to retire to my country seat in West Sussex. We'll remain there throughout the winter."

Violet tried again. "No."

One tiny word, no more than a breath, and again, no one heard her.

Lady Chase, who seemed to have suddenly realized the granddaughter who'd sworn she'd die a spinster was on the verge of becoming a countess, quickly recovered from her swoon. "We'll have a wedding breakfast, of course. If it's to be done, we'll do what we can to see it's done right. If word gets about it was rushed, the ton will gossip."

Iris and Hyacinth turned to Violet, their faces stricken. She met their gazes and began to shake her head, and once she started, she found she couldn't stop. "No."

Hyacinth rose unsteadily to her feet. "Violet—"

"No."

She couldn't marry Lord Dare. She'd lied to him, used and deceived him, and when he looked at her now, his gray eyes were cold, so cold. *Those cold gray eyes will break my heart...*

Violet rose now, too, though her knees still threatened to collapse beneath her. "No. I-I beg your pardon, my lord, but I can't...I won't marry you."

Lord Dare's icy gaze swept over her, and there wasn't a shadow of understanding or empathy in his face. "I'm afraid I'll have to insist, Miss Somerset. I don't intend to be put to the trouble of embarking on a new courtship because of your deception, and it's only a name, after all. Hyacinth or Violet—what difference does it make? *You're* the lady I've been courting. *You're* the lady I compromised, and *you're* the lady I'll marry."

Every word he spoke was like another blow. The chasm in Violet's chest opened until she thought she might be sucked into the gaping hole and disappear into the abyss. "No—"

He seized her arms in a merciless grasp. "*Yes.* Need I remind you, Miss Somerset, that you've involved your younger sister in your deception? If I choose to make this matter known to the ton, it won't only be your reputation that's ruined, but hers as well. I'm certain you don't wish her to suffer for your foolishness."

Violet jerked her gaze to Hyacinth.

Her youngest sister, the baby of the family. Hyacinth had always been more fragile than the rest of them, the one who could never sway or bend—the only one of the five sisters who seemed forever on the verge of breaking. Yet everything about her was kind and pure, natural and true, and she deserved only good things.

She's our family's dearest treasure...

Hyacinth was shaking her head, her eyes pleading with Violet, but it was too late. It was already done. "No, I...you're quite right, Lord Dare. I don't wish for that. I—I accept your proposal."

"Then I'm the happiest of men." He took her hand and brushed his lips over her glove, but the gesture was perfunctory, and his face was blank.

And that was it. It hadn't even taken an hour, but Violet's fate had been decided. Whether she wanted it or not, in less than a week's time she'd marry a man she hardly knew, and become the Countess of Dare.

Chapter Sixteen

Violet's sisters did all they could to introduce a note of gaiety to the occasion, but despite their best efforts, the wedding was a grim affair.

Violet was numb and quiet, her bridegroom severe and unsmiling. Lady Westcott listened with sober attention as her nephew uttered his vows, and Hyacinth looked as if she were about to succumb to floods of tears at every moment. The only one who appeared well pleased with the proceedings was Lady Chase, and even there it was difficult to tell, as she took to her smelling salts partway through the ceremony, and never lifted them from her nose again until it was finished.

Then there was the wedding breakfast to get through. It was nearly over when Delia, Lady Carlisle and the eldest Somerset sister, nudged Mrs. Lily Sutherland, the second-eldest, and tilted her chin toward the staircase. Lily understood at once and prodded Hyacinth, who tapped Iris's shoulder and gave her a meaningful raise of the eyebrows.

Iris shot to her feet, caught Violet by the arm, and offered a gracious smile to the rest of the company. "Please do excuse us. We'll just take Lady Dare upstairs and ready her for her journey to West Sussex."

Once they reached Violet's bedchamber, Lily closed the door and folded Violet into her arms. When she drew away, her lips were curved in a determined smile. "Well, Violet, that was just…lovely."

"Lovely!" Iris, who'd thrown herself onto the bed in a full sprawl the moment they entered the room, struggled up onto her elbows to glower at Lily. "For pity's sake, Lily. I've attended funerals more joyous than that."

"Hush, will you, Iris?" Hyacinth hurried across the room to Violet, who was staring at herself in the dressing-table mirror with a lost expression. "Lily's right. It was a perfectly lovely wedding." She wrapped an arm around Violet's shoulders. "Lord Dare is so handsome, and I've never seen you look lovelier, Violet."

Violet gazed at her reflection without answering.

She did look lovely, in her silver tissue gown with the puffed Belgian lace sleeves and the tiny embroidered violets scattered about the bodice and hem. Her sisters had insisted on dressing her hair themselves, and they'd taken great care to weave handfuls of dark purple violets into her heavy curls in a graceful, artistic manner.

She did look lovely. Lovely, and unlike herself.

But then she wasn't herself anymore, was she? She was the Countess of Dare now, wife to a man who'd had to force himself to look at her when he'd said his vows this morning.

She loved him. Dear God, she *loved* him, and he didn't love her, and she was terrified.

"What do I…I don't know what I'm supposed to do now."

Even her voice sounded strange, so dazed and forlorn, so unlike the Violet she'd been a fortnight ago, when she'd been so certain no one would be hurt by her deception.

"Oh, my dear." Delia crossed the room and urged Violet to sit in the chair in front of the dressing-table. "It looks rather grim now, I confess, but it will sort itself out, I promise you."

"Of course it will." Lily knelt to take both of Violet's hands in hers. "It's not the courtship that matters, but the marriage. It will come right in the end. You'll see."

"Courtships are dreadful things. You witnessed my courtship with Finn, Violet—it was an utter misery, but you see how happy we are now." Iris rose from the bed to press her cheek against Violet's, smiling at her in the mirror.

"They are dreadful, aren't they? Robyn's idea of a proper courtship was to risk taking a ball between his eyes in a duel." Lily shook her head. "Once I was certain he was safe, I nearly shot him myself."

Delia laughed. "Alec was no better. He chased me on horseback from London halfway to Surrey in the midst of a dreadful downpour. By the time he caught up to me at last and dragged me from the carriage he was covered in mud, and utterly furious. I thought he was a highwayman! Come to think of it, I *hoped* he was a highwayman. A villain with a pistol would have been easier to manage than Alec at that moment."

"Gentlemen are impossible when they're in love, especially possessive, imperious gentlemen, which seem, alas, to be the sort of gentlemen the Somerset ladies are fated to fall in love with. Indeed, each one of our successive husbands is more high-handed than the last." Iris gave Hyacinth a sly grin. "Well, my dear, I wish you luck with *that*."

"I daresay you're right." Violet forced herself to smile at her sisters, but inside her chest her heart was sinking. Her elder sisters' courtships hadn't been smooth, no, but they were nothing like her situation with Lord Dare. Alec, Robyn, and Finn were in love with her sisters, and had been from the start, before the duel, and before the carriage chase.

Lord Dare didn't love her. Why should he? She was a bluestocking who'd been destined for spinsterhood. She wasn't suited to be a wife, especially not the wife of a man like him, who could have had London's most celebrated belle for the asking. She'd only become Lady Dare because she'd cheated fate with a lie.

He didn't love her, and now her heart was his to break.

"All you can do now is beg Lord Dare's pardon, Violet." Delia rested a cool palm against her cheek. "Once you've done that, simply take every day as it comes. Lord Dare can't hold a grudge forever, after all, and I'm certain you'll find a way to make it up to him."

"Oh, yes. I can think of any number of ways she could do so, particularly in the bedchamber." Iris's lips quirked in a grin. "For example, she could try—"

"Iris! For pity's sake!" Delia tilted her head toward Hyacinth. "Do we need to have this discussion *now*?"

"I don't see why not. Hyacinth's bound to end up with the most demanding husband of us all, so she'll have to hear it sooner or later. But not to worry, Hyacinth." Iris squeezed her youngest sister's hand. "I have some books for you to read that will explain all you need to know about the bedchamber."

Hyacinth's face went pink. "Yes, ah…well, perhaps another time, as I'm certain Lord Dare is anxious to set off for West Sussex. Fetch Violet's traveling dress, won't you, Iris? And her cloak as well, Delia? Lily, will you run to the attic and see that Violet hasn't left any of her papers there? I'll help Violet out of her gown."

Once their three elder sisters were gone, Hyacinth stepped behind Violet and began to loosen her buttons, and their eyes met in the mirror. "I should never have agreed to deceive Lord Dare, Violet. I knew it was wrong, but I went along with it instead of stopping you as I should have, because I was afraid of…" Hyacinth blew out a breath. "I don't even know what I was afraid of, but I seem to always be afraid of something, and look what's come of my cowardice this time."

Violet spun on her chair, wrapped her arms around her sister's waist, and laid her head against Hyacinth's stomach. "You're *not* a coward, and this isn't your fault. You tried to dissuade me from my foolish scheme, but I wouldn't listen, and now here we are."

Hyacinth shook her head, but she didn't argue. She only sighed and stroked Violet's hair.

"I'm sure it won't be as awful as I imagine." Violet turned to face the mirror again, her eyes pleading, and it occurred to her she was trying to convince herself. "Lord Dare isn't a wicked man, or an ill-tempered one. Indeed, in the short time I've known him, he's been..."

Everything an honorable gentleman should be.

"He's *kind*, Hyacinth. Perhaps it's not the first thing one notices about him, but he has kindness in his heart." Violet looked down at her hands as a familiar dry ache pressed behind her eyes. He'd been kind to her, and she'd offered him nothing but lies and betrayal in return.

"Then he'll be a kind husband, won't he?" Hyacinth settled her hands on Violet's shoulders until her sister met her gaze in the mirror. "Promise me something, Violet. You don't..." Hyacinth drew in a breath. "You don't always have to be brave. If he isn't kind, or if he unintentionally hurts your feelings, you must let him know it, or else he won't know not to do it again."

Violet reached behind her to grip Hyacinth's hand. "I'll try."

* * * *

By noon the wedding cake had been reduced to crumbs, the champagne had run dry, and the new Countess of Dare's trunks were packed and waiting in the drive for the servants to load them into the carriage.

Within the next hour, Nick and his new bride would be on their way to West Sussex.

He had his countess, just as he'd planned, and he'd gotten her more quickly and with far less bother than he'd dared hope for. He should have been satisfied, but as he and his aunt waited in the entryway for Violet to appear, gratification was as distant as it had ever been. So distant, in fact, if the Marquess of Huntington pressed a gun to his temple at this very moment and demanded he appear joyful on his wedding day, Nick couldn't have forced his lips into a smile.

He *should* be satisfied, but he wasn't.

Lady Westcott had been quiet all morning, but now she laid her hand on Nick's arm and pinned him with the same penetrating gaze he remembered as a child—the one that seemed to see right through him. "Miss Somerset looked terrified when she greeted us before the ceremony this morning. Her face was quite gray, and the poor thing looks as if she hasn't slept in days."

Nick flinched. Did his aunt think he hadn't noticed? Only a brute could fail to see how pale and exhausted Violet looked. He had his flaws, but Nick was no brute, and the moment he'd laid eyes on her this morning a weight had settled on his chest. "I noticed."

"You might have said something to comfort her, Nicholas. The young lady is distraught, and a few words from you would ease her. I know you're still angry, but it isn't like you to withhold your forgiveness to punish someone, least of all a frightened young woman who's clearly sorry for what she did."

"Punish her?" Nick gaped at his aunt, aghast.

He wasn't trying to punish Violet, but if his aunt believed he was, then mightn't his bride think so, as well? Is that why she'd been unable to meet his eyes when she whispered her vows to him this morning? "I'm angry she deceived me, yes, but..."

But he understood why she'd done it, perhaps better than Violet understood it herself. It wasn't just because she'd wanted to get the sketches for her book. No, he'd offered her far more than that with his courtship—he'd offered her something a lady like Violet Somerset was helpless to resist.

Freedom. Knowledge, and an unmatched chance to pursue it. It was such a simple thing to want, and one she shouldn't have to fight for. How could he hold it against her that she had?

"I don't wish to punish her, Aunt. I just...I'm not sure how..."

I care for her, and I don't know how to go on.

He'd been stunned and angered by her deception, certainly, but any lingering resentment paled in comparison to the regard he had for her—

Regard?

Nick shook his head in disgust. If he couldn't even find the proper words to explain to himself how he felt about Violet, how would he ever find the words to explain it to her? How could he make her understand she was unlike anyone he'd ever known? That he was stunned by her? That her blue eyes made his knees weak, and he dreamed about her smile?

When she talked about bare-knuckle boxing, he wanted to ravish her. Her ink-stained fingers drove him mad, and he was sure she was the only lady in England who could make cobwebs look enticing. He'd stand in the Thames all day for her—he'd ruin every pair of boots he owned if she asked him to. Christ, he even wanted her to sing for him again, and if that wasn't love, then he didn't know what was.

How could he ever explain how grateful he was to her?

She would always be the lady who pulled every string, who seized every chance so she could turn it over and over in her hands until she saw it from every angle. The man he'd been—that lonely man still frozen with grief, so weary of life and so certain it had nothing left to show him—since he'd met her, every moment had become an opportunity, a wonder, another chance to be amazed.

Because of *her*.

She was everything, and he was a tongue-tied, besotted fool. "I don't know how to show her, or how to make her understand that I..."

His aunt's gaze softened, and Nick knew she understood what he didn't know how to say.

"Oh, Nicholas. It's so much easier than you think it is. Talk to her. Reassure her of your affection for her. She's wary of you now, and ashamed of having deceived you. You can hardly blame her for being skittish, given the circumstances, but despite her reticence, it's plain to see she cares for you."

Nick's heart leapt with hope, because at one time he'd thought she cared for him, too.

That day at the Hunterian Museum, those moments afterwards in the carriage, when she'd kissed him...that hadn't been a lie. There'd been nothing false between them then. He'd known it, had felt it with every brush of her lips against his, in every frenzied beat of his heart. The moment she'd kissed him, Nick knew he belonged to her, and now...

She was *his*, just as surely as he was hers.

But he hadn't touched her in two weeks, and every time he looked at her he was flooded with memories of how her hands had felt tangled in his hair, the exquisite touch of her lips on his, and the way she'd held him as he'd shuddered with pleasure in her arms.

It wasn't above a five- or six-hour journey from London to Ashdown Park, his country estate in West Sussex, but Nick planned to take his new wife to an inn in Guildford tonight, regardless. He was half wild with wanting her already, and five hours alone in a close carriage with her seemed an interminable amount of time to wait. Despite their odd courtship, he'd won her, and he intended to have and hold her as soon as he possibly could.

That is, if he could find her. He'd been waiting for her in the entryway for the past twenty minutes, and she still hadn't appeared. "Where the devil is she?" He turned a frustrated frown on his aunt. "How long does it take to dress one small lady?"

Instead of scolding him for the curse, his aunt laughed. "When five sisters are set to the task, far longer than you'd think. I'm sure she'll be down directly. Will you accompany me back to the dining room? I'd like to offer my congratulations to Lady Chase before we depart." His aunt was accompanying them to West Sussex to help her new niece settle into her home.

"Yes, I'll come in a moment." Nick leaned down to kiss his aunt's cheek. She went off toward the dining room, where most of the party was still lingering over the last of the champagne. Nick rounded the grand staircase and strode from room to room, but his search for his wife proved fruitless.

He was just about to return to the dining room himself when a hesitant hand touched his arm, and he turned to find Hyacinth Somerset standing there, an anxious frown on her face.

"Miss Hyacinth?" Nick raised an eyebrow, taken aback by her sudden appearance. Hyacinth was much more subdued than her four elder sisters, and so painfully shy she'd never yet worked up the courage to look Nick in the eyes. He was surprised she'd sought him out now.

"I beg your pardon, Lord Dare." She sank into an awkward curtsy. "Forgive the intrusion, but I wanted to have a word with you, and this was the only time…"

She trailed off with a swallow, and Nick hurried to reassure her. "Of course. It's no intrusion at all, Miss Hyacinth. What can I do?"

"It's, ah, it's about my sister. I—this won't take long, my lord, but I thought you should know Violet is…well, she's very clever, as I'm sure you've realized, and brave, as well—much braver than most ladies of her age and experience."

Nick's lips twitched. "Yes, I couldn't help but notice that. I don't know many young ladies who'd engage in a false courtship so they could dash about London taking sketches of gibbets. Your sister is…quite remarkable."

Hyacinth Somerset must have been heartened by this comment, because her eyes lit with hope, and she dared to venture a step closer. "She is, yes, but she's also…softer about the heart than she appears to be. She's so clever and brave, you see, it's easy to overlook how vulnerable she is. I thought it quite important *you* should be made aware of it, my lord, so you know you must take care with her feelings."

Nick blinked. Hyacinth Somerset, who really was the most timid young lady he'd ever come across, had taken it upon herself to warn him not to hurt her sister. Surprise made Nick fumble over his reply. "I—yes, of course I'll take care to…"

He trailed off as he tried to think of what to say to reassure her, but Hyacinth grew agitated when he hesitated, and she rushed on, her words tumbling one over the other.

"She's far more easily hurt than you'd ever suspect, my lord. The gentlemen of the ton haven't always been kind to her, or the ladies either, come to that. Her intellectual turn has earned her a good deal of mockery, I'm afraid, and—"

"It's all right, Miss Hyacinth." Nick took her hand and pressed it between his own. "I appreciate your concern for your sister, but I assure you, the last thing I would ever do is hurt her, and I won't suffer anyone else to do so, either."

She searched his eyes as if to gauge the truth of his words, then her lips curved in a shy smile. "I'm vastly relieved to hear you say so, my lord. I couldn't bear to think Violet's heart would be broken again."

Again? Nick frowned. Had someone broken Violet's heart?

"There's Violet now, my lord, just there." Hyacinth pointed toward the stairs. "I'll go tell my grandmother you're about to depart."

She went off toward the dining room, and Nick peered around the side of the staircase. There, tucked under the stairs that led to the kitchens below, was a tiny alcove he hadn't noticed before.

A gentleman in a dark blue coat was there, bowing over a lady's hand. It was Lord Derrick, and the lady, half-hidden by the curved wall of the alcove...

Lady Dare.

Nick's shoulders tensed. His new bride didn't look as if she'd been searching for *him*. No, she was smiling up at Lord Derrick, a faint blush on her cheeks, and she looked quite content to remain where she was.

A strange, unfamiliar feeling seized him—something hot and sharp that made his hands fist and his stomach clench. Something that made him stride toward them, grasp his wife's elbow, and draw her away from Lord Derrick.

"Ah, here you are, Dare." Derrick turned to him with a cheerful smile. "I was just offering your countess my heartfelt congratulations on your marriage. She tells me you leave this afternoon for West Sussex."

"That's right." Nick's face felt hot, and he was sure he must be glaring at Derrick. "In fact"—he pulled Violet's arm more firmly through his—"we need to leave at once if we plan to reach Guildford before dusk. Are you ready to go, Lady Dare?"

If Lord Derrick noticed the possessiveness with which Nick uttered those last two words, he didn't acknowledge it. "Safe travels then, Dare." He took Violet's hand in his once again and raised it to his lips. "And Lady Dare. I'm very happy for you both."

"Thank you, my lord." Violet was obliged to call these thanks over her shoulder as Nick hurried her down the hallway, away from Lord Derrick. "My lord? Why are you dragging me down the corridor?"

"Your grandmother is looking for you." The lie rose easily to Nick's lips. "I promised I'd bring you to her before we leave."

They found Lady Chase in the dining room, flushed either with victory at having successfully married her granddaughter to an earl, or perhaps from too many glasses of champagne. When Nick and Violet came to bid her goodbye, she heaved herself to her feet with the help of her cane and held her arms out to Violet.

"My dear child. I see your husband is anxious to leave, so I must bid you goodbye. Well, well, Violet, I don't mind saying you've made me proud today. There now." She patted Violet on the back, and when she drew away her eyes were glistening.

Violet took her grandmother's hand and held it for a long moment. "I'll miss you, Grandmother, and my sisters..." She trailed off, and her mouth twisted as if she were holding off tears. "I'll miss you all."

Lady Chase raised a hand to pat her granddaughter's cheek. "It will get easier, child. I promise you that. Your husband will take care of you. Despite what you may believe, Violet, I wouldn't let you go for anything less."

Violet nodded and clutched at her grandmother's hand as her sisters and friends all crowded around her to fold her in their arms and bid her a final goodbye. Then Nick ushered her out the door, handed her into the carriage, and they were on their way.

Lady Westcott had decided to ride in her own carriage, and after the noise of the wedding breakfast and flurry of good wishes, the silence of Nick's carriage seemed deafening. Violet sagged against the squabs and closed her eyes as if she were exhausted, and she didn't open them again.

Nick remained quiet, watching her. He might have believed she was asleep, but her tense jaw and the rigidity of her shoulders gave her away. She was nervous to be alone with him again, and given what had happened between them the last time they were in his carriage, Nick couldn't blame her.

She must know how much he wanted her. Perhaps she thought he'd ravish her as soon as the carriage door closed behind him? He wouldn't, of course. He was a gentleman, and a gentleman didn't leap upon his innocent bride like a savage.

No matter how lovely she was, or how breathless she made him.

And she *was* lovely—rather pale, yes, and with shadows under her eyes that spoke of sleeplessness—but even so, Nick's breath had caught the moment he first laid eyes on her this morning, and he hadn't yet regained it.

For the ceremony she'd worn a silvery gown with some sort of dainty, sheer fabric draped over the top of it that floated around her when she moved. Nick wasn't versed in ladies' fashions, but he knew what he liked, and his mouth had gone dry at the sight of the creamy skin of her bosom revealed by the wide neck and tiny puffed sleeves of her gown.

He was going to buy her dozens of such gowns—tens of dozens of them—just for the pleasure of easing those maddening little sleeves down her arms and pressing kisses on her bare shoulders.

She'd changed into a carriage dress and heavy cloak for the journey, and not a sliver of her skin was visible, but even so he couldn't take his eyes off her, and if he could judge by the nervous flutter under her eyelids, she was well aware of it.

And yet her eyes remained closed.

The moments passed slowly into an hour, then two, until at last they were within five miles from the inn at Guildford, and she still hadn't opened her eyes, or uttered a single word.

The rain slashed against his window, and as they lurched over every soggy rut of the Great North Road between London and Guildford, Nick could no longer deny the truth to himself.

His aunt was right. His wife was miserable, and he couldn't bear it another moment.

He still didn't know what to say to comfort her, but he had to say something—*anything*—to make her open her eyes and look at him.

"You're fatigued," he murmured at last.

He half-expected her to ignore him, but she didn't. After a moment's hesitation she opened her eyes and offered him a wan smile. "A bit, yes."

"You didn't eat much today. We're but half an hour's ride from Guildford. We'll order dinner once we arrive, and then you can rest."

Her hands twisted in her lap. "Thank you, but I'm not hungry. I…there's something I have to say to you, Lord Dare."

"Not Lord Dare, Violet. Nicholas, or Nick. We're husband and wife now, and it's time you called me by my given name."

"Yes, I—yes, of course. Nicholas. I need to tell you that I—I'm…" She stuttered to a halt, but then she drew a deep breath and met his gaze. "I'm so sorry for deceiving you these past few weeks, and I most sincerely beg your pardon. I wanted to tell you the truth, and I tried to, every day after that night on Cockpit Steps, but I was afraid…"

Nick leaned closer to her—closer than he should have if he intended to keep his hands to himself, because as soon as he caught her warm scent, he was helpless against the urge to stroke the backs of his fingers against her cheek.

"What? What were you afraid of, Violet?"

She stared at him, her eyes huge. "I was afraid if you knew the truth you'd refuse to see me again."

Nick's hand stilled on her face.

The night of the rout, when he found out she'd lied to him—he'd burned with humiliated fury over her deception. But there'd been something else there as well, under the fury, and it was worse than wounded pride, and more powerful than anger.

Hurt.

She'd hurt him. That day, at Wapping Old Stairs, with water seeping into his boots and the sun catching at her hair as she frowned down at her sketchbook—she'd been lying to him that day, and every day before and after, and the lie hurt him more than he'd ever imagined it could.

But even in the midst of his pain and fury, he knew he was no better. He'd been so determined to find a bride as quickly as possible he hadn't even known which lady he was courting. Could he really blame her for using him, when he'd done the same to her?

Their courtship began with a lie, yes, but that didn't mean they had to start their marriage with one, and he needed the truth from her now. "You were afraid I'd refuse to see you, and you wouldn't be able to get the sketches you needed for your book? The book, Violet…was it the only reason you wanted me?"

The question had been tormenting him for the past week. He was desperate to hear her answer, but half-afraid of it, too.

She swallowed. "At first, yes, but then…"

"Then?" He held his breath.

A faint flush rose in her cheeks, and her words emerged in a sudden rush. "And then it wasn't about the book anymore."

She didn't say anything else, or even explain what she meant, but the breath Nick had been holding since the moment he'd discovered her deception left his lungs in a heated rush. "Tell me what it *was* about, Violet."

She gave him a shy glance, but her dark blue eyes were hopeful. "That day we spent at Wapping Old Stairs…after that day, I just wanted…*you*."

The last word was soft, a whisper only, but Nick heard it, and his eyes drifted closed.

"But I know that's no excuse for lying to you, and I—"

"It doesn't matter." He opened his eyes, reached for her hand, and pressed his lips to her palm. "I forgive you. It's done, Violet."

Her eyes went wide. "I—but you were so angry that night. I thought…I didn't think you'd ever forgive me."

"I *was* angry." He stroked his thumb over her cheekbone. "But even then I knew I'd forgive you."

Wonder lit her face, and for the first time since they'd become betrothed, the smile she gave him was genuine. "I don't know that I deserve such a forgiving husband after my deceitful behavior, but it seems I'm to be rewarded with one, after all."

"Is it a reward, having married me, Violet?" His voice was soft. "A reward, and not a punishment?"

Her eyelashes swept down to hide her eyes. "I could ask you that same question. I daresay you never expected to marry a lady like me. No gentleman wants a bluestocking for a wife."

He cupped her face in his palm. "*I* do."

Her eyes filled with questions, but Nick didn't give her a chance to ask them. Instead, he lowered his mouth and hovered his lips over hers, making it clear he wanted to kiss her, but still giving her a chance to pull away.

She didn't. She curled her fingers into the lapels of his coat and parted her lips in invitation.

Nick groaned as he took her mouth with his. He'd only kissed her twice before, but he already knew the shape of her lips, had memorized her sweet taste, and it felt as if he'd been kissing her for years.

Or for a lifetime.

He lifted her arms to twine them around his neck, another groan tearing from his throat when she sank her fingers into his hair. She sighed when his mouth opened over hers, and that breathless little sigh undid him.

He darted his tongue out to trace her bottom lip, and a faint whimper rose from her throat at his urgency, but she didn't pull away from his hungry kiss. Her fingers closed into fists in his hair, and when his lips moved away from her mouth to brush dozens of open-mouthed kisses along her jaw and behind her ear, she responded with a desperate tug.

Her passion, the tiny sting of pain made Nick wild to have more of her. "Violet, let me…" His hands moved restlessly over her back, then settled on her curved hips. "Hold onto me, sweet."

Her tongue met his in a single shy stroke, such an innocent caress, and yet her eagerness had him breathless and panting as he surged inside, his tongue searching for more of her silken warmth.

She grabbed his shoulders with a gasp when he lifted her in his arms and set her down on his lap. He nudged her legs gently apart with his thigh to make a space for himself between them. A helpless moan escaped his lips when he remembered how she'd straddled him in the carriage, stroked him between her thighs again and again until she'd made him shudder with pleasure in her arms.

His cock hardened painfully, and oh, God, he wanted to do that for her, here and now—to make her come again and again as he held her, her breathless cries in his ears as she trembled against him. He slid his hands under her skirts to stroke her thighs, crazed with love and desire, but just then the carriage rattled as they jolted over a deep rut in the road, and it jerked him from his sensual haze.

"Not here, Violet...we're almost at the inn, sweetheart."

Violet's arms tightened around his neck in protest as he slid his hand out from under her skirts. He'd only meant to kiss her gently, to reassure her, not to attack her like an animal. For God's sake, she was his wife now, and as soon as they retired to their bedchamber at the inn he could take her in private, as many times as they both wished.

Surely he could wait another few minutes?

They were both panting, and she was gazing at him with such an adorably confused expression it took all of Nick's self-control not to snatch her back into his arms. "I, ah...I nearly forgot I was a gentleman." He offered her a sheepish smile. "Carriages seem to have that effect on me now."

Her cheeks went even pinker, and she let out a soft laugh that was so charming, and so utterly unlike anything he'd ever heard from her before, Nick couldn't prevent a rush of masculine pride, and he found himself grinning back at her like a besotted fool.

He was going to make love to her tonight, and when they were both sated and she was lying in his arms, he was going to dream about her smile, and that flirtatious little laugh. Tomorrow he would make her laugh again, and for every tomorrow afterwards, whenever that laugh was on the edge of her mouth, he would catch it on his lips.

Chapter Seventeen

"You've hardly touched your dinner, Lady Dare."

Violet jerked her head up, but when she found her husband's warm gaze fixed on her she lowered her eyes at once and resumed pushing her food from one side of her plate to the other. Every time she met his darkened eyes across the table her belly leapt with nervous anticipation.

Dear God. She'd been anxious enough when she wasn't certain what would happen when they retired to their bedchamber. The tension between them, the awkwardness of the wedding ceremony, and his anger over her deception—it was enough to make any young lady dread her wedding night.

But the tension between them had dissipated when she'd begged for his forgiveness, and he'd so graciously offered it in return, and then there'd been all the kissing, and touching, and now, well…whatever interest her husband had in dinner had given way to his interest in *her.* He was twirling the stem of his wineglass between his long fingers, those smoky gray eyes of his fixed on her as if he were anticipating another kind of feast altogether.

Now she was quite certain she *did* know what would happen when they retired to their bedchamber, and she was more nervous than ever.

Not that she hadn't imagined this moment. She had imagined it, more times than she dared to admit even to herself. But now it was here, and he was *there*, and somehow his shoulders looked broader than they ever had before, and his chest and arms more powerful, and wasn't there just the faintest hint of ferocity in the curve of his lips? And soon he wouldn't be *there* at all, but *here*, and…well, it was rather overwhelming.

"May I pour you more wine, my lady?"

His low, rough voice teased along her nerve endings, and a shiver shot up Violet's spine. "No, I—no, thank you."

"Are you ready to retire then?"

He sounded…eager. Violet risked another glance at him and found him watching her, one corner of his full mouth curved in a sensuous grin as he studied her flushed face, and her belly quivered with a delicious ripple at the hot look in his gray eyes.

Nick had ordered their trunks brought up and unpacked while they dined, so when they retired to their room, all would be ready for them. The sheer white nightdress her sisters had chosen for her would be laid out on her bed, and—

No. Not *her* bed. *Their* bed.

"Lady Dare? I asked if you're ready to retire."

Not just eager. Impatient. Dear God, that poor flimsy nightdress would be reduced to shreds. Violet's hand trembled as she laid her fork beside her plate. "Yes, my lord. I'm ready."

"There's no need to look so terrified, Violet." He smiled, and his warm hand covered hers. "I'm not quite the animal you seem to think I am."

Violet bit her lip. Perhaps not, but he *did* have very large hands.

His voice dropped to a low rasp. "I promise I'll take exquisite care of you, sweet."

Violet swallowed. He'd never been anything but gentle with her, and she knew he'd never hurt her, but she might have felt more reassured by his words if his tongue hadn't curled around the word "exquisite" with such sensual promise.

Neither of them spoke as they made their way up the deserted staircase to the bedchamber, but Violet shivered again at the heat of his body close behind her, his warm breath on her neck, his hand brushing against her hip as he reached around her to open the door, and—

"Oh!" A young maid with her hair scraped back into an enormous white cap was standing at a table by the fireplace, but she whirled toward the door when they entered, and dropped the papers she held in her hand with a guilty flush.

"I beg yer pardon, my lord." She bobbed a quick curtsy. "I were jest readying the room for ye." She began to sidle away from the table, her gaze darting toward the open door. "Ring if ye need anything else, aw right? Good night, my lord. Yer ladyship."

Nick raised an eyebrow as the door slammed behind the maid. "What was that all about? She scurried away like a pack of wild hounds was after her. Are we so menacing as that?"

Violet glanced around the room, but nothing seemed to be amiss. Her white nightdress had been draped over the coverlet, as she'd expected, and the small trunk Bridget had packed for the one night's stay at the inn was lined up neatly next to Nick's at the end of the bed. It didn't look as if anything had been taken, but the girl had clearly been anxious to escape—

"What's this?" Nick strolled over to the small table near the fireplace, where the housemaid had been standing when they came in. It was likely placed there for private dining, but now it was covered with dozens of papers that looked as if they'd been hastily shoved into an untidy pile.

Violet's brow furrowed in confusion, but then she froze, her throat closing as her frantic gaze moved over the familiar papers. A few sketches lay scattered across the top of the table, as if the maid had been studying them, and then tossed them aside in a panic when she heard the door open.

"Wait, my lord—"

But it was too late. Nick was already across the room. He'd picked up one of the sketches and was studying it with close attention, an amused smile curving his lips. "Wapping Old Stairs. A perfectly good pair of boots were sacrificed for this sketch." He set it aside, then picked up the one underneath. "Cockpit Steps. Ah, now I see the trouble. The housemaid was nosing about your sketches. Impudent chit, but I doubt she's ever seen anything like these before. It's not surprising such skilled drawings would catch her eye."

Violet hardly heard him as she stumbled over her feet in her rush to get to the table before he could see any more of her sketches. Dash it, how had the housemaid gotten hold of her book? The footmen had been directed to bring up the overnight trunks only, but somehow her sketchbook had come up as well, and—

Oh, no. Please, no...

Violet's throat worked as she realized her private portfolio was there too, open and gaping like a gutted fish, all its contents disgorged and scattered haphazardly across the table like bloody entrails. The girl must have thought she was meant to unpack it, and she'd done a thorough job of it. It looked as if every page of the book had been pulled loose.

Nick was turning the pages over one by one, the smile still twitching on his lips as he paused for a moment to study another sketch. "Bunhill Fields Burial Ground. This is one of my favorites. May I compliment you once again on your excellent rectangles, Lady Dare?"

Violet darted forward and began to snatch the pages up. "The servant has made a mess of them, I'm afraid. Why don't you warm yourself by the fire, my lord, while I gather them all up and put them away."

But Nick was studying a page in his hand, and didn't appear to hear her. "This is your list of sketches? My God, I had no idea there were so many. I haven't seen even half of these. You'll have to show them to me, my lady, but not tonight. I have another form of entertainment in mind for us this eve—"

He fell abruptly silent as one of the papers on the table caught his attention. He set the page in his hand aside, grabbed the corner of the sketch, and slid it out from under the pile. Violet saw at once which one it was, and her heart surged into her throat with a nauseating lurch.

Everything seemed to slow down then, much as it did when one was caught in a nightmare from which they couldn't wake. Violet could only watch in numb horror, her lips moving in a desperate prayer as he studied the page, his brows drawn together in confusion.

Please, please don't let him see—

But her prayers were destined to go unanswered. Fate had caught up to her again, and she was determined to reveal every one of Violet's mistakes, every one of her sins.

Violet didn't want to see his face, didn't want to watch, but part of her must have known she deserved this, because she couldn't tear her eyes away. She saw every single moment of it unfold, and as long as she lived she would never forget the look of puzzled hurt in his eyes when his mind could no longer deny what his eyes so plainly showed him.

For a single, frozen moment he seemed to plead with her—to beg her to reassure him what he saw couldn't possibly be true—but before she could breathe a word, his face hardened.

"The Selfish Rake?"

Violet stumbled the rest of the way to the table and reached out a shaking hand to clutch at his coat. "I drew that sketch the morning after Lord Derrick's dinner party, after you mistook me for Hyacinth. That was weeks ago, Nick. It was dreadfully unfair of me, and it's been weeks since I've seen you in such a way—"

He shook her hand off. "I'm flattered, my lady, to find I was a subject of your intellectual musings, and not merely an escort. Ah, and look. There's an essay to go along with the sketch. Shall we see what opinion you hold on selfish rakes?"

"I didn't...I never meant to..."

But Nick's gaze was already moving over the page. When he reached the end, his head jerked up and the page fell from his fingers and drifted back to the table. "You heard me with Lady Uplands in Lord Derrick's library that night. You...*watched* us?"

Violet squeezed her eyes closed. "I—I'm sorry. I should never have—"

"Why ever not? Come, Violet, we're both aware of how curious you are, and I did bring it on myself with such disgraceful behavior. But you must have been thrilled to witness such a salacious debauchery. Tell me, why didn't you include a description of my cock in your essay? Oh, but wait. Perhaps if I look through the rest of the sketches, I'll find a drawing of it."

"Please, Nick. You don't understand. Once I knew you, I intended to burn that sketch. You must know I don't feel that way about you anymore—"

"Oh, but I understand perfectly, sweet." He smiled at her, but it was an ugly twist of his lips, and his eyes remained cold. "The sketch is a good likeness of me, I'll give you that, and God knows there's no better example of a selfish rake in all of London. Isn't that right, my lady?"

"No. You're not…that's not true, Nick."

Her voice was nearly inaudible, no more than a choked whisper, and he ignored her and snatched up the list of sketches again. "Let's see…no, I don't see 'The Selfish Rake's Cock' here—rather a waste, since surely a talented artist like you could draw it accurately. But there *is* something else here I didn't notice before. You have a chapter entitled 'The Perfect Gentleman.' Well, I suppose if you're going to have the rake you need the gentleman as well, for comparison purposes. But I wonder, Violet—which sketch goes with that chapter?"

Violet's blood ran cold. Oh, God, she'd forgotten about that sketch. If he should find it, there was no explanation she could offer he'd ever believe. She dove forward and scrabbled for the remaining pages on the table, desperate to snatch the sketch away before he could see it, but once again fate was determined to have this moment out to the bitter end, because just as she stumbled into him and grabbed the table to steady herself, Nick found the sketch.

"Ah. Here it is."

She lunged at him to grab it, but he held it out of her reach, and when he saw who it was…

A choked whimper tore loose from Violet's throat as his face drained of color. When he turned to her his lips were white, and his eyes were shadowed with pain and fury. "Lord Derrick."

Since the moment she'd met Nick, Violet hadn't given Lord Derrick a second thought. All of her thoughts, all of her emotions, were tangled up in the man standing in front of her, and whatever she'd once felt for Lord Derrick had faded into insignificance.

It hadn't been love. A girlish infatuation perhaps, an appreciation for Lord Derrick's kindness, but not love. She knew that now. The way her heart soared with joy when Nick smiled at her, the constant ache she felt to touch him, the urge to brush his hair away from his eyes or take his hand—*that* was love, and she'd never felt any of that for Lord Derrick.

Only Nick.

She had to tell him, to make him understand—

"I offer a compliment to your taste, Lady Dare. Derrick's a worthy gentleman. There's none better in all of London, in fact. I should have guessed it, of course—two of your sisters mentioned something about your broken heart. Pity, but it does you credit Lord Derrick should have been the one to break it. Your sisters seem to think your heart is mended, but perhaps you haven't quite overcome the disappointment? You were happy enough to linger with Derrick in the alcove today, and he appeared to be more than satisfied to have you to himself."

Violet recoiled as if from a slap. "No! You don't think…you can't possibly be implying something improper occurred? It's been weeks since I cared for Lord Derrick in that way, and Lady Honora is my friend—"

"And I'm your husband, Lady Dare, but you didn't seem to recall that when Lord Derrick's lips were on your glove, did you?"

"He was offering his congratulations on our marriage, my lord. Nothing more—"

But Nick went on speaking, as if she hadn't offered a word in her defense. "Well, my lady, don't despair. You may yet have a chance to mend your shattered heart. Lord Derrick may tire of his new wife, and you'll be rid of me soon enough."

"Rid of you?" Violet pressed a hand to her stomach to ease the sudden sickening twist there. "What do you mean, I'll be rid of you?"

He shrugged, but the despair in his eyes was at odds with the casual gesture. "Oh, did I forget to mention it? As surely as you used me, I also used you, Lady Dare. I needed a wife, you see, and you happened along at just the right time."

Violet reached out a hand, but there was nothing to grasp, nothing to steady herself with. "You…used me?"

For one instant he seemed to flinch at the question, but then the hard mask descended again, and when he spoke it was with the same casual unconcern as before. "I'm afraid so. Not very gentlemanly of me, I confess, but then I'm a selfish rake, and one can't expect much better from such a man. I've just acquired a new Italian mistress, you see, and I'd hardly had a chance to enjoy her before my aunt dragged me back to England and refused to let me return to the Continent until I'd found a wife. Most inconvenient timing, it not being the season. I'd reconciled myself to a long, dreary stay in London, but then I stumbled upon you, and once I determined you weren't mad, I decided you'd do as well as any other lady."

A tiny gasp of pain escaped Violet's lips, but it was a faint, choked sound—too faint for a sound that felt as if it had been torn from her very soul. "You're…leaving England? You intend to return to Italy at once?"

"As soon as I get an heir on you, yes. It won't be as pleasant a task as we both might have hoped, but it's another requirement of my aunt's, you understand."

Violet kept her gaze fixed on a point just over his shoulder.

Oh, God, I can't look at him…

"We won't attempt the business now, however—not when you look so… distressed. Fatigue, I daresay. Go to sleep, my lady. We leave for West Sussex early tomorrow morning." He gave her a mocking bow, then he strode to the door without sparing her another glance, and closed it behind him.

Violet stood in the middle of the room after he'd gone, still and silent, her body numb, her mind a blank. What was she meant to do now? She didn't know, couldn't think…

Long, silent moments passed before the answer came to her, and when it did it brought no comfort.

There was nothing she *could* do. Not tonight. Perhaps tomorrow, when he'd calmed down, then she could explain, persuade him…

But the tiny flicker of hope stuttered and died before it could spark to life.

His eyes, when he'd looked at her…she'd never seen such coldness in his eyes before, like two frozen gray stones…

She pressed a hand against her mouth to smother the sob that rose to her lips and stumbled toward the bed, her movements stiff and mechanical as she discarded her clothing and donned the sheer white nightdress. She cringed as the silky fabric slid over her skin, but aside from the clothes she wore, it was all she had.

Sleep. She'd go to sleep, just as he'd bade her, and perhaps tomorrow it wouldn't all seem so hopeless.

She was about to slip under the coverlet when she remembered her sketches were still scattered over the table. She dragged herself across the room to gather them together, but she didn't linger over them—didn't look at them at all. She simply shoved them into an untidy pile and stuffed them back into her portfolio.

Papers and ink, nothing more, just as Hyacinth had said. It seemed incredible to Violet she ever could have felt so passionate about them—that she could have ever believed they were so important. What was paper, compared to flesh and bone? Her book—the book she loved so dearly—had it ever been anything more than an excuse, a poor substitute for the only things in life that truly mattered?

She blew out the lamp, crawled between the cold sheets, and lay there for a long time in the silent darkness, trying not to think of Nick.

Where he'd gone, what he was doing, whether he was alone...

She didn't realize she was crying until she felt the wetness on her face. She squeezed her eyes closed to keep the tears from falling, but they persisted, sliding under her closed lids, dampening her eyelashes and streaming down her cheeks until at last, weary from weeping, she fell into an exhausted sleep.

* * * *

Hours later, she awoke with a start. There'd been a noise, a soft click—the door opening?

There was a muted thud, then a second one, the sound of a pair of boots dropping to the floor, then a faint rustle of clothing, and unsteady footsteps approaching the bed.

Nick had returned.

Every muscle in Violet's body drew taut as he stumbled across the room and paused by the bed. A glimmer of light shone under the crack in the door, but it was too dark to see his face. She heard him, though—each one of his deep, rasping breaths as he hesitated beside the bed.

What would he do? Would he crawl in beside her and turn away at once, or—

His hand dropped to the bed, and Violet held her breath as he lifted the edge of the coverlet and slid underneath.

She didn't move—not so much as a twitch—but her heart was racing.

The bed was a large one, and he kept a respectable distance between them, but his body felt enormous next to hers. His side of the bed sagged under his muscular weight, and Violet found herself clinging to the edge of the mattress to keep from rolling into him.

He made no move to touch her. He lay as still as she did, but she could sense him in the dark, the rise and fall of his chest, and his scent, that hint of amber and wood seemed to surround her. Tonight there was something else as well, something rich and slightly sweet that made her want to inhale deeply...

Whiskey.

Had he been drinking all this time? He'd stumbled a bit when he'd crossed the room, and then he'd collapsed into the bed as if someone had shoved him from behind. He must be in his cups—

Violet froze as he shifted on the bed. He rolled onto his side, facing her, and a moment later a large, warm hand touched a lock of her hair. A low, husky sound rumbled from deep in his chest, and then he was stroking her loose hair, his long fingers sliding through the heavy locks, his touch careful, gentle.

He didn't say a word, and Violet, who wouldn't have known what to say even if she could have spoken, also remained silent. Perhaps he thought she was asleep, and wouldn't have touched her at all if he knew she felt every movement of his fingers, heard every one of his heavy breaths rasp through his lungs.

He caressed her hair for a long time, until the rhythmic strokes of his hand had nearly lulled her back to sleep, but then she felt the back of his fingers slide across her cheek.

His breath caught, and his entire body went rigid beside hers.

Violet didn't move, couldn't breathe as he stroked his fingertips across the sensitive skin under her eye. As he touched her face, a low, broken sound tore from his chest.

That's when Violet understood.

She'd been weeping in her sleep, and his fingers had come away wet.

"Don't cry." It was a whisper only, more of a breath than a sound, and slightly slurred from the whiskey, but that small, unexpected kindness made more tears sting her eyes.

He slid to the middle of the bed, draped his arm across her body, and buried his face in her neck. Violet tensed at once, uncertain what was happening. Had he forgiven her, and intended to consummate the marriage, or, dear God, had he *not* forgiven her, and intended to consummate it anyway? She was his wife, and it was his right to do so, but the thought of being so vulnerable to him even as she knew he despised her made a desperate whimper rise to her lips.

"Shhhh." He nuzzled his lips against her ear and caressed her shoulder in long, soothing strokes. "Just want to touch you."

His words were slurred, but his touch remained gentle despite his incoherence, and it felt so good to be held by him Violet let herself melt against him.

Once he felt her relax, Nick slid her nightdress off her shoulder and traced his fingertips over her bare skin. "So soft…"

Violet gasped a little when he leaned over her to press his open lips where his fingers had been, and his mouth grew greedy as he kissed and nipped the tender skin there. He dragged his lips lower, his hand cupping one of her breasts as he suckled at the pale skin just above the low neck of her nightdress.

Violet shifted under him, her hands clutching at his shoulders, but he eased her back down to the bed with a hand in the middle of her chest. "Lie back."

He smoothed his palm over her stomach, then grasped a handful of her nightdress in his fist and raised it over her thighs. He paused to gaze at her after he'd bared her, and a low, hungry groan broke from his lips. His breath quickened and deepened as he slid his hand up the inside of her thigh, nudged her legs open, and brushed a fingertip over her curls.

Violet nearly rolled off the bed at the sensation, but Nick held her, his mouth closing over the tip of her breast as he stroked between her legs again, his thumb circling the tender flesh where she ached the most. His touch was light, but the combination of his hot mouth over her nipple and that slow, maddening finger made her body arch and tighten with anticipation in a way Violet had never felt before.

Whatever her body was doing, Nick seemed to approve of it, because he let out a long, hoarse groan and circled faster, his touch more insistent. When her hips began to arch against his hand he groaned again, and sank one long finger into her, moving it in and out in careful thrusts until something inside her gave way and pleasure rushed from between her legs and over her entire body, so intense she cried out as she twisted beneath him.

After it was over she lay there, dazed, a light sheen of sweat covering her body. Nick smoothed her nightdress down over her legs and drew the coverlet over her. Then he sighed, and something about the sound was so lonely, so hopeless, the tears swelled in Violet's throat again, choking her, until at last she gave way to them, and her body shook with silent sobs.

Nick didn't touch her again, and he never said another word.

When she woke the next morning, she was alone in the bed.

Nick was gone.

Chapter Eighteen

Nick's head was throbbing, his eyes were gritty, and his neck was so sore from being jammed against the carriage window all night that if there'd been any blood to speak of, he would have sworn he'd been decapitated.

And yet despite all this pain and annoyance, his cock remained as hard as a slab of marble.

He ran a weary hand down his face. He didn't recall everything that happened last night after he'd stormed out and left Violet alone in their bedchamber, but he did recall that the rest of the evening involved a great deal of whiskey, and he'd stumbled upstairs in a haze of liquor, vowing to fall into a drunken stupor before he could do any more damage.

Except he hadn't fallen asleep. Instead, the moment he'd slipped between the sheets he'd been overwhelmed by his lust for his wife, and instead of resisting his baser instincts as he'd promised himself he would, like most sotted scoundrels, he'd yielded to temptation.

He'd touched her. Stroked and caressed and tasted her until she'd cried out, then come to a quivering release in his arms. The way she'd arched and squirmed under his fingers, her slick heat—

Christ. He'd been hard ever since, which seemed a fitting punishment for a man who'd reduced his new bride to solitary weeping on their wedding night. When he'd touched her face, and his hand had come away damp with her tears...

Had she been crying for him, or for herself? Or for Lord Derrick?

It shouldn't matter. Her tears couldn't make him forget what she'd done, yet those drops on his fingertips felt like a blow to the chest. His heart was still reeling from it.

He let his head fall back against the squabs and squeezed his lids closed over stinging, bloodshot eyes. He and Violet had been wed for less than one day. Already there were enough lies and betrayals between them to doom their marriage, and now there was the drunken, illicit touching, as well. To make matters worse, after he'd given her pleasure, he'd behaved like every other sotted rake who's committed a debauchery—that is, he'd slunk off to sleep in his carriage.

He should have stayed away from her last night. He should have known as soon as he lay down next to her and inhaled her warm, seductive scent he wouldn't be able to keep from touching her.

That there would be more touching was a foregone conclusion, of course, since touching was a necessary component of getting an heir upon one's wife, and getting an heir upon his wife was a necessity if he was ever going to escape England. But *that* touching would be of the clinical, detached sort—the sort one engaged in only as a means to an end.

Purposeful, not passionate.

Last night he'd given in to the hungry, urgent sort of touching, but it wouldn't happen again. There would be no more stroking her hair, or whispering in her ear—no more tenderness or passion. He'd be respectful of her, of course, but anything more than that would only encourage Violet to believe there was a chance they could overcome the obstacles between them.

There wasn't.

Nick pressed a hand over his closed eyes, but it would take far more than his hand to erase the image of those sketches. They were burned into his brain like a brand, so deep even a scalpel wouldn't excise them. He'd nearly drowned himself in whiskey last night, and even that hadn't been enough to make him forget that drawing she'd done of him.

The Selfish Rake.

Christ, what a fool he was. That day they'd visited the Hunterian, when she'd wrapped her arms around his neck in his carriage afterwards and begged to touch him...

I want to. Not for a sketch. For you. Just for you.

He'd believed her, every word. She'd kissed him so sweetly, and he thought he'd felt truth in every stroke of her hands. He'd been out of his mind with desire for her that day, but his hopes had all disintegrated into smoldering ashes last night when he discovered what she really thought of him.

Just for you...

What had been moments of exquisite tenderness for him was likely nothing more than an experiment for her—a salacious chapter for the bluestockings.

How to Break a Rake's Heart.

At least she hadn't taken a sketch of him when he was shuddering to release beneath her. He supposed he should be grateful for that much. But then perhaps it hadn't been about him at all. Perhaps she'd been thinking of Lord Derrick the entire time, imagining it was *his* hands stroking her, *his* lips tasting her skin...

Nick dug his fingers into his scalp, but there was no escaping it.

Violet had been in love with Lord Derrick. Perhaps she still was.

Lord Derrick had broken Violet's heart when he married Lady Honora. Perhaps it was still broken.

Lord Derrick. Graham's best friend, and so like Graham one could hardly tell them apart when they were boys.

Lord Derrick. Such an ideal gentleman. So perfect in every way.

So much more like Graham than Nick had ever been.

Than he ever could be.

Whatever the state of his wife's heart, it didn't belong to *him*. She might feel affection for him, attraction even, but no lady who'd loved Lord Derrick could ever fall in love with him. It was absurd to even hope for it, as absurd as...

As imagining he could take Graham's place.

He'd already tried, and he'd failed, and his father had never forgiven him for it. He'd learned to live with the burden of his father's disappointment, but if the same were to happen with Violet, if he should fail her as he'd failed his father...

If?

A bitter laugh broke from his lips. There was no question he'd fail her. How could he not? He couldn't be Lord Derrick, any more than he'd been able to be Graham.

Nick tapped his clenched fist against his forehead. Just thinking about Violet and Lord Derrick drove him mad. It made him want to hurt Violet as badly as she'd hurt him. Last night he'd succeeded, but her tears hadn't made him feel any better.

They'd made him feel as if his heart were being ripped from his chest.

What a pity his father wasn't still alive. The old earl would have been so gratified to find he'd been right all along—that Nick was no better a husband than he'd been a son.

There was no future for him and Violet now—no going forward from this. He'd been a fool to think a marriage that began with a lie would ever become anything other than that. He'd done as his aunt asked. He'd married, and he'd remain in England long enough to fulfill the rest of his promise to Lady Westcott, but after that he was leaving England, where it was cold and wet and he'd be forced to make peace with his new brother-in-law, the haughty Marquess of Huntington.

He'd return to Italy, where the sun bathed everything in its warm rays and he could lose himself in Catalina's willing flesh. The sooner Violet accepted that, the better it would be for both of them.

They'd consummate the marriage and make a reasonable attempt at getting an heir, but he'd perform his duty to his title with his usual cool detachment. Surely he could bed his wife without falling into paroxysms of love for her?

He was a Selfish Rake, after all. He'd had plenty of practice.

With any luck the business would be concluded quickly—

"Good morning, Lord Dare. I see you're anxious to be off this morning."

Nick had collapsed into a slouch against the seat, but now he jerked up and glanced through the window to find his aunt peering at him, her lips tight with displeasure. Violet was beside her, but she lingered a few steps behind Lady Westcott, and she didn't meet his eyes.

Damn it. What were his chances of getting an heir on her if she couldn't even bring herself to look at him?

"I await your pleasure, Aunt." He did his best to sound courteous, but his frustration was evident in his curt tone. He did manage to drag himself from the carriage and offer a half-hearted bow, but his aunt didn't look at all impressed with this effort. No doubt his crumpled cravat and disheveled hair dampened the effect.

Lady Westcott arched an eyebrow at him. "It would please me, Lord Dare, if you had appeared the morning after your wedding day looking like a gentleman rather than some bleary-eyed sailor reeking of whiskey, but I see that's rather too much to ask."

"Far too much, Aunt, so I advise you to lower your standards and make your peace with it."

Her face reddened with irritation at this rude reply, but his aunt had always been attuned to his moods, and she knew better than to argue with him when he was so close to the edge of fury, as he was now. "Very well, then. Once the servants deliver the baggage, we're off. That is, if you're ready for the journey to West Sussex, Lady Dare?"

Lady Westcott gestured toward the carriage, but Violet hesitated. "Have you dined?"

She still hadn't met his eyes, and it took Nick a moment before he realized she was addressing him.

His lip curled. "Such touching concern for my welfare, Lady Dare. But I'm not hungry, and I'd just as soon get the journey over with."

She flinched at this cool reply, and Nick blew out a hard breath. It would only make things more difficult if he was rude to her, and yet as soon as he laid eyes on her this morning, frustration and anger began to thrash like a wild thing inside him.

Why must she look so lovely, and why couldn't he tear his gaze away from her lips? They were pinker than usual, a touch swollen, and when he looked at them, every breathless sigh she'd uttered last night, every soft moan, echoed in his head.

"I believe I'll ride with you and Lady Dare the rest of the way to Ashdown Park." His aunt held out her hand, and Nick dutifully took it and helped her into the carriage. He turned to offer his hand to Violet next, but she refused to notice it, and boarded the carriage without his assistance.

Nick waited until the servants finished loading the baggage, then he threw himself into a corner of his carriage and lapsed into a moody silence. His head ached like the devil, his aunt was in a snit, and his bride couldn't bring herself to touch him.

It promised to be a delightful journey.

His aunt and wife ignored him in favor of making polite conversation between themselves, which suited Nick just fine. He closed his eyes and tried to will the tension from his limbs, and for a while it seemed to work, but as they approached the border of Surrey and made their way into West Sussex toward Ashdown Park, Nick's hard-won peace deserted him.

It had been nearly three years since he'd been to his childhood home. Avoiding the place after Graham's death had been the only thing he and his father had in common, but now here he was, back again.

It felt as if no time at all had passed, and yet at the same time, everything had changed.

Graham was gone, and whatever fond memories Nick cherished of his time in West Sussex had been lost in a sea of pain and grief. Nothing short of a permanent escape to the Continent could ever have induced him to set foot near the place again.

But the Dare name and legacy must be preserved at all costs, mustn't it? And Lady Westcott, with her strict sense of propriety and her piles of money, must have her way in all things, no matter who it hurt.

His fury began to build until at last Nick's eyes flew open. He needed an outlet, a target for his rage, and as soon as his gaze settled on his aunt, he found it. Her hands were clasped neatly in her lap, every fold of her gown falling in perfect, graceful lines, and she was watching him.

Waiting.

A grim smile stretched Nick's lips. She'd known all along he'd explode. She'd simply been waiting for it to happen, and he wouldn't dream of disappointing her.

"I see my father was too busy drinking and wagering away my fortune to waste any of his precious time here. I confess I didn't expect much of the old pile, my lady, but it's even shabbier than I imagined it would be."

"Yes, well, it's been sadly neglected, I'm afraid." Lady Westcott's tone was even, neutral.

It infuriated Nick she should be so calm while his stomach churned with anger and pain. "I suppose no one saw much reason to keep it up after Graham was murdered. Once the heir is dead, what's the point, after all?"

He used the ugliest words he could, and made his voice as harsh as possible. Violet sucked in a shocked breath, but his aunt never flinched. "The heir *isn't* gone, Nicholas. You're Lord Dare, and you're right here."

"Me? Oh, come now, Aunt. I'm nothing but a poor substitute for the true heir—a last resort, as it were. A disappointing son, a disappointing nephew, and now destined to become a disappointing husband, as well."

Violet gasped. "No! I never said—"

He interrupted her with a short laugh. "You didn't have to say it, Lady Dare. You wrote it down, remember? Christ, you drew a bloody picture of it."

God, he hated this. Hated the look of despair on her face, hated that he'd been the one to put it there, and hated himself for his pettiness. He hated this place, and he hated his father, and he hated that no matter what he'd done, or how hard he'd tried, he'd never been good enough to take Graham's place.

"It's a pity, truly, that I should have proved such a disappointment, but anyone would have proved a disappointment in comparison to Graham. Except, perhaps, Lord Derrick. He is, after all, the perfect gentleman. Isn't that right, Lady Dare?"

A flush of red colored her cheekbones. "I've had enough of your insinuations, my lord. I told you last night how I feel about Lord Derrick. If you have doubts about my affections, why don't you say so? I'd be more than happy to reassure you."

"Oh, I'm sure you would, but then you have a history of lying, my dear, and about the most inconsequential things. Your name, for instance."

Violet stared at him, her mouth working, but before she had a chance to say a word, Lady Westcott spoke, her tone matter-of-fact, as if everyone else in the carriage hadn't just succumbed to hysterics. "I daresay you're a bit distressed to see your new home in such a dilapidated state, but I can assure you, Lady Dare, despite the air of neglect, it's a beautiful property. It takes its name from Ashdown Forest, you know, which lies just to the west of the estate, in the heart of the High Weald area."

Violet blinked at the abrupt change in topic. "I, ah—I'm anxious to see it, my lady."

"The house is Elizabethan," Lady Westcott went on. "Quite comfortable, or it will be again once you and Nicholas take it in hand. Oh, and there are four acres of lovely gardens."

Violet nodded politely, but she looked as if she didn't know quite what to say to this recitation. "I—it sounds lovely."

"Oh, it is. I grew up there, of course, just as Nicholas did, and it's a wonderful house for children. My brother, the late Earl of Dare, and I used to run quite wild about the grounds, and it was the same for Nicholas and his brother Graham. Graham was two years older and a faster runner, but Nicholas was the better shot. It was Nicholas their father relied on to bring home braces of pheasants during the season."

"That's enough, Aunt."

Nick's voice was hard, with a note of warning underlying it, but if his aunt heard it, she chose to ignore it. "Hunting and fishing, and of course riding, especially Nicholas. Graham was the more studious of the two boys—always with his nose in a book—but Nicholas was too restless to sit still for long, and as a child he enjoyed riding above all things. I suspect that's still true. Do you intend to ride a good deal while you're here, my lord?"

"Stop it." Nick struggled to pull breath into his lungs, to clear the sudden lump from his throat. "I know what you're doing, and it won't work."

"I'm telling your bride about your childhood, Nicholas. Nothing more." Lady Westcott gazed steadily at him for a long moment, then turned back to Violet. "Nicholas wasn't above five years old before it became clear he would become an avid sportsman. Does your family hunt, Lady Dare? Perhaps we'll host a fox hunt this fall—"

Nicholas slammed his fist against the roof of the carriage, making both ladies jump.

Lady Westcott braced herself against the seat as the driver drew hard on the ribbons and the carriage came to a sudden, crashing halt. "Nicholas! What are you—"

Nick wrenched open the carriage door and leapt to the ground. The manor house was an easy walk from where they'd stopped, and he couldn't bear to sit in the carriage for another minute. "I'll walk from here." His face felt numb as he met his aunt's eyes. "I wish you ladies a pleasant afternoon."

* * * *

He should have wished his bride a pleasant evening, or perhaps bid her goodnight, because the sun had set and the house was shrouded in darkness long before Nick saw her again.

He spent the day prowling the grounds of the estate, and by that evening he'd locked himself alone in his father's study with a bottle of whiskey, his hands shaking as he raised glass after glass to his lips.

But the drunken stupor he wished for eluded him.

Ashdown Park, his memories of Graham and his father, his aunt, his *wife*—Jesus, how had he ended up back here, and how long would it be before he was buried so deep there was no longer any hope of escape?

Damn it, he had to do *something...*

He staggered to the desk and fumbled through the papers he'd brought from London. The servants had stacked them neatly on top of the desk, but he tossed them aside one by one until the desk and floor were littered with them.

Then, at last, crumpled beneath a stack of old ledgers, he found what he was looking for.

Nick rummaged through the drawers until he found a quill, then he quickly signed and dated the document. He stared at his signature scrawled across the bottom of the page for a long time, but the relief he'd hoped for didn't come.

He threw the document down and tore through the desk again, snatched out a blank piece of paper, and began to write a letter, but he only managed to scratch out a dozen words before the quill fell from his hand.

Catalina's face...he could no longer recall it. Her dark eyes insisted on turning blue in his mind's eye, and the sleek black hair kept giving way to a memory of fair curls, so soft and heavy against his fingers...

He shoved the papers into the desk drawer and let his head fall into his hands.

The fire had died by the time Nick grabbed his whiskey bottle and made his way up to his bedchamber. He stripped down to his breeches, but instead of climbing into his bed he found himself with his ear pressed to the door that connected his apartments and his new countess's bedchamber.

All was silent on the other side.

He hadn't intended to pay his wife a midnight visit, but what if she was weeping again?

Damn it, she was his wife, and he had a duty to see she was comfortably situated in her bedchamber and not on the verge of hysterics over that ugly scene she'd witnessed in the carriage this morning, or the dilapidated state of Ashdown Park.

He had another duty, as well—consummate his marriage, and get a child on his bride. The sooner he undertook the business, the sooner he could crawl free of the weight of his wife and aunt's smothering expectations and leave England behind.

It wasn't as if he had to linger over it. A quick, efficient consummation was all that was required. Surely he could manage that much.

He winced at the creak the door made as he eased it open. Aside from the dying fire the room was dark, but he could just make out a small, still shape huddled in the middle of the enormous bed.

A quiet breath left Nick's lungs as he crept across the room and paused beside the bed. She was asleep, her fair curls spread out across her pillow. There was no trace of tears tonight, and yet even in sleep, she looked…sad.

Before he could stop himself, he reached out to stroke a stray tendril of hair away from her forehead. The muted orange light from the fire played over her, and he'd never seen anything as beautiful as her face, with her mouth so soft in repose, and her long eyelashes resting against her pale cheeks.

She stirred but didn't wake, and Nick eased onto the bed beside her, his palm moving over the silky strands of her hair again and again, his chest tight. She looked far too young, too lovely and innocent, to be doomed to such a hopeless marriage.

Her chest rose and fell in a soft sigh, and she shifted closer to him, instinctually seeking more of his soft touches against her hair, the stroke of his fingertips across her cheek.

And he…he was weak and debauched, because as soon as she settled on her back beside him with her warm hip pressed against his thigh, his gaze was drawn to her curves, the dark pink of her nipples peeking through the sheer white nightdress, the shadows between her legs.

But this was what he'd come for, wasn't it? She was his wife, and a husband was obligated to take his wife's innocence. He needed an heir, and he wouldn't get one by gazing stupidly at her while she slept.

He watched her face as he traced the tip of his finger around one of her nipples, the softest touch only, just enough to make the tender bud rise so he could lean down and dart his tongue over it. She let out a soft sigh, still half asleep, but when he dragged his tongue over her nipple again, her eyes fluttered open.

A faint cry left her lips when she saw him hovering over her, and she struggled to sit up, but Nick shook his head, and wrapped a gentle hand around her shoulder to ease her back down onto the bed. "Let me touch you. I won't...no matter what's happened between us, Violet, I will never hurt you."

The whispered lie burned on his lips, because he *would* hurt her—had already hurt her, as surely as she'd hurt him, and he'd do so again when he left her behind.

She didn't answer, but when he leaned over her to lick and kiss her nipples, her fingers slid into his hair. He teased the tip of his tongue over that pretty peak again and again until he couldn't hold back any longer, and opened his ravenous mouth over the straining bud to draw her deep inside. She gasped as he suckled first at one nipple and then the other, and her fingers tightened in his hair.

Not to push him away, but to pull him closer.

Nick caught his breath at this unexpected show of trust—a trust he didn't deserve, but one he'd take, because he couldn't make himself do anything else. He buried his face between her breasts for long moments, inhaling her warm scent before he began to kiss and nip his way down her stomach, his tongue tracing her skin as he eased lower and opened his mouth to taste the pale flesh of her belly, right above her curls.

He hadn't come to her tonight to taste her, or to bring her to pleasure with his mouth, but even as a distant part of Nick's brain acknowledged this wouldn't get him the heir he needed, he didn't stop. For all his promises to himself to remain detached, to take her quickly, to keep a distance between them, he couldn't stop.

Jesus. He couldn't stop.

He needed to have her like this—to feel her grow wet against his mouth, to make her come apart on his tongue.

She tensed when he moved between her legs, and grabbed his wrist to stop him from raising the silky fabric of her nightdress, but he made a soothing sound in his throat and pressed a tender kiss to her thigh, and after a moment her grip relaxed.

"So pretty right here," he murmured, dragging a finger through her curls before probing delicately between her thighs to open her for his mouth. She cried out, pushing at his head and trying to squirm out from beneath him, panicked at the first stroke of his tongue, but Nick held her thighs open to him, his hands gentle, and burrowed between her folds until he found her sweet center.

She let out a small cry and jerked against him, her thighs going rigid in his hands as he teased his tongue over her damp pink flesh. His strokes were light but steady and insistent, his tongue circling that tender bud until the unfamiliar sensations overwhelmed her and she began to gasp and squirm against him.

He groaned, so hard for her he was thrusting against the bed as he darted his tongue over her again and again, maddened by her breathy gasps. "Taste so sweet…want you to come on my tongue."

She clutched at his hair as her hips moved against his face in a silent demand, chasing his tongue, her cries growing more desperate as the pleasure continued to elude her, until Nick captured the tiny bud between his lips to suckle hard, letting his teeth graze her as he sank one long finger inside her.

A low sob broke from her lips and she writhed against him, and Nick stayed with her as she arched her back with pleasure, his lips and tongue gentling when he felt the tension leave her body.

When she went limp against the bed, he rested his head against her thigh to catch his breath, his eyes closing when she reached for him to sift her fingers through his hair.

Now. Take her now.

Her breathing was slow and even, her body boneless, and he was so hard for her, aching to sink into her damp heat. He could hold her in his arms and move inside her, listen to her sighs and moans as he coaxed her to another release. All it needed was for him to slide up her body, ease her legs apart, lodge his hips between them, and it would be over with a few careful thrusts.

But none of it would happen tonight.

Nick rolled onto his side, away from her, and threw an arm over his eyes.

He would take her innocence, and he'd get his heir, because he didn't have any other choice, but not tonight—not when he could still feel the soft drag of her fingers in his hair, still taste the sweetness of her release on his lips.

Tonight, no matter how much he might wish to, he couldn't fool himself into thinking she was his. It didn't matter that she was his wife, that her innocence was his to take. It didn't matter that she was obligated to bear him an heir, or that he was the earl and she was his countess, or that they were both responsible for the Dare legacy.

Even now, while she was still breathless from the pleasure he'd given her, she wasn't his.

She would never be his, because the specter of Lord Derrick would always be between them, and Nick, who'd spent his entire life being second in his father's eyes, couldn't bear to be anything but first in hers.

He drew her nightdress down to cover her and rose from the bed, but before he could turn away he caught her eyes, so wide and hopeful in her flushed face, and he paused to cup her cheek in his hand.

"I wish I could be…I'm sorry I'm not a better man, Violet."

She made a small, pained sound in her throat, and Nick thought he saw her reach out to grab his hand, but the fire had died to embers, and the darkness pressed upon his eyes, and before he could be sure, he made himself turn away.

Chapter Nineteen

When Nick touched her, it felt like a dream. When her body was arching under his hands, when he was wringing sighs from her lips, Violet could almost convince herself it was one.

But her mind knew better.

His warm breath in her ear, his soft murmuring, his fingers stroking her damp flesh—underneath the sweetness, the bliss—her mind recognized the truth.

This was no dream. It was a nightmare.

They'd been married for two days, and he hadn't made love to her. Their marriage remained unconsummated, and her virginity, if not her innocence, very much intact.

He'd given her pleasure tonight, the kind of sweet, aching pleasure Violet had thought only existed in dreams, and then he'd slipped out again without taking his own release, and without making her his.

She lay still, her limbs melting into the soft bed, her body still humming with ecstasy from his touch. Sleep tried to pull her into its arms, to wrap her in soft, gray oblivion, but she'd never been one to ignore the whisperings of her mind, and her eyes remained open, her unblinking gaze fixed on the heavy silk draperies hanging from the canopy above her.

Nick's face, when he'd seen those sketches...oh, she couldn't bear to think of the hurt, the betrayal in his eyes when he'd raised his gaze to hers. Tears leaked from the corners of Violet's eyes and kept falling until they dampened the hair at her temples.

I'm sorry I'm not a better man.

Violet gasped at the pain of it, the irreparable tear it left in her heart. She rolled over onto her side and clutched a pillow to her chest, her furious tears scalding her cheeks, falling so fast now she thought she might drown in them.

It would be easier that way—easier to curl up and weep while her husband lay alone in his bed believing his bride preferred another man to him, that she didn't care for him—but Violet had discovered long ago she wasn't destined to tread the easiest path.

She'd had to struggle to get anything that had ever mattered to her, and nothing had ever mattered to her as much as Nick. She wanted all of him, his body and his heart, and not just this ghost who crept into her room and then disappeared again before she could see his face, as soon as the darkness gave way to dawn.

Violet slid her feet to the cold floor, dressed herself, and sat on the edge of her bed with her fingers wrapped around her sketchbook. She waited until the patch of sky in her window lightened to a pale gray, then she rose, slipped out her door, and padded silently down the hallway to Lady Westcott's room.

It was early still—far too early to disturb her ladyship in her bedchamber—but Lady Westcott opened on the first knock, and she didn't look surprised to see Violet standing there.

"Good morning, Lady Dare." She stood aside and gestured for Violet to enter. "You're awake early this morning."

Violet didn't mince words. "I never went to sleep. I've done something dreadful, Lady Westcott, and I—I don't know how to fix it. I need your help."

It was an ominous enough declaration, but Lady Westcott didn't blink at it. "Something dreadful? How unfortunate. Perhaps you'd better sit down and explain it to me."

Violet took a seat on a settee, pulled the sketches of Nick and Lord Derrick from her sketchbook, and handed them over to Lady Westcott. "I did the one of Lord Derrick months ago, and haven't thought of it since. The other…" Violet hesitated, her face flushing with misery. "I'd known Lord Dare for less than a day when I drew it. I don't see him that way at all now, and haven't for some time, but—"

"But Nicholas saw these sketches, and now he believes you're in love with Lord Derrick." Lady Westcott gave her a sharp look. "*Are* you in love with Lord Derrick, Lady Dare?"

"No. I never was. I mistook friendship for love, but what I felt for Lord Derrick was nothing more than a childish infatuation. I know that now. I tried to explain it to Lord Dare, tried to tell him—"

"But he didn't believe you. No, he wouldn't, I'm afraid." Lady Westcott met Violet's gaze, and her gray eyes were shadowed with pain. "Nicholas's elder brother, Graham—has he ever told you anything about how Graham died?"

"No, never. That is, I know his death was sudden and tragic. Nick's never spoken of it to me, but if he cared for his brother as I care for my sisters, he must have been devastated by the loss."

"He was. We all were, particularly my brother, the previous earl. He doted on Graham—we all did. Graham was…well, it's difficult to do justice to him in words, but he was the best of men. He was killed by a highwayman on his way back here, to Ashdown Park to assist his father with repairs to the estate. Both my brother and Nicholas blamed themselves for his death—the previous Lord Dare for calling Graham here, and Nicholas, well…because he lived, I suppose. Graham was meant to be the heir, of course—Nicholas never expected to become Lord Dare, and he's never felt worthy of the title."

Violet's body went cold.

That ugly scene in the carriage between Nick and Lady Westcott yesterday—the throb of despair in Nick's voice when he spoke of his brother, that dark laugh when he'd said he was nothing more than a poor substitute for the true heir.

"Nicholas tried to become everything to his father after Graham's death. He came back to Ashdown Park and did all he could to be the son my brother demanded, but nothing he did was ever good enough. It breaks my heart even now to think of how hard he tried." Lady Westcott's voice roughened, and she trailed off.

Violet took Lady Westcott's hand in hers. "He gave up, and went off to Italy?"

"No. I could see what his father was doing to him, and I sent Nicholas away to the Continent before it could destroy him. My brother wasn't a wicked man, Lady Dare, but the death of his wife when Graham and Nicholas were young, and then Graham's sudden death…life ruined him, and he took his misery out on Nicholas."

Violet squeezed Lady Westcott's hand, her eyes burning with tears for her husband.

Two years of struggling with his grief, two years of living in the long shadow cast by his brother. Two years in Italy, hiding from the pain of his father's disappointment, and two years of believing he wasn't worthy of his father's love. The title, the estate, the expectations—all of it thrust upon him by the sudden, tragic death of a beloved brother.

It must have tasted like ashes in his mouth.

"You must understand, Lady Dare. I love Nicholas with all my heart. I never wanted or expected him to try to take Graham's place. I've only ever wanted him to find his own happiness, but Nicholas's father tainted everything for him, even the way he sees himself. These drawings..." Lady Westcott picked one up, and her hand was shaking. "They confirm his deepest fears. I know you never meant to hurt him, my dear, but when he saw these he would have felt, once again, that he was to be forced into another man's place—that you judged another man as more worthy of your love than him."

I'm sorry I'm not a better man...

For Nick to come back to England at last only to find himself wed to a lady he believed loved another, and to be trapped with her in a crumbling estate that should have been his brother's...

Dear God, what had she done?

"I love him, Lady Westcott, more than I ever thought I could love anyone. Please." Violet clutched at the hand in hers, her heart fluttering with panic. "I have to fix this. Tell me how...tell me what to do."

Lady Westcott's eyes were glistening with tears. "Oh, my dear. If you were any other lady I'd say there's nothing you can do, but you're special, Violet, and Nicholas feels that in you just as surely as I do. He's different with you, you see. If there's a lady in England who can help Nicholas find his way, it's you."

"*Me?* But I don't...how, my lady?"

She wasn't special, and she never had been. She wasn't a seductress or a belle, or some irresistible beauty like Lady Uplands. She wasn't charming, and she hadn't the first idea how to tease or flirt or coax a man with soft words and beckoning smiles. She was awkward, impatient, and abrupt. As far as London society was concerned, she'd never been anything more than an oddity, tedious at best and mad at worst. She was a bluestocking, with ink stains on her hands and dust in her hair, and—

She was a bluestocking.

Violet went still, her gaze finding Lady Westcott's.

Of course. She was a bluestocking, and bluestockings had something better than charm, or beauty, or a perfect flirtatious smile.

Knowledge.

She didn't ask herself whether it would be enough.

It *would*, because it had to be.

Violet gathered the sketches together and shoved them back into her sketchbook. "I have an idea."

Lady Westcott's lips curved in a hopeful smile. "What will you do?"

Violet squeezed Lady Westcott's hand, then rose and walked to the door. "The only thing I know how to do, my lady."

No one saw her as she made her way down the grand staircase and slipped into the library. She closed the door behind her, and immediately erupted into a sneezing fit that left her nose red and her eyes streaming with tears.

When she could see again, the first thing Violet noticed was the dust. It covered every surface, and no doubt lingered between every page of the thousands of books on the tall mahogany shelves. It looked as if the servants had simply closed the room after the family left, and hadn't set foot in it since.

Well, that wouldn't do, but at the moment the dust wasn't her first concern. Nick was, and as every bluestocking worth that title knew, a good plan always began with a visit to a library.

She might not be a belle, and she might not know how to charm, seduce, or court her husband, but she could use the talents she *did* possess to help him set Ashdown Park to rights again. She'd read about modern farming practices, and she'd accumulated other bits of knowledge in her studies that might prove useful. If Nick could make this place his home again—if he could see it as *his* and not as a legacy he'd stolen from his dead brother, then perhaps he could begin to see himself as more than just a lesser version of Graham.

As more than just The Selfish Rake.

Violet took a determined step toward the first set of shelves. A book on estate management might give her some ideas, and something about how to organize servants, and how to care for a grand manor house, as well.

Violet sneezed again, and drew her sleeve across her eyes to clear them. It *was* a great pity no one had ever thought to write a book on how to court one's husband. Perhaps one day she'd write one herself, but until then...

She'd never let a little dust stop her before.

* * * *

By the time Violet finished in the library, peeked into every neglected corner on the ground floor of Ashdown Park, and filled five pages with scribbled notes, the sun had risen and was doing its best to emerge from a sky full of dark December clouds.

She was ready for Nick.

She soon found out, however, Nick wasn't ready for her.

For her, or anyone else.

Violet spent over an hour pacing from one end of her bedchamber to the other, tensed for any sound on the other side of the connecting door, but there was nothing but tomb-like silence.

She managed to hold off for a second hour, then a third, and then, overcome with impatience, she finally rang the bell for Bridget.

Her lady's maid appeared a short while later, and the moment she crossed the threshold and got a good look at Violet, she set the tea tray in her hands down, jabbed her fists onto her hips, and announced, "Ye look a perfect fright. What have ye been doing, crawling about the attics on yer hands and knees?"

Violet made a feeble attempt to tidy her hair, felt at once it was useless, and shrugged. "No, the library."

"Well, I might a' known." Bridget pointed an accusing finger at Violet. "Ye're covered in dust an' grime. I daresay ye've ruined that gown, and—"

"Oh, for pity's sake, will you hush? I have other gowns, and I need you to help me into one of them at once."

"I'll do no such thing until ye have a wash and let me brush yer hair, and ye have yer breakfast like a proper countess does."

Violet recognized the stubborn look on Bridget's face and let out a groan. "But I've so much to do this morning, Bridget. I haven't time—"

"Ye'll find the time, and no arguing, miss. This isn't yer grandmother's house, and I won't have ye running about like a savage. Yer a married lady now, and a countess. Besides, do ye really want that handsome husband of yer's seeing you looking like ye've been drug through a knothole?"

That gave Violet pause. She'd never lingered much over her toilette, preferring to keep it brief and practical, but she *was* a married lady now, and she was wed to a devastatingly handsome man who'd shown far more appreciation for her appearance than she'd ever dared hope he would. If he should have a mind to stroke her hair again as he had last night, she didn't want him coming away with a handful of cobwebs for his efforts, did she?

A blush crept into her cheeks, and Bridget noticed and let out a loud cackle. "That's what I thought."

As it happened, Violet needn't have worried about the time, because even after she'd washed, dined, changed into a fresh gown, and let Bridget brush her hair until it shone, Nick still hadn't stirred from his bedchamber.

"For goodness' sake, what's the matter with him? Why doesn't he rise? Bridget, go down and see if you can coax Gibbs into waking him."

Bridget sniffed. "Never known a man more full of himself than that Gibbs. He's stiffer than a corpse, my lady. He won't stir a step to help me, or you either, you may depend upon that."

"Why, Bridget, there was a time when you could harass a corpse out of its coffin, but if you mean to say you've met your match at last, then—"

"Met me match, indeed." Bridget snorted at the very idea. "Certainly not, leastwise not in that dry old stick. All right, then, I'll get him up here quick enough, but don't think I don't see what you're doing, my lady."

Violet had no idea what Bridget did to persuade Gibbs to do her bidding, but when the maid returned she was flushed with triumph, and not five minutes later Violet heard Nick's bedchamber door creak open, and muted male voices on the other side of the wall.

"Bridget, you're brilliant! However did you get him to—"

Crash!

The loud noise made them both jump, and Bridget slapped a hand over her mouth. "Oh, mercy. It sounds like he knocked the tray—"

"Out! And don't bloody come back until you're called!"

Violet blanched at Nick's furious roar, but she couldn't quite prevent a grin at such a shameful display of unapologetic bad temper. "Well, it, ah—it sounds as if his lordship is awake at last."

Bridget's eyes were wide. "We were better off when he weren't."

"Yes, please do go down and offer my apologies to Gibbs, won't you, Bridget? You may assure him I'll never ask for that favor again."

No, if Nick was going to fall into tempers and shout until the windows rattled, then he could shout at her. From now on, she'd handle her husband herself. How fortunate she had such quick reflexes. One wouldn't think she'd need them for a courtship, but here they were.

Once Bridget had scurried out the door, the tray rattling in her hands, Violet crossed her bedchamber, and, throwing her shoulders back with determination, she opened the connecting door and slipped into Nick's room, closing it with a soft click behind her.

Nick's hearing was evidently as acute as her reflexes, because he bolted upright in the bed, a frightening scowl on his face. "Damn you, Gibbs, I told you to *get out*—"

His mouth dropped open when he saw Violet standing there. "What the devil are you doing in my bedchamber?"

Violet hadn't expected him to be overjoyed to see her, but the short speech she'd planned to deliver froze in her throat as she stared at him, unable to say a word.

His chest was bare.

Oh, dear God, where was she meant to look?

Violet's brain might not have known the answer to that question, but her eyes certainly did. His shoulders were so…and the hard muscles in his arms were like…and his chest, the solidity of it…she'd felt it before, slid her palms over it, but even so she never would have guessed it was so, so…

And his skin. Smooth, stretched taut over all those hard angles, and dark hair, just enough to be intriguing but not enough to overwhelm, and…

Nipples. Strangely tempting.

Violet jerked her gaze away, her face bursting into flame.

"Lady Dare? I asked you a question. What are you doing in my bedchamber?"

His voice had deepened to a low rasp and her skin prickled with awareness. "I thought we might…that is, I thought you might…"

"Yes? You thought I might *what*, my lady?"

Was she imagining the suggestive note in his voice? "Take me on a tour of the estate. Your aunt showed me the gardens and the house yesterday, while you were…otherwise engaged, but I'd like to see the park, as well."

It was the wrong thing to ask, because Nick's face went hard. "Have my aunt take you today, then. She's far more enthusiastic about the place than I could ever be."

No, his tone was not at all suggestive, or even friendly. It was dismissive. Violet's chin rose a notch. "I'd prefer to go with you, my lord."

His gray eyes narrowed. "You'd best get accustomed to disappointment, Lady Dare. I'm fatigued, and don't choose to ride out today."

Today, or any day.

He didn't say it, but Violet could see Nick's future unfolding before her eyes as clearly as if she were looking into a gypsy's glass ball. He'd spend his days sleeping and his nights drinking until, inevitably, he put a child in her belly, and once he did, he'd leave England and never return.

She didn't doubt he was fatigued. Despair led to a numbing, exhausting inertia, and if she let him succumb to it today, it would be that much more difficult to rouse him tomorrow. But how to convince him? He clearly considered the matter settled, because he'd already disappeared back under the coverlet.

This courtship wasn't going at all well.

Violet turned back toward the door with a frown, ready to retreat and marshal her forces for the next day, but she paused with her hand on the door.

That day he'd taken her to Execution Dock, he'd insisted on standing between her and the Thames while she took her sketch. His brow had furrowed with increasing anxiety with every step she'd descended, until at last he'd sacrificed his boots to a watery ruin to position himself so he'd catch her if she slipped.

His lordship might feign indifference, but underneath it he hid a fiercely protective streak. Perhaps it wasn't quite fair to use such a noble trait against him, but it *was* for his own good.

"Very well, my lord." Violet took care to keep her tone bland. "I beg your pardon for disturbing you. I can tour the estate alone. If I'm back by teatime, perhaps we can—"

She didn't get any further.

"What the blazes do you mean?" He shot upright in bed and fixed her with a ferocious glare. "You will *not* tour the estate alone, Lady Dare."

"Why ever not?" Violet lifted her shoulder in a shrug, and did her best not to stare at his glorious chest, which was once again on display. "Now I think on it, it's been ages since I've had a ride alone in the country. It sounds just the thing."

"You'll take my aunt and a groom with you, my lady, or you won't go at all."

"Oh, no. I'm afraid that won't do. Your aunt is fatigued from the journey yesterday, and intends to spend the day resting." Violet bit her lip guiltily, but then she didn't know for certain it was a lie. Perhaps Lady Westcott *was* fatigued. "And I prefer a solitary ramble. But you needn't concern yourself, my lord. I'm an accomplished rider."

He snorted. "You could be the bloody cavalry, and I still wouldn't permit you to ride out alone."

Violet jabbed her hands onto her hips. "The cursing is unnecessary, my lord, and as to my riding alone, you're being silly. I'll be perfectly fine—"

"Silly!" He sputtered with indignation. "There's nothing silly about—"

"Oh, go back to sleep, my lord." Violet turned her back on him and reached for the door again, but before she could open it, his low growl stopped her.

"Not one step further, Lady Dare."

Violet heard a rustling as the bedcovers were tossed to the floor, and pressed her face against the door to hide a smile.

* * * *

Nick thought they'd take an easy trot over the grounds closest to the house, and then make a quick visit to the stables. Violet would ask a few simple questions, he'd answer them, and that would be the end of it.

Bloody foolish of him.

This was Violet, after all. He should have known better.

She kept him out for hours, riding across field after field, inspecting the farmlands and assessing the fencing and equipment. She quizzed him about tenants, livestock, turnip and clover crop rotations, nitrogen in the soil, acreage in arable lands, fertilizers, and wheat, barley, and oat yields at length and in such precise detail Nick decided she must have read *The Complete Farmer* from cover to cover.

Surprisingly enough, he'd retained more than he imagined from his brief time on the estate before he'd left for Italy, and he managed to answer a good many of her questions, though for the life of him he couldn't have said how many lambs they'd had the previous year.

When they at last returned to the house, both of them soaked to the skin from a sudden downpour, Nick, who'd been fantasizing about a fire and a bottle of whiskey for the past four hours, instantly set off in the direction of his study.

He hadn't made it more than half a dozen steps before she stopped him. "Where are you going, my lord?"

Nick reacted how one might expect a man with freezing cold water trickling down his neck *would* react. With irritation. "Why? Are you waiting for me to deliver a report on shearing schedules? The ploughboys' first and last names?"

She cocked her head to the side, considering it. "No, that won't be necessary. That is, I'm sure the land steward can answer those questions."

"Land steward? What bloody land steward?"

"*Your* land steward, my lord. Mr. Quarles. I sent word to him this morning asking for a review of estate business. He's waiting for us in your study. It shouldn't take more than a few hours."

Nick's mouth fell open. "A few *hours?*"

Violet shot a cheerful smile over her shoulder as she made her way down the hall to the study. "No more than three, certainly."

Mr. Quarles was a man of impressive efficiency, but even so, it did take more than a few hours—four, to be precise—and by the time he ushered the man out the door, Nick was ready to collapse with exhaustion.

Violet, however, still looked as lovely as she had when she'd stormed his bedchamber this morning. She'd taken a seat in front of the fire to scribble something in a small book she'd carried with her all day, but she looked up when he offered her a glass of port.

"Industry agrees with you, my lady," he murmured, taking in the color in her cheeks as he joined her on the settee.

She held his gaze as she parted her lips and sipped at her port. "Repose does not?"

Nick tensed, but he let his glass dangle carelessly from his fingers as if he didn't follow her meaning.

He did, of course, but what did she want to hear him say? That no matter what she did, whether she were sleeping or waking, he thought her beautiful? That he wanted her, and last night when he'd left her room without taking her he'd cursed himself for his cowardice? All of those things were true, but saying them aloud wouldn't make any difference. It wouldn't change anything between them.

Nothing could.

Nick held up his glass to the fire and turned it, watching the dark amber liquid swirl in the bowl. He thought of Violet as she'd been last night, her shadowed blue eyes on his face as he stroked his hands over skin so fine and pale and smooth he could almost believe he was dreaming when he touched her.

"You're like a dream when you sleep." He stared at his glass for another moment, then brought it to his lips and tossed the whole of it back, his face expressionless as it burned his throat. "Troublesome thing about dreams, though. One always wakes up."

She leaned toward him, her blue gaze steady on his face. "You're awake right now, my lord, and I'm no dream. I'm your wife."

"You're the Countess of Dare." He dropped his empty glass on the table and rose from his seat. "But you're not really mine at all, are you, Violet?"

He went to the door, then glanced back at her, but what was there for him to say? For either of them to say?

In the end, he said the only thing he could:

"Good night, Lady Dare."

Chapter Twenty

One week later...

He was touching her. Every inch of his eager body was pressed against hers, her legs wrapped tightly around his waist as he moved inside her. His mouth was on her throat, her neck—dear God, she had the softest skin he'd ever kissed—and her long, silky hair spilled over his hands. She was murmuring to him, her lips brushing against his ear, breathless words of desire and love broken with quiet gasps as he loved her with slow, steady strokes, careful with her, so careful not to hurt her when he made her his...

Nick woke with a start, a sheen of sweat covering his body, thrusting his throbbing cock against the sheets. It took a moment for him to realize Violet wasn't in his bed, but once he determined he was alone, a defeated moan broke from his lips and he buried his head in his pillow. Another dream, one that dissolved, as they always did, into a lonely, disappointing reality.

Nick rolled onto his back and threw his arm over his damp brow.

He still hadn't taken her. She was his wife, damn it, and he wanted her desperately. He'd crept into her room again last night, as determined to take her as he was every night, but the moment he laid his hands on that pale, smooth skin, doubts assailed him. Was she thinking of Lord Derrick, and wishing it was *his* hands caressing her instead of Nick's? Was she imagining it was *him* in her bed?

He'd be trapped in England for eternity if he didn't get an heir on his wife, but in a twist of fate so ironic he might have laughed if he weren't so bloody miserable, London's most selfish rake was incapable of making love to his own wife as long as he believed she cared for another man. But he also couldn't keep his hands off her, so every night he'd creep into her bedchamber to touch her. He'd bring her to a gasping, panting release with his hands, his fingers, his mouth, and then he'd pull her nightdress back over her thighs, draw the covers over her, and retire to his own bedchamber with an aching cock, a curse on his lips, and a head and heart full of doubts and recriminations.

He couldn't keep on like this. He was going mad—

"My lord?" A soft, tentative voice intruded on his thoughts, followed by a light knock on his bedchamber door. His first confused thought was it was Gibbs, and he was one breath away from giving voice to a fearsome bellow, but he managed to bite back his furious demand to be let alone before it left his lips.

Gibbs's voice didn't have that soft, teasing note, and the knock was coming from the door that connected his bedchamber to Violet's, not the hallway door. Despite his relentless bad temper, it seemed his lovely bride was anxious to spend time with him, because she'd made quite a habit of venturing into his private bedchamber while he was still abed.

There seemed to be no end to her enthusiasm for improving Ashdown Park, and she pursued those improvements with an unflagging optimism he would have put down to drunkenness if he'd witnessed it in anyone other than Violet.

Yesterday she'd demanded a lesson on the paintings in the portrait gallery, then she'd dragged him up to the attics to see what other paintings were stored there that they might have the servants bring down for hanging. The day before that it had been a stroll through the formal gardens—was he fond of roses, or did he prefer wildflowers?—a wander through the stables—wouldn't he tell her each of the horses' names?—a visit to the library—not surprisingly, Violet had a great many ideas about how to improve the library—and then a carriage ride past the neighboring estate and a visit to town to view the rectory.

Lady Dare was nothing if not determined. Cheerful, too, resolutely so, and unendingly pleasant and patient. She met every one of his sour comments with a good-humored shrug, every bout of ill temper with an angelic smile, despite the fact he'd complained and pouted his way through each of these outings like a petulant child. It was difficult to oppose someone who was so unfailingly obliging, and at some point he'd given up resisting her. And then, despite his every effort to keep it from happening, his greatest fear had been realized.

He'd begun to enjoy the outings.

To enjoy *her*, much as he had when they'd spent those weeks touring burial grounds and gibbets in London. Just as he had then, he began to see Ashdown Park through Violet's eyes. The delight he took in her—it was both beautiful and exquisitely painful at once, because as much as he needed her, as much as her presence was becoming as necessary as air to him, he wasn't at all certain *he* was necessary to *her.*

It made him surly, distant, but then the night would come, and he'd creep into her room and touch her, drown in the sensation of her hot, slick folds against his fingers, his mouth, and then he'd creep away again like a thief, a coward too afraid to make love to his wife.

"My lord?" There was another soft knock.

Nick emerged from the coverlet and propped himself against his pillows, fighting the temptation to toss his blankets aside so she could see how hard he was—so she understood what she did to him. After all, such an impatient lady should be made aware of the perils of invading her husband's bedchamber so early, when a man's body was primed for his wife's affection.

Of course, *his* body was always primed for her, always hungry...

If he threw the covers off and felt her gaze on him when he was so stiff and hard for her, perhaps his desires would override his foolish misgivings, and—

"My lord?" The door creaked open a crack. "Are you awake?"

Awake, aroused, erect—whatever she wished to call it, he was all of them. "Yes. Come in."

"Good morning, my lord." Violet entered the room with brisk efficiency, and went at once to the window to pull aside the drapes.

"Damn it." Nick jerked his hand up to shade his eyes from the offensive sunlight pouring through his window. In that respect he was very much like every other fashionable rake in London. He despised daybreak, and the earlier it arrived, the more detestable it was. The last thing a rake wanted to see first thing in the morning was the bloody sunrise.

"What do you think you're doing, Lady Dare? For God's sake, close those bloody drapes."

She didn't move or reply, and her silence continued to drag on until Nick's eyes at last adjusted to the light, and he moved his arm away from his face. "Did you hear me, my lady? I didn't allow you into my bedchamber so you could assault me—"

His words dissolved on a quick, hard breath.

She was staring at him, her hungry gaze moving over every inch of his bare chest. "I, ah..." Her cheeks flushed as she met his gaze. "I wanted..."

Nick nearly groaned aloud when her pink tongue darted out to wet her lower lip. She tried to look away, her frantic gaze darting from the washstand to the fireplace to the window, but her eyes were drawn back to him again and again, as if the sight of his bare flesh mesmerized her.

Nick knew Violet wanted him. He'd known it since the first moment he touched her. Her body craved his, just as any young, healthy body craved the touch of another. He'd felt her desire in the way she writhed beneath him, in every needy moan that left her lips, but he'd never before *seen* it—he'd never watched her lips part, her eyes darken, or the fevered flush bloom on her cheeks when she looked at him.

Nick's cock swelled to painful dimensions, and his hips shifted restlessly against the coverlet. He swallowed, but when he spoke, his voice was hoarse. "Now that you've woken me, what do you intend to do with me, Lady Dare?"

If she crossed his bedchamber right now, slid into his bed, and pressed her warm lips to his, his desire for her might well override his doubts about her affections. A part of him wanted that—wanted her to make the decision for both of them.

Yet even as his body tensed with anticipation, bitter regret made his chest tighten. It didn't matter how often he told himself making love to her was only a means to an end, or that she didn't need to love him for him to put a child in her belly—it *did* matter.

Perhaps she saw it, that spasm of indecision on his face, because she straightened her spine and raised her chin. "I, ah—yes. I wanted to…to… oh, yes. I recall now. I wanted to know what do you intend to do about the conservatory."

He'd half-wished for such a mundane reply, but it was unwelcome nonetheless, and Nick's lips turned down in a scowl. "*Do?* Why should I do anything about it?"

"Because a half dozen panes of glass are broken, another dozen are about to break, and those that are left are so filthy the few plants inside are shriveling from want of light. It seems rather a shame, when you could have such lovely exotic plants and shrubs. Don't you care for shrubs, my lord?"

"Shrubs?" Nick blinked. She was talking to him of shrubs? He hadn't ever given shrubs a second thought. "I don't care for them or *not* care for them, Lady Dare. I have no opinion at all regarding shrubs."

She frowned. "No? How odd. Fruit, then? There's an orangery, as well, though it's not in much better repair than the conservatory, I'm afraid. Do you care for oranges? Or lemons, or pineapples?"

She'd woken him for *this?* Because she wished to discuss fruit? "Oranges are all very well, but I don't see what—"

"Oh, good. Oranges and pineapple, then. I'm fond of pineapple." She pulled out her sketchbook, which accompanied them on every outing, no matter how brief or inconsequential it might be, and she was forever scribbling in it.

She wrote something down, and then offered him a beaming smile. "Well, it's a beginning, at any rate. Will you escort me to the conservatory now? You can tell me more about what you'd like when we're there."

Nick made a rude noise, then lay back down and pulled the blankets over his head. "That's not necessary, my lady. It will save a great deal of time and fuss if you simply go yourself, and then *you* can tell me what I want, since that will inevitably be the outcome of this experiment."

"If you insist, my lord, of course I'll leave you to your rest. It's only…"

He poked his head up from the nest of blankets, annoyed. "What is it *now?*"

"Well, it's just occurred to me one of the loose panes of glass could come crashing down upon me while I'm wandering about in there. I daresay I'm being foolish, but a number of them are only attached at the corner, you see. But no matter. If one of them *should* fall on me, I'm certain one of the servants or Lady Westcott will hear it and rescue me before I succumb to a swoon and crack my head on the stone floor."

Nick let out a heavy sigh. Damn it, it was bloody nonsense, and she knew it as well as he did. She was no more likely to be hit by a pane of glass than she was to be trampled by a herd of cattle.

But if the unthinkable *should* happen, and a broken window should come loose just as she happened to be standing beneath it…

The panes were heavy—heavy enough to knock a much larger person than his petite wife unconscious, and that was to say nothing of the risk of cuts, or worse, a stabbing, and the conservatory was at one end of the house, far enough from the main rooms it was more than likely no one would hear the sound of shattering glass.

Nick kicked at his covers and let out a frustrated groan. He may as well do as she asked, because he'd never get another wink of sleep now she'd put that image in his head. "I deserve this, for being foolish enough to take a clever wife."

Violet met his irritated grumbling with a pleased smile. "Does that mean you'll escort me, my lord?"

"I don't see I have much choice. I'll meet you downstairs in the entryway, my lady—unless, of course, you wish to wait here while I dress?"

He didn't give her a chance to move or reply, but tossed the coverlet aside and rose from the bed, a slow grin spreading over his lips as her gaze moved over his chest, and then down, down, down…

"Oh, my." She gaped at him, her eyes wide, but then she jerked her gaze away with a breathless squeak. "No, no, I—that is, that's quite all right, my lord. I—ah, I suppose I'll just leave you to…"

"What's the matter, my lady? Not embarrassed, I hope? As I recall, at one point you seemed quite interested in male arousal, and I am your husband, after all. If you insist upon invading a man's bedchamber while he's abed, it stands to reason you'll see bare—and often rigid—flesh."

Bright red color suffused her cheeks, and Nick grinned as she scurried out the door like a rabbit with a stolen carrot in its mouth.

He despised rising with the sun. His retinas were likely permanently damaged, his cock was still hopefully erect and showed no signs of subsiding, and if the truth were told he wasn't all that fond of oranges, but none of that mattered a whit now.

It was all worth it.

For the first time since he'd met her, he'd rendered his wife speechless.

* * * *

"It's rather like a jewel box, isn't it? Small, but perfect in its own way."

Violet tilted her head back to admire the domed ceiling. The conservatory was a bit unusual in that it had been done in a circular design, with oblong panes of glass set into a heavy, ornate cast iron frame.

The whole of Ashdown Park was rather like this room—simple, but beautiful and unique, and like this little jewel of a room, it only wanted polishing. There was so much for Nick here—so much joy and peace within his grasp, if only he believed he deserved to reach out and take it.

"Hardly perfect, Lady Dare. At least a dozen panes of glass are shattered."

Despite this denial, Nick's voice was thoughtful. Oh, he'd been surly enough for the first hour or so, but as they'd strolled around the conservatory he'd forgotten himself enough to relax, and a slight smile had been hovering at the corner of his lips ever since. It had been days since she'd seen even a ghost of a smile on his face, and Violet's heart leapt with hope.

"My father wanted to build my mother a great monstrosity of a conservatory," he went on, "but she never wanted anything sprawling or extravagant—just something simple and beautiful to grow her flowers."

"What kind of flowers did she prefer?"

"Gardenias, jasmine, myrtle—the usual sort of thing. She wanted to add arching trellises following the roof line so she could grow climbing vines." He pointed up at the curved ceiling. "But she died before it could be done."

Violet hesitated, but he'd never spoken of his mother to her before, and she couldn't let this opportunity escape her. "How old were you when she died?"

He was quiet for a moment, and she thought he might not reply, but then he sighed. "Nine. Graham was eleven. After she died, my father refused to ever set foot in this room again, and you see what happened. Shattered glass and withered plants."

Shattered hearts, withered dreams...

Violet glanced up at the broken panes of glass, at their jagged edges glittering in the sun. The glass wasn't the only thing that had been shattered when the previous Lady Dare died.

She went over to the table where she'd left her sketchbook and pencil, sat down, and drew a few hasty lines. "Trellises like this, you mean?"

Nick crossed the room and peered over her shoulder. "Something like that, yes." He sounded surprised.

She sketched in another dozen or so lines, murmuring to him as she drew. "The vines could be planted in containers below. It would take no time at all for them to climb the trellis. Once they grew in, it would be like having a separate little garden above your head. As for the rest of it..." Violet waved a hand around the room. "Broken glass is easily repaired, and we can plant new flowers. We could have gardenia, if you like, and jasmine, just as your mother did."

Nick didn't reply. He wandered to one end of the room and stood there for a long time, his arms crossed over his chest, staring out into the garden. Violet could only see his profile, but he didn't look angry. He looked...wistful.

Her breath caught as she gazed at him. The light pouring down from the roof set fire to the strands of auburn hidden in his dark hair and emphasized his strong jaw and the sensuous curve of his lower lip.

Quietly, Violet turned to a blank page in her book and began to sketch him, taking care to make certain every line and every curve of his face was true, so when she showed the sketch to him, he could see himself as she saw him. Not as a selfish rake, but as the man he was—a man of strength and compassion, yet always with that hint of sadness about him, of wounds not quite healed.

Those wounds, that trace of grief in his eyes he'd likely carry with him always...

Did he understand they only made him more beautiful?

"Everything seems different when I see it as you see it."

Violet's pencil stilled on the page, and she slowly raised her gaze to him.

He wasn't looking at her—he was still staring out the window, as if he were watching something she couldn't see. "It was that way in London, too." The perfect curve of his lips softened with a faint smile. "Burial grounds, gibbets, ghosts..." He shook his head. "I never would have believed there was more than one way to see those things, but I was wrong."

Violet hesitated, unsure what to do. They were the first kind words he'd spoken to her since their disastrous wedding night, and she was afraid to disturb the quiet tenderness of the moment, but at the same time she'd waited weeks for him to offer her even the smallest opening, and she couldn't let her fear stand in the way of taking it.

She closed her sketchbook, laid it aside, and went and stood before him, close enough so her body brushed against his. She didn't speak, but lay her hands on his chest, gazed into his extraordinary gray eyes, and hoped with all her heart he'd see the truth in hers.

He stared down at her, searching her face. "Seeing things as you see them, looking at every moment as a possibility, as another chance to be delighted… it feels like waking up from a drugged sleep. It feels like breathing again."

Violet didn't move, and she didn't breathe. She only looked into his eyes, a silent prayer hidden on her lips.

Please let him see, let him understand…

He trailed a finger down her cheek and rested it under her chin. Violet didn't make a sound until his lips brushed over hers, then a long, deep sigh escaped her.

His mouth was soft at first, gentle, but when he stroked his tongue over her bottom lip and she opened for him without hesitation, he sank his hands in her hair to hold her still to take her mouth over and over again, his kiss desperate.

Violet whimpered in dismay when he drew away, but before she could bring his mouth back to hers he trailed his lips over her neck to kiss her throat. His chest heaved with his panting breaths as he slid his hands from her hair to tear at the buttons on the back of her dress. He loosened them with shaking fingers, then tugged her bodice down to kiss and nip her collarbones and the smooth skin of her chest.

He nipped and licked at her until her knees went so weak she had to grip his hair to keep herself from collapsing. "Please…"

He was kissing the tops of her breasts, his mouth ravenous against her damp flesh. "Do you want me, Violet?" He eased the muslin lower, groaning when the pink of her nipples appeared. "Tell me."

"I want you." Kissing him, touching him…it felt like drowning and surfacing at the same time, and Violet wrapped her arms around his neck to keep from being swept away.

"Who am I, Violet?" His voice was a low growl in her ear. "Who's kissing you, touching you right now? Say my name."

"*Nick…*" The word left her lips on a sob.

He tore his mouth from hers, grasped her shoulders, and held her away from him so he could see her face. "Who do you belong to? Say it, Violet." She took his face in her hands. "*You*, Nick. Only you."

A low groan shuddered through him, and he took her mouth harder then, as if he sought to punish her with his tongue and lips, but his hands were careful as he touched her, his fingers gentle as he tangled them in her hair, and for one breathless moment she understood him as surely as if she'd caught a glimpse inside his heart.

This man she'd wounded so deeply, whose heart she'd been so careless with—he'd never punish her. He'd never try to hurt her in return. It wasn't who he was, but she...oh, God, she'd been so unfair to him, so hurtful, and her heart swelled with the need to take that hurt away. She had to make him understand she loved him, had never loved anyone but him.

Words began to pour from her lips in an incoherent rush. "You...you're more to me than everything, Nick...more than anyone. No one has ever... not Lord Derrick, no one but *you*—"

He'd buried his face between her breasts and was sucking at the tender skin there, but her words made him freeze, and in the next moment he yanked her bodice up to cover her, then pushed away from her.

"Nick?" Violet opened her eyes, dazed, her heart thudding in her chest.

"You dare to say his name to me?" His face was white, his voice shaking. "You *dare* to say his name to me while I'm holding you in my arms, touching you? While I'm thinking of nothing but *you*, you're thinking of *him?*"

Violet stared at him in horror as it dawned on her she'd made a terrible mistake. "*No*—Nick, no. I could never...I'm sorry. I only wanted you to know there's no one else I've ever—"

"No one? Come now, Lady Dare. We both know that's not true."

She grabbed his arm, her grip frantic. "It *is* true. It's been true from the moment I met you. Please, Nick." She curled her fingers into his coat. "The drawings—I don't see you that way now. I..."

She wanted to tell him she loved him. The declaration hovered on her lips, but his eyes had hardened into cold gray stones, and Violet knew it wouldn't be enough. He wouldn't believe her. Why should he? She'd lied to him and hurt him, and a few whispered words weren't going to change that.

He jerked his arm out of her grasp. "Of course you see me that way, sweetheart. Why shouldn't you? 'The Selfish Rake.' It's what I am."

"No! You were *never* that. I never should have—"

"Not much of a rake now, I grant you. I can't even make love to my own wife." He let out a bitter laugh. "Ironic, isn't it? But even so, I'm not quite the paragon Lord Derrick is."

There was a long pause while they stared at each other in silence, but then Violet shook her head. "No, Nick," she whispered. "This isn't about Lord Derrick. It never has been."

"No?" He gave a harsh laugh. "Who, then? Are you in love with another man, in addition to Lord Derrick?"

Violet's gaze never left his face. What she was about to say to him...oh, she didn't want to say it. It would hurt him, and she'd already hurt him so much. But it had to be said, and it had to be said by *her*. His wife.

"None of this is about Lord Derrick, Nick. It's about Graham. When you say you're not Lord Derrick, what you really mean is you're not Graham. But I don't want a man like Graham, or one like Lord Derrick. I only want you."

He stared down at her, his throat working, his face growing paler by the second, and then without a word he shoved past her, leaving her alone in the conservatory.

Violet stood quietly for a long time after he left, but she was still shaking when she made her way back over to the bench and sank down onto it. Her eyes slid closed, and her head sank into her hands.

But she didn't let herself stay there for long.

When she'd wanted to finish her book she'd schemed and plotted and lied to get it done. Would she do less now, when the stakes were so much higher? If she wanted Nick to forgive her—if she wanted him to give up his plan to flee to the Continent, to abandon her for his Italian mistress—she had to do better than this.

She had to *show* him she loved him.

Violet raised her head, and her gaze fell on her sketchbook. She dragged it closer and began to turn the pages one by one, her hands trembling.

It was filled with drawings of Nick. Dozens of them.

Nick, his hair wet and his cheeks flushed, mounted on an enormous black stallion, his expression earnest as he pointed toward some distant fields. Nick, firelight flickering on his face, a glass of port dangling carelessly between his fingers. Nick in his bed, blankets twisted around his hips, his chest bare, his hair disheveled, and dark stubble shadowing his jaw.

Violet straightened her shoulders and rose from the bench, her lips pressed together with determination.

This courtship had just begun.

Chapter Twenty-one

Once Violet determined Nick hadn't left the house, it wasn't difficult to figure out where he'd gone. As she mounted the stairs to his bedchamber, she tried to persuade herself to consider the scene in the conservatory from her usual practical angle, but her heart sank lower with each step.

For the first time since she'd arrived at Ashdown Park, her optimism was threating to give way to hopeless exhaustion. Nick desired her, but he didn't trust her, and he wasn't any closer to forgiving her than he'd been when he'd first discovered those sketches. Nearly a fortnight had passed, and he still refused to talk to her, or allow her to talk to him.

Perhaps he never would. Perhaps her marriage had ended the very day it began, and nothing she could ever do or say would earn his forgiveness.

The thought made Violet's shoulders sag with fatigue, and as she slipped into her bedchamber, she let her gaze wander longingly to her bed. How easy it would be to give in to the need to sink down onto it and lose herself in a dreamless sleep. How peaceful to forget, if only for a little while, the icy disdain on her husband's face right before he'd left her alone in the conservatory.

She didn't yield to the temptation, but squared her shoulders and crossed the room to the connecting door. She raised her hand to knock, but before her fist met the wood, she paused.

If she knocked, he'd only send her away.

Violet squeezed her eyes closed, wrapped her hand around the knob, and twisted. Her eyes flew open in surprise when it turned obligingly in her palm.

Nick hadn't shut her out.

The unlocked door—it must mean he wanted her to come after him, mustn't it? Oh, if only he'd give her a chance! If only he'd look at her, and truly *see* her. He need only look into her eyes to believe he was the only man who'd ever held her heart.

Violet eased the door open, hope flaring in her breast for the first time in weeks...

Only to sputter and die again when she stepped into Nick's bedchamber. It was dark—as dark as if the sun had never risen this morning.

He'd drawn the heavy drapes over the windows to shut out the light, and Violet blinked in the sudden dimness. Was he here? Perhaps Gibbs was mistaken, and Nick had ridden out after all—

"Get out."

She jerked her head toward the voice, and after a moment her eyes adjusted enough so she could make out Nick's solid bulk on the bed. He'd pulled the coverlet over him, and it was clear from his tone he didn't intend to crawl out from underneath it anytime soon.

"Didn't you hear me, Lady Dare? I said get out."

Violet took two halting steps toward the bed, but Nick's angry hiss made her freeze. "Christ, you're worse than Gibbs. Neither of you seem to have the least idea what *out* means."

Violet didn't answer, because a hot, tight knot rose in her throat, and she couldn't say a word. She didn't realize she'd closed her hands into fists until she felt the sting of her fingernails biting into her palms.

"Are you confused, my lady? Allow me to clarify my meaning. I *don't* wish to see you, and I *don't* wish to speak to you, so I fail to see why you're still standing in my bedchamber."

The knot in Violet's throat grew so thick it threatened to choke her, but by now she recognized it for what it was, and once she gave way to it, it swept all before it. Her exhaustion, her hopelessness, her fear—all gone in one single, powerful rush, like one wave swallowing the next and hurtling the water back out to sea.

It left a single thing behind in its wake.

Anger.

No, fury. Sudden, sharp, cleansing fury.

When she still didn't move, Nick jerked up in his bed and let out an ear-splitting roar. "Damn you, I said leave my room at once!"

Such a frightening bellow would have sent a meeker woman running for the door, but Violet hadn't ever been afraid to stand her ground, and she didn't intend to start now.

"No."

"No?" His lordship was accustomed to having his bad temper indulged, and his voice rang with disbelief. "*No?*"

"I believe you heard me perfectly well, my lord." Violet didn't spare him a glance, but marched across the room toward the windows. "I wish to speak with you, and I won't do it in the dark."

Nick threw the coverlet aside and leapt from the bed. "If you lay a single finger on those drapes, Lady Dare, I swear I'll—"

He didn't get any further, because Violet dove for the window, snatched one of the heavy silk drapes in her fist, and jerked it open with a quick snap of her wrist. A narrow beam of sunlight spilled across the room, but before she could grab the other one he was there, his bare chest at her back, and his powerful arms wrapped around her, trapping her against him. "Do you suppose I won't toss you over my shoulder and carry you out myself? You should know better than that by now."

Violet shivered as his warm breath drifted over her ear, but she kept her voice cool and steady. "I don't pretend to know what you'd do, my lord. I hardly know you anymore."

A soft, mocking laugh fell from his lips. "Oh, but you do know me, my lady." He turned her to face him and wrapped his fingers around her wrists. "I'm The Selfish Rake, remember?"

Violet blanched as she stared into his cold gray eyes. A part of her wanted to do exactly as he ordered—to flee this room, and leave Nick in the darkness to battle his demons alone, but two years of solitary struggle hadn't freed him from his ghosts. He'd never be free of them—not until they were torn loose with bare hands.

Very deliberately, Violet began to prod at the rage inside him. She *wanted* his fury—she wanted to make it heave and shudder and swell until there was nothing left to feed it, and it burned itself out.

"You *are* selfish, my lord. I thought I'd wronged you with that sketch, but only the most selfish of men neglects his wife and abandons his every honorable impulse to wallow in self-pity."

"You...I..." Angry red color rushed into his cheeks, and he was so furious he couldn't form a coherent sentence, but Violet didn't even consider a retreat. Now that she'd begun, she'd finish, and face whatever consequences fate dealt her.

"Is this how you envisioned our marriage, my lord? When you insisted I become your wife, did you imagine yourself sneaking into my bedchamber each night to touch me, without ever making me yours?"

The color drained from Nick's face. "You want me to make you mine, my lady?"

Violet raised her chin. "We both want—"

He jerked her hard against his chest. "Oh, I *want*, my lady. I want to toss you onto my bed right now, spread your thighs and sink into that lush heat I've dreamed of every single damn night since I first laid eyes on you. I want to put my hands all over you. I want to make you sigh, and moan, and beg me to take you, and I want to hear you scream my name when I do."

Heat rushed over every inch of Violet's skin at the dark desire in his voice, but even as seductive warmth bloomed low in her belly, she wanted to beat her fists against his chest in frustration. "Yet you'd deny us what we both so desperately want because of a *sketch?* I'm your wife, Nick. *Your wife*. You insisted on this marriage, and now you're content to let it wither away like your mother's dead flowers in the conservatory? If you want me, then take me."

He laughed, but it was a dark sound, filled with despair. "I want you, sweet—I want to take you more than I want to breathe, but when passion overwhelms you and you do cry out a name, I'm afraid it won't be mine."

It won't be mine...

He'd whispered the last words, but they echoed inside Violet's head long after the room had gone silent. She went limp against him as the hope drained out of her, and with it any urge she had to keep fighting. She was tired, so tired, and this battle had already been lost, hadn't it? It was lost before she had a chance to fight it—lost in a single blow.

The exhaustion she'd been struggling against fell over her again, and dear God, it was so heavy this time, heavy and wet and suffocating—far too heavy for her to fight it. She could scream until her voice was gone, beat her fists until they were bruised and aching, drop to her knees and beg, and still it wouldn't be enough.

He was never going to forgive her, and she...

Oh, how could she ever have believed Lord Derrick had broken her heart? How could she have thought that tiny scar was anything like this wound that cleaved her heart in two? She'd never mend it, and she'd never recover from it. It was hers now, and she'd never crawl free of it.

He was staring at her, his chest heaving. "Do you think this is what I want, Violet? Do you think I *ever* would have insisted on this marriage if I'd known what you truly thought of me? Christ, if I could go back to that night in my aunt's sitting room and make a different choice, don't you think I would, for both our sakes?"

Violet forced words through her numb lips. "You wish you hadn't married me."

"Don't we both wish it?"

She stared up into his handsome face. His eyes were so beautiful they'd win any woman's heart, but she'd known that from the start, hadn't she? She'd known he'd take her heart, and that he'd break it. And yet it was strange, so strange to find it could be broken again and again, in the time it took to say a single word.

She dragged in a few short, shuddering breaths, but she couldn't swallow back the tears stinging her eyes. They would spill over, fall down her cheeks, and she didn't want him to know, didn't want him to see...

But he did see, and his face went ashen. "Violet."

He tried to pull her against his chest, but she tugged her wrists from his grasp.

"Violet, please." He reached out his hand to her, but she backed away and flew across the room to the door.

She never got it open, because in the next breath Nick was there.

"No." He braced his arms on either side of her shoulders, trapping her between the door and his body. His chest was bare, his skin warm, and within seconds her senses were swimming with his scent, that impossible, wonderful scent of amber and wood, and...

I can't do this.

Deep inside, Violet began to tremble. She jerked at the door knob, desperate to get away, but Nick reached down to cover her hand with his, and stopped her from turning it. "No."

He was too close—so close she could feel the vibration of that one quiet word against her back, and he wouldn't let her go, and she was tired, so tired...

Tears began to spill down her cheeks, and Violet gave into them. She let her forehead fall against the door, let the despair take her, but for all her heartbreak these were quiet tears, her weeping silent in the still room.

But Nick heard her. He heard, but he didn't try to stop it. He didn't say a word, but pulled a long, shuddering breath into his lungs, then slowly, as if he were afraid he'd frighten her if he moved too quickly, he wrapped his arms around her and gathered her against his chest.

He held her for a long time, until at last the final tear was wrung from her and her gasping sobs quieted. She was too exhausted to struggle with him, so she simply stood, every muscle in her body trembling with fatigue, and waited for him to release her.

He didn't. He brushed the hair away from her neck with gentle fingers and buried his face in the sensitive curve of her shoulder. Violet tensed, but before she could shy away from the unexpected caress, Nick made a soothing noise in his throat. "Shhhh."

His lips ghosted over her neck, his kiss so soft Violet wasn't sure she hadn't imagined it until he followed it with another, then another. His mouth moved over her, dropping dozens of tiny kisses on every bare inch of skin he could reach—her neck, the curve of her nape and the arch of her shoulder. His lips were so tender, so sweet and gentle, Violet's eyes filled with tears again.

Nick held her through every shudder, every ache—he took her pain into himself until at last the tension left her and she sagged against him.

And still, he never spoke a word.

He let his touch speak for him.

He caught her hands in his and placed her palms flat against the door, and then, one by one, he loosened the buttons on the back of her gown. A low, hungry sound rumbled in his throat when he saw she wore only a thin shift beneath. He traced his fingertips up her spine to the heavy coil of hair at her neck and slid the pins loose, his breath catching on a quiet gasp when her hair spilled down her back. He gathered the heavy curls in his fists and buried his face in them, inhaling deeply before he draped them over her shoulder and brought his open mouth back to her neck.

His lips were warm as they tasted her skin. Violet could feel the tension vibrating in him, the barely leashed desire in his body, and a soft cry left her lips. Nick went still for a moment, then he nuzzled his face into the curve of her shoulder. "Shhh."

He soothed her with soft murmurs, much as one might soothe a distraught child, but he touched her with passionate purpose—the way a man touches a woman he desires—a woman he intends to have.

He was going to make her his, and it was going to be *now*.

"My lord—"

Violet tried to turn then, to face her husband, but he curved an arm across her shoulders and held her still. "Shhhh."

She opened her mouth to reply, but his lips drifted over her neck, and all that emerged was a breathless sigh, and…oh, dear God, she couldn't catch her breath as Nick slipped his fingers into the open back of her gown. He drew the soft muslin over her shoulders and down her arms, then lower, down her back and over her hips, baring her skin to his gaze, until at last he tugged the gown free of her body and tossed it aside.

He let out a low groan when she stood before him in only her shift, then he sank to his knees behind her and pressed his lips to the arch of her back.

Violet curled her fingers into the hard wood and bit her bottom lip to keep from whimpering as he plucked at the bows on her garters and slid her stockings down her legs, but nothing could silence her cry when he rose from his knees behind her with the hem of her shift caught in his fist. But she didn't protest, and she didn't hesitate. She raised her arms and let him drag her shift over her head.

When she was bare before him, he took her shoulders in his hands and turned her to face him. His lids had gone heavy over those shadowy gray eyes, but even in the dim light Violet could see the way they darkened with desire as he took in every flushed inch of her skin, lingering on her bare belly, her breasts, her throat and neck.

Her mouth.

His eyes burned as he leaned toward her, and Violet tipped her head back against the door, parted her lips, and let her eyes drift closed, her body trembling in anticipation of his kiss.

But it never came.

He drew in a harsh breath, and Violet opened her eyes to find he'd gone still. He stared at her for long moments without speaking, then he reached forward and traced the remnants of her tears on her cheeks.

"I'm sorry I hurt you." His voice was low and choked. "Whatever happens between us, this…" He brushed his thumbs under her eyes to dry the last of her tears. "It ends now."

He didn't wait for her reply, but gathered her into his arms, crossed the room, and lay her gently on his bed. He didn't join her, but stood motionless by the side of the bed, gazing down at her as if he'd never seen her before.

Because he hasn't.

The realization came to Violet with a pang of bitter regret. He'd touched her intimately, tasted her, and brought her to release in his arms, but he'd never before seen her spread across his bed. She was his *wife*, and he'd never before seen her body bared for his pleasure.

Broken words formed on his lips. "Beautiful." He reached out as if in a daze to stroke a tentative hand down her calf. "Softest skin I've ever touched." His gaze darted to her face, and a shadow of doubt lingered in his eyes. "Is this what you want, Violet? Do you…" He swallowed. "Do you want me?"

He even had to ask? His uncertainty made a sob rise in Violet's throat, but she choked it back and held out her arms to him. "Yes."

He let out a long, slow breath, then kneeled beside her and lay his hand against her throat. He stroked it down her body, lingering between her breasts and on the gentle curve of her belly, a faint smile appearing at the corner of his lips when she stretched like a lazy cat under his touch.

He never took his eyes off her. His hot gaze followed every arch and twist and shiver of her body as she undulated like a wave across his bed. "Such a pretty flush here." He dragged a fingertip across the tops of her breasts. "Cup your breasts in your hands, sweet," he murmured when her nipples grew hard under his gaze.

Violet didn't think to deny him, but slid her hands up her stomach and cupped her breasts in her palms. Some instinct made her squeeze gently and lift them, as if she were offering them to him, and Nick's lips parted on a harsh groan. "Stroke your nipples for me."

Her flush deepened, but the fierce desire in his eyes left no room for embarrassment. She dragged her thumbs over her nipples once, then again, but her touch wasn't enough—not when she could remember the sensation of his hot mouth against her, licking and teasing.

A soft plea tore from her throat. "Please…"

"What do you want?" Nick's bare chest heaved with each breath, but he held back, watching her writhe against the bed.

He was waiting for something.

He needs to hear me say it, to say how much I want him.

"Your mouth," she gasped as she circled her nipples again. "I need your lips on me, your tongue—"

He grasped her wrists and tore her hands away, and then his mouth was there, devouring her. He darted his tongue over the straining peaks again and again, then wrapped his lips around her and sucked, hard. Violet thrust her fingers into his hair with a cry, twisting and pulling with each delicious tug on her nipple, but she couldn't have said whether she wanted to end his exquisite torment, or urge him on.

Nick didn't give her time to decide before he slid his hand up the inside of her thigh. "Open your legs, sweet." He growled when Violet spread her thighs for him. "Put your hand between them." He bit down gently on her nipple when she hesitated. "Your hand, Violet." He groaned when she slid her hands between her damp curls. "Now stroke your fingers…*yes*, just like that. Are you wet for me?"

Violet brushed her fingertips between her legs, just as he'd done when he touched her, and warmth flooded her core. "*Yes.*"

With that one gasped word, Nick's control seemed to snap. His hand dropped onto her belly to hold her still and he buried his face between her legs. "Yes, so wet and sweet," he murmured, stroking his tongue between her slick folds. When Violet arched her hips against his mouth he tightened his fingers around her thighs and opened her wider. He sucked her sensitive bud between his lips and worked it with the tip of his tongue, circling and darting and licking at her until her body drew taut, and with a shuddering sob she came apart against his lips.

Violet was still struggling to catch her breath when Nick kissed his way up her body, but when he lowered himself over her, his hips between her legs, she blinked in surprise. "Are you..." She frowned with confusion at the sensation of buckskin rubbing against her thighs. "My goodness, are you still wearing your breeches?"

"I, ah...I became distracted before I could remove them."

Nick caught his breath on a groan when she squirmed closer and rubbed her core against his hard length. His hips jerked against her in a restrained thrust that nevertheless brought another desperate groan to his lips. His cheekbones were flushed, his mouth open, his face drawn into harsh lines of need.

He wanted her, desperately. His rigid flesh jerked insistently against her thigh, yet he made no move to discard his breeches. Violet brought her hands to his face, but he refused to meet her eyes, and all at once she saw the next few minutes unfolding as if they'd already happened.

He's going to leave me again.

He was going to ease away from her, rise from the bed, and leave her alone in his bedchamber, without taking his own pleasure, and without making her his.

Before he could move, Violet turned his face toward hers, and words began to fall from her lips. "I belong to you, Nick. You and no one else, and I want you to make me yours."

He shook his head, but Violet moved quickly then, before he could pull away. She wrapped her legs around his waist and arched against the tantalizing column of hard flesh nestled between her thighs.

Nick threw his head back and sucked a sharp breath between his teeth. "Violet..."

He reached behind him to untangle her legs, but she locked her ankles behind his waist, wrapped her arms around his neck, and held on.

Nick caught her wrists and pinned her hands over her head with a growl. "You think to play with me? Damn you, Violet, this isn't a game."

This isn't a game, Miss Somerset.

That day they'd gone to the Hunterian Museum, he'd said the same thing. He'd insisted desire wasn't a game, and warned her not to tempt him...

Right before she'd shamelessly ridden him to release.

A gentleman's arousal isn't something to play with...

He'd begged her to stop, had tried to push her away, but then he'd become so aroused he could no longer think of anything but his desire, and he'd given himself over to her. He'd been hers in that moment, and even now, as he struggled with her, his hips were moving, and he was growing harder with every nudge between her legs.

He'd be hers again.

She cinched her legs around his hips and bit down gently on his earlobe. "I want you, Nick, and I know you want me. I can feel it. I can feel *you*." She dragged her nails over his chest and down his bare stomach to the waistband of his breeches. "You taught me about a man's arousal. Do you remember?" She twisted the buttons on his falls and slid her hand under the loose fabric. "I know you want to be inside me."

Both of them gasped when her hand slid lower and her palm brushed against the head of his cock. Nick pumped into her hand with a helpless groan, and Violet's eyes widened at the sensation of this hot, rigid part of him pushing into her fist. She'd never touched him like this before, so intimately. His ragged breath in her ear, his swollen flesh cradled in her hand—dear God, it was heady, and her fingers tightened instinctively around him as she began to stroke him.

Another desperate groan left his lips. "Violet...ah God, *yes*, sweetheart..."

At his panting moans and frantic thrusts, heat rushed through Violet until she was as aroused as he was. She tugged at his breeches in a frenzy to get closer to him, and by the time she'd dragged the fabric down his hips there was no more talk of games, and no more hesitation. Nick reached down, spread her thighs apart, and slid into her—just a few inches, but it was enough to make Violet go still, amazed at the strange sensation of him moving inside her.

"Don't want to hurt you..." Beads of sweat formed in the hollow of Nick's throat, and he was panting with the struggle to remain still. "Can't bear to hurt you..."

Violet's heart melted at his tender concern, but she took his face in her hands and held him until his eyes met hers. "I need you. It hurts me not to have you." She hitched her legs higher on his hips, and his eyes closed as he slid in another inch. "Please, Nick. I need you."

He crushed his lips to hers as his hips snapped forward, and he surged inside her with a single, forceful thrust. Violet gasped at the sharp pain, but it was mere moments before it faded into a soft warmth, and then there was only Nick, his arms wrapped around her and his body buried deep inside hers. She scratched her nails lightly down his sweat-slicked back and turned her head to murmur in his ear. "More."

He took her lips in another passionate kiss, and then...

Then he began to move.

Restrained, shallow thrusts at first, but faster and deeper when broken pleas began to fall from her lips. Violet writhed against him as the tight knot inside her began to unravel in waves of exquisite heat. Nick held her hips to the bed when she began to meet his thrusts, and took her harder, coaxing her toward the peak with every sinuous movement of his powerful body until she shattered beneath him. The moment he felt her release he tensed, then he buried his face in her neck with a harsh groan as his body convulsed with pleasure over hers.

He collapsed on top of her a moment later, and Violet wrapped herself around him, holding him to her as tightly as she could as their breathing quieted.

For Violet it was enough to be close to him, her fingers toying with his damp hair, his chest pressed to hers and their hearts beating in time together, but after a moment Nick stirred, then rolled away from her onto his side. He propped his head on his hand and gazed down at her, searching her eyes, and even in the muted light Violet could see doubt still haunted him—the shadows of it flickered in those gray depths, and with them a truth she couldn't deny.

She had his body, but she still didn't have his trust.

Without his trust, she'd never have his heart.

Despair threatened, but instead of allowing it to suck her into its dark depths, she urged Nick's face down to hers, and soft words rushed from her lips. She hardly knew what she said, but it didn't matter. It only mattered they were words of reassurance, and forgiveness, and love, and that every single one of them was true.

"I noticed your eyes first. Such an extraordinary silvery-gray, and with those black irises." She laughed softly. "Every night before I fall asleep, I think about your eyes and try to decide what color they are. Gray, or silver, like a bird's wing? But they're clearer than that, aren't they? Like water in sunlight."

His eyes drifted closed, and Violet leaned toward him and pressed gentle lips to his eyelids. "No gentleman I've ever known smells as divine as you. You smell like amber and fresh wood. Did you know that? Your scent makes me dream of forests."

A shudder passed through him, and his head fell back against the pillow.

But Violet didn't give up. She lay her palm flat against his chest, over his heart. "And here, Nick. You're good and kind, right here inside your heart."

She stroked his hair and murmured to him for hours, until his chest began to rise and fall in slow, even breaths, and she knew he'd fallen asleep.

Violet didn't sleep—not for a long time, and when her eyes did drift closed at last, she dreamed of clear water in sunlight, and a love as deep as the deepest forest.

And prayed it was deep enough.

* * * *

It was dark when Nick woke.

Before he even opened his eyes, he knew everything was different. Violet was next to him, curled against his side, her long lashes resting against her smooth cheeks, and he thought, as he always did when he watched her sleep, that she looked like an angel.

Like a dream.

But she was no dream—not this time. She was here, in his bed, her warm body pressed against his, her hair lying in tangled curls on his pillow.

And she was his.

He turned his head to the window, surprised to see only darkness. They'd slept for hours. A maid must have come in at some point because a fire had been laid, but it had long since burned to embers, and its faint glow wasn't enough to chase away the pressing darkness.

Nick slid out from under the coverlet and rose from the bed, careful not to wake Violet. He padded across the room, squinting in the dark, but his dressing gown was draped over the end of the bed, as always, and he snatched it up and shoved his arms into the sleeves.

He needed time away from her, away from her tempting body and her seductive warmth, or else he'd take her again. God knew it was tempting to bury his fears and doubts, much as he'd buried himself inside her sweet body tonight, but his heart was still wary, even if his cock wasn't.

He needed a drink.

He fumbled in the dark, tripping over discarded clothing as he went. He'd nearly reached the door when he stepped on something, and looked down to find he'd trod upon Violet's gown. He took it up and discovered there was something in the pocket—something square and hard. Curious, Nick reached in, pulled the object out, and held it up to the faint light of the fire to see what it was.

Violet's sketchbook.

She'd taken it with her everywhere since they'd arrived at Ashdown Park, and she was forever scribbling in it. Nick hesitated, but then he slipped the book into the pocket of his banyan and crept from the room, closing the door quietly behind him.

He didn't open the book until he'd reached his study and had a full glass of whiskey at his elbow. He wasn't sure what he expected to find inside those pages, but the whiskey seemed a good idea, just in case.

On the first page of the book was a sketch of him, mounted on his horse and surrounded by a sodden field. His lips were pulled into a sulky line, and his hair was damp with rain. She must have taken it the day after they'd arrived at Ashdown Park, when she'd wheedled him into escorting her over the grounds. Despite his pout, he looked rather vigorous and lively in the sketch, which was odd, since he didn't recall having been terribly enthusiastic about that outing.

Nick lifted his glass to take a deep swallow of his whiskey, but then set it aside again as he turned to the next page, blinking in surprise when he found it was another sketch of him, this one a close drawing of his face. He wasn't smiling, but there was a softness in his eyes he would have thought utterly out of character for him.

He turned to the next page, then the next, and then he quickly flipped through every page, his eyes widening with disbelief.

The book was filled with sketches of him.

Some of the drawings were rough, and there were a few of just his eyes, or his mouth, but there were dozens of them. Close sketches of his face, profiles, and detailed sketches of him in settings around the estate. There was one of him in the portrait gallery, strolling among the paintings, and another of him in the attics, pulling a cloth off a portrait of his mother that had once hung in the dining room. After her death his father couldn't bear to look at it, and he'd had it packed up and stored away, but Violet had persuaded Nick to bring it down and re-hang it. There was a drawing of him in the carriage, and another in the churchyard in the village, pointing up at the steeple.

And then, at the end of the book was a sketch she'd taken this morning, when they'd been together in the conservatory. It was only half-finished, but something about it made Nick's breath catch.

His arms were crossed over his chest and he was staring out the window, his face wistful. What had he been thinking of when he'd been staring out that window this morning? What had put that look on his face, that look of such yearning—

Her. He'd been thinking of *her.*

The book slipped from his fingers and fell to the desk.

All these drawings…

She must have started the book on the day after they'd arrived at Ashdown Park, because the first sketch was from the day he'd escorted her over the estate, and there was a sketch for every single day since. All this time he'd been berating her, hurting her, and she…

Had she intended to give the book to him?

He'd hardly thought the question before he realized he already knew the answer.

She'd done this for him.

A gift. An impossible gift, one he never dreamed he could ever receive, from anyone.

Himself.

But the sketches were of him, and yet not him at the same time. That man in the conservatory—he wasn't The Selfish Rake.

Nick's hands shook as he picked up the book again and turned back to the final drawing. There were lines of grief etched into this man's face, but there was strength and resolve as well, and even though his eyes were shadowed with pain, there was kindness and patience in them.

Was this…was this the way *she* saw him?

The Selfish Rake.

She'd sworn over and over she hadn't thought of him that way almost from the first moment she'd known him, and yet he'd refused to hear her, refused to listen, refused to believe.

"The Selfish Rake"—perhaps it had struck at his heart not because he believed it was how Violet saw him, but because it was how he saw *himself.*

But now…

She'd shed light on two years of smothering darkness. Gibbets, ghosts, the dreary streets of rain-soaked London—she'd turned them all on their heads, and given him a new way to see them.

Was it so unbelievable to imagine she could help him change the way he saw himself?

And if he could do that, if he could be strong enough to believe he was a worthy man—not Graham, or Lord Derrick, but a worthy man in his own right, like the man in these drawings—then surely there was still hope for him and Violet?

He thumbed slowly through the pages again, but this time when he looked at the sketches he didn't only see his own face.

He saw hers.

He saw her as she'd been tonight, with her hair cascading over her shoulders, her face alight with hope as he moved inside her. He heard her—the way she sighed for him, her cries as she shattered so sweetly beneath him, and later, when she'd whispered in his ear…

Your scent makes me dream of forests.

Nick slipped the book back into his pocket and left his study, his whiskey still untouched on his desk. When he reached his bedchamber he crept to the bed and slipped under the covers. Violet murmured in her sleep, but she burrowed into him and nestled her head against his chest.

Nick pressed his lips to her hair and settled her against him, just as if he'd never left her at all.

Chapter Twenty-two

Four weeks later...

Nick woke with a sleepy smile and reached to the other side of his bed, but instead of handfuls of warm, tempting wife, his arms closed on empty air.

Where Violet should have been, he found only cold, deserted bedsheets.

Damn it, where—

"Good afternoon, Lord Dare."

Nick thrust his head out from under the cocoon of blankets, and every appendage that had been swollen with hope only moments before deflated at once. "Damn it, Gibbs. You're not my wife."

"No, my lord. I'm afraid not. I beg your pardon for disappointing you."

"Disappointing me? You flatter yourself. It's not a disappointment, it's a bloody tragedy. Where the devil *is* my wife?" He'd fallen asleep with her cradled in his arms, and he preferred to wake up that way, as well.

Gibbs hesitated. "I believe I overheard her lady's maid, Bridget, tell Lady Westcott her mistress is indisposed this morning. Lady Westcott is with Lady Dare now."

"She's indisposed again?"

Violet had been *indisposed* a number of times over the past few weeks, and so fatigued she'd taken to resting in her bedchamber before dinner. This behavior was so unlike his vibrant, energetic wife Nick suspected illness wasn't the cause of her discomfort at all, but until Violet confided in him, he forced himself to subdue the wild leap of hope in his heart.

"Perhaps a quick wash, my lord, and simple attire for the day, so you may attend Lady Dare as soon as possible?"

Nick glanced at Gibbs in surprise. "What, leave my bedchamber without a properly tied cravat, Gibbs? Have you lost your wits, man? People will think I'm a savage."

"Yes, my lord. I mean *no*, my lord. That is, no one could ever mistake your lordship for—"

"For God's sake, Gibbs. I'm only jesting. There's no need to become flustered. I'll attend Lady Dare after I've breakfasted and properly attired myself." He didn't want to encourage the notion he was so besotted with his wife he'd scurry from his bedchamber to go chasing her all about the house.

Except...

Nick glanced at the cold, empty place next to him in his bed.

He *was* besotted with his wife. What was the use in pretending otherwise? She'd only left his bedchamber a few short hours ago and he already missed her. The truth was he'd go much farther than her bedchamber to see her. He'd chase Violet from one end of Ashdown Park to the other if he had to.

Or one end of England to the other, come to that.

He was wildly, madly, frantically besotted with her. He could spend a lifetime with Violet and she'd never cease to surprise him. He could devote all his years to peeling back one intriguing layer after another in search of her elusive center, and she'd remain a mystery to him still, but he knew one thing with the kind of bone-deep certainty that wouldn't be denied:

He *was* besotted with her, and he had to tell her.

He'd been careful these past few weeks not to make promises to Violet he wasn't certain he could keep. It was only in the past week he'd realized he'd never fully lose his grief over Graham. The memories of his father, the other ghosts that haunted him—he'd never be completely free of those demons. He'd carry some of that sorrow with him always.

And it didn't matter.

The only thing that mattered was Violet, and she'd never asked him to be perfect. She'd never asked him to be anyone other than who he was. All she'd ever wanted was him.

He was hers. He had been from the start—he was just too confused to see it.

He belonged here, with her. She was his life now, and those distractions he'd thought so important at one time—his mistress, his villa in Italy—they'd never been anything more than pale substitutes for a life he'd thought he wasn't worthy to live.

He'd wasted enough time on doubts and regrets. It was time for him to focus on his future with Violet, and even now his child might be growing in her belly...

"Never mind the cravat, Gibbs. I've changed my mind. I will go to Lady Dare at once. No breakfast." Nick threw off the coverlet, overwhelmed with the sudden urge to see his wife. "Just a wash, and fetch my clothes. Oh, and Gibbs? That matter we discussed, about the surprise for Lady Dare? You've seen to the details?"

"Yes, my lord. The footmen will bring in the tables and shelving today, and the draperies and furnishings you requested."

"Good. I'll come see it this afternoon and give my final instructions. I intend to leave very early tomorrow for London, and I want the thing done before I go. I wish to present my gift to Lady Dare tomorrow night, when I return."

"Yes, my lord. I believe she'll be quite pleased with it."

"Good man, Gibbs. I wouldn't have trusted the thing to anyone else."

"I—why, thank you, Lord Dare."

Nick glanced up at the odd note in Gibbs's voice, and his lips quirked. Dear God, it looked as if there was actually the hint of a smile on the old man's face.

A brief silence fell, then Nick cleared his throat. "Ah, my clothing, if you would, Gibbs?"

Gibbs blinked, then recalled himself with a grimace. "Yes, of course. Right away, my lord."

* * * *

"How much longer do you intend to keep up this charade, my dear?"

Violet didn't like to lie to Lady Westcott, so she settled for feigned ignorance in place of a blatant falsehood. "Charade? What charade is that, my lady?" After all, Ashdown Park could be rife with charades Violet knew nothing about.

Lady Westcott crossed the room, sat down on the edge of the bed, and took Violet's hand with a sigh. "My dear girl, it's apparent to anyone who's paying the least attention that you're with child."

Cold beads of sweat popped out on Violet's forehead. If Lady Westcott had guessed her secret, then mustn't Nick have guessed it as well, in spite of her silence on the subject? He hadn't said a word to her, or even so much as hinted at it, but she spent nearly every moment with her husband, and God knew he paid attention to her.

A great deal of rather marked attention, indeed.

Lady Westcott went on as if she'd read Violet's mind. "Nicholas is far from a neglectful husband. I daresay he's well aware of your condition, but if not, then I imagine he must be concerned for your health by now. You don't wish for him to worry about you, do you?"

"No. I wish nothing but happiness for Lord Dare, my lady."

The trouble was, she wished for happiness for *herself* as well, and all her happiness depended on Nick. And if Nick's happiness should depend on an Italian villa furnished with a seductive Italian mistress, what then? All Violet's hopes for a life with him would come crashing down the instant he discovered she was carrying his heir.

Lady Westcott patted her hand. "Then tell him, my dear. It's such wonderful news. I'm certain he'll be delighted."

Violet didn't doubt he *would* be delighted. Delighted to escape England, and Ashdown Park, and a marriage that had disappointed him from the start.

Delighted to escape *her.*

"Dash it, not again." Violet wiped at her eyes with the back of a shaking hand. Dear God, she could hardly go an hour without becoming weepy and overwrought these days. She didn't know whether it was the baby, or Nick, or if love reduced even the most unshakeable among them to whimpering fools, but she seemed to be forever dissolving into floods of tears, and that was to say nothing of the nausea and the dizziness.

She didn't recognize herself anymore. Violet Somerset had hardly ever been ill, but Lady Dare...well, Lady Dare wasn't nearly as stalwart as Violet had been. No, Lady Dare seemed to be forever on the verge of a swoon, and she'd almost cast up her accounts all over the dinner table last night.

Quail eggs, it seemed, no longer agreed with her.

She'd swallowed the nausea back only to be overcome with an extreme bout of dizziness that had nearly sent her face first into her dinner plate, and now here she was again, sniveling and hiccupping like a hysterical child.

"Oh, my dear. Look at me." Lady Westcott leaned forward and gently drew Violet's hand away from her face. "Tell me what's upsetting you."

"Don't you see, my lady? Nick has fulfilled the last of his promises to you. Repairs are underway at Ashdown Park, and his countess is now carrying his heir. There's nothing to keep him in England any longer."

"Oh, Violet, how can you say so? Why, one need only look at Nicholas to see he's madly in love with you. Surely you must know how dear you are to him. Has he ever given you any reason to think he intends to leave?"

Violet's breath hitched. "N-no, but he's never given me any reason to think he intends to stay, either."

Nick hadn't mentioned Italy or his mistress since their disastrous wedding night, but he'd also never made Violet any promises. Even when he held her tightly in his arms throughout the night, or when she woke to find him gazing down at her while she slept—even then, when she swore she could feel his love wrapped around her—even then, he made her no promises.

And that wasn't the worst of it.

Violet met Lady Westcott's eyes. "He's been…secretive lately. More than once I've caught him whispering with Gibbs, and when I entered his study the other day he whisked some papers off his desk so I couldn't see them. He disappears for hours at a time, too, and I've no idea where he goes—somewhere in the house, I think, but I can never find out where."

Lady Westcott's brows drew together. "That *is* rather odd, but it may be perfectly innocent, and even if he does intend to leave, hiding your condition from him only postpones the inevitable, Violet. He's going to discover the truth soon enough, if he hasn't already."

Violet knew Lady Westcott was right, and yet it seemed for all that she'd drawn Nick as The Selfish Rake, she was the one who was selfish, because she wanted to keep him with her for as long as she could. "I know. I promise I'll tell him soon, my lady, but—"

They were interrupted by a soft knock on the door, and a moment later it opened and Nick peered around the corner. "Violet, I—oh, good afternoon, Aunt."

"Ah, Nicholas. Good afternoon." Lady Westcott gave Violet a meaningful look, then patted her hand one last time and rose from the bed. "Now that you're here I'll leave your wife to your care, as I've letters to write this afternoon."

Once Lady Westcott was gone, Nick joined Violet on the bed. "You look pale, my lady. Do you feel better?" He cupped her cheek in his hand and lowered his voice. "I was lonely this morning when I woke and found you'd gone. Poor Gibbs got the brunt of my disappointment, I'm afraid."

His sheepish grin, his hand on her face, his soft voice…it was difficult to look into his warm gray eyes and believe he didn't care for her. Perhaps he didn't intend to leave at all, and she was worrying herself over nothing.

"I'm sorry I left you alone. I woke very early feeling ill, and I didn't wish to wake you."

"It's all right, sweet. You've, ah…you've been feeling unwell for several weeks now. Perhaps we should call in a doctor."

His eyes met hers, and Violet knew at once Lady Westcott was right—Nick already suspected she was with child. He was only waiting for her to tell him, and she was being terribly unfair, keeping it from him. He was her child's father, for pity's sake, and no matter how afraid she was, he deserved to know the truth.

She drew in a deep, shuddering breath, reached for his hand, and laced her fingers with his. "Yes, perhaps we should, but I'm not ill, Nick. I'm... we're going to have a child."

She'd imagined he'd react with pleasure—no matter what his intentions regarding their marriage, a child was welcome news—but she hadn't expected his face to transform as if a beam of sunlight had fallen across it, and she couldn't have foreseen the way his beautiful gray eyes softened and darkened with emotion.

The joy on his face, the wonder there...

Violet gazed at him, wild hope leaping into her throat. "Nick? Are you—?"

Before she could say another word, he seized her hand, brought it to his lips, and smothered it with kisses. "I thought perhaps...but I didn't dare hope. Such a gift, Violet. I couldn't be happier."

He tried to say more, to swallow the emotion that made the words tangle in his throat, but his voice broke, and after a moment he simply lay down beside her, drew her into his arms, and urged her to rest her head on his chest.

Violet melted against him as his fingers sifted through her hair, and the breath she'd been holding for weeks eased free of her lungs at last. He cradled her against his chest for a long time, and Violet's eyes had just begun to drift closed when she felt the rumble of his voice against her cheek. "I'll leave you here to rest for a while, sweet. I've some business with Gibbs this afternoon, but I'll come see you when I've finished."

Violet tensed. "What business?"

"Oh, it's just...I don't like to bore you with it."

Sudden nausea crawled up Violet's throat, but this time it had nothing to do with the child. What was this mysterious business with Gibbs that had taken so much of her husband's time these past few weeks, and why was Nick so determined to hide it from her?

"Nothing you do could ever bore me." Violet made an effort to keep her voice light. "It's just not like you to be so secretive. What does this business entail?"

A journey to the Continent? Italian villas, and Italian mistresses?

Nick laughed, but he shifted restlessly beneath her as if he wished to be away. "It's nothing you need worry about, but I'm afraid it will take me to London tomorrow. I intend to leave at first light so I can be back at Ashdown Park the same evening."

He tried to ease her head off his chest, but panic made Violet cling to him like a burr. "London? But...it's so sudden. You never said a word about it until..."

Until I told you I was with child.

"…until now."

"I know, sweet. I'm sorry, but it can't be helped, and I won't be gone long—just a single day."

Violet's head had gone dizzy with fear, but she pulled herself from his arms and struggled to a sitting position so she could see his face. "Take me with you."

Nick looked startled at this abrupt request. "I don't think that's a good—"

"I'd welcome the chance to see my grandmother and sisters, even if just for an afternoon," Violet added, trying to control the note of hysteria in her voice.

He shook his head and laid a tender hand on her belly. "No, sweet. It will be a cold, wet journey, and I don't like for you to exhaust yourself when your health is delicate. It's best if you stay here and rest."

His tone was kind, but Violet heard the finality in his voice, and she gave him a weak nod. It was nothing, after all—just a quick journey to London. She was foolish to get so upset over what was no doubt a simple errand.

It wasn't as if…

It wasn't as if he'd leave tomorrow and never return.

"Violet?" Nick took her chin in his hand with a frown and turned her face up to his. "Why are you so distressed? It's only for a day. I'll be back before you even realize I've gone."

"I—it's just that I'll miss you dreadfully."

His face softened, and he trailed the back of his fingers over her cheek. "I'll miss you, too. Rest now, and I'll be back before long to check on you, all right?" He pressed a kiss to her forehead, and Violet, who hadn't any idea what else she could do, let him ease her back against the pillows.

He did come back and check on her, much later, but he seemed distracted, and Violet fancied he avoided meeting her eyes. She suffered another bout of nausea in the evening and was forced to leave him on his own for dinner. She took a tray in her room, bathed, retired to her bed, and waited for him to come to her.

Waited, and waited, and waited…

After hours spent staring at the canopy above her, she at last crept through the connecting door into Nick's bedchamber, only to find it cold and empty.

He wasn't there, and he never came to her that night. For the first time since they'd made love, her husband left her alone and untouched in her bed.

It was hours before Violet succumbed to a troubled sleep, and when she woke the next morning, Nick was gone.

Chapter Twenty-three

The sun was struggling to shine through a heavy bank of clouds, and the normally cheery breakfast parlor was dull and dreary.

"Won't you take a bit more sustenance, my dear?" Lady Westcott cast a worried glance at Violet from the opposite side of the table.

The entire house was dull and dreary, and Violet was the dullest and dreariest thing in it.

It would have saved everyone a great deal of trouble if she'd given in to her initial impulse to stay in bed, but she'd forced herself to rise, wash, dress, and join Lady Westcott for breakfast, despite the nausea churning in her stomach and the heavy depression that hung over her spirits.

No wonder Nick had left her for his mistress.

His mistress would be beautiful, of course—mistresses always were, especially the Italian ones. Beautiful and sensual, and…accommodating. A lush, dark-eyed enchantress who didn't burst into tears at the slightest provocation, or cast up her accounts at the dinner table—

"Violet?" Lady Westcott's brow creased in a frown as she took in the dried crumbs on Violet's plate. "Surely you can manage a bit more than a few bites of toast?"

Violet sighed. She was being absurd. Nick had promised he'd return this evening, and she had no reason to doubt him. "Perhaps a bit later, my lady. I believe I'll retire to my rooms and rest for a while."

"Yes, I think that's wise, my dear. Shall I come up in a few hours, to see how you do?"

"Yes, please."

Violet offered Lady Westcott a wan smile, then set her napkin aside and wandered out into the entryway, intending to retire to her bedchamber and let sleep eat up the long hours until Nick's return, but instead of mounting the staircase she found herself roaming the hallway toward Nick's study. She slipped inside, closed the door behind her, and drifted over to his desk, sighing as she sank into his deep leather chair.

It smelled lovely in here, like Nick, but with a rich, faintly smoky undertone of whiskey and fine port. Violet inhaled deeply, letting the scent fill her head and spill around her until she could almost imagine Nick himself was here.

Her eyelids felt weighted, and she let her eyes drop closed. Perhaps she'd rest in here for a bit, instead of retiring to her bedchamber...

"Oh. Lady Dare. I beg your pardon. I didn't realize anyone was in here."

Violet blinked open her eyes to find Gibbs standing at the doorway of the study. "It's all right, Gibbs. Do you need something?"

"Yes, my lady. The land steward Mr. Quarles is here, asking for the bill of sale for some farm equipment Lord Dare recently purchased. Apparently there's a dispute about a missing plough."

"Yes, I know the one you mean." Violet glanced over the papers scattered across the polished surface of the mahogany desk, but she didn't see it, so she rummaged about for the key, unlocked the desk, and slid open a deep drawer on the right where they kept the papers related to the farm and tenants. "Ah, I think this is what you need."

She held out the paper to Gibbs, who accepted it with a bow of thanks and left to deliver it to Mr. Quarles.

Violet slid the drawer closed, locked it, then tossed the key into the shallow top drawer, but when she tried to push it closed, it jammed halfway, as if something were blocking it. She pulled the drawer back out and squirmed her hand into the small space behind it, patting around until her fingers closed on a few crumpled papers wedged between the drawer and the back of the desk. After a struggle, she managed to pull them loose.

She smoothed the pages flat on the desk, her brow furrowing with confusion. She was as involved in the management of the estate as Nick was, and she'd seen every paper that crossed this desk, but she didn't recognize these.

She skimmed over the first document. Odd. It looked like a lease agreement. As far as she knew they didn't lease anything, but Nick's signature was scrawled across the bottom of the page, so there must be—

Casa di Bella Mare, a San Felice Circeo.

House by the Beautiful Sea.

Violet blinked down at the name, then blinked again, but the words continued to swim in front of her eyes. Nick had never told her the name of the house, but she knew at once there was only one thing this could be.

The lease to his villa on the Italian coast.

Violet's breath stuttered in her chest as her gaze darted down to the bottom of the page. She must have known what she'd find, in the same way one knew a dream was about to disintegrate into a nightmare, because her breath had already frozen on her lips before she even read the words.

But knowing didn't keep her heart from breaking.

The paper drifted from her nerveless fingers and fluttered to the desk. He'd renewed the lease on his villa.

The agreement was dated weeks ago, in November, on the day after their wedding—the day they'd arrived at Ashdown Park. He'd sat at this desk in this study and signed that agreement, and then that night he'd crept into her bedchamber and touched her, made her cry out for him—

Made her weep for him.

All this time—all those nights he'd held her, stroked her hair as he whispered in her ear—all along this paper had been sitting in his desk, waiting for the moment when he'd done his duty to his aunt and his title and could be free of her at last.

Had he sent a copy of the agreement back to Italy weeks ago, when he'd begun to suspect she was with child? Or had he taken it to London with him today? His mysterious trip to London—the trip that had materialized only after she'd confirmed she was carrying his child.

But it didn't much matter when, did it?

What mattered was he'd never intended to stay in England, and once he was gone, he never intended to return. There was only one date on the lease—the signing date. In the place where the lease's end date should have been written, Nick had scrawled the word "indefinitely."

Violet was shaking so badly now the pages felt slippery in her hands, but there'd been another sheet of paper wedged at the back of the desk. She didn't want to look—God, she didn't want to know, but even as her heart pleaded with her to leave the single, crumpled sheet unread, she was sliding it out from under the lease…

A name was scrawled at the top left corner of the page. A woman's name. *Catalina di Foscari.*

No doubt Nick's mistress—*Catalina*—was as beautiful as her name, dark-haired and passionate, and of course she must be in love with Nick, madly so, because why wouldn't she love him? Any woman would love Nick, any woman would want to keep him for her own.

There were very few words on the page, but what was there made Violet gasp from the pain slicing through her heart.

My dear Catalina,

It feels as if years have passed since I last saw you, but it won't be long before—

That was it. The last word trailed off in a smear of ink, but once again, it didn't matter.

She'd seen enough.

She dropped the papers onto the desk, not bothering to replace them in the drawer. Let Nick find them there. Let him know she'd seen them when he returned—

If he returned.

When she rose from the chair at last, her limbs felt heavier than they ever had before, but no tears came this time, and why should they? She'd known all along she wasn't destined for a great love, so she really hadn't lost anything, had she?

Her hand went instinctively to her belly then, and she pressed her palm protectively over the flat surface. No, she'd gained something. Someone, and it was more than she'd ever hoped to have. That someone was already so precious to her, crying self-pitying tears would be nothing less than blasphemous.

Violet left Nick's study without a backward glance. She spoke to Lady Westcott first, then went in search of Bridget. Not more than two hours later her trunk was packed, and she and Lady Westcott were bundled into her ladyship's carriage and on their way to London.

* * * *

Nick's only thought when he burst through the door of Ashdown Park later that evening was Violet. He was so anxious to see his wife he didn't even notice Gibbs hovering in the entryway, wringing his hands like some kind of morbid gatekeeper waiting to announce the arrival of doomsday.

"Lord Dare, a word, if I may—"

"Not now, Gibbs." Nick took the stairs two at a time. Dear God, an entire day away from Violet had felt like a lifetime. The gift he'd brought her weighed down the leather satchel slung across his back, and he couldn't wait to see her face when she opened it.

"My lord, I beg you to—"

"I really must speak to Lady Dare about hiring a butler. We can't have you hanging about in the entryway in this ghoulish manner, Gibbs. You'll frighten the visitors away."

"That's what I wish to tell you, my lord. Lady Dare is—"

"Lady Dare is *what*, Gibbs?" Nick paused on the landing and waved an impatient hand at his valet. "For God's sake, get it out, would you? Or better yet, whatever it is, let Lady Dare tell me herself. I'd much rather stare at her lips than *yours*."

"Lady Dare's lips aren't here—that is, Lady Dare, my lord. Lady Dare isn't at Ashdown Park."

Nick blinked. "Not here? What the devil do you mean, Gibbs? Of course she's here. Where else would she be?"

"London, my lord. She left early this afternoon with Lady Westcott, in her ladyship's carriage."

The first shiver of foreboding darted down Nick's spine, and he descended a few stairs, his full attention now fixed on Gibbs. "Why, Gibbs," he asked, his voice dangerously quiet, "would my wife be in London?"

Gibbs, who prided himself on his unflappability, became as flustered as a debutante at her first ball of the season. "I don't know what happened, Lord Dare. One moment she was dozing in your study, and the next she'd summoned her lady's maid, packed her trunks, and set off for London."

Panic was creeping upon Nick, threatening to send his thoughts scattering in a thousand useless directions. He gripped the bridge of his nose between his fingers and tried to think. It wasn't at all like Violet to suddenly walk out the door without a word of explanation to anyone.

No, something must have happened.

Nick came down the stairs as quickly as he'd gone up, and rushed down the hallway toward his study, Gibbs on his heels. He threw the door open, expecting to find something awful, but the study looked much as he'd left it this morning. A bit messier, perhaps, with some loose papers flung about on top of his desk, but—

Nick's gaze landed on a page with a few lines in his handwriting scrawled across it, and he moved closer to the desk, his brow furrowing. What—

Oh, Christ.

He leapt for the desk, understanding slamming through him as he caught the papers in his fist, but there was no need to read them. He already knew what they were, and his heart sank like a lead ball into the pit of his stomach.

The lease for *Casa di Bella Mare,* with his signature scrawled across the bottom, and dated the day after his marriage to Violet.

And underneath the lease...

Nick squeezed his eyes closed, but he could see the words as clearly as if he were holding the paper in front of his nose.

My dear Catalina, it feels like years since...

He'd signed the lease and written that fragment of a letter in some sort of petty, childish bid to return the hurt he'd felt over Violet's sketch, but even as sotted as he'd been at the time, he'd known he'd never post either of them, so he'd shoved them into his desk drawer and forgotten all about them.

Until now.

"Burn these." He thrust the crumpled papers at Gibbs, then turned for the door.

Gibbs clutched them to his chest as he followed Nick into the entryway. "But…where are you going, my lord?"

"To London, to bring my wife home."

* * * *

"What the *devil* is that infernal racket?"

The Marquess of Huntington wasn't the sort of gentleman who enjoyed surprises, and he especially didn't care for them when they were loud, unexpected, and arrived in the dead of night when he was enjoying uninterrupted private time with his wife.

"Bloody hell! Stop that hammering!" His lordship tightened the tie on his robe as he stomped down the few remaining stairs and marched across the hallway. He threw open the door, ready to leap upon whoever stood on the other side, but when he saw who it was, shock made him freeze. "Dare? What the devil are *you* doing here? I thought you were in West Sussex. For God's sake, man, it's the middle of the bloody night—"

Nick thrust Finn aside without a word of apology and shoved his way through the door. "Where's my wife?"

Finn stared at him for a moment, his mouth wide open with shock, then he crossed his arms over his chest and fixed Nick with a cold stare. "You're asking *me?* You mean to say you don't know where your own wife—"

"Damn you, Huntington. Is she here, or not? Tell me at once."

"No. She isn't here." Finn seemed to notice Nick's wild panic then, and his anger faded to baffled concern. "Why should she be in London?" His eyes narrowed. "Oh, Christ. What have you done, Dare?"

Nick let out a bitter laugh. "Let's just say your lack of faith in me has proved prophetic, Huntington, and leave it at that, shall we?"

He turned for the door without another word, but a voice pitched high with distress stopped him before he could escape through it.

"Lord Dare?"

Nick paused, and he and Finn looked up the stairs to find Lady Huntington standing on the landing above them, her face pale and her hand twisted in the silk dressing gown at her throat.

"Has something happened to my sister? Is she…is she all right?"

Nick dragged his hands down his face. "I—there's been a misunderstanding between us, but if I can just *find* her, I can set it to rights."

Finn glared at Nick. "What sort of misunderstanding?"

"If it's all the same to you, Huntington," Nick replied with a scowl, "I'd rather discuss it with *her*."

"Wait!" Iris's voice echoed in the entryway. "Where are you going?"

"To Bedford Square, to Lady Chase's. If Violet isn't there, then to my aunt's. Lady Westcott and Violet left Ashdown Park together."

"And if she isn't at either place? What then, Dare?"

Nick met Finn's gaze without blinking. "Then the rest of London. All of bloody England, if I have to."

Finn studied him for a moment, then to Nick's shock, a corner of Finn's mouth lifted in a smile. "Good man, Dare."

"I'm coming with you."

Finn's smile faded as he glanced back up the stairs. "No, Iris. Go back to bed—"

"I *said* I'm coming with you. You will wait right there for me to dress, Lord Dare, and *you*, Lord Huntington." Iris gave her husband a cool look. "You may stay or go as you please, but I *will* accompany Lord Dare, with or without your approval."

Finn shook his head, but his lip quirked again, and after a moment he threw his hands up in the air. "To Lady Chase's, then."

* * * *

"Well, Lord Dare. Here you are, and I can't say I'm surprised to see you." Lady Chase looked him up and down, her lips pinched together with disapproval. "Already made a mess of it, have you? Not as charming a husband as you were a suitor, eh?"

Nick hardly noticed the insult. It was clear Lady Chase had been expecting him, and that meant Violet must be here. It took all of his restraint not to nudge the old lady aside and tear the house apart until he found his wife, but manhandling her grandmother wouldn't improve his chances with Violet, so he offered Lady Chase a hasty bow instead. "I beg your pardon, my lady, but—"

"Yes, yes. I know all about it. Fools, the both of you." Lady Chase stood aside and gestured Nick into the entryway. "And here are Lord and Lady Huntington, too. I suppose you dragged them from their beds first. Well, well, come in, then."

"My wife? Where—"

"She's in the old schoolroom, on the third floor." Hyacinth Somerset stood at the bottom of the staircase, her arms crossed over her chest. She gestured with her chin toward the stairs, but she made no move to step aside when Nick approached. "You promised you wouldn't hurt her, Lord Dare."

Nick had had quite a few hours on his return journey to London to think about his behavior toward Violet over the past weeks, and he'd already concluded he'd been a brute and a scoundrel, but never was he more ashamed of himself than when he looked into Hyacinth Somerset's reproachful eyes.

"If I could take away her hurt—take it into myself—I would. I can't, but I vow to you, Miss Hyacinth, I'll never hurt her again."

"You failed to keep that vow once. Why should I believe you'll keep it now?"

"Because I'd rather die than hurt her. Because I love her."

The quiet words came straight from Nick's heart, and Hyacinth must have understood that, because after a brief hesitation, she stepped aside.

Nick bounded up the four flights of stairs, but when he reached the door to the schoolroom and saw Violet he stopped, his breath heaving in and out of his lungs.

She was sitting in an old leather chair, staring straight ahead. She turned at the sound of Nick's boots on the wooden floor, and he crossed the room until he was standing in front of her. He pulled his hat from his head and stood there silently, twisting the brim between his hands.

Violet looked up into his face, and her breath left her lungs in a quiet sigh.

And that sigh undid him. The grief of it, the exhaustion and despair— that tiny sigh sliced through his heart. He slid to his knees before her and buried his face in her lap. "Would you leave me, Violet? Would you abandon me, and break my heart?"

She was quiet for a long moment, and when she did speak, her voice was the softest whisper. "I left you before you could leave me. I broke your heart before you could break mine."

He wrapped his arms tighter around her legs and pressed his face against her belly. "No. I won't leave you, Violet. Not ever."

She stiffened. "I saw the letter. The lease, Nick, and the…the letter to—"

Nick had to close his eyes against the pain in her voice. "I never sent them."

"But you must have thought you would, eventually. Why else would you keep them, hidden away in your desk?"

He didn't release her, but he raised his face to hers. "Listen to me, Violet. It was a moment's madness only. The lease, and the letter…I was hurt and confused, but the ink hadn't even dried on the page before I knew I could never leave you. I shoved the papers in my desk and never thought of them again."

She drew in a shaky breath, but she didn't speak, and she didn't touch him.

Nick grabbed her hand and pressed it to his cheek. "Please, Violet. Italy, Catalina—the moment I met you, they ceased to exist for me." He dragged her hand down to his chest and pressed her palm against his heart. "You must know how much I love you. So much that breaking your heart would be the same as breaking my own."

She'd kept very still since he touched her, but a tremor passed through her at his words, then slowly, so slowly he thought his heart would cease beating, a tremulous smile lit her face. "You love me?"

Nick wrapped his hands around her waist and eased her from the chair into his arms. "Madly. How could I not? I've loved you since the day you took me to the burial grounds and demanded I hand over my walking stick so you could dig for bones."

That made her smile, but it faded quickly, and Violet hid her face against his chest. "I—I'm sorry, Nick. I shouldn't have left Ashdown Park without speaking to you first. I thought…well, it doesn't matter now." She let out a ragged sigh and wrapped her arms around his neck.

"What did you think? I don't want any more secrets between us." She tried to look away, but Nick tilted her face up to his with a fingertip on her chin. "Violet?"

"It's just that you've been so secretive lately, and then there was this sudden trip to London, and you didn't come to me last night. When I saw the papers, I…well, I put all those things together, and assumed the worst."

"I didn't come to you, sweet, because you were unwell. I'm not such a brute I'd force my attentions on my ill, exhausted wife. Though perhaps I am a brute, after all, because I nearly yielded to temptation a dozen times that night. I had to move to another bedchamber, because it was driving me mad knowing you were just on the other side of the connecting door."

She flushed, but her eyes were sparkling. "I'm never too ill to receive your attentions, my lord."

"No?" His gaze dropped to her lips just before he lowered his mouth to hers, his kiss tender and demanding at once. When they broke apart at last, they were both breathless. "As far as my being secretive, well…I've been working on something for you. A gift."

Violet's eyes widened. "A gift? You mean the whispering with Gibbs and the sneaking about the house was all because you were planning a gift for me?"

"Yes. I have part of it here with me, but you'll have to wait until we return to Ashdown Park to see the rest of it." Nick urged her to sit down in the chair again, then fetched the leather satchel he'd dragged all the way back to London and pulled a large, paper-wrapped package from it.

Violet eyed it with interest. "It's heavy."

Nick grinned. "I know. I've carried it to London and back twice now. Open it."

He laid it carefully in her lap, and Violet slid her fingers under a flap in the paper covering and smoothed it back. "Oh, my," she breathed when she lifted the book from the wrappings. "It's so fine." She smoothed her palm over the dark green leather binding and traced a reverent finger over the gilt-edged pages.

"I think you'll like the frontispiece." Nick knelt next to her chair and opened the book to the title page.

Violet gasped softly, then reached up to press a shaking hand against her mouth. "Oh, my goodness. Oh, *Nick.*"

He brushed his lips over her ear. "Read it to me, sweet."

It took Violet a moment to catch her breath, but at last she whispered, "*A Treatise on London for Bluestockings and Adventuresses.*"

"All your essays, and your sketches." Nick turned over a few pages until he reached a page entitled *List of Illustrations.* "Cockpit Steps and Execution Dock—they're all here. The publisher, John Murray, was astounded at how much information you'd gathered. He's already asked to see your next work, and...Violet? Don't *cry,* sweetheart."

She looked up at him, her lower lip trembling. "I just...I can't believe you did this for me."

He looked surprised. "But...don't you know, Violet? I'd do anything for you."

Violet stared down at the book on her lap, running her fingertips over the page, her eyes swimming with tears.

Nick tipped her face up and caught the drops on his fingertips. "More tears? What's the matter, sweet? Don't you like it?"

Violet turned her face to press a soggy kiss into his palm. "I love it. I love *you,* so much, Nick. More than I can ever tell you."

"Oh, love. You don't need to tell me." He brushed a soft kiss on her lips, then lay his hand gently on her belly. "You've already shown me."

Chapter Twenty-four

"It smells like paper, and fresh ink. Have you given me my own library?" Violet reached behind her head and tried to tug off the scarf Nick had tied around her eyes. "Take this off, Nick! You've made me wait long enough to see it."

Nick, afraid an immediate return journey to West Sussex would exhaust her, had insisted they remain at Lady Chase's for the night, and Violet had spent the entire carriage ride from Bedford Square to Ashdown Park teasing him to tell her about her surprise.

Nick took her by the shoulders and guided her across the room. "It's not a library, but perhaps it will be, someday. And you've waited less than a day to see it, sweet," he added with a chuckle. "You only found out about it last night. I don't recall you ever being this impatient before."

"I'm only impatient for surprises from my husband, and if this is anything like my book, then I can't wait another moment!"

"Do as I say and you won't have to. Stand here. This corner has the best vantage point. Yes, good. Are you ready?"

Violet let out a little squeal of anticipation. "Yes! I've been ready!"

He chuckled again and pressed a kiss behind her ear, then reached up, untied the knot, and slid the blindfold away.

"Oh, my goodness." Violet's voice was hushed, and for a long moment she seemed unable to move. She didn't utter another word, but stood quietly, her gaze sweeping from one end of the room to the other, her hand over her mouth. At last she took a step forward, but then she stopped again, as if she weren't sure what to touch first.

Nick cleared his throat. "I had extra tables brought in and arranged in a row so you'd have room to lay out pages side by side if you liked. You can use them as writing desks, too, but I had that one brought in in case you preferred it." He gestured toward a massive mahogany desk situated in a corner of the room, next to a window. "It gets quite a lot of natural light in that corner."

Violet took a few hesitant steps toward it. "It's beautiful," she murmured, running a hand across the polished surface.

"The shelving is deeper than standard shelving, so you can store whatever you like in it. Your sketches, or books..." He trailed off, watching as she crossed the room to study the floor-to-ceiling shelves against a long wall of the room.

"So many supplies." Her voice was faint. "Paper of every size, ink, drawing pencils...you had all of this brought in for me?"

"Of course, sweet. I imagined you'd want to write more books, and as fetching as I find your cobwebs, I didn't like for you to be isolated in some dusty chamber on the third floor. There's this sitting area, of course, and a place for you to sketch, there by the other window."

He waved a hand toward another corner of the room, where a smaller table had been set up, and with it a chair covered in a cheerful print of purple violets. Violet drew closer, and a soft gasp fell from her lips when she saw the handsome drawing box sitting on top of the desk. The lid was open, and inside was a collection of brass and ivory drawing instruments.

She traced a finger over the inside of the cover. "You had it inscribed."

"Violet Balfour, Her Ladyship, the Countess of Dare, a gift from her loving husband Nicholas Balfour, His Lordship, the Earl of Dare, 1817." Nick recited the inscription as he crossed the room to her. "It's all very proper, but I like this one better." He removed the top tray of instruments, then eased out a piece of wood that had been fitted to the bottom of the box.

Violet smiled. "A false bottom."

"And another inscription. Read it to me, my lady."

He wrapped his arms around her waist as Violet read quietly. "For Violet. Your love taught me to see again. I am ever yours, Nick." A sob tore loose from her throat, and she turned in Nick's arms and pressed her cheek to his chest, her voice breaking. "Oh, Nick. It's so much. Too much—"

"No. It's not enough." He kissed the top of her head. "Open the top drawer of the desk, sweetheart."

Violet kissed the hollow of his throat, then wiped her eyes. "Oh," she murmured in surprise when she saw what was in the drawer. "I wondered where this had gone. I thought I'd lost it." She drew out the small sketchbook she'd started the day after they arrived at Ashdown Park. "Have you had it—"

"The whole time? Yes. I'm sorry I didn't tell you."

She smiled. "It's all right. I made it for you, as a gift. I always intended for you to have it."

"A gift only you could have given me. You're the only person in the world who could ever have understood it was the one gift I needed more than any other. I love you so much, Violet."

He held out his hand to her, and she flew to him and threw herself into his arms. "Oh, I love you too, Nick. Thank you for my book, and for my writing room. I'll have to come up with a new project to do it justice."

"Did you know parts of West Sussex are said to be haunted with ghosts and fairies? That would make an interesting book, wouldn't it?"

"Hmmm. Yes, but I think I'd like to spend some time on sketches first. I've an idea for a new sketchbook, and I'd like to do that before I start anything else."

He gave her a teasing smile. "Oh? What sort of idea? Horses, or dogs? Flowers? Kittens in a basket, perhaps?"

"No. I have something else in mind. I think you'll like it." She took his hand to lead him from the room. "Come with me, and I'll show you."

* * * *

Nick was sprawled in a chair beside the fireplace and Violet was sitting on the floor at his feet, her white night rail falling off her shoulder, the only sound in the room the faint scrape of her pencil across the page.

She was taking a sketch of him, but it wasn't just any sketch. This one was for a private sketchbook, for their own personal pleasure. He was dressed only in his banyan, his legs spread wide, the heavy silk gaping over his bare chest. "What will you call it? 'The Besotted Husband'? 'The Satisfied Earl'?"

Her mischievous blue eyes flashed as she peeked at him over the top edge of her sketchbook. "Perhaps I'll call it 'The Bluestocking's Triumph.'"

"A triumph, indeed." He watched with interest as her hand moved over the page. "Will you write an essay for it, as well?"

She shrugged. "As you know, my lord, I treasure words, and I flatter myself I know a good many of them, but the adjectives that come to mind at the moment hardly do you justice."

His lips curled into a smile as her avid gaze lingered on his bare chest. "What adjectives are those, my lady?"

"Well, I suppose if I *must* make do..." She cocked her head as she studied him. "Let me see. Broad, powerful shoulders, and a trim waist.

A taut, flat belly, and…" She tapped her pencil against the page, drawing the moment out to tease him.

"Yes?" Nick let his legs fall open a little wider, his body hardening with anticipation. "Anything else?"

Her gaze darted lower. "Lean, muscled legs, a sturdy pair of knees, an intriguing sprinkling of dark hair, and I've never noticed it before, my lord, but you have lovely, ah…feet."

"Feet!" Nick tried to sound outraged. "Come now, Lady Dare. Surely you've overlooked *something*—something deserving of an adjective or two, at the very least."

"Hmmm. Well, I suppose there is *one* other thing, but paying it too much attention is dangerous, rather like staring too long at the sun."

The "it" in question twitched insistently against his stomach, determined to earn its adjectives. "Indeed? And why is that?"

A sly grin flitted across her lips. "The more attention one pays to it, the more attention it demands."

Nick chuckled. "I don't deny it's a greedy appendage. Perhaps you should ignore it."

She darted her tongue over her lower lip. "Impossible, my lord. It's quite good at making its presence known. Why, even now, when we're not paying it the least bit of attention, it's grown long and thick and…swollen."

The firelight caught at the sheen of moisture her tongue left on her lips, and the last of Nick's restraint ignited into flames of desire. "Put down the sketchbook, Violet."

"But I've nearly finished—"

"Oh, you've finished, my lady." He reached out and plucked the sketchbook from her hands.

She squealed as he scooped her into his arms and carried her to the bed. "Why, Lord Dare. I was under the impression you wished to encourage my intellectual endeavors. But if you recall, my lord, I did warn you, no gentleman would ever want a bluestocking for a wife."

He held her gaze, his gray eyes twinkling as he slid her night rail off her other shoulder. "You were wrong, sweet. Nothing less than a bluestocking would ever do for me."

Notes

1. *The Punishments of China*, illustrated by twenty-two engravings, by George Mason and Henry Dadley, 1801. This book might well have been on Lady Chase's library shelf, but the "death by a thousand cuts" illustration is a creation of the author's imagination. There is no such plate, though a number of other punishments, including Bastinade and the Rack, are depicted.

2. *Casanova Blowing up a Condom*, c. 1754.

3. The description of the condom is taken from the Hunterian Museum catalogue. The museum currently displays a prophylactic device dated 1776, but it's not clear whether the condom would have been part of the collection during the Regency period.

4. The origin of the word "condom" isn't known, but the term was in use as early as the early eighteenth century.

About the Author

Anna Bradley is the author of The Sutherland Scandals novels. A Maine native, she now lives near Portland, Oregon, where people are delightful and weird and love to read. She teaches writing and lives with her husband, two children, a variety of spoiled pets, and shelves full of books. Visit her website at www.annabradley.net.

Printed in the United States
by Baker & Taylor Publisher Services